THE SHARDS OF THE MOON

Books by Brendan Noble

The Frostmarked Chronicles:
A Dagger in the Winds
The Trials of Ascension
The Daughters of the Earth
The Deathless Sons
The Shards of the Moon

Frostmarked Tales:
The Rider in the Night
The Lady of Rolika

The Realm Reachers:
The Crimson Court
The Crystal Heir

Realm Reacher Novellas:
The Amber Dame

The Prism Files:
The Fractured Prism
Crimson Reigns
Pridefall
White Crown

To Rick Riordan, whose works taught me to love mythology at a young age.

Author Note: Trigger Warning

The Shards of the Moon contains elements that may be triggers or traumatic to some readers, so please proceed with caution if any of the below are so for you. I have done my best to treat these serious topics carefully and with respect.

- Torture

- Graphic injury

- War/War Trauma

- Death

Godly and Demonic Marks

Marzanna - Frostmark
Winter, Disease, and Death

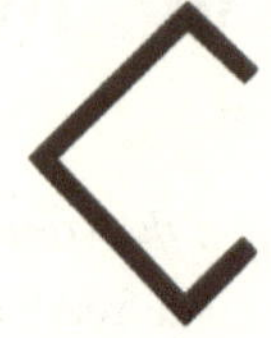

Dziewanna - Bowmark
Wilds, Hunt, and Spring

Jaryło - Springmark
Spring, Agriculture, and War

Mokosz - Mothermark
Women, Divination, and Earth

Perun - Thundermark
Thunder, Justice, and War

Weles - Serpentmark
Underworld and Lowlands

Czarnobóg - Darkmark
Death, Darkness, and Corruption

Dadźbóg - Sunmark
The Sun

Otylia - Moonmark
Endings and Moon

Wacław - Eclipsemark
Storm Demon (Płanetnik)

Pronunciation Guide

Major Characters

Wacław Lubiewicz: Vahtswahv Luubeeayvihch
(Little Name) - Wašek: Vahshehk
Otylia Welesiakówna: Ohtihleeah Vehlehseeahkohvnah
(Little Name) - Otylka: Ohtihlkah
Andrij: Ahndrey
Narcyz: Nahrsihz

Gods

Czarnobóg: Charhnohbohg
Dadźbóg: Dahdzbohg
Dziewanna: Djehvahnah
Jaryło: Yahrihwoh
Marzanna: Mahrzahnah
Marzyana: Mahrzeeahnah
Mokosz: Mohkohsh
Perun: Pehruun
Swaróg: Svahrohg
Trygław: Treegwahv
Weles: Vehlehs

Other Terms

Alatyr: Ahlahteer
Chort: Khohrt
Grudzień: Gruudjehn
Jawia: Yahveeah
Krowik(ie): Krohvihk(ee)
Kryzhana: Kreetshahnah
Kwiecień: Kvihehchehn
Naw(ie): Nahv(ee)
Nawia: Nahveeah
Październik: Pahjshdjihehrnihk
Płanetnik: Pwahnehtnihk
Sierpień: Shihehrpihehn
Smorodina: Smohrohiinah
Szeptucha: Shehptuuhah
Wrzesień: Vrzehshehn
Žityje: Zhihtyeh
Żmij: Zmee

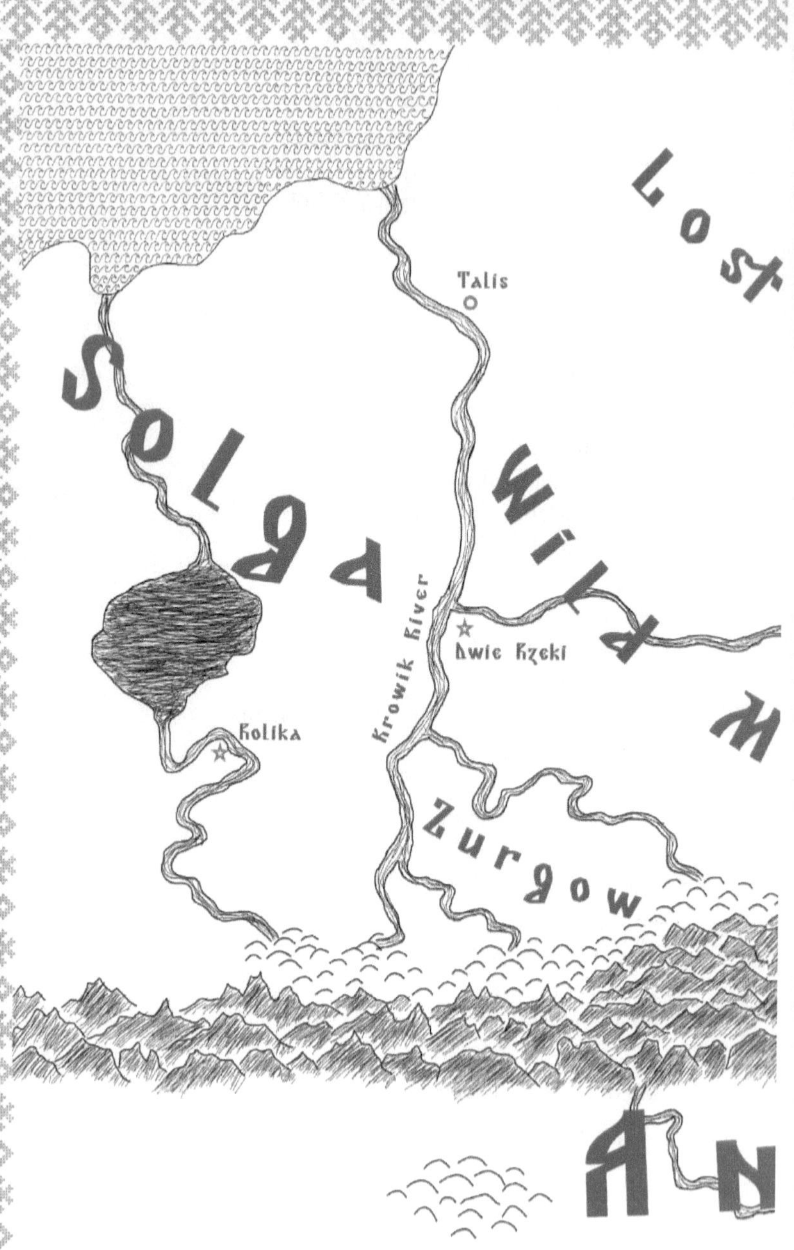

Lost
Solga
Wild
W
Talis
Krowik River
Dwie Rzeki
Holika
Zurgow
An

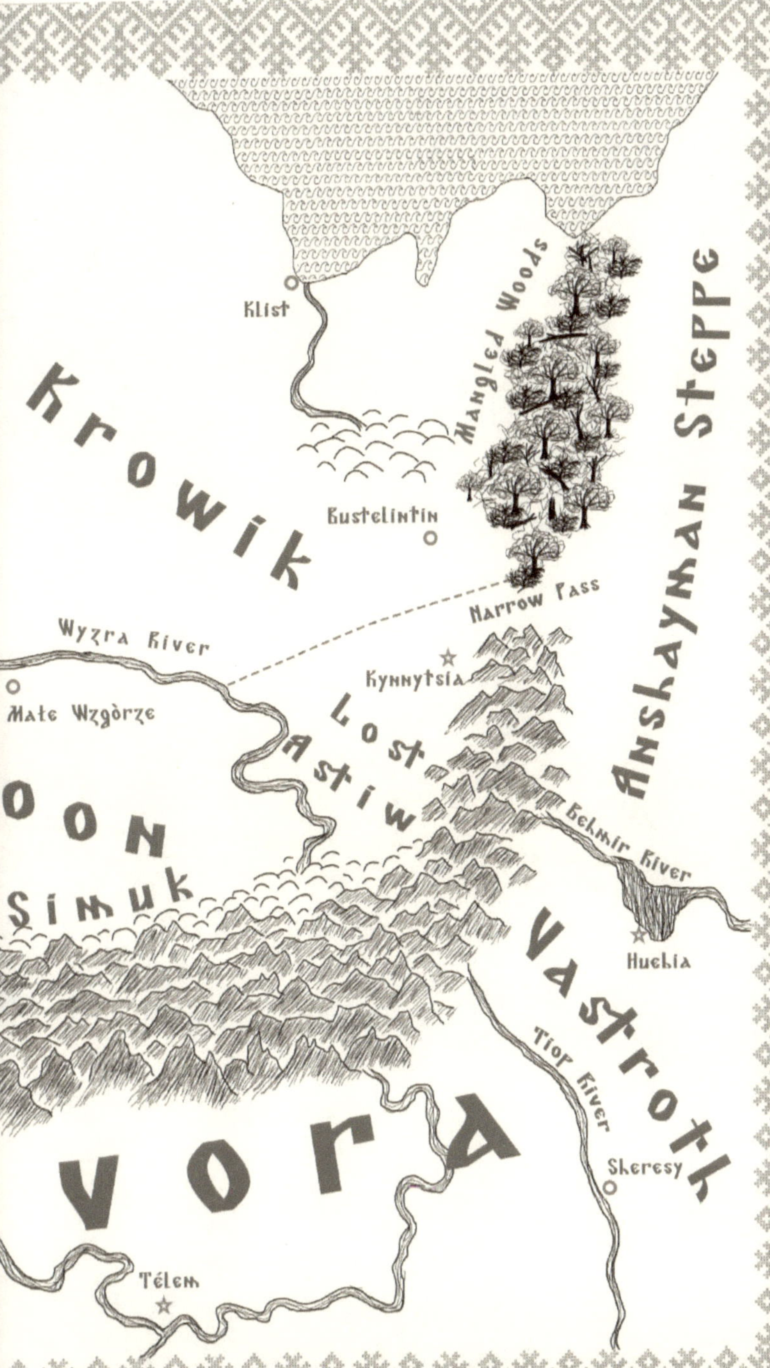

Klist
Mangled Woods
Anshayman Steppe
Krowik
Bustelintin
Narrow Pass
Wyzra River
Kynnytsia
Małe Wzgórze
Lost
Astiw
OON
Behmir River
Simuk
Vastroth
Huebia
Vora
Tior River
Sheresy
Télem

THE SHARDS OF THE MOON

BRENDAN NOBLE

The Story So Far

FOUR YEARS AFTER BEING TORN APART from each other, a young warrior named Wacław and his once best friend, the witch Otylia, reunited on the spring equinox. It was supposed to be the day to celebrate the death of the winter goddess, Marzanna, but the goddess tempted Wacław into accepting her Frostmark. This mark soon awakened latent demonic storm powers within him, and with winter rising beyond its bounds, they sought to stop Marzanna's forces in the east.

During their travels, they encountered a demon hunter named Juri who helped them on their way, but he was actually the spring god, Jaryło, who'd hidden his identity from them. He showed them to a lake that exposed Otylia's true birth as a goddess, the daughter of Dziewanna of the wilds and Weles of the underworld. Jaryło then betrayed them, killing Otylia to send her to Weles in the afterlife of Nawia.

While Otylia sought Ascension into her true godhood to escape Nawia, Wacław led the eastern nomadic clans through toil and conflict as they fled Marzanna's Frostmarked Horde. All east of the mountains burned, but he focused on finding a way back to Otylia. He wrestled with his twin demonic and mortal souls while Otylia did the same with her godly one to complete her Trials of Ascension.

The Trial of Life and Death had her face the dark żmij (shapeshifting dragon) Czarnóbg for the first time, realizing he'd entrapped Dziewanna with Marzanna. The final trial of Love and Loss forced her to admit her love for Wacław, then steal his mortal soul, but because of a ritual they'd conducted in their earlier travels, a final fragment of that soul now remained in her. They reunited in Nawia, escaping Weles and a weakened Jaryło before appearing in a desert land.

They had intended to return home, but the Heart of Nawia sent them instead to the southern land of Vastroth. Many worshipped the Great Mother, Mokosz, there. Marzanna's forces occupied the lands, though, and a Moonstone of Alatyr exerted influence over people and Wacław's demon. It drove him mad as Otylia worked with Mokosz's allies to overthrow Marzanna. Only through her taking part of Wacław's corruption could he find some peace and control.

The pair then followed clues from Otylia's newfound abilities and headed off to find Dziewanna. Despite their rescue, the goddess of the wilds had been drained of her power, and only the eldest god, Rod, could restore them. So they headed to the realm of the gods, Prawia, in hopes of doing so.

But Marzanna and Czarnobóg had plotted while they were away in Nawia, Vastroth, and now Prawia. Demons and undead men of the Frostmarked Horde, led by the necromancer Koschei the Deathless, ravaged Krowik. They corrupted the sun god, Dadźbóg, as well to turn the world dark as Czarnobóg himself attacked Prawia. Only the united efforts of the gods could repel Czarnobóg, but he stole Weles away in his retreat, threatening the realm of the dead.

The avatar of Death forced Otylia to kill Rod before they left Prawia, repaying a debt she'd owed to save Wacław's life earlier. Rod had foreseen his fate, but the other gods weren't so kind, banishing Otylia from Prawia forever. She returned to the living realm to face Koschei's Horde with Wacław and her mother, outwitting Baba Jaga to uncover the secret to Koschei's immortality before defeating him and a projection of Marzanna in the final battle.

Wacław was crowned king for leading the victory over Koschei, and Dziewanna now rules the living realm of Jawia. The Frostmarked Horde is defeated. But Winter's grip remains, and the god of darkness holds Nawia's lord…

Part 1
The Way of Souls

1

Wacław

Even gods die in the end.

MARZANNA'S SNOW SPIRALED THROUGH THE TREES on the out-skirts of the village of Dwie Rzeki. I knelt amid them, my fur hood drawn down to reveal my windburned cheeks and nose. After so many moons of endless winter, the cold had become a familiar foe, and warmth wouldn't change what I must do. Nor would it change the past.

Branches littered the ground—nature's relent to the weight of Marzanna's brutality. I had silently arranged many of them into Rod's Wheelmark and now could only stare at the symbol of the eldest god, wondering. What lay ahead without Rod's guiding hand to ensure balance within the Three Realms?

Otylia scoffed whenever I asked her a question like that. The pain in her gaze was obvious, knowing she'd been the one to drive her silver spear through Rod's chest, but she hardly believed the Three Realms had been balanced before. If recent moons had taught me anything, though, it was that there were forces far beyond our understanding. We meddled in the affairs of gods and beasts so ancient that mortal lifespans were mere blinks to them. Yet not even the gods could grasp the truth of every force working within the realms. Maybe that was for the best.

"Your wheel always turns to what comes next," I prayed to the absent creator. "Otylia says she's seen Destiny herself, yet I feel as if I stumble through each day. The people… *my* people… have named me king. I fail them every day Marzanna consumes this realm and Czarnobóg curses the afterlife."

No answer came.

Of course one didn't. The gods had never answered my prayers before, so why would Rod reply when he was dead? It was only a demon's call. A Naw's plea. My power came from Rod's force, but he had not created two-souled mortals willingly. If Balance as a pure force was out there somewhere, despite Rod's death, could it not answer one of the few Nawie left to fight the corruption that tainted us?

A familiar ball tightened in my chest. Footsteps crunched behind me moments later, but I need not look back to see who it was.

"It's quiet out here," I said, raising my gaze from the Wheelmark to the rising light. Dadźbóg, god of the sun, had betrayed us all by falling to Marzanna's temptations, but Swaróg contained his rogue son for now. Each morning was a reminder of the never-ending night we'd faced during his betrayal. The gods granted us gifts which could be taken away at any time.

"It's dead." The sharp scent of mixed herbs wafted through the trees as the footsteps stopped beside me. Otylia lay her hand on my back, pressing hard enough to reveal her frustrations. "Mother's wilds should be full of boar and deer and wolves. The birds should sing to each other and scream at us to *stay away*, but the only song now is the croaking of dying trees. That changes today."

I leaned back into her hand and enjoyed her touch. Working the fields my entire life had given me strength, but the stress of kingly duties made my body feel like that of a sore old man. I allowed myself only a moment of the luxury, though, before hopping to my feet.

When Otylia was in this kind of mood, I'd learned many years ago not to make her wait. "Is Dziewanna ready for the ritual?" I asked her, taking her cheek and tracing the crescent scar upon it. Goddess of endings and moon. My goddess. My love.

She pulled away. "Yes, but some idiots decided calling to Marzanna is better than helping Mother banish the winter."

"What have they done this time?" Marzanna's cultists had been exiled for years, but discontent had led a desperate few to believe she and Czarnobóg, the shapeshifting draconic żmij who commanded darkness, were the only hope to end their suffering.

Otylia wrinkled her nose. "It's better that I show you."

She stormed off so quickly that I had to jog to catch up. Her simple gray dress hemmed in black resembled her old szeptucha attire more than a goddess. Clothes couldn't hide that she was different to the outcast witch she'd once been, though. Silver strands strung through her raven black hair instead of bone amulets, and the moonlight emanating from her skin made them shine despite her grim demeanor this morning. Her aggression, too, was from determination more than spite. I'd felt her fury plenty enough to know the difference.

"You could have called for me," I said, taking her hand and intertwining our fingers. Even through our leather gloves, the ethereal bond between us revealed how her heart quickened at my touch. Mine echoed its drum. "But it's cute you came to get me instead."

"Not the time," she replied.

A smile tugged at the corner of her mouth. Of course she was mad—that was practically her state of being—but I took great pride in being the one who could bring out the soft side of her, if only for a fleeting moment.

She dragged more than led me through the makeshift outskirts of Dwie Rzeki. It was now the capital of our fledgling Kingdom of the Wild Moon, but its roots remained that of our old Krowikie tribe. The space beyond what had once been the main village wall was now filled with wooden houses, their thatched-roofs sloping toward the ground and their floors sunken to keep the earth's warmth through the winter moons.

Simukie and Zurgowie from the eastern steppes filled the path as they strapped saddles to their horses in preparation for a hunt. Days before, it would've been desperate at best, but we'd spent a moon gathering sacrifices to strengthen Dziewanna's *żityje*, the life force that fueled all beings and our magic. If the wild goddess's ritual worked, much of our land would be free of Marzanna's grip. Dziewanna herself didn't know how far her power would reach, though, and none of us dared ponder what lay ahead if she failed.

Behind the hunters, children of every skin shade and hair color darted under remnants of what had once been a farm fence. An elderly woman stomped a warped wooden cane and shouted after them, but they just giggled and continued their chase.

Life goes on, I reminded myself.

Refugees had arrived from tribes and nations both familiar and not in the aftermath of the Frostmark Horde's rampage. We'd defeated Koschei's main army in our desperate defense, but Marzanna's forces had wreaked havoc far beyond what had once been Krowik. Besides Dwie Rzeki, Kostroma's protected area around Rolika, and what we'd managed to protect in Vastroth, there were few settlements that hadn't fallen to the Horde. Resources were scarce, so those of us left had banded together out of necessity more than desire. Tribal rivalries mattered little when we were all on the brink of starvation.

I greeted those familiar to me, but many gave wary glances.

"The king," they whispered in various tongues. "The demon."

Absently, I traced the dark, decaying lines that ran across my face and body. Accepting I was a two-souled Naw tasked with protecting the natural cycle—not cursed as a demon—had taken time for me. It would be longer until I could banish the rumors spreading among my people. When I resembled some decrepit beast of a man, that would be all the more difficult.

We soon passed through Dwie Rzeki's eastern gate. Warriors now patrolled the outskirts of the village itself, rather than standing guard at the gates, but a smirk flicked at my lips as I remembered slipping past in my invisible soul-form as a child. It disappeared at the sight of the gray-haired priest awaiting me.

"The council has been calling you," Dariusz insisted, snatching the arm his daughter hadn't already wrangled. "There has been a blaze at one of the barns."

"The sacrifices!" I exclaimed as my heart sunk.

Otylia's nails dug into my skin. "We needed those for Mother's ritual!"

They both dragged me deeper into the village. *Like father, like daughter…*

Before the eternal winter, Dwie Rzeki's air had been a battle between the stench of mud and aromas of baked bread and sizzling meats. Instead, there was only reeking wood-rot and smoke. Fire couldn't banish Marzanna's fury, but it could at least keep your fingers from succumbing to frostbite for a few hours longer.

A crowd blocked our path when we approached the village center. Someone shouted from near the longhouse at the far side. I couldn't see, so I pushed through until I had a clear view of the familiar raving man standing upon a wooden cart.

"We can't keep living like this!" Conall's voice carried, echoed by the crowd. "The king would have us starve, but there's one who can stop the winter. They'd shoot me with an arrow if I dared mention her name, but you know who I speak of!"

"Marzanna," I answered.

A hush spread as Conall reeled back, a hand clutching his weathered cloak of reeds. He had bright hair like the changing autumn leaves, and his skin would've been pale enough to camouflage with the snow had his cheeks not been burning in his fury. Pargiawi like him from the far northeast refused to use animal products in their clothing, substituting them with plant fibers that required so many layers that they seemed to swallow him whole.

"So, the king does hear his subjects!" Conall spat, his accent over-emphasizing every *ooh* sound. "Not afraid of the goddess? Then why not call her aid?"

I spoke to the crowd more than him as I continued my advance. "You would have me plea to the goddess who slaughtered your people, swallowed the summer? If we'd failed against Koschei and his Frostmarked Horde, they would not have spared any of us. We're nothing more than sacrificial blood at the death goddess's altar!"

"And your *wild* goddess is nothing compared to Marzanna and Czarnobóg!" He threw out his arms. "She claims to wield fire, but we have nothing but snow and dark demons!"

A *crack* answered him, spires of flame rushing overhead as Dziewanna emerged from the longhouse. Clothed in a burnt red riding dress with a bear pelt draping from her shoulder, she sneered at Conall as fire crackled at the ends of her clothes. Antlers rose from her head to crown her queen of the wilds. Beneath them burned all the fury of nature's wrath.

"You wanted Marzanna's aid?" she snapped, summoning an arrow and nocking it on her elaborately carved bow. "Why don't you meet her, then?"

Conall stumbled off his cart and landed on his back. "Spare me, Lady Dziewanna! I only wish to feed my daughters, be free of this frost."

Dziewanna scoffed. "The only freedom you will earn from my sister is that of death. If you desire it so, then I am perfectly capable of granting you the same. Czarnobóg would happily corrupt your dying soul into a demon."

"Mercy!" Conall pled.

"Wait," I insisted, crouching before him. He twitched as I called the winds to amplify my voice for all the crowd to hear. "My father wasn't known for mercy with Marzanna's worshippers, but if you tell me who burned the barn, maybe I'll consider it."

"I…"

I reached over my shoulder and drew Grudzień. The blade of the twelfth moon glinted like obsidian in the morning rays as it slid from its scabbard with a brutal shill. Each of its colored teeth resembled that of a sawblade, eager to bite into flesh.

"Consider your next words *very* carefully," I told him, blade to his throat. Dziewanna's threat was likely enough, but I was the king. People needed to see that I could lead with strength.

Trembling, Conall pointed into the crowd. Otylia followed his gaze, then leaped to action as a group fled. The mass of people blocked their retreat, and Otylia grinned with her hand raised.

"*Byt!*"

Żityje shot from her fingers in a flurry of silver and entrapped the five Marzanna worshippers, paralyzing them where they stood. The rest of the crowd backed away to form another circle around the group. Good, no one wanted to look attached to them. If we faced resistance now, then dissent was worse than we'd feared.

"Bring them here," I commanded my guards stationed around the village center. My old Simukie mentor, Xobas, was among them, and he grabbed two of the paralyzed Marzanna worshippers by the arms. Their eyes exposed their fear as he and the other guards dumped them beside Conall.

The Pargiawi man held out his hand pleadingly, so I nodded to the side. "Go, Conall. But do not speak another word in favor of Marzanna. We will know."

He nodded rapidly before rushing toward his family and disappearing into the audience.

Dziewanna replaced him beside me, drawing sweat across my brow from both nerves and heat. The wild goddess kept herself out of most business within the village, but when it involved Marzanna, she loomed like the summer sun. Yes, I was king. With two goddesses at my sides, though, I was not the true power here.

"You must kill them," Dziewanna said of the Marzanna worshippers.

"That could inspire more resistance," I replied. Death would mean handing them over to the goddess they worshipped and the dark dragon's corruption. Was there a better way to make use of them?

Otylia's moonlight pulsed as she spoke silently through our bond, *"Force them to offer a small blood sacrifice to replace the lost żityje. Just killing them would be a waste."*

My stomach churned, but she was right. Execution would do nothing for us except spread fear. A small token offering was not enough of a punishment, though, so sweeping my blade toward Marzanna's worshippers, I chose a third way.

"You burned our sacrifices to Lady Dziewanna. You betrayed every person in Dwie Rzeki and beyond, and for that, there can be no forgiveness." I drew an iron dagger from my belt. "You each have a choice: Die for your crimes or slice your hand, offering your blood to replace the *żityje* for Lady Dziewanna. All who choose the offering shall face exile instead of execution."

Otylia released them from her magic, and they cried out together until she raised a fist. "Enough!"

"Please!" one of the men protested. "Exile is no better than death." From old northern Krowik, he had more hair on his neck than his head, and his scalp was red from the chill.

Otylia scoffed. "You sabotaged us for Marzanna, but cannot trust her to save you from her winter? Coward."

"You have a choice," I said. "Make it quickly, so that we can fix what your goddess has wrought."

The northern man bowed his head, tears dripping to the snow. "I'd rather die quickly than suffer."

My chest tightened. I had hoped each of them to choose exile, but all who survived had been through much. To suffer alone was a greater toll than some could pay. He'd chosen, though, and only a weak ruler refused to carry out his sentence.

"Then so be it," I whispered, raising Grudzień. "May Nawia grant you rest."

It took all my strength not to avert my gaze as the blade fell. I'd killed plenty of men who'd faced me on the battlefield, but executing an unarmed foe was another matter entirely.

Grudzień struck true. Its teeth pierced him in a gruesome, inconstant cut that failed to sever the neck completely, but the deed was done. When I turned to the others, they clambered to offer their blood to go free. Their gazes twitched from their fallen comrade to the blood bowl that Otylia's Zurgowie friend, Ara, brought to her.

Thank the gods…

Yes, they had worshipped Marzanna and burned valuable offerings for Dziewanna's ritual, but it felt *wrong* to strike down people on their knees before me. Enough blood had fallen upon the snow in recent moons. If we were to survive the trials ahead, we needed unity, not more conflict. I just hoped the path I'd chosen was the right one.

I waved for Andrij, who stood at attention by the longhouse, a commander's silver cape hanging over his shoulders. He thumped his chest in reply before signaling to Xobas and the other guards.

"Bind the prisoners and take them east," he ordered.

Xobas nodded, grabbing the worshippers and instructing the crowd to part for them. In leather, sleeveless armor and with a curved cavalry blade at his side, he was a strange sight compared to the Krowikie guards, but I was grateful for him. It was hard to know who to trust in times like these. Xobas, though, would stand by me until time's end.

Narcyz leaned against the wall behind and watched Andrij with a heavy gaze. He chewed on a dry reed, which twisted around his finger as he huffed and followed his lover. Andrij marched with the discipline I needed in my captain of the guard, but Narcyz advanced like a grunt ready to knock out his opponent's teeth. Like fire and ice, both had their uses.

The crowd dispersed with the disturbance at its end. Were they pleased? Disappointed? I couldn't tell as I stood by the empty hole that had once held Jaryło's Heart of Jawia—known as Perun's Oak before we'd learned the truth of Jaryło's deception. Bone amulets would once have rattled overhead, the winds speaking through them, but all was uncomfortably still for the moment. The day had just begun, and the twisting in my stomach told me our problems were far from over. So, for the little time I had, I closed my eyes and breathed in the chilled air.

Now, we banish the frost from our lands.

2

Otylia

This had better work.

I HATED RULING. People were always mad about *something*. Whether chickens got loose, someone's neighbor dumped waste too close to their fence, or Marzanna worshippers burned down a barn, no decision pleased everyone. I so badly wanted to silence the objectors with a glare and a moonblast, but we had to be diplomatic, genial.

It was awful.

Wacław took the brunt of people's sting as king, but he'd taken to the role far more quickly than me. I wasn't queen yet. But I *was* a goddess. My word carried weight.

Prayers had rattled my sleep-deprived mind each night while I lay by Wacław's side in the longhouse, staring at the moonlight as it crept through the shuttered windows. So many hopes. So many fears. Most came from within Wild Moon's narrow lands, but I sensed people praying from further—those who, like me, stared up at the moon and searched desperately for a way to fix things. The people of our kingdom were Wacław's to protect. All the world was mine.

Mother had been little help in understanding the weight of a goddess. She'd spent so long fighting Perun and then Marzanna, so few had ever worshipped her when Jaryło was a far more pleasant option.

With Jaryło exposed and weak, she was the only spring deity left, and she was even worse at handling people than me.

Having Mother, the queen of Jawia, and Wacław, the king of Wild Moon, under one roof had left me in an odd position. Wacław was far less brutal than Mother. His decisions the morning of the ritual proved that. Both he and Mother called me to take their side, but I didn't want to be in charge. I just wanted to fight our way to Marzanna in Nawia and end this stupid winter. That couldn't happen until we finished Mother's ritual.

I jumped on the first chance to begin preparations. Wacław was busy dealing with Mother criticizing him for not executing the Marzanna worshippers, so I could build the ritual circle in blissful isolation.

Politics was hard, but time passed smoothly when I prepared my rituals. Each skull, bone, head of wheat, tuft of wool, or drizzle of blood had its place. Witchcraft was a formula, a puzzle like the potions Mother had taught me as a child. I found comfort in every step of the process.

"What's that symbol mean?" a voice rang.

I bit my cheek *hard*, nearly ripping the belladonna I'd been delicately placing between two opposing ends of the circle. "Awakening," I muttered, giving Ara a harsher side-eye than she deserved.

Dressed in her usual hunter's trousers and woolen coat, she hardly embodied the lover of the Simukie marzban, Zakir. She'd consented to wearing the Simukie's tan single-shoulder cape, and that small signal revealed a deeper care for her role, but she'd never abandon the simpler garbs of her Zurgowie clan.

"It's fascinating how similar your magic is to Zurgowie traditions," she said, kneeling beside me and fixing the break in the belladonna line I'd made when I jolted. "We all search for the same answer in different ways."

"And what's that answer?" I asked.

"You're the goddess." She surveyed the crowd, and I winced at the sight of my Moonmark pulsing on her neck. It still felt *wrong* to have branded one of my closest friends, even if it allowed her to wield my power. "We're all looking to you for guidance in this strange situation we've found ourselves in."

Of course. Unlike Zakir and me, she understood people at a glance. The Simukie and many Zurgowie had joined our Kingdom of the Wild Moon, but their once nomadic people remained connected. We needed her insights into the clans' cultures.

I followed Ara's gaze to a small, raven-haired girl who peeked out from behind a fencepost. When she realized I'd spotted her, she giggled and tucked back, believing like a cat that she was hidden as long as she couldn't see me.

But I kept watching. By blood and power, I was a goddess, and as that girl peeked again, I extended a hand toward her.

She scampered to me, leaving her mother deep in conversation with another woman. I'd anticipated her taking my hand, but she bypassed it to entrap me in her arms. If I hadn't known better, I would've thought she were a mighty beast wrestling me to Mokosz's earth. No. There was passion in that grip, adoration in her eyes.

"You can't hide from the gods," I whispered, embracing her after my initial surprise. "At least some of us care, even when you don't see us."

The girl just squeezed harder. Her nose ran from the cold and left an unsightly mark down the front of my dress. Yet I didn't pull away, and instead channeled the force of endings as I stroked her hair.

Smoke consumed reality.

I descended into End's visions, stepping from a funeral pyre and into a tundra. Only a scorched tree broke the ever-white plain as darkness smothered all other light. Its boughs hung like the scraps of a fallen roof, and the final ones clung to the trunk by a few thin strips of fibers. Terror echoed from it. Not audible, but piercing nonetheless, a cord wrapping tight around my heart.

A single sob tore me from the tree's bitter chill and back to the pyre's breath. The smoke covered a figure no taller than me, a torn hat flopping over her ears and eyes of Vastroth's rich sandstone studying me, narrow. The girl, now a young woman, tugged her heavy coat tighter around herself. Her gaze never left me as the wind tugged her hair free from its loose braid, joining with the fresh snowfall.

No powerful terror radiated from her. Her eyes said enough.

"You weren't there."

I ripped myself from the vision, taking a sharp breath and meeting the girl's wanting gaze. Who would she lose? Her mother? Everyone?

Those eyes haunted me as I released the girl. "What are you called?" I asked her, swallowing my fear, at least on the outside.

Her reply was lost to my ears, the tree's terror ringing in my mind instead. Asking her again would make it seem I hadn't listened, so I just smiled, summoned a silver wisp against her cheek, and sent her on her way.

"I'm not going anywhere," I promised.

She looked back, brow raised. "What?"

Her mother called for her before I replied, so I just waved for her to return to where she belonged. Czarnobóg's dark corruption permeated every part of my vision. But Preparations for the ritual came first, and ruminating about End's visions wouldn't fix anything. Dwie Rzeki would fall to Marzanna's winter without Mother's ritual. I couldn't let that happen.

Except Ara's own brow distracted me from my work. Furrowed, it unsettled me.

"A goddess can't hug a child?" I asked her, shifting to a gap in the ritual circle. It was a precarious arrangement, with portions that would burn to light the offerings and others that would remain grounded. Mother had trained me well, but this was more complex than any I had made before.

Ara copied my placements nearby, but I felt her gaze on me. "Oh, Otylia. If you believe I couldn't see your eyes flash white, then you don't know me as well as I thought. I'm your szeptucha and your friend. It's obvious when you're unsettled."

My fingers shredded a tuft of wheat. I huffed, sitting back on my heels and shutting my eyes, picturing that scorched tree. "I saw a barren winter in the future. That girl mourned someone at a funeral pyre, and there was this tree… It screamed out to me for help, but it was already dead."

"Do you think we fail?" she blurted out.

"End's visions can mean anything," I told her as much as myself. "Some are true, and others are just possibilities. I don't know which are which, but I'll do anything to avoid what I just saw."

She turned back toward me. "Why did you call End with that girl?"

I continued my work, nose wrinkled, as I considered that question. Why had I? Much had changed for me since my Ascension. Every time I thought I understood it all, something else crept in, and this silent force within me was the greatest question yet. I hadn't noticed it during the distractions of recent moons, but slow time in Dwie Rzeki had made it apparent. The force of endings guided me. I didn't understand how or why. When End reached out for me, though, I knew it in my soul, and I needed to answer.

"Destiny has her reasons, I guess," I replied.

Some time later, we finished the preparations with the help of a dozen other women. The ritual encircled the entire village center. Wheat and wool woven designs of the old tongue like roots intertwined beneath a dense forest. With blood and bones marking the end of one symbol and beginning of another, I stood in awe that this was allowed in the village now. My rituals had once been scorned.

Now, they were our only hope.

3

Otylia

Awaken the wilds, Mother, so that I can finally rest.

MY HOPES TURNED TO BURDENS beneath the purple skies of dusk. The moon renewed the strength in my soul, but it couldn't pierce the winter. Only Dziewanna could do that.

Mother stood atop the longhouse's step, the winds nipping at her flaming dress. She banished the cold for a hundred strides, and not a flake of snow fell upon Dwie Rzeki as I approached with a bowl of blood. This blood was symbolic. Her newly chosen szeptuchy had already burned the offerings we'd collected, granting her the power she needed, but the Marzanna worshippers' blood remained an image of Dziewanna's victory over her winter sister.

Before her, I felt like nothing more than a serving szeptucha. My skin reflected the moonlight, and my cloak of autumn leaves seemed to burn with her power. But she was ancient—a goddess carrying centuries as a warrior hardened with each battle. I was a child grasping at the forces of the divine.

Mother looked at me with pride, but sorrow crept into her eyes. She averted her gaze as she took the bowl, then raised it for the gathered crowd to see.

"My sister's winter has gripped this realm for far too long. Though we have vanquished her army and banished her to Nawia, the underworld cannot contain the corruption she unleashed through Czarnobóg. It spreads like the disease bearing her name, and I will do what I must to push back, to allow Jawia to breathe life once again."

Silence answered as she drank.

The tension in my chest hung over the entire village. Mother dropped the bowl, allowing it to shatter, and strode past me. Smoke drifted in her wake, and I hesitated at the memory of the girl's vision. Why had it rattled me? I'd seen so many visions of destruction, death, but this girl I'd met for mere moments gripped me tighter than most. End was telling me something. What?

Mother's szeptuchy held bowls of burning herbs along the rim of the circle. I closed my eyes, taking in their piercing scent as Dadźbóg's light disappeared over the horizon. Dark again. We'd survived the long night, and when the sun rose again, we'd have pushed back Marzanna.

Except End tugged on my soul. Like a child demanding attention from its mother, the pressure would not fade as I followed Mother to the circle. She stepped within, but I couldn't follow.

"All great acts require sacrifice," she said to me, glancing over her shoulder. "Listen to your force. My worst failures came when I ignored the will of the wilds."

Sacrifice?

I snatched at her arm, but she pushed onward to the heart of the circle, fire dripping from her fingers and igniting each symbol of the old tongue within the circle's layers. Any trace of Marzanna's chill vanished with the blaze. Power lingered in the old tongue, and where mortals saw mere flames, vibrant *žityje* flashed before me in a thousand colored wisps. Mother split them in her slow, ever constant charge until she held a hand before her.

"Jawia must thrive as it was meant to!" she declared. "A land for the living, not consumed by such death."

The winds paused at her voice. My chest tightened in the stillness, but she was too far now. Pushing for an answer would change nothing, and when she finished, the wisps circled her.

Faster and faster, they whipped through the flames and into her hand. Her willow wood hair rose and tangled in her antlers as she whispered in the old tongue. Light pulsed from her eyes. Flames surged from her skirts into her very body, setting her alight.

She slammed her palm into the earth.

A shockwave threw me onto my back. Wacław scrambled to me from the longhouse doorway as darkness overtook the ritual circle, ash replacing flame in an instant. He helped me up, but I staggered alone toward the dim figure now kneeling amid the ritual circle.

Ash consumed Mother. Her skin and once fiery dress were gray, and her eyes were no longer radiant with the *žityje* she'd consumed. Where her palm met the ground, streaks of deep green shot across the dirt like cracks in a frozen lake. But roots rose from those streaks and entangled her. Sweat beaded down her brow, and her neck bulged with effort as she looked up at me.

"Mother?" I cried out, dropping to my knees and reaching toward the roots. They grew up her body. Soon, they would trap her completely.

Her green eyes sharpened. "Don't! This is my prison, my cost for commanding Jawia."

I shook my head. "Why? I don't understand."

"Rod deemed Jawia to be free from the complete control of a single god, but the balance is gone. I have claimed the living realm to push back against Marzanna's corruption. It will grant your people hope for a time, but Jawia will feed on me as long as Marzanna's winter also claims this realm."

The roots tightened around her neck, each breath becoming a gasp.

"You can't just leave me. Not again!" I screamed with tears stinging my eyes. "I just got you back."

Mother smiled proudly. "Find the remaining shards of Alatyr. Unite them, and I will never leave you again."

Her eyes glazed over as the roots covered her head, locking her away from me yet again. I sat back with my fists dug into the ground. They shook from both anger and fear. This ritual was supposed to buy us time, but I needed Mother to help me face Marzanna. *She* was the real goddess. *She* was the queen of Jawia. And she'd left me to fend for myself.

"Why do you never tell me your plan?" I asked her still form. "What do I have to do to earn your trust?"

I flinched as a hand fell lightly on my shoulder.

"I'm sorry," Wacław whispered, kneeling beside me and taking me in his arms.

My moonlight exposed his own tears, and beyond the circle, torches lit the forlorn faces of our people. They'd looked to Dziewanna for hope, for a future. Mother seemed to believe her ritual had repelled Marzanna's power, but to these mortals, it appeared that their goddess had failed despite their offerings.

"No." I forced myself to stand and meet their gazes. Despite my pain, they needed to see that I had hope, that they still had a goddess to guide them. Grief could come in private.

"Lady Dziewanna has bound herself to Jawia," I announced, wiping away my tears. "She has pushed back Marzanna's power at a great cost, but we *will* defeat Marzanna and free our realm of Czarnobóg's corruption, freeing my mother from this toll."

My words found only gasps and shaking heads. I'd told them the truth, and if they still feared, then so be it. There was plenty to fear when we faced a corrupted goddess and a three-headed dragon who'd fought all Prawia's gods and nearly won.

Now, I somehow had to defeat them both without Mother… Wonderful.

The crowd mulled about for some time, grumbling as Father, Wacław, and the szeptuchy tried to reassure them, but I couldn't give any more. My shoulders felt as if the mountains rested upon them. Half of me wanted to scream and punch at Mother for abandoning me again without warning. The other half wanted to curl up in the longhouse and pretend this day had never happened.

"Do you need a moment alone?" Wacław asked through our bond, catching my eye from amid a group at the far side of the village center. He didn't wait for an answer. *"Go. I'll handle the crowd and join you when they're calmed."*

Thank you, I replied, head dropping as I turned back to the long-house.

But I didn't want to be alone, just away from the crowd. Though I was more powerful than Wacław, being with him made me feel safe. He let me speak my mind without judgment. Besides him, only Ara could make me bare my heart, and they had *very* different approaches.

The expansive interior of the longhouse's main room swallowed me in its shadows as I hurried across it. End's familiar tug called for me to answer, but the last thing I needed today was another vision. Mother had insisted I listened to my force, yes, but she'd not given me the chance to listen to her. I'd follow its call when I was ready. Not a moment before.

Memories of the spring equinox festival filled my mind. The long-house had been lighter then, chiefs and commonfolk alike celebrating the new season in ignorance of what would soon come. Andrij's arrival had sparked their interest in the eastern clans as a threat, but Jacek and the other chiefs had missed the true horror beyond. They were dead because of it. There were no celebrations in this hall now, just arguments about our lack of food and what to do about Marzanna and Czarnobóg.

The main door creaked open behind me.

I spun, channeling bright *žityje* and ready to launch a moonblast. A woman cowered in the doorway with a yelp.

"Please, Otylia, it's just me."

I dismissed my power. "Lubena?"

Wacław's mother stepped into my moonlight with her radiant blonde hair aglow and her sky-blue eyes as caring as her son's. She took my hands, bowing her head. "I am sorry to intrude, but I couldn't let you be alone. Especially not after all you suffered the first time Odeta... Dziewanna... left you."

My defenses fell. I embraced her, sobbing into her shoulder while she stroked my hair. Why couldn't I be the strong goddess my mother demanded I be? She needed me to kill Marzanna, but I couldn't even hold myself together in front of a crowd.

"I never wanted to be a goddess," I mumbled. "Nobody ever needed me before. It was easier that way."

Lubena chuckled. "It is better this way, though. What would we be without you?"

"But I can't kill Marzanna." I stepped away, arm held across my waist. "We barely managed to defeat the sliver of her power she sent to aid Koschei during the battle, and she'll have Czarnobóg now."

"Dziewanna said that her sister was different before Jaryło's adultery, right?" she asked. When I nodded, she gave a knowing smile. "Then maybe she can change again—gods know both you and Wacław have in recent moons. Any mother fears to see it, but this was where you two were meant to be, and I know you'll find a way. You need her Moonstones, not her death."

"Her Moonstones are the other shards of Alatyr we need to mend the seal between the Three Realms and Oblivion, but she's the one who tore it in the first place. We'll have to kill her somehow."

She squeezed my shoulder. "Then I pray her end is final. This long winter has my skin more fragile than your father's pride."

That brought a smile out of me. How did she do it so easily? It was only a moment's relief, but it felt like an oasis in the Vastrothie desert.

We parted with another embrace, but I so badly wished that touch were Mother's instead. Even when present, though, she was never so gentle. Wildfires blazed through the forests. Lubena was the trickle of a creek during a spring drizzle.

The shadows returned as I headed down the side hall to the chamber I now shared with Wacław. We'd seen Jacek exile him from these walls at birth, but he was king now. Someday, I would be his queen. First, I needed to fulfill my promise to our people and end Marzanna's wrath. Mother had given them a reprieve.

I would end their trial.

I threw open the room's window and rifled through my old herb bag. Few usable ones remained, but enough to form a small ritual circle along with the small bones that I'd once decorated my braid with. The circle was unnecessary to reach into End's power. After tonight's uncertainty, though, it was an act of solidarity with Mother. For until I did my part, she would be trapped in the circle I'd helped craft.

Moonlight streamed over me as I sat crossed legged, closing my eyes. Emotions stirred in my soul, but I focused only on End's whisper. That constant hum that demanded I listen.

Show me. Tell me how to save Mother and end this.

4

Wacław

The ritual worked, but it sure as Oblivion doesn't feel like it…

DADŹBÓG'S LIGHT ROSE OVER A CHANGED LANDSCAPE the morning after Dziewanna's ritual had left her paralyzed in magical roots. Moods throughout Dwie Rzeki were varied, but most mourned the goddess's sacrifice. Ironic, as few had offered a prayer to her moons before.

Much had happened since the equinox, though, and now, the villagers around me sang Dziewanna's praises as we stared at the thawed forests and farms. In a few hours, the air had warmed and the snow had melted. It was Sierpień, autumn in the natural cycle, but even the middling temperatures were a relief compared to the brutal frost we'd faced.

But our true joy came from the appearance of leaves, critters, bird songs, and flowers. Red poppies swarmed the areas where our warriors had fallen. Widows and widowers wept by the reminders of their loved ones, while children rushed alongside our red fox, Sosna, through the fields with their cheeks bright in the sunlight. Where death had conquered was now full of life.

For now.

We'd all seen the toll Dziewanna paid for such vibrance. The goddess hadn't warned Otylia, and my heart grew heavy knowing how she suffered. I'd consoled her all I could last night. She'd still insisted on going into the woods alone, and she never took no for an answer.

So I let myself enjoy the morning with the others. Little Nevenka, my half-sister, circled me with her indecipherable giggles as she swung about some kind of woven toy resembling a cross between Kuba's old jackal body and a firebird. Occasionally, she shouted her nickname for me, Waci, before resuming her dance. I tried to join in, but she insisted that I was doing it wrong. So I stuck to watching and pondering what came next until Otylia emerged from the woods.

She was covered up to her knees in mud, and much of it had splattered across her face too. Sosna yapped and ran through her loose, roughspun trousers as my old tunic hung nearly down to her shins. Mom would've been aghast if I'd treated my clothes like that, but I dared not question a goddess, even if she'd borrowed my clothes.

Some deities rose radiant above the earth. Others became one with it. Otylia could do both, and gods, I loved that dirtied witch stomping through the fields like a miawka out for vengeance.

She hauled two overflowing bags of herbs to me and threw them down with a huff. They interrupted Nevenka's circle, but the girl just hopped over them as Otylia grinned at me. Her green eyes were as bright as the lively wilds as she laughed. *Laughed.*

"I haven't collected this much birch in *years!*" she exclaimed, pulling out twigs and then countless leaves. Sosna inspected each with a greedy sniff as Otylia explained each herb's uses, and it took Nevenka distracting the fox to give her enough space to lay them all out.

It was far too much to comprehend so quickly, but I loved every moment of Otylia's passion. Last night, she'd been a ball of rage and sorrow. This, though, was the Otylia I'd known as a child and the one I'd fallen in love with over every year since. It didn't matter if I understood the herbs. I'd give her every moment of joy she could have.

Nevenka stopped randomly throughout Otylia's explanation to point at an herb and shout, "What's that one?" or "Why's that one puwple?"—she still struggled with her R sounds—before skipping off for a bit. I expected Otylia to snap at her for interrupting constantly, but she seemed to enjoy the dose of chaos.

A rare moment indeed.

"Dziewanna said the ritual would push back winter," I said, waving my arms to all the changes around us, "but I didn't expect all of *this.*"

Otylia's nose wrinkled. "She has a habit of not telling us everything."

"All the gods do, it seems."

"But she's supposed to be different."

"I'm sorry she left," I said, cupping her cheek as I tugged at the wooden Mothermarked necklace Mom had given me. "But besides Mokosz, how many other gods would surrender so much to protect Jawia?"

She leaned into my hand. "How can she protect Jawia when she's trapped? She insisted this ritual would only work temporarily."

"Which is why you listened to her and reached out to End, right?"

Sosna's yapping interrupted her reply. A stumbling young man burst from another section of the woods to the south. Clutching a javelin in each hand, his bare torso was more mud than skin, and his smile was as jubilant as the spring sun.

"Oh gods," Otylia muttered, pinching her nose as Nevenka mimicked the gesture and fled. "Is that mud or manure?"

Kuba hopped over a pasture fence and stopped before us. He reeked of everything nature had to offer. "This is awesome! I forgot what it felt like to hunt."

"Based on your empty pack," Otylia replied, "you forgot how to hunt too."

He stuck out his tongue before turning to me. "She's just jealous that I caught *three* deer in one morning. These are my last two javelins, thank you very much! Got Narcyz's brutes carrying the carcasses back. We're going to have a feast for sure, right?"

Otylia gave me a pleading look. "We can't feast while Mother is like that."

"Isn't she a patron of hunters?" I asked with a shrug. "The people need something to celebrate, and we can dedicate a feast to her honor before we set off to face Marzanna."

Kuba dropped to his knees to beg, earning an obnoxious fox kiss from Sosna, but Otylia dug in her heels. "Why do you resemble a dog now more than when you were one?"

I chuckled. "Kuba has a point for once. We should store what we can from our gains, as this won't last forever, but a small celebration as thanks to Dziewanna is in order." Otylia's glare turned to me, but I took her hand. "We'll address her failure to communicate *after* we free her. Until then, we need to accept she gave us a chance."

"Fine," Otylia muttered, a smirk slipping through as she glanced at Kuba. "But a *small* celebration. I have enough supplies now to brew some herbal teas like Mother always did too."

Kuba hopped up and slapped her on the shoulder. "That's the spirit. Meat and… err… tea for celebrations. Nope, no oskoła or beer at all."

"Get drunk tonight all you want," she said. "But if you're too hungover to come with us and face Marzanna, we're leaving you behind."

He jabbed his javelins into the ground. "Oh, yes! Where are we going? Who do I stab?"

Otylia rolled her eyes. "We'll talk more about the plan later. Just know we're going back to Nawia, and somehow, I expect our trip to be less pleasant than last time."

"Sounds fun." He scanned the gathered people. "Have you seen Maja? She'll be so excited."

"She was with a group of women by the tannery last I saw," I replied. "Maybe wash before running through the village, though. We have some eager hunters, and you look like a demon more than a man."

Kuba ran a mud-covered finger across the demonic veins on my face, pursuing me despite my attempts to pull away. "Says the actual demon!"

With my face thoroughly muddied, he grabbed his javelins and hopped more than ran after his lover. Otylia shook her head, but I couldn't help smiling.

"He's been to Prawia and Nawia alike, died, turned into a jackal, and found the fern flower," I said, "but he's not changed one bit."

"Mother used to say that even rocks change over the ages," Otylia said, "but I don't think Kuba ever will."

I picked up one of her bags, which she protested before resorting to carrying just one, following me toward the village. "I hope he doesn't. We need him to remind us that not everything is about gods and demons."

"Except it is."

"For now, but what about after all of this? There is still life to live, especially for those with shorter lifespans than the two of us."

She raised a brow. "You seriously can think about what happens after? We don't even know that there will be an after."

"There will be," I said with a nod to the guards at the gate. They looked forlornly to the forests, wishing to join the festivities. "As long as you are determined to do something, it'll happen. Nothing can stand in the way of Nemiza, *Calamity*." The Vastrothie had named her Nemiza in honor of the destruction she'd brought against Marzanna's forces in their country, but she'd insisted on her true name as a goddess.

She drew a long breath before clenching her fists at her sides. "We stopped Koschei. We escaped Baba Jaga. We beat Czarnobóg once. So we can do it again."

"What do you think they're doing to Weles?" I asked. Czarnobóg had dragged Otylia's blood father, the god of the lowlands and cattle, into Nawia. It was likely the underworld had fallen with its god.

She sneered. "Hopefully punishing him for being the worst father to ever walk the Three Realms. I'll free him too, but then he'll answer to Mother and me for what he's done."

We passed Dariusz's house and bands of hunters comparing the pelts they'd already earned. Sosna ran up to each and demanding they scratch her head or neck, and even the toughest hunters complied. I couldn't laugh, though. Not when I feared these gifts wouldn't last long.

"Then to Nawia we go," I replied. "I already know where the evening gate is in the west, so we can pass through when we're ready."

"No." She hoisted her bag further up her shoulder. Despite just being herbs and twigs, each one was heavy, and it was impressive she'd carried both with ease. "Marzanna and Czarnobóg will expect that. They'll have an army guarding it like a chokepoint. There's no way we'll get through."

"Huh. You've been listening to Xobas."

She nodded as we passed Ara and Zakir's group of Simukie, who gathered around the smithy owned by Narcyz's parents. Zakir studied the farrier as she shoed the horses in preparation for the clan's next hunt. Ara seemed content to just be by his side and occasionally whisper into his ear.

"Xobas has experience," Otylia said, "and we can learn from the clans. They were smart enough to bond with Mother's horses after all."

We stopped at the edge of the village center, Otylia's face paling. "Mother told me to listen to End, and she was right. Our only option is the Way of Souls. Follow the dead, and we'll find the goddess of death."

I followed her gaze to Dziewanna's paralyzed form. Like a statue, she knelt amid the streaks of green that now stretched across the ground for miles. "What else did End tell you? You were secretive about it last night, and if you're mad about Dziewanna keeping secrets, then—"

"I'm not keeping secrets," she interrupted. "It's just... I saw what could happen. End's visions aren't continuous, but I know what we can't do and what might work. Putting them together is what's hard.

Just trust that I'm doing what I must to avoid all the ones where Czarnobóg burns you to a crisp before my eyes, okay?"

The pain in her voice pulsed through our bond. It had been apparent the night before as well, but I'd tolerated her silence as part of her mourning. Though not knowing the whole plan was irritating, End hadn't shown her everything either.

"So, the Way of Souls then…" I said, trying to calm my tone. "Dogoda told me it was another way when I was trying to get to you, but she didn't say how we follow the dead." The kind west wind had joined part of my journey to the evening gate, and I winced remembering her falling in the battle against Czarnobóg in Prawia.

Otylia hoisted her herbs. "That's what these are for. Did you think I collected them just for fun?"

"Well, I considered you might've enjoyed ruining my clothes."

She went onto the tips of her toes to kiss my cheek, then wiped away some of the remaining mud from Kuba's attack and hurried ahead. "Of course I did, but we'll need a large ritual circle to convince Jawia our spirits are dead."

"Who else are we bringing?" I asked, following her to the longhouse. "I assume End showed you which groups are most likely to succeed."

Andrij stood with his jaw jutted out by the longhouse doors. Narcyz leaned against the wall on the other side, arms crossed, decidedly not looking at his partner.

"In fact, I have exactly the crew," Otylia said, nodding at Andrij. "Are they gathered?"

The guard captain thumped his chest. "I did my best. Everyone is here except for Kuba and Ara."

"I'm here!" Ara called out, throwing her arm over Otylia's shoulders. "Sorry. I was wishing Zakir luck on his hunt with the Simukie."

"Thought he didn't like hunting?" Narcyz grumbled. He still refused to look toward Andrij, and there was a slice in his pantleg that was already crusted with dry blood.

Ara flexed her bicep. "He's tough. Besides, he said it would be a 'fascinating study of the realm's changes' or something like that."

"So just Kuba's missing, then," I said with a glance at Otylia. "You should've said we needed him."

She tapped her nose. "I don't want that reek in our longhouse. We both spent the morning in the forest, but I didn't come out wearing half of it."

I pointed at her trousers. "Right, just a quarter of—oof." Her fist jabbed my side, so I relented the joke. "Who else is here?"

Otylia pushed open the door. "Why don't you come and see?"

5

Otylia

Everyone in this room is at risk. Their lives are in my hands.

LIGHT STREAMED THROUGH THE LONGHOUSE WINDOWS, and candles in the chandeliers above banished the shadows that had followed me the night before. I was no longer alone. Our friends had gathered at my command, each chosen based on End's visions.

Meeting their faces made me shudder. My ritual had given me clarity, but so too had it shown me the deaths of everyone I loved. Some were distant, others nearer. None were certain.

Mother had tasked me with collecting the twelve shards of Alatyr, each a Moonstone for the twelve moons. Seven shards were gathered here:

Narcyz held Kwiecień: the golden shard of the fourth moon.

Kuba held Maj: the green shard of the fifth moon.

Sabina held Czerwiec: the white shard of the sixth moon.

Marzyana held Sierpień: the orange shard of the eighth moon.

Ta held Wrzesień: the violet shard of the ninth moon.

Ara held Październik: the gray shard of the tenth moon.

And Wacław held Grudzień: the black shard of the twelfth moon.

I had surrendered the shard Lipiec to the dragon Garafena in Buyan until we returned with the rest. That left four of the twelve in

Marzanna's grasp. We'd only succeeded in taking Grudzień from her in Vastroth, and the other seven had once been Jaryło's. That gave us more than she had, but she had wielded them for centuries. Only a god could access the true power within a Moonstone. That meant only Marzyana—the goddess of the harvest—and I had complete control over the form a shard took. For the rest, they remained as a Moonblade.

Andrij joined us as well, his power as Mother's first szeptun—the male version of a szeptucha—giving him enough to be an asset with the bow she'd gifted him. His eyes were still ashen despite Mother's healing, but at least his sight had effectively returned. Few others in our journeys had been so lucky.

The nine of us were hardly an army, but End's visions had shown that too large of a group would draw attention on the Way of Souls. Whenever anyone else showed up in the visions, we failed. That didn't guarantee success with this group, but it meant we at least weren't doomed. I'd take it.

"We need no introductions," I said, standing with Wacław in the room's center as the others sat at various tables. "Each one of you here has faced Marzanna's forces in one way or another, and you carry a power that can help us defeat her. Whether Moonblade, channeling, or some other ability that Destiny wishes you to use, you are the group I saw in my visions. Together, we can succeed."

Sabina raised her small nymph hand, and her wings fluttered when she spoke. "Wouldn't it be better to give the Moonstones to you? You're a goddess, and most of us aren't warriors."

"Even I, being a goddess, do not feel that I should be part of this mission," Marzyana said from her seat alone at a table near the door. The harvest goddess wore a simple brown dress, and she looked ashamed as she held the sickle-like blade of Sierpień. "Your mother's gift was a great one, and the people of Jawia need me here to ensure it can be protected to its greatest extent. Though her power far exceeds mine, perhaps I can provide some guidance and life to the crops that are so late in their planting."

"End's vision—" I began.

"Is the will of your force," Marzyana replied, standing. "My own guides me to stay with the living realm, where I am most needed. Take Sierpień, Otylia, and allow the shard of this moon to strengthen you during its final days. We had at one time three goddesses to guard this fledgling kingdom. If we both leave, there will be no one left to protect Jawia should Marzanna conspire here once again."

I bit my cheek. "They'll have no protection if we fail."

"In my heart, I do not believe you will," she said sweetly. "You have my blessings, and now, you have my Moonblade. Use it well." She approached, holding Sierpień out for me to take. "Fight well, daughter of the wilds."

I grimaced as I took the blade, running my finger along the flat and the amber symbols of the old tongue etched into it. "We'll miss you, but I can't force you to come."

"Much more can be accomplished through cooperation than force."

The goddess left. Her auburn soul wisp drifted behind her, invisible for all but me, and I resisted the urge to touch it. Would her decision sway our ends for good or ill?

We were in the last third of the Sierpień moon, and the Moonblade hummed in my grasp. Plentiful *żityje*, ready to be channeled at a moment's notice. But my silver spear served as my weapon, so I touched the pool of *żityje* and willed the sword to shift into a Moonmark temple ring, to be worn from my headband as I'd done with Lipiec before. I could channel the shard's power from there or embed it into the tip of my silver spear whenever I summoned it.

"So that's it, then," Narcyz said, holding his own Moonblade like it were a delicate child. "Eight of us against a goddess and a dragon that had even Perun shaking in his boots… perfect."

"It won't be easy," Wacław said, "but we defeated Koschei together. We drove off Czarnobóg too."

Kuba sat back with his hands behind his head. "With the fern flower's luck on our side, we can't go wrong. It'll lead us right to Marzanna's little hideout, and then *WHAM!*" He stabbed the air with his blade. "Right in that empty heart of hers. Wish we had Perun's golden apples, though. Those things were like lightning in… well, you know… an apple."

"That's the point, air brain," Ta quipped, spinning one of her glass-bladed rings between her fingers. "Ya know, as the god of lightning and everything."

"Oh…"

"Who trusted Kuba with a Moonblade anyway?" Narcyz added. "He'll probably stab one of us before—"

Kuba shot to his feet, sword raised as Narcyz rose to meet him. "Wanna find out what I can do?"

I stared up at the ceiling and whispered a prayer before pulsing my power. A wave of harmless moonlight washed across the room, stopping the boys in their tracks. Their eyes widened as I tapped my foot. "Are you finished? Or would you prefer to keep squabbling while holding *shards of the stone that literally created the gods?*"

The boys shied back to their respective tables, heads tucked so far to their chests that any semblance of their necks disappeared. Wacław nodded to me, so I continued.

"The Way of Souls is a dangerous path meant only for the dead. Based on the legends, it follows Weles's lowland rivers into the ground. Guardians ensure anyone who is still alive no longer has the pleasure by the time they reach the fiery Smorodina River at Nawia's edge."

Sabina raised her hand. "How… How do we go through, then? We're not dead."

"That's the problem," I confirmed. "We're not dead, except for Wacław." His tension pushed through our bond, the Trial of Loss far too recent not to sting. I'd taken his mortal soul to Ascend, but that would work in our favor now. "Rod told me that Nawie were meant to protect the Way of Souls against corrupted demons, aiding the dead on their journey. The guardians should see him as an escort to us if we appear dead."

Ara's face contorted. "You want us to *die?* Kuba has already done that once, and it didn't look fun."

"It wasn't!" Kuba exclaimed, gesturing at his body. "I just got out of that jackal body. I don't want to go back."

One look from me sent him cowering again. "Let me finish before you panic. We only need to appear dead, not be actually dead. Based on End's visions, Wacław being a Naw should be enough to prevent the guardians from seeing past our ruse."

"And if it doesn't work?" Ta scrambled to ask. "What're these guardians? Demons? Dragons? Massive fish with eighty teeth and venom oozing from each one?"

Sabina's jaw dropped. "That is horrifying…"

"Your horror," Ta replied. "My dream. Imagine riding something like that. Even Marzanna would be afraid."

Wacław waved a hand in their direction. "I think we're getting off topic. Whatever the guardians are, we don't want to fight them. We'll have enough trouble facing Marzanna and Czarnobóg without being drained first."

Thank you, I told him through our bond before continuing out loud, "Wacław is right. End showed me flashes of some shadows' forms, but little else. It doesn't matter what they are. As long as my plan works, they won't attack." I raised my herb bag with some effort before setting it back down. "Which brings me to how we appear dead to the guardians: tea and an old ritual Mother described to me once."

"It can't be oskoła?" Narcyz asked.

"Try it," I snapped, "and then let me know what it feels like to have the Way's guardians ripping your soul from your body."

Andrij rubbed Narcyz's back. Narcyz didn't shy away, so I hoped whatever lovers' quarrel they'd gone through earlier was over. We had enough problems without fighting each other.

"What will this tea and ritual do?" Andrij asked. "I imagine we will resemble the spirits of the dead?"

"The tea slows your heart and cools your body," I replied, recalling Mother's use of it many years ago to aid a child whose chest ached from exertion. "By itself, it isn't enough, because the guardians will sense our *żityje* like Wacław can. The ritual will stop that by taking our *żityje* and placing it in a skull we'll each carry." Any witch knew that bones could carry remnant energy, so if the guardians tolerated our Moonstones, they would hopefully ignore the skulls carrying *żityje* too.

"Won't that kill us?" Ara asked. "*Żityje* is life force, so how can we live without it?"

I winced. End's visions had been clear that this part would be a struggle for all of us: god, Naw, nymph, or mortal. "We'll give up all but the little *żityje* we need to exist until we reach Marzanna's castle at Nawia's edge, which means we'll be basically at death's door until we're safe to draw our *żityje* back from the skulls."

Wacław cursed under his breath. "You want them to go through what I do each time I'm drained?"

"No. The rest of us don't have a demonic soul, so we'll just be weak." I wrapped an arm around him, trying my best to be reassuring. "You won't go through the ritual. Nawie always have *żityje*, so the guardians won't care about you."

Ta nodded. "Good idea, after what happened in—" She stopped herself there, but Wacław clenched his fists. His bloodthirsty slaughter in Vastroth had been mere moons before. All he'd done since was fight the part of him we called the Płanetnik, but even with me forging a new pact to calm his demon, we both knew the presence would linger as long as he lived.

"So," Ara said with a forced cough. "We drink this tea and put ourselves at death's edge, then walk past some creepy shadows. How hard could it be?"

Sabina took flight, sword raised, but her arm shook until she gripped the hilt with both hands. "We can do this together!"

"Ah, the power of friendship," Narcyz muttered. "That'll do it."

"If there aren't any more pressing questions," I said, "then spend the day preparing. *King* Wacław has ordered a small celebration with the thaw." I winked at Wacław, and he chuckled at my formalities. "But be careful. We leave at dawn tomorrow. Mother's power wanes every day, and I'd rather use Sierpień before we return to Marzanna's moons."

Andrij thumped his chest, smiling wryly. "As Lady Otylia commands."

"Don't call me that. You know better."

"I know, but some of us need to counter Narcyz's lack of decorum." He grabbed Narcyz and hauled him to his feet. "C'mon. Let's get ready, then drunk. I don't want to think about death teas until morning."

The others followed them out, leaving Wacław and me alone. He looked ill as he circled to the throne and sat with Grudzień's jagged black blade balanced across the armrests. The thin streaks of colors arcing across it shimmered in the light, and even mad, his eyes glowed with it.

"Why didn't you tell me about the ritual sooner?" he asked. "I don't want you or them to suffer without *žityje*. I've endured it enough."

I took his Moonblade by the hilt, then replaced it on his lap. His expression softened as I read the old tongue symbols on its flat, "*Finality. Darkness. Hope.* Grudzień describes exactly what we'll face on the Way of Souls, and it'll be up to you to give our friends that hope. I know the plans, but you're the one that can make it not seem like we're doomed."

"Are we?"

"I don't know." I laid my head on his shoulder, still admiring the blade. "You have no idea how badly I want to ram this through Marzanna's chest."

He wrapped his arms around me. Demonic soul or not, his touch was soft, and it calmed the fire within my chest. "You'll have to fight most of us for the honor. It's frightening how much she's done to us in only half-a-year." He held out his once Frostmarked palm. Below it pulsed our joined Moonmark and Eclipsemark on his forearm, mirroring the one on mine. "I can't believe I was desperate enough to listen to her, to give into her temptations."

I set down the sword and intertwined our fingers. Our bond allowed us to experience the other's senses, so moments like this were a cycle of pleasure from the slightest contact. It threatened to pull me in, but there was so much to prepare for our journey.

"She's had centuries to perfect her craft," I whispered. "I'm not so well practiced, but luckily, you weren't all that difficult for me to tempt."

I kissed him, enjoying his touch a few heartbeats longer before forcing myself to pull away. His gaze lingered on me as I headed toward the door. *Good.*

"I need to start brewing the teas," I said, smiling back at him. "Keep our friends alive through the celebrations for me. This will get even more difficult if they're actually dead."

"As if this weren't already difficult," he replied.

I traced our shared mark. "Beyond this, everything is."

6

Wacław

In the legends, they leave out the part where the hero's stomach aches in fear.

MUSIC FROM NEARLY A DOZEN TRIBES AND CLANS FLOWED through Dwie Rzeki's trails that night. Meats and berries filled the tables of my longhouse and the village center beyond, and people raised mugs of oskoła, beer, and wine in honor of the bounty Dziewanna had brought us.

As I sat on my father's old throne, watching people dance through the night, I couldn't join their revelry. It felt wrong just to call this longhouse mine. Celebrating Dziewanna's sacrifice only made the feeling worse, and I feared what my friends would endure come morning. The Way of Souls was the rare place a Naw belonged. Why couldn't I take their burdens on the journey?

The others had no such qualms about what came next. They laughed among warriors and hunters, displaying their Moonblades like trophies. What had Alatyr looked like while united? Maybe we'd see soon.

Each of our friends drank their share, and Ara had to pry Ta's fourth or fifth drink from her fingers. At thirteen, the girl put up quite the fight. Krowikie tradition dictated that children could enjoy alcohol as they pleased, but we didn't need her first hangover ruining what would already be a perilous quest.

Gods, she's just a child, and I'm dragging her into battle against gods.

Nausea halted my effort to raise my mug to my lips. My people feasted today, but I couldn't bring myself to. Friend or stranger, each of them was my responsibility. This was about more than our personal grudges against the winter goddess and her dark dragon. The Kingdom of the Wild Moon was at stake—and all of Jawia with it.

Grabbing Grudzień, I stood, drawing the gaze of some. That last symbol on its blade, *hope*, burned in my mind. Otylia had said it was my responsibility to keep the others going while she planned, so while I couldn't celebrate, I would do my duty.

"Dziewanna has given herself so that we may fight on," I shouted, silencing the songs. All eyes were on me now, and I realized I had no speech planned. What words could be enough anyway?

"Tonight is not a celebration of what we have accomplished," I continued. "It is a remembrance of the sacrifices that have allowed us to make it this far. Mortals, gods, and even demons have fallen so that we may create a new future for Jawia, so that we can defeat the taint that grips the Three Realms." I rolled up my sleeves to expose my demonic veins, a web of the very corruption we fought. "I would say 'gods help us,' but Perun and his allies don't care. It's up to us now. And I don't intend to fail you."

Drunken cheers answered me, but my shoulders slumped. Hope would keep them going for a time while we were gone. It didn't change the steep challenge we faced.

Many in the crowd patted me on my shoulders or bowed as I made for the doors. A hundred supporters. On our last night before we joined the dead, though, there was only one person I wanted to see.

Dancers stomped and twirled to the beat of the drums outside. Motion filled the village center in a flurry of light and shadow, but the center remained deathly still. Dziewanna knelt amid the roots, alone. Could she see the joy she'd created? Or did pain consume her every moment as she waited for us to free her?

Either way, I promised myself the queen of Jawia would be unbound again soon. Jawia needed her. We all did.

I found Otylia where our troubles had begun all those years ago. The ring of trees I'd drained moons before were vibrant once again, and I sensed *žityje* shifting through the underbrush. Would the wolves dare attack us again? Before, I'd been a foolish boy with nothing more than a stick for a weapon. They would not fare so well against a god's blade.

"You should be with your people," Otylia said from the center of a candlelit circle. She knelt before a kettle which boiled over a small fire surrounded by skulls, just as elders' stories described a witch.

Except in those tales, the witch wanted to eat you or tempt you with power. This one made me want to lie by her side for eternity, forgetting the world's troubles as her chest rose and fell with mine.

She furrowed her brow. "You're staring at me like that again."

"It's hard to look away from you," I replied as I stepped carefully into her circle. But a putrid smell struck me the moment I neared the kettle's steam. I gagged and backed away, knocking over a candle in the process.

Exhaustion sunk Otylia's face as she stared at the extinguished candle with her ladle dangling from her fingertips, as if on the precipice. I used another's fire to re-light its wick, but she remained like a statue. Silence crept over the forest beyond the kettle's bubbling. Some part of me wished to break it, but I felt her empty sorrow. No rousing speech could change that.

I rounded the fire and rubbed her back. Rigid as a board, she resisted at first before sinking into me, her emerald eyes glinting with moonlit silver.

"If you won't celebrate with them," she said, "then you should rest. Destiny knows when we'll have the chance again."

"Sleep is still a stranger to me," I replied, sitting behind her and allowing her to lay her head in my lap as she stared up at the stars. Each was a living soul, and there were far less than when the spring equinox had come five moons before. "It's strange to always be in my soulform now, willing people to see me instead of being invisible."

"Your soul-form never slept before," she said. "I don't understand why it must now that you're always in it."

"Even gods sleep, I guess. Maybe it's our souls rejoining with the forces of the realms for a time." I closed my eyes, talk of sleep reminding me how exhausted I was after the last couple days. "Rising from my body was both a curse and a gift. It was freedom, but those were the loneliest hours. For a third of my life, I was completely alone, invisible to the world. I sometimes wished for it when Mikołaj or Narcyz would beat me and mock me. I realize now, though, that I didn't want to be invisible."

Otylia reached up and ran her fingers across my stubbled chin. Gods, my heart ached at her touch. "You wanted to be seen."

"Yes," I said, a surge of painful memories swelling within me. They were miniscule compared to the threats we faced now, but a hundred cuts hurt as much as a mighty strike. "I didn't need attention. I just wished someone would see that I was more than my father's rejected son, more than just a cursed outcast."

"I see you," she whispered.

I held her hand against my cheek. "Why did I take so long to tell you? I didn't want Father to exile you for your channeling, but we lost so many years…"

"You were a child. We both were. What's done is done, and you're not responsible for Jacek's failures."

"We found each other in the end," I said. "That's what matters."

She sighed, then pushed herself back up to stir the tea. "I know what you're doing. Distracting me won't work."

"Won't it?" I continued to rub her back and shoulders. "I feel what you do, remember? You're more relaxed than before."

"Yet you're tense now."

"I'm worried about you… and everyone."

She scooped the tea in her ladle and took a whiff, not showing the slightest disgust. "Good. Something's wrong if you're not worried, and I have enough problems without something being wrong with you."

A weight left my shoulders at that. Strange. For my entire life, I'd been ladened with the weight of my supposed curse, then being a demon. Rod revealing the truth about Nawie had changed that more than I realized.

"You're thinking about something," she mused. "Whatever it is, it's helping, so it's either about me or someone I intend to stab."

I chuckled, then kissed her on the cheek, rounding the fire to take a seat. "The last thing on my mind is other women, but if you intend to stab whoever I'm thinking of, you'll have to stab me. You just made me realize that I'm not carrying the weight of being a demon anymore. Sure, I need to feed to not become drained, but you've lessened the burden of my demonic soul. It's almost normal… or as normal as someone with the power to control the winds can be."

Otylia looked up from her tea with half a smile. "We all have our demons, Wacław. Yours are just more literal. They don't go away, but we can heal. We've done that together, for both of us. I was afraid to love after Mother's death, and I think I forgot how to love myself too. You reminded me that I was more than Dziewanna's vessel." Her voice cracked, but she laughed through it. "Gods, so much has changed. But none of it matters if we don't finish this."

"We will. Together."

"Go to bed," she said. "You're leading us into the Way of Souls tomorrow."

I lay back instead, staring at the stars and her moon. "I spent sixteen years without sleep. One more night spent awake with you sounds wonderful."

We gathered around Otylia's kettle come sunrise. Eight friends, seven Moonstones, a goddess, a Naw, a nymph, and a witch's brew to take us to the underworld—just a normal morning.

"So that's the stuff," Narcyz said, wandering over to the kettle and sniffing as the others kept their distance among the trees. His frown deepened until his brow resembled the great gorges at the far end of Nawia itself. "You drop a dead cat in this or something?"

Otylia scooped the tea into a clay cup. "Thanks for volunteering." She shoved it into his chest, eyes sharp enough to cut. "Drink fast. By the time you see the bottom, it'll start to take hold."

"Wait!" He glanced at the cup, then at me. "How are we even getting to the Way of Souls? I'm not standing around like a ghoul while you stumble through the river for a way to Nawia."

Otylia's eyes flashed white, and the Threads of Life appeared around us, binding each of us to our families and loved one. A sea of colors wound and weaved together with vibrant life. She took hold of one Thread dangling from her chest. While the others took direct routes, like the one binding her to me, this one slithered across the ground on its way toward the Wyzra River.

"Simple," she replied. "Marzanna has Weles, so we follow his Thread. Wacław can see them as long as I open my sight to them too. Even if I'm weak, he'll show the way."

Yet another part of the plan she hadn't told me, but I had no choice. Following Weles's Thread would be simple while Otylia had the meager *žityje* to keep it visible. I had no desire to help the crotchety old god of the afterlife, but at least he had his uses.

"Does his Thread show you anything about where Marzanna is keeping him?" I asked.

She shook her head. "End shows me flashes, but in his Thread, I just see a dark place. Cold."

"Really?" Kuba quipped. "The winter goddess has him in a cold place? Now we'll know exactly where to find him."

"Your fern flower is our back up plan," Otylia said, "so keep it close. I'd hardly call Weles a treasure, but it could show us the way if my *žityje* runs out."

Ara crossed her arms over her sleeveless hunter's shirt. Despite the temperatures being far from summer's, she showed no sign of a chill. "If you're out of life force, then I doubt Kuba's ability to interpret a magical flower will save us."

"Enough talking," Otylia insisted. "Drink, Narcyz. We still have the ritual to complete."

As he did so, she passed out cups to the rest of the group before drinking herself. Only I didn't have to consume the tea, and my friends' vile expressions made me glad of it. Their faces paled. Their movements became sluggish. But the demon in me sensed their *žityje* still, as Otylia claimed the guardians would.

Otylia appeared unphased by the tea's effects as the others wavered. She grabbed my hand and Narcyz's, instructing the others to do the same.

She began chanting in the old tongue the moment our circle was complete. Whatever she said must've excluded me, because I felt nothing as the others gasped. The skulls surrounding the firepit glowed, as if stealing the light from the candles which extinguished one-by-one. Our friends dropped with them. I gripped Otylia's hand to warn her what was happening, but she chanted on until an emptiness struck my chest. Otylia's exhaustion crept through our bond. Her legs failed as the final skull pulsed before her with blinding radiance, and when she fell to her knees, the forest fell silent with her.

Beneath the shadowed boughs, the seven skulls held an ethereal light that both drew me in and terrified me. My demonic soul hungered for the *žityje* lingering within them. They were more than vessels for my friends' lives, though. Each represented their fragile morality, risked to join us on this journey.

I'll protect them, I promised myself silently.

I helped each of them rise as they collected their skulls with glazed over eyes. The ritual had felt so quick, but the fire had already dwindled to ash. Where our friends had once held vast amounts of *žityje* before, I barely sensed any now. It was as if the screaming sounds of life had dulled to the quietest whisper, and I doubted I'd have even sensed them if I wasn't focusing so heavily on doing so.

Kuba threw his arm over my shoulder, huffing. "You were always too tall…"

If it had been anyone else, I would've been concerned, but jokes meant Kuba still had his wits. I half-carried him as I followed Weles's

Thread toward the Wyzra, glancing back at Otylia. Her eyes were still white to keep the Threads visible. Even that simple channeling had her clenching her fists from the effort, but she showed less strain than the others' haggard steps.

How are we going to make it through the Way of Souls like this?

I kept the question to myself. Those I loved were at death's door, and expressing my doubts would make their journey even more difficult. Luckily, following Weles's Thread was far simpler.

The Wyzra's gurgling grew louder until we reached a point just downstream of where Nevenka and I had promised to cross the stones together moons before. We were less than a few minutes' walk from where we burned and drowned Marzanna's effigy every spring. Was the nearest entrance to the Way of Souls why our ancestors had chosen it? I held to that pondering to distract me from my friends' slow gates.

"The Thread enters the river here," I said, stepping into the water, but stopping before it poured over the top of my boot. "Should I search ahead?"

Otylia pushed past me. She was trying to be strong, but the current threw her off her feet, forcing me to catch her. "The Way of Souls can't be far," she said, jaw clenched. "There are thousands of entrances for souls, and if you're drawn in, you won't be able to come back to show us."

"Then we move slowly, carefully," I insisted.

I grabbed the Thread before it disappeared underwater, following it further into the Wyzra's flow. The river here was far shallower than the Krowik, but it soon rose to my stomach. Rocks littered the bed. For me, they were little obstacle, but my friends struggled to keep pace. The whole expedition would be over before it had begun if we didn't find the entrance soon.

Weles's Thread tingled in my grasp. Power lingered in these bonds, but it was unlike channeling that could be used. There was another force at work here, something that warmed my entire body until the Thread suddenly arced downward.

The shift nearly threw me off balance as I clung to the now taut Thread. It clearly went deeper into the riverbed, but a quick search with my feet uncovered only more rocks.

"Please tell me you found it," Ta said, the water nearly up to her chin. Andrij had to hold her arm to stop her drifting away as his eyes pleaded for me to say yes.

"I think so," I replied, "but I don't feel anything here. I'll have to go under to look."

"Then hurry up!" Narcyz grunted, barely coherent.

I ducked under the surface. My motion disturbed the water, so I kept as still as possible until the bubbles cleared, revealing the Thread's route directly into a rock. Drifting closer, I ran my hand over the surface. A gentle force tugged at it.

My fingers sparked, lightning bursting between them without my calling. No *żityje* left me, but the lightning grew until it crisscrossed the entire stone in a series of unfamiliar symbols. My lungs began to ache for air. I stayed, though, watching as a sixth sense told me to place my hand in the stone's center. It was neither a voice nor a push, but an instinct that was familiar as knowing how to walk. Had some part of my Naw nature done this before?

Slowly, I surrendered to the urge. The stone was hot against my palm, and the moment it touched, the lightning burst outward with a *crack*. I recoiled at the sound, reaching for Grudzień, but no attack came. Instead, the rock was gone, replaced by a strange surface of pure darkness.

A hand pulled me back to the surface, and my lungs rejoiced at the arrival of air as I came face-to-face with an exasperated Kuba.

"You gonna drown or find it?" he asked. "What were you doing with lightning down there? Nearly shot off poor Sabina's feet—not that she really needs them with those nymph wings of hers."

Sabina opened her mouth to object, but I replied first, "I found it! There's a portal of some sort. We just need to swim through, I think."

Narcyz pushed his way to the front. "It's always 'I think' with you two. Bloody gods and demons." He dove toward where I'd been and vanished a moment later.

"Maybe we should just shut the portal now," Kuba said. "Marzanna can have him."

Andrij swam past. "Speak for yourself."

When he disappeared, the rest followed except for Otylia, who lingered with her hand in mine. "How did you open it?" she asked.

"Lightning just came from my hand without me telling it to," I said with a shrug. "It was like it knew me."

"Maybe it did."

"Well, my mortal soul died already." I squeezed her hand tighter. "Time to follow it."

We dove together, and I let her take the lead as we plunged toward the black portal. Swirling, it called me in. To answer what I was, what I had always been.

A protector of the dead souls' path.

7

Wacław

What guardians await us?

THE PORTAL TURNED US ON OUR SIDES and flung us into a deep gray river with sleek stone banks. Our friends were already there, pulling each other onto the dim shore. Sabina fluttered overhead, but drifted ever-downward as she encouraged those still struggling.

Otylia's eyes flickered back to their usual green. She fell into me, so I picked her up and trudged through the hip-high water. It felt thicker than normal, resisting each step.

I leaped to shore with a push from the winds and set Otylia down. Like the rest, her skin was cold, and I felt her slow heartbeat in my chest. The tea was working. Whether that was a good thing or not, though, I wasn't sure with the trials still to come. We'd struggled to reach the Way of Souls, and I could only hope my friends had to strength to continue through it.

"How are you all feeling?" I asked with a quick survey of the group. None were injured at least. "Can we keep moving?"

Narcyz waved an absent hand instead of his usual appeals. Ta and Ara nodded too, so I took the replies as enough. With even Ta's darker skin turning ghastly gray, they certainly passed for dead spirits to me. We'd have to see whether the guardians agreed.

The gray river cut through what appeared to be a canyon of some kind, different layers of rock rising to either side of us until they were merely shadows far above. The portal had disappeared, and only the murky water offered any reminder of Jawia. There was neither sun nor moon, and the air was stale, as if we were trapped within a deep cavern. The winds *had* answered my call, though. That gave me some relief. I was the only one with any *žityje* to channel, and it would be useless without the winds to come to my aid.

There were no other routes forward, so I led the group downriver. It had to lead to Nawia eventually, right? Where else did souls go when the waters of Jawia dumped them here?

Time was difficult to track without the sun, but we walked for what had to be a few hours. Nothing changed besides the occasional small crevices which offered alternatives to the river's winding path. They were dark, though, and my skin crawled at just the thought of heading down them.

"Should we not check the Threads of Life?" Sabina squeaked from alongside Otylia as we reached a larger fork in the path. The two held hands, Otylia half pulling Sabina along as her frail nymph body sagged. "Maybe one of these routes away from the river is the right one?"

"As long as Otylia has the energy," I said.

Her eyes turned white without a word. The Thread binding her to Weles appeared, revealing a loose brown strand following the river through its center. My heart sunk. I wasn't sure what I'd hoped for, but the thought of continuing through the dreary cliffs had my legs dragging.

"The river will go to the Smorodina," Otylia said. "All souls must cross the flaming river, so this is probably a tributary."

Kuba raised his brow. "A what?"

"A small river that'll feed into the larger Smorodina River." Otylia started walking again. "C'mon. The less time we spend in this dreary place the better."

But as we journeyed on, we found little else but stone and water until a humming came from the river upstream.

"Stop," Otylia commanded. She raised her fingers to the skull in her pack, ready to pull its *žityje*, but I stepped in front of the group with Grudzień ready. We couldn't waste our preparations so quickly.

The humming grew as a figure bobbed through the current. Vaguely in the shape of a person with a bird's beak, it sat back into the water, staring above with deep brown eyes and hair that seemed to become one with the river. It held no *žityje*, but there was an unmistakable presence to it as it passed us by.

"A dead soul," Otylia said, holding out a hand toward it, the other held over her heart. "May your passage to paradise be swift. May Nawia be kinder than it was to me."

"What's the beak for?" Kuba asked. "I didn't get one of those. Or… I don't think I did."

Otylia's head dropped slightly. "Most souls spend forty days in Jawia before they take the Way of Souls, but you went to Nawia faster than that. Either Weles intended to use you to his ends against me, or Marzanna knew you were our friend and wanted to take you."

"Then it's good that Kyustendil and Ivan found me first."

I patted him on the head. "It is. We might've had you stuck as a pup for a time, but I'm glad you're back."

"Hey, I wasn't a—"

"Uh, guys…" Ta stammered, pointing down a crevice to our right. "There's something coming."

Four birds circled through the peaks of the crevice's cliffs: a raven, a crow, a nightjar, and a stork. They flew single file, not heading in our direction, but downstream. They swooped overhead of the dead soul ahead as it still bobbed along without bother. Whatever the birds saw was enough, because they flew on.

"Are those the guardians?" I asked Otylia.

She narrowed her eyes at them. "I don't know, but those types of birds carry souls after they die. It would make sense if the Way of Souls' guardians took similar forms, maybe to be familiar to the dead."

"They don't look like a threat," Andrij replied. "But I've learned not to trust my eyes nowadays."

"Good call," Otylia said.

I took a long breath and stared down the river, the walls of stone on either side seeming to press ever closer upon us. Shadows hung over them with higher layers jutting out to form overhangs where the crow perched for a moment. It surveyed the river again before carrying on its way.

"If the guardians are here," I said, "we're making progress. Keep close in case they get suspicious."

The guardians strayed out of sight whenever we reached another crevice for them to investigate. My heart raced each time until they returned to swoop over any souls that passed in the river. Each check was quick and without aggression, yet they didn't do the same to us. Did they know I was a Naw? Or did they know we were faking?

We soon reached a larger intersection, where many routes split off downstream, and two gray streams merged into our river. They were smaller, barely a stride wide, so we hopped over them with ease to keep on our path. A pair of bird guardians swept into sight for a moment upstream of each before disappearing. They showed no interest in us, but the original four guardians still circled nearby.

"They're watching us," Otylia said through our bond. *"Don't warn the others—they're worried enough—but make sure you're ready."*

I gave her a subtle nod. *Let me handle them if they come. The moment you take back your žityje and channel, they'll know you're a goddess. They could alert Marzanna.*

She tensed at that, but relented. *"Fine, but if they poke my eyes out, I won't be able to fix your unruly hair anymore. We'll have King Matted Head."*

Matted Head? I asked. *You can do better than that.*

"Not like this. I can barely think."

Our river widened with every tributary it met, and no matter how far we went, the guardians were always searching nearby. I slowed, ensuring my friends couldn't stray too far behind. The hairs on my neck rose. From this far, it was impossible to tell, but my senses said they were watching me specifically. That was fine. As long as I kept their attention, the others were safe from their judgment.

The stork and nightjar landed on a stone arch over the next confluence, the crow and raven taking alternate positions on segments
higher up that jutted out from the cliffs. The others noticed too. I
sensed their tension, and Kuba yelped as his foot struck a rock. He
tumbled until Andrij caught him.

The guardians' heads snapped around at the sound. We froze,
their dark eyes watching us. I slowly reached back for Grudzień and
readied the winds as the crow cawed.

Then the guardians dove.

I rose on the winds to meet them. Grudzień lacked its usual sheen
in the dull light, but it was still a god's blade. Birds needed to fly, and
I would throw them from the sky if they dared threaten those I cared
for. Guardians of the natural path or not, they wouldn't stop us after
all we'd endured.

The four encircled me beyond the blade's reach. Together, they
spoke, their voices echoing through the narrow canyon. "We have
not seen one of your kind for many moons. Have you truly returned?"

"All the other Nawie I know have been corrupted by Marzanna,"
I replied. "I am going to face her."

"Yet you bring the dead?"

"I am protecting them, so that they reach Nawia safely."

The guardians quickened their pace. "They are strange. They do
not follow the river."

I glanced at my friends, who were waiting for the confrontation's
result. "Do all dead souls do so? They follow my guidance on the
land instead."

"They have *żityje*," the stork replied, drifting lower.

"They have Moonstones," the crow added as it spun in excitement. "*Shiny* swords."

The raven and nightjar landed on my shoulders, but I didn't attack. They seemed curious, not aggressive, for now. "Who have you
brought to the Way? A goddess? A nymph? Have they *truly* perished?"

Their voices echoed from each shoulder and hammered my mind, pressing me to answer. But I had faced gods. These guardians would not intimidate me.

"I know the way of things," I said.

"Then answer our questions…"

I spun to throw the birds off my shoulders, then held my blade toward the nightjar. The air hummed around me. All I needed was a pulse to throw away these guardians. "With me are a goddess and a nymph along with mortals, yes. You can sense as well as I that their souls are drained. The *żityje* they carry is in skulls as an offering to the spirits of Nawia."

"An offering?" the guardians asked together. "May we have a taste?"

I swung Grudzień about. "You threaten the dead. It is my responsibility to protect them. Leave us be, or I will fight."

"Hmmm. Continue on, Naw, but we shall watch."

"Very well." I dropped back to the others. Instincts told me this wasn't over, so I gripped my blade. The guardians kept their distance, but kept to their elevated positions, watching. What threat did they actually pose? They had more *żityje* than most animals, but they were hardly powerful beasts from what I could tell.

Yet, *żityje* of a threat or not, my nerves danced on their ends under the guardians' gazes. I silently told Otylia what they'd said, but motioned for no one to speak. Whatever cover we had left was minimal.

The river grew ever wider as our legs dragged and the empty sky darkened further. Like a veil slowly falling over the Way of Souls, it drowned the gray sky before reaching an orange hue which rose over the cliffs far downstream. Otylia and I exchanged glances.

Is that what I think it is? I asked her through our bond.

She nodded slowly, her nose wrinkled.

Should we rest, *then? The Smorodina—*

"*Will lead us the rest of the way,*" she interrupted. "*If we rest, the tea will wear off. I doubt the ritual will be enough with the guardians watching us so closely.*"

I waved a hand toward the others. Ta leaned against Ara, and Andrij had his arm over Narcyz's shoulder, nearly dragging his trailing foot. *They're barely standing! If the guardians come, I'll deal with them.*

She threw down my arm. *"We're not sleeping here."*

Her ferocity gave me pause, and I studied her, reaching into our bond to feel the source of her panic. *What did End show you? What are those things?*

"Keep walking. Just trust me."

I continued alongside the river, but the guardians had drawn closer during our pause. Enough souls had passed us to reveal that we were more than a fluke. None of the dead acted like this. I feared the guardians were just biding their time before they struck.

Tell me, please, I pled to Otylia as I called on the winds. They spiraled around my fingers, eager to be commanded. *If we don't act now, we might not have a choice.*

She took a sharp breath. *"They're called chorty—troublemaking beasts that feed on powerful souls. Mother said they were Weles's way of allowing only the dead to pass, but not the ones not too strong to challenge him. A chort shouldn't stop a Naw."*

I swallowed, studying the chorty. Did they see me as a powerful source, or did they seek the Moonstones and skulls? *Weles commands them,* I replied, *and Czarnobóg captured Weles.*

"Wacław!"

Kuba's shout tore me from Otylia. The guardians surrounded us, their bird forms shifting into horned beasts with goat-like legs and torsos the size of an ox. They struck the stone hard enough to throw my friends off their shaky feet. At full speed, they would be upon us in seconds.

I stopped Otylia as she reached for her *żityje* skull. Lightning cracked between my fingers.

"Duck!"

8

Otylia

The visions must be wrong.

I SHOOK AS WACŁAW THREW OUT A WINDBLAST, but it wasn't the chorty who frightened me. End had showed me countless outcomes of our journey. Many defeats. Few victories.

When we fought the chorty, someone always died before we reached Marzanna.

The guardians snarled at the blast throwing them back. It wasn't enough. They recouped quickly, two striking at Wacław as the others charged the defenseless group. Grudzień's dark blade slashed through the first with ease, but our friends lagged with their heavy Moonblades.

I called Sierpień to my hand as a sword. My light spear would take *żityje* I didn't have, and the chorty's gnashing teeth were already upon us.

Ta sloppily swiped at the first, missing but buying me a moment to close the gap. The chort didn't notice my advance. My arms ached as I drove Sierpień into its side, and the weak strike failed to pierce more than a finger length through its hide. Dark blood oozed from the gap as it turned with incredible speed and elbowed me in the face.

My nose snapped. Such a strike wouldn't have mattered normally, but without *żityje*, I toppled into the river, losing my grip on Sierpień.

The viscous water, now strangely warm, washed over me. It was as if hands pulled me down as I fought for freedom. My drained body refused, and a scream sent a shiver down my spine. Who had fallen because of my failure? I'd foreseen guardian attacks, but the tea and ritual should have stopped it!

Should didn't matter with Wacław's desperation and mine flooding our bond. These chorty were ferocious, and when his sharp pain slashed across my shoulder, it took all my will not to draw my *żityje* from the skull. End's visions flashed through my mind again—a reminder that if I channeled on the Way of Souls, all the guardians within it would descend upon us once they caught a goddess's scent. Not four… hundreds.

I caught hold of a rock along the shore, clinging on as the chorty forced my friends to the river's edge. Wacław swooped overhead and shot a lightning bolt through the second beast, but the final two had nothing more than knicks and scrapes. And one held Sierpień.

The sight sent a jolt through me. It wasn't much, but I hauled myself to shore, heaving. Gods, why had End shown me what I couldn't do? I was weak, useless to save my friends.

Goopy liquid clung to me in globs—definitely not water—as I staggered my way back toward them. Wacław turned on the remaining chorty, but the one with Sierpień met him. Drained, my Moonblade-wielding friends could barely keep the remaining chort at bay. I was too far, and so was Wacław.

The chort charged Sabina at a speed greater than any animal I'd seen. She sang in her strange nymph song, but no power answered as her wings carried her mere inches off the ground. Her Moonblade could do nothing to stop the chort's horns from plunging into her chest.

"NO!" I shouted, my voice strained.

Sabina collapsed into the river amid a pool of blood. Gray turned crimson, my Moonmark upon her neck dulling by the second.

Take your żityje from the skull! I called through my szeptucha connection to her.

"I'm so tired," she replied, her voice drifting.

Wacław slayed the third chort and sent Sierpień sprawling as Narcyz managed to stab the final one in its stomach. The beast lashed out with a deafening shriek. One claw raked across Ara's face as it lowered its head and rammed into Narcyz. Together, the pair dropped into the river beside Sabina.

They'll die without me.

Rage burned away my fear. I shoved away End's visions and grabbed my *żityje* skull, drawing my strength from it and soaring over the river with moonlight arcing at the tips of my fingers. End's wisps revealed the final chort's intention to burst from the river, so I cut off its path.

Just as the chort emerged, I summoned my light spear and slammed its base into the stone. The chort's force was immense at full stride, but the braced spear sliced through its sternum as I released a moonblast into its face. Combined, the strikes split the towering beast in half. But there was no time to celebrate its death.

Light radiated from Sabina as she drew her *żityje*, but she still bled as the current caried her on. Ara, too, screamed in a ball, cradling her gashed face, and Narcyz had disappeared beneath the river's surface.

"Go get Narcyz and Sabina!" I told Wacław as I scrambled for a poultice in my herb bag. "And the rest of you, drain your skulls. The other guardians will sense me, so there's no use trying to hide."

Wacław didn't hesitate for once, diving straight into the river while I covered Ara's wounds the best I could. The legends said all gods could heal in some way, so I sent more moonlight than was prudent into the wounds. I couldn't lose Ara. Gods, I'd doomed us according to End's visions, but what was victory if we had no one left? We'd figure it out. We had to.

It seemed an eternity before Wacław dragged a sputtering Narcyz from the river. They were barely on shore before Wacław took flight to track down where Sabina had ended up, and I prayed to Mother that she was safe. Sabina had suffered the worst of every realm for me. If she'd died from my plan's failure, I couldn't have forgiven myself. But I felt her presence as my szeptucha. She lived, and I would ensure Ara did too.

"You need to take your *žityje* back," I told Ara, cupping the skull into her hands. She spasmed against the cold stone, but I held her down as Mother had done with so many of her patients. The poultice was working. The *žityje* would give it the time it needed.

Her lips opened slightly, and silver wisps emerged from the skull. They poured into her mouth, her heart quickening with the burst of life. Her eyes remained closed.

"Yeah, give *her* all the help," Narcyz groaned, bleeding from his stomach. Based on the amount of blood, the wound was deep, and Andrij and Kuba were doing their best to keep it covered.

I cursed and grabbed another poultice. Every moment we spent healing was another the guardians had to surround us, but what choice did we have? These were more than our friends—they were our family.

Yes, even Narcyz.

"Stop complaining and bite down on this," I scolded, sticking a root in his mouth so that he didn't bite off his tongue as I applied the poultice. His cries pierced the root and turned into a roar when I channeled my moonlight into him.

Ta tended to Ara as Andrij and Kuba kept Narcyz still. I could hold Ara down by myself, but Narcyz fought. After restoring his *žityje*, he was tough to pin down, even for a goddess. Soon, though, he stopped resisting and dropped unconscious. He'd lost a lot of blood, and the wound was right next to the one he'd suffered in battle against Koschei's forces. It would take time for his mortal body to recover. I forgot sometimes how much of a luxury it was for my own *žityje* to heal me at will.

A gust of wind marked Wacław's arrival with Sabina in his arms. Her eyes were shut, and I sensed her *žityje* waning as I grabbed the last of my poultices and rushed to them. Wacław set her aside from the rest of the group, his head bowed.

"I'm sorry," he mumbled. "I tried to find her, but the river turned to rapids farther down. She'd already struck the rocks…"

I quickly applied the first poultice to her chest wound from the chort's horn before using a second on the gash along her temple. What energy I'd felt from her before had faded. The horn had at least pierced her lung, and head wounds were never easy to treat, channeling or not.

Light poured from me as Sabina's wisp lowered. A vibrant green, it usually danced about on the gales, but it barely moved now. What color it had possessed faded to the dull gray of iron, and her rosy cheeks paled with it. *Žityje* still resided in her soul. How much, though, I couldn't tell as I worked, pouring my power into her wounds with all the moonlight I could muster underground. Silver emanated from me in a blinding array, my immense *žityje* draining into a body that should never have been exposed to such forces. But the wounds wouldn't close fast enough.

"HEAL!" I screamed into the gray skies, slamming my fist into the stone hard enough to bruise.

Wacław tried to embrace me, but I tore myself away just to see the others fading. Ara had been on the mend. Narcyz had stabilized. Both of their wounds now peeked beyond their wrappings, the edges festering and discolored.

This place is killing them…

9

Otylia

We need to break its hold on them…

I CLOSED MY EYES, feeling the gods' forces around me. They were everywhere, even when the gods themselves weren't present, as I focused on the river's pull toward the flaming Smorodina.

Toward death.

I cursed. How had I not sensed it before? Marzanna and Czarnobóg's power altered Weles's guardians, and the Way of Souls bordered her castle at Nawia's edge. Death came before paradise, so was it not her force's role to ensure all who entered Nawia through the Way were actually dead? Poultices would do nothing against it. My channeling could save one of them, maybe two, but I was already draining myself quickly. I refused to choose between them. There had to be another way.

When Wacław took hold of me again, asking how he could help, I caught an amber glint over his shoulder. *That's it!*

Again, I pushed past him and sprinted to Sierpień. Wacław had used Kwiecień to bring back his mother moons before, and she'd been already dead. With a goddess to wield it during its moon, Sierpień had to be enough to heal two wounded mortals and a nymph.

The Moonblade hummed in my grasp as I willed it back into its temple ring form. I needed my hands to work with the wounded like Mother had, and the heavy blade would only slow me. My legs no longer dragged. My heart no longer waited for each beat. This was life or death for my family, my szeptuchy, my closest friends. No lasting effects of a magic tea would stop me.

I tapped into Sierpień's *żityje* before I reached Sabina, and its energy struck me like a bolt of Wacław's lightning. Without meaning to, I took flight, silver light filling the sky along with the wisps and Threads of every soul passing through the Way. Every moment of their lives flashed before me. Even beginnings were another end, and centuries filled my mind in a blink.

The power was blinding, distracting me for precious moments until I forced myself to gaze upon my fallen companions. They appeared like ants beneath me. What *żityje* they had left was swallowed by my light, but I sensed something else in the distance. *Somethings.*

The other guardians were coming.

I dropped to my injured friends and placed my hand on each of their brows, releasing part of my power into them. This much *żityje* made it impossible to know how much they needed, but I continued until their wounds closed. Death was everywhere. I couldn't risk it tainting them again.

The moonlight faded with each healing, but by the end, I still held more *żityje* than ever before. My mind was abuzz, as if reaching this threshold granted me extra godly senses that I couldn't yet grasp. It wasn't until Ara and Sabina hugged me that I regained my presence.

"There's no time for that," I said, slipping out of their grasp. "More chorty are coming—too many. They know I'm here, and if we don't get to the Smorodina, we'll have no cover."

"What about our plan?" Andrij asked. "How will we get into Nawia now?"

I summoned my light spear again, embedding Sierpień into its tip before pulling the entire group into the air. Those with wings or their own channeling soon flew under their own power, and I pressed them onward at full speed.

"We break down the door," I called back. "I'm done knocking."

Keeping with the group took more concentration than I was used to as I sped along faster than ever. This *žityje* was immense, but finite, I reminded myself. We still had a long way to go. I'd risked everything by pulling from both my reserved skull and Sierpień so soon, and using it all now would leave us hopeless. If we weren't hopeless already…

The guardians swept from every crevice and confluence we passed. All were upstream, but did that mean the Smorodina was safe or too dangerous for even the guardians?

We had no choice but to follow the path of the dead souls. Our newfound speed sent us past most guardians, a few strikes from Moonblades, lightning, or moonlight scattering the rare one who got close enough to threaten us. My speed waned with the more *žityje* I expended, though, and more closed in.

I focused instead on the souls in the river as we pushed onward. Each we saw appeared more whole, as if its new body was taking shape for Nawia. Was that the point of the river's odd liquid? Preparation?

The cliffs straightened to reveal the Smorodina's flames bursting to life ahead. It wasn't a separate river, but a continuation of the ones we followed. I'd thought it no more than a couple minutes' flight away, but it was apparent now that the towering height of the fires had made it appear closer than it was.

The guardians were closer, shifting into half-chort, half-bird forms while we remained airborne. At this rate, they would surround us before we reached the fires.

"What do we do?" Wacław asked from my flank. His bright eyes reflected the flames, and our bond revealed his anticipation of battle. How was he excited after what we'd just faced?

"Form a ring below me," I ordered the others. "Keep them off my legs, and I'll handle the rest."

Kuba scanned the advancing chorty, their numbers enough to blot out the gray horizon. "By yourself? I mean, you're a goddess, but—"

"Shut up and do what I say for once!" I snapped.

His cheeks turned as red as poppies, and they all took their positions. In truth, this plan wasn't well thought out, but it was all I had. The others would fight better as a group. They would only get in the way of my channeling, though, and this gave me clear space to prepare a moonblast, holding its power tight in my free hand.

When the chorty struck, so did I.

My moonblast shook the air as I screamed and tore apart the first wave with my silver light. These were creatures of death, of endings, but they did not serve me. So they perished instead.

The second wave of guardians followed close behind. My wisps revealed the intended ends of their movements before they acted, hundreds of shadowy forms surrounding my friends. But they never reached their goal.

My eyes flashed white. I grabbed their Threads of Life, shredding them with touch and spear by the dozens. Their freakish cries haunted the air as they crashed into the river.

Some broke through to duel with the group below. They were few, though, and with plentiful *żityje*, my friends dealt with them easily. Oh, how *żityje* changed everything.

But it wasn't infinite, and any channeling by my szeptuchy or me took from my reserves. Those first immense moonblasts had killed most of the chorty, draining me with them. I still held far more *żityje* than normal. End's visions had revealed it wasn't enough to face what lay ahead.

The remaining guardians were scattered between half and full bird forms, clinging to my friends to keep airborne as they struck with their jagged claws and horns. Wacław's winds sent many tumbling, but others ganged up on Sabina. Her dodges and slashes were hesitant after her earlier injury. I ensured the chorty couldn't take advantage.

Striking from above, I drove my spear straight through the skull of the closest chort to Sabina, then re-summoned it to my hand and moonblasted away another pair. She went back-to-back with me, her breaths heavy.

"They were so fast…" she said. "I thought I could channel better, but—"

"You're fine," I insisted, smacking the butt of my spear into the head of a guardian who lunged from below in bird form. "Wait for them to surround us again, then we moonblast together on my signal, okay?"

"I'll try."

So we waited as the chorty gathered around us again. They saw her as the weakest target and me as the most valuable, drawing their attention away from our group. That allowed Wacław and the others to spar with the rest as I gathered my power in my hands. I didn't need as much of it this time, but it shone brilliantly as Sabina did the same.

"Now?" Sabina asked, shaking against me as the chorty's numbers grew to twenty, then thirty.

I waited until they charged before unleashing my power. "Now!"

A flash split straight through the ring of chorty just as the tips of their horns neared us. They seemed to fall in slow motion, and a *snap* echoed in my chest. I leaned back, a sense of peace greeting me among the forces of this strange connecting place between the realms. Death had reigned here before, but it was silent now. Had Marzanna extended her grip here through those beasts?

"Otylia?" Wacław asked, rushing to me, his winds sending my hair drifting as if I were floating atop the river itself. "What's wrong?"

I laughed in relief. "Those weren't guardians!"

"You're telling me we've got to fight more of those beak brains?" Ta asked.

"No," I replied. "Whatever guardians were here are gone. Marzanna used Weles to control these beasts and corrupt the Way of Souls. Close your eyes and tell me what you feel."

Ta shrugged. "Nothing's different."

"It is," Ara said, breathing in deeply. Her face was remarkably clear of her earlier wound, as if she'd never been struck at all. "The air is lighter, and there isn't this darkness pulling within me."

"That's our empty stomachs," Narcyz said.

I smiled, not annoyed with his antics for once. "We've pushed out the corruption, at least for now, so we can finally rest and eat. I'm sure we're all hungry."

Relinquishing my power to lower us felt like a surrendering of sorts. Fighting such numbers with ease was glory, divinity. Their absence had cleared the corruption, but so too was it disappointing to have no immediate target for the rest of my *żityje*. A part of me craved to unleash it, to search the ends around me and alter them to my will.

This is how the gods change, I told myself. *Each offering brings them higher above their worshippers until they cannot see a single mortal.*

Ara scooted beside me, nudging my arm. "You all right?"

"I don't want to forget who I was before I Ascended," I replied. "That much *żityje* is intoxicating."

"And powerful. Think about all the good you could do once we've defeated Marzanna. With enough worshippers, you could help us rebuild Jawia without worrying about Perun and his cohort."

I watched Wacław check on the others. He did it naturally, as a king should. The last moons with him had taught me much about myself and what it meant to be a friend. Those lessons were a journey, and I was far from finished.

"Rod's dead," I said, "but destroying what little balance he held won't make things better. Strife between the gods caused this. I refuse to make it worse."

"What if Perun decides he doesn't care?" Ara asked.

I lowered my head. "We'll fight if we must, but honestly, I could use a few decades of peace. Maybe centuries."

She pulled away. "I'll die someday, and you'll still be here."

"I know."

"There's just this question that… you know… normal people have to live with: Will anyone miss me when I'm gone? You'll meet tons of people like me, and I know you'll forget me someday." She bit her lip, a fist held over her heart. "Just know you'll always be the one who cared about the strange Zurgowie girl when everyone else made fun of me. You're going places I know I can't follow, but if you ever need me after all this, I'll be there."

I hesitated, an old part of me wishing to back away from her vulnerability that demanded I be open with her too. But Ara had trusted me from the beginning. She'd cared about the outcast witch as much as I'd cared for her, probably more. Before I even knew I needed a friend, she'd been there.

"I'll never forget you," I said, leaning into her and pointing to the night sky… except it wasn't there, so I made my own lights instead. "And I won't let Jawia either. The souls in the sky will create a portrait of you—*The Huntress.*"

The little lights rearranged above us until they showed Ara with a bow aiming at a monstrous woman. Like any constellation, it required some interpretation, but I would ensure her story was known.

"When your clan was beaten back and your new tribe was on its back foot," I said, "you were brave enough to stare down Marzanna *as a mortal.* How many others can say they shot a goddess and lived?"

Ara grinned. "Well, it wasn't Marzanna in her full power, just a projection."

I waved my hand and allowed the lights to disperse. The motion was unnecessary, but it felt like a dismissal of Ara's death for a time. Yes, she was mortal. We were both young, though, and I would do everything to protect her until she was ready to pass into Nawia.

"The legends always exaggerate," I said. "Why can't yours?"

"Then why not claim I slayed her myself?" she exclaimed, lying back with her hands behind her head. "The Huntress shot Marzanna, then descended the Way of Souls to finish her off!"

Kuba stuck out his tongue from nearby. "Hey, I helped get us here too."

"Fine," Ara replied. "Otylia can add a pup next to me, and people can decide whether it's Sosna or you."

"I suggest you take that as a win," Andrij said, nudging Kuba. "*The Huntress* could've shot you instead."

We all laughed, and the two rejoined Wacław to cook some boar we'd brought along. There were no trees for fire, so Kuba decided to mime building a fire as Narcyz held the boar's meat and Wacław zapped it with his lightning. It was a… unique… idea. Whether it charred the meat or just cooked it in the center, I didn't know, but it had Sabina giggling and the group overjoyed at their attempt. That was better than any meal.

Though, my stomach was rumbling. Ara noticed as she lay her head on my lap.

"Goddesses get hungry?" she asked. "I swear. Unless you're drinking blood from the offering bowl, I never see you eat nowadays."

"When the world is on your shoulders, you don't think about food that often," I said. "I have *žityje* to heal me if I starve. Everyone else in our kingdom doesn't."

Ara huffed. "Well, I insist you take the first bite of your lover's concoction. We all drank your tea, so you can eat the boar."

"That is a terrible idea."

But it was too late. Sabina met Ara's gaze, and they jumped into action, bringing me a chunk of discolored meat. Half of it was black as obsidian, the other still pink. *Wonderful.*

I must've had a wild look in my eye, because Wacław swept up behind them, throwing his arm over Sabina's shoulder. Considering she was no taller than his armpit, it was quite the sight. "Let's not poison our only hope of surviving this trip, shall we?" he quipped before whispering, "We might not survive the night if she's mad anyway."

I shot to my feet and tackled him. He was far taller and bulkier than me, but the move caught him off guard, sending us tumbling into a heap alongside the river, the hard ground skinning our hands. We laughed anyway, and as Wacław kissed me quickly, I hoped the distraction would keep me from having to eat that disgusting food.

Unfortunately, Sabina awaited me when we rose. She cackled like a child who'd tricked someone for the first time, and knowing her, I wouldn't have been surprised if it was the first time.

Wacław shrugged and side-stepped away. "I can't stop what's been put into motion."

So Sabina handed me the insult to all that was right in the Three Realms. Flakes of black broke free from the meat's center at my touch, yet the outer sections sent juices trickling between my fingers. Gods, it took all my strength not to gag. Mother probably would've killed a worshipper for wasting a hunted boar like this, but my friends insisted, so I took a bite.

And it wasn't bad.

I wrinkled my nose, checking I'd taken a bite out of the boar meat and not something else. It was as inconsistent as Kuba, but the second bite was good too… flavorful? How hungry was I that I actually liked it?

"Hah!" Kuba exclaimed. "See? It worked."

Narcyz smacked him on the back. "Imagine if we told others about it. A whole new way of making fire: lightning fast. No more bending over a forge, hitting metal with a hammer for me. We'd be rich!"

"Aren't you, you know, carrying a god's sword?" Ta asked, arms crossed and hip out. "How much you think you can sell ugly looking meat for?"

"Enough." Narcyz glanced at the golden blade of Kwiecień, tucked away in its scabbard. "Besides, it's not like I can sell that sword anyway. Otylia would have my head."

I took a couple more bites before passing off the charred portion of meat to Wacław, who gave it a disgusted look. "Thanks…" he mumbled.

"I'd have your head," I told Narcyz, "and then I'd come down to Nawia and make sure you spend eternity getting chopped to bits by golden swords."

Narcyz just smiled. "Glad to see Wacław hasn't softened you up too much."

We finished eating and settled down to sleep, with Andrij offering to take first watch. The dim light hadn't changed with time, and the Smorodina still burned in the distance, taunting us. I stared at it as I lay on my bedroll alongside Wacław. End had warned me what would come by the flaming river if I exposed my power too early. I'd done it anyway, and when I closed my eyes, I saw everyone I loved consumed by fire and frost.

10

Wacław

There are so many…

WHERE THE CLIFFS ENDED, gray, half-formed souls filled the black sands alongside the Smorodina's flaming waters. Thousands of them mulled about, limbs dragging and faces covered with holes which revealed muscles beneath. None wandered back into the shadows of the cliffs, and more souls climbed from the river to join the crowd.

"What *are* those things?" Kuba asked from the air beside me, staying back from the start of the Smorodina. Otylia's *żityje* would attention if anything waited in ambush, so I'd taken him and Narcyz to scout ahead on the winds. We'd hoped to find an end to the Way of Souls, but one strange landscape merely replaced another.

I shook my head and lowered, examining the border of the river we'd followed and the Smorodina. I dared not cross over the sands without Otylia. There was some power lingering there, hovering over the souls. Sopping ash dripped off those climbing from the flames, their bodies forming like molten glass that had cooled too quickly. None left the river until they were in the fires, and even then, they did so without haste. Was this some natural process?

"The souls seem trapped," I said. "It's like they escaped the river before they were ready."

Narcyz pointed ahead, slightly to the left of the Smorodina. "They're not moving randomly. Looks like they're heading that way, just real slow."

The longer we lingered, the more that became apparent. That constant shifting made room for new souls to emerge while still having entered the Smorodina itself, but the souls stretched on for as long as we could see. Where were they going? And why were they walking on these black sands?

And why did this feel so familiar?

Hairs rose on my arms as I closed my eyes, searching for the last time I'd seen sand like this. Marzanna had pulled me in with her Frostmark and threatened me from the Smorodina's edge. Black sand had consumed the horizon, and despite the flames, her chill had frozen my very soul. We were close.

"This is Marzanna's doing," I said. "She showed me her home here once… or at least part of it. The dead must pass here, and from the looks of it, she doesn't want that to happen."

Kuba gasped. "She's making an army of souls."

"Why can't we have the army for once?" Narcyz asked, teeth bared as he reached for his Moonblade's hilt. "We should slice 'em down now, before she gets a chance to do whatever in Oblivion she wants to."

I rested a hand on his arm. The demon within me desired to fight too, but it was well sated with the *żityje* I'd taken from the hearts of the fallen chorty yesterday. "These are the souls of the people we fought to protect in Jawia. If we kill them now, they'll never enjoy paradise in Nawia."

"I'm telling you, if we don't kill them now, then we'll do it later when they're a lot stronger."

"Half our village is probably down there, my brother included," I pleaded with him. "I understand why you want to do this, but don't. Every single one of their eternal deaths will be on your conscience for the rest of your life."

He pulled his arm free and drew Kwiecień half out of its scabbard. "Better my conscience suffer than all of us. We've saved demons, but not in a goddess's own realm. We're way out of our depths here, even Otylia."

"Hey," Kuba said. "We'll figure it out without killing a bunch of innocent people." He pulled out the fern flower, its vibrant colors dulled. "Maybe the flower or Otylia's force can make sure they don't fall under Marzanna's control. We've gotta try, right?"

Narcyz huffed and sheathed his blade. "We'll see."

With him abated for now, I messaged back to Otylia that she was clear to follow with the rest of the group. If any more guardians were near, they would sense her, but I neither saw nor sensed anything but the souls. They held no *żityje*. It seemed the natural process, but I wondered what sustained their strange bodies until they reached Nawia.

The others arrived a few minutes later, and Ta didn't hold back her disgust.

"Gross. Is that what happens after we get old and saggy—we get older and saggier?"

"I fail to believe this is supposed to happen," Andrij replied. "Kuba, you said nothing like this happened to you?"

Kuba shrugged. "I'd have lost my mind, looking like that."

Otylia drifted toward the Smorodina, preparing to cross over the sands. "We've established well enough that we don't know what's happening. These souls shouldn't be here, so let's figure out why, shall we?" She nodded to me. "This is your realm, my lovely Naw. Lead the way."

I drew Grudzień and slipped past her. The closeness gave me a renewed confidence, pushing back the dread that weighed me down. So many we knew were among these suffering souls, and my heart ached for them.

Until I fell.

The winds surrendered the moment I crossed the border between stone and black sand, sending me tumbling toward the souls. No matter where I reached, the winds refused to answer. They were distant, trapped beyond the sands. Even Otylia couldn't rush to my aid.

Her moonlight shot toward me, but faltered at the same border that the winds had. Powerless, this would've been a death sentence before I'd gained the ability to heal with *žityje*. I still flinched at the potential of being surrounded by a thousand souls who could be used by Marzanna. Grudzień was a god's blade, but without the winds, what hope did I have against such numbers?

The ground came despite my best attempts. I crashed onto a poor soul, my arm snapping from the impact, but the soul showed no reaction except to fall. I was grateful for that, as its body dispersed the impact.

Except my body didn't get the message that it could've been worse. I groaned, unable to move my sword arm, and my ribs screamed at any attempt to sit up. *Žityje* worked quickly for smaller wounds. For ones like this, though, I could only stare up at the souls and the dark sky beyond, waiting for the healing to finish.

The souls seemed unbothered by my presence. Even the one I'd struck wobbled back to its feet, adjusted an exposed hunk of spine sticking from its neck, and continued on its meandering way.

I wish I could do that.

My friends' shouting soon broke through the crowd. I hadn't realized how loud it was, but thousands of shuffling feet through the sand created a calamity of sound from my position on the ground. The souls themselves didn't speak from what I could tell, but they lacked the glassy black eyes of the undead people Marzanna's servant, Minna, had controlled in Vastroth. That was a good sign, I hoped.

"You all right?" Kuba asked, slipping through the nearest souls and helping me stand. I winced with my ribs aching, but his support helped. Him wincing every time a dead soul touched him, though, sent my still mending arm into another of the mangled things.

"Please," I muttered. "Stand still for once."

He forced a smile. "Right... sorry."

Narcyz shoved over a few souls to reach me, creating a gap for the others to pass through. "Nice work, Half-Chief. You fell like a real champion."

"I did my best," I quipped as I glanced past him. "Where is Otylia?"

Sabina fluttered overhead, as her wings didn't rely on channeling. "She is studying one of the natural souls, I think."

Otylia's black hair became visible in the gap Narcyz had created. She darted between the souls, picking and poking at their skin with her nose wrinkled. It always did that when she was focused, and it would've been adorable if dead people weren't surrounding us.

Ara prodded another with the flat of her sword to keep it away. "At least they aren't trying to kill us. I'll take it."

"Yet…" Narcyz grumbled to himself until Andrij stepped to his side.

"Whatever this is," Andrij said, "it is a step in the right direction. Marzanna wouldn't be disrupting Otylia and Wacław if we were headed the wrong way."

Otylia appeared by my side with her arms crossed. "It is the right direction. I checked Weles's Thread last night, and it leads this way." She turned to me. "Remember the Catalyst's force in Vastroth?"

I glared at Grudzień, which Marzanna had used to suppress the Vastrothie population and ignite the demonic Płanetnik inside me. "How could I forget?"

"This feels the same," she said. "It's a Moonstone—or multiple—suppressing our powers. I'm sure of it. Only a shard of the stone that created the gods could stop one from channeling."

"Let's do the same to Marzanna," Narcyz said, shoving aside another soul and toppling a row of them. "We've got seven of them. That's got to be enough."

Otylia sighed, thumbing Sierpień at her temple. "It's not that easy. Sure, the Moonstones are powerful, but I barely know how to change one's form. She's managed to use at least part of their powers outside their moons. That shouldn't be possible."

"Uh, guys?" Kuba squeaked. He backed toward us as a new wave of souls smacked into him, and more emerged from the river behind. "Can we talk about this as we walk? I'm not liking all this undead skin-on-skin contact."

"Get used to it," Otylia replied. "We've got a ways to go on foot."

We headed into the denser crowd, and despite my best attempts to find suitable gaps, the lumbering souls closed them before the whole group could get through. Even my height wasn't enough to keep track of everyone. Luckily, our mental connections were unaffected by Marzanna's dampening of our powers, so we at least could communicate.

It soon became clear that we had no idea which direction we were going. The Smorodina's flames rose vaguely to our right, but with the size of the crowd of souls, we could've been straying away from the Thread path Otylia had seen. We had little choice, though, but to continue in hopes we would get close enough. If only the souls would wander in their intended direction instead of into us.

No matter how well I timed my movements, limbs struck me every few heartbeats. The souls had no apparent intent, but their misshapen bodies flailed about like drunken dancers as they stumbled in the sand, leaving me with dozens of bruises. None were all that painful. Still, they did a wonderful job reminding me of their presence each time I met another soul's elbow.

Nawia was supposed to be paradise, so what was this? Some eternal punishment? Damnation to wander on this torturous plain? This couldn't have been the intent of the Way of Souls.

My legs dragged as the sand grew shin deep, slowing both the souls and us. A long while had passed, and there was no way to tell how far we'd gone with the Smorodina filling the sky with smoke. Behind, there was no sight of the rivers we'd left. And ahead, there was only unending darkness. I lost all reference to time and exhaustion, gripping Otylia's hand as some grounding to life. Our heartbeats quickened together, and I took some solace in knowing I wasn't the only one out of my depth.

At some point, Otylia yanked me back. "Ta says we need to stop. She found something."

"Where?" I asked, my mouth dry. The trance I'd been in had made me forget the labors I'd placed on my body, but the soreness, hunger, and thirst struck me like a punch in the gut. How much longer could we endure this?

Otylia led me and the rest of our group toward the Smorodina. The chill remained no matter how close we came to the river, and our labored breaths fogged the air as we stumbled into Andrij and Narcyz, who held back the souls for Ta. She knelt beside a hip-high tower of stones. Each shimmered in the light that radiated from Otylia.

"Thunderstone," Otylia said, tracing the edge of the rocks. "This tower is like those the northeastern tribes said they use for marking a trail. What do they lead to?"

"Don't know," Ta replied. "We could've passed others, but with all these dead guys around, it's hard to tell."

Sabina drifted overhead. "It is strange. The souls seem to wander everywhere but near the tower. Should they not have knocked it over by now, just by chance alone?"

"She's right," Narcyz said, ready to shove away any souls, but none bothered us. "They just go around."

I shut my eyes to sense *žityje* or any other forces, but there was nothing new. "There doesn't seem to be anything special around the tower itself."

"Maybe it's not magic," Otylia said, taking the top stone. "Thunderstone is created where Perun's lightning meet's Weles's earth. These stones hold plenty of power on their own, and the souls must sense that somehow. Wait…" She kicked the sand and bit her lip. "Is this *all* broken down Thunderstone?"

"Gods…" Narcyz's eyes widened. "Imagine all the weapons we could make from this. The stuff's nearly as good as Moonstone for a blade."

Andrij scooped up the sand in his gloved hand, letting bits drift between his fingers. "What could have created this much of it? That would take a lot of lightning."

"The war between Perun and Weles consumed the Three Realms for centuries," Otylia replied. "The Way of Souls is a connection to Nawia, so it only makes sense that Perun would attack here to drive Weles away from Jawia, especially if Marzanna has a hold here. She's Perun's daughter, even if she's a corrupted one. You all have seen the gods' willingness to use anything to their advantage."

"Thunderstone drains someone," I said, drawing my Thunderstone dagger and examining its black blade. "Moonblades absorb the *żityje* to add to its reserves, but Thunderstone destroys it from what I can tell. I've felt it." I looked to Otylia. "What if these souls avoid the Thunderstone tower because they have no *żityje*, and these stones are potent enough to sap whatever they gain? Their souls are exposed in these unfinished bodies, and they're trapped in a field of Thunderstone sand. It could be draining them constantly."

My heart grew heavy. All around us were souls searching for paradise, many after suffering against Koschei's Frostmarked Horde. Instead, they'd found sands that devour the little life they sought to regain in order to enter Nawia at all. Death hadn't allowed them to escape Marzanna, but walk into her trap.

"That's a possibility," Otylia replied with a curled lip. "But we can't know that for certain."

"Touch them and ask End," I insisted.

She held out her hands. "My power is as useless as yours here."

I took them, intertwining our fingers. "Yet the bond between us is still there. End uses that connection to allow you to see others' ends. Use that, or at least try. If I'm right, the Thunderstone could be what's dampening our power too—maybe with a Moonstone or by itself."

"We're all tired," Ara said. "Let's think on it before trying to connect with the dead."

Otylia stared at me, and though I expected her to speak through our bond, she said nothing. Instead, curiosity brewed within us both.

Whatever had happened here had changed the landscape long ago, and it may hold the answers to the sands.

"I'll do it," she finally said after a minute, squeezing my hands before stepping away. "Worst-case scenario, it doesn't work."

Ara scowled. "The worst-case scenario is the dead fighting back in your head. Those visions mess with you every time, and they're not usually tormented souls!"

Otylia rested a hand on her shoulder. "I'll be fine, and if I'm not, then I'll have all of you here to help me. Save your fight, Huntress."

Her eyes flashed white as she neared the parting souls. They left no more than a two-stride gap on any side of the tower, so when she reached out, her hand found a suitable soul with ease.

Then she collapsed.

11

Otylia

Why can these visions never be gentle?

EMPTINESS OVERTOOK ME.

I'd been drained before and exhausted to the point of collapse. But this… It was worse than anything. All consuming, a force ripped my *żityje* from my soul and tore my limbs from my body until I was nothing, floating in the abyss.

"This is not the first age where balance vanished," Rod's voice echoed in my mind.

"What happened to the Way of Souls?" I asked. "Why is it draining the dead?"

He hummed an unfamiliar tune. *"When all the realms were birthed from the World Egg, there was unity, balance, and a natural way. Ironic, then, that I broke my own force's will with the creation of Swaróg, who was to aid me in protecting the realms. He used Alatyr to create but more of us. They warred, and scars now litter my realms. What of it, though, when I am gone?"*

Regret twinged in my stomach, but it was nothing compared to the agony I already endured. Each breath stabbed at my lungs when I replied, "You aren't gone if you're talking to me. Help us! What's happening to the souls, to our forces?"

"When two forces of equal strength collide, there is either a combining of both, or the destruction of both. What is left desires to attain what it once had, but such loss cannot so easily be replaced."

"Can we fix it?"

"Oh child… Not all that can be broken may be mended to its original form, but nor is it broken beyond the creation of a new balance."

That glimmer of hope clashed with the dread of what I'd seen on those sands, what I feared was happening to the souls. "Show me how."

Rod gave a fatherly chuckle. *"I cannot teach you what you already know. Unite Alatyr and banish the corruption."* He hesitated. *"I have used your connection to the soul you touched to speak with you, but your force's power is weak here. I must go. Know that what you will see is not pleasant."*

"Wait!"

The void vanished, and I struck a solid surface at full force, sending my head spinning. All around me were colors of every kind. Wisps drifting freely through the gray as they headed together toward a bright horizon, and whatever pulled them dragged me along the ground too. Their movements were slow at first, but grew quicker the further they went, strands of color appearing from the air around them and joining with the wisps.

That horizon grew closer. I hoped it wasn't the Smorodina, but its flames soon became apparent. The current pulled me toward them. My body was still useless to fight it, so all I could do was hope the vision's effects didn't reignite my agony.

The wisps took near human shapes when they struck the Smorodina, crystalline bodies slowly forming around them in brilliant shades. Each started in a different place, and *žityje* began to flourish within them until black smoke fell over the river. It choked the crystalline progress and forced them to flee. We'd seen the souls do this, but we hadn't *felt* what came next.

Emptiness returned, drowning me as I followed them onto the sandy shore without a choice. A strange force burned my throat and eyes, and I joined the wispy souls in a brutal cry.

This wasn't loss. I'd endured plenty of that in my life, both in the Trials and beyond. No, it was the absence of everything somehow ripping each of us apart piece by piece—devouring the little *żityje* the souls had managed to collect. There was no hope. There was no light. There was only the void within and without.

A humming rose in the distance.

We shifted toward it out of a desire to feel *something* else. A gentle song, it reminded me of the lullabies Mother would sing to me as a child, and I wished for the comfort of her embrace. No such comfort came. The endless plain of sand continued tearing through me until another force tugged on my soul. Gentler, it lulled me away from the humming.

"Otylia, come back," Wacław said through our bond. *"You need to leave the visions."*

I closed my eyes, allowing the opposing forces to pull me as they wished. The pain in my body and soul was too much to comprehend his words or what I was headed toward. This is what I'd asked for when I'd touched the souls—to experience what they did. This was their slow march toward some end. Was I trapped with them?

Wacław's pleas echoed louder and louder. They prodded at my conscious mind and demanded I listen, but the agony was familiar, constant. To leave would be to confront the unknown that lay beyond, along with the enemies that lurked there. Would that truly be better?

A mental haze lingered over me until a force repelled me to the side. Not the sea of sand, but a pillar of black, wispy tendrils reaching for any soul who drew too near.

The tower. My friends.

I threw my mangled body towards it, willing myself to wake up from End's nightmare. The wisps struck my chest like the sharpest blades and skewered my soul. Though I did not bleed, my own wisp of green and silver drifted from me as the darkness consumed its power.

Then I awoke.

Cold flooded my veins and coarse sand dug into my skin. I coughed, rolling over to find myself held back. Wacław's and Ara's voices called for me to lie still as misshapen feet stamped inches from my nose. Their pain was no longer mine, but I spasmed at the shock of being torn from the vision.

"The sands are torturing them," I stammered, falling back into my friends' arms. Tears stung my eyes. I tried to wipe them away, but my hands trembled.

"You're okay," Wacław whispered as he cradled my head against his chest. "You're free from the visions."

I gritted my teeth. "It's not just a vision! This place is destroying them. I felt it…" Wacław winced, and my heart sunk at the realization he'd likely felt everything I had through our bond. "But you know that. You know what they're going through, then, and the force that lulls them?"

"It was hard to understand," he replied. "What happened? You were out a long time."

I repeated Rod's explanations for the Thunderstone and the broken balance before telling the rivers' journey through the souls' eyes. The gods had destroyed so much in their wars, but to do this… Could they not try and mend what they'd broken? The souls probably weren't supposed to leave the Smorodina so soon, unformed, but why allow such destruction to border paradise?

"Perun's a vindictive asshole," Narcyz said, stomping on the sand, as if it would be some vengeance for the damage done. "We all saw that. This is his fault, but we're here dealing with his mess for him *again*."

"Master Weles was likely at fault as well," Sabina replied. "He is not one to forget a wrongdoing, and even now, I heard him speak often about ensuring Jaryło rules Jawia in his favor."

Andrij gave the tower a distrustful look. "Excuse my worry, but if this sand is draining the souls and dampening your powers, could it not be feeding upon our *żityje* as well? Are our bodies truly enough to protect us?"

"I don't know," I said, standing with Wacław's help and brushing the dark sand off my clothes. "But the less time we spend here the better. We need to figure out what was making that humming sound I heard in the vision and destroy it before it lulls all these tortured souls into serving Marzanna."

"Will that restore the balance Rod spoke about?" Sabina asked with her fingers pressed hopefully to her lips. "What would replace this?"

I sighed. "I doubt there will be any balance until we beat Marzanna, but let's see what we can do about this Thunderstone field first."

"No resting, then?" Ta huffed. "Just our luck."

"Sure, sleep in the soul-sucking sand and see how you feel afterward," Kuba quipped. "I'm following Otylia."

I jabbed him. "Just not too closely. A dip in the river would've helped your stench."

Wacław grabbed a stone off the top of the tower and tossed it to Kuba. "If each of us holds onto one of these, the souls should keep their distance. I've been elbowed enough for one day."

"The souls are tortured enough without us carrying Thunderstone near them," I replied.

"Will these stones keeping them away actually hurt them?" he asked with his Thunderstone dagger drawn. "They're deep in Thunderstone sand, so I doubt we can make it much worse."

"Fine." I grabbed a stone. "Just don't touch them with it."

Once everyone had a chunk of Thunderstone, we headed toward where I'd heard the humming. I hated holding the stone with the knowledge of what it could do to the souls—and maybe us—but Wacław's inclination was right. We made progress far more quickly with the way ahead clear. It was only for a few strides at a time, but at least we weren't constantly bruised by the souls' random movements.

The souls began to change the further along we went. They were far more densely packed, and their eyes began to blacken. Dark veins like Wacław's crossed their malformed bodies, bringing with them less humanlike shapes.

Wacław pointed to one fur-covered soul near the Smorodina. The fires gave it an aura that made it look aflame itself, its jagged teeth on just the left side reflecting the light. Half of it was beast, the other a combination of twisted, incomplete limbs that forced it to hobble.

"That one looks way too much like a wilkołak to be a coincidence," he said.

I nodded. "There's more than emptiness here now. That humming is loud in my soul… I can almost hear it in my ears even. Marzanna's Moonstone must be close."

"She'll have an army of demons far larger than Koschei's if we don't hurry."

But the twisting of my gut told me we were too late already. Marzanna had captured Weles a moon before, and anyone who'd died since could've been trapped by her pull. Weles had mentioned some corruption of the dead before, so it may have been longer still. Even with our powers and Mother's aid, we'd barely survived against the Frostmarked Horde, and we would have neither if these ever-more demonic souls decided to turn on us.

Kuba tapped me on the shoulder a few minutes later and presented his fern flower. "I think the flower is telling me where the Moonstone is. It's a treasure, right? Super valuable."

"Just tell us where," I said, my patience run through.

"It's in the ground somewhere." He pointed in the direction of the humming, but downward. "I've got this feeling that there's a door in the sand around there. The fern flower usually isn't all that specific, but the Moonstone is definitely underground."

Narcyz kicked through the sand. "How you expect to find a door in all of this?"

"Very carefully," Kuba quipped.

"What about the markers?" Ara asked. "If I needed to find a shelter under the snow, I would use something like those towers to mark it."

I held up my piece of Thunderstone. "There was nothing around the one we found."

"Right, but there could be others. We haven't exactly been looking for them."

Wacław shrugged and looked at me. "It's worth trying, don't you think? If we form a line, we can search together and clear a large path through the souls."

"I concur," Andrij added. "It would be a good use of what we've found, and though a sweep might take longer, I doubt it'll be worse than wandering randomly in hopes of finding a door."

Sabina stood up on her tip-toes. "I can also fly overhead. If I know to look for towers like this in gaps between souls, I should be able to help."

"Just be careful," I said, earning a giddy smile from her as she flew off.

I nodded to Wacław, so he took lead, organizing us into as long a line as possible without the stones losing effectiveness between us. We extended for around fourteen strides and marched together. I still had my doubts. Soon, though, a tower appeared from the crowd of souls nearest to the Smorodina.

As an experienced tracker, Ara helped estimate the connecting line between the previous tower and this one, sending us in a more direct route than the sweeping motion we'd taken before. It felt a bit silly to walk in the line together, but results were results.

We found three more towers in quick succession with some adjustments in direction from Ara. Each was taller than the previous one, now stretching to the top of my head. I wasn't the tallest in the group, though, and even Wacław couldn't see further towers over the souls. We had to be close.

The constant drumming in my chest confirmed it. So did the increasingly distorted souls, their forms turning to demons of every kind we'd seen before and beyond. These were innocents who never should have been twisted by such corruption, but End had shown me Marzanna's call bringing them ever closer. They had no choice.

"Be ready," I told the others as we moved on from the last tower. "The demons might attack if we get too close to the Moonstone."

Andrij drew his blade with the others. "What's the plan if that happens?"

"Don't die," Narcyz replied. "I've got your back."

Andrij grimaced. "That's appreciated, but there is no way we can fight this many."

"Then we force the door open and close it behind us," I said. "If they try to follow, all we can do is hope it holds."

"No," Narcyz said. "I'm not trusting a hunk of metal, but it'll create a chokepoint. I'll block it with Andrij and Kuba."

Kuba rubbed his neck, laughing uncomfortably. "Yeah, thanks for volunteering me. Happy to die protecting a door."

"I'll stay back with you three," Wacław said. "Better that we have numbers in case someone ends up in a pinch."

More and more souls resembled demons as Sabina waved from the air ahead. All kept their distance from us, but darkness lingered in their eyes. I'd seen that change in Wacław during our time in Vastroth. Soon, the demon would wrestle control away from whatever humanity remained in the souls.

Sabina lowered between two towers at our approach. They kept the souls away, but no door was immediately obvious in the open area.

"It's here," Kuba said. "The fern flower is sure of it."

Without powers or any other tools, we dug with our hands. End's vision and a full day of walking through the deep sand had taken its toll, and soreness gripped me. It couldn't compare to the torture I'd endured among the souls. They needed to be free, and I would do whatever it took to free them. Being a goddess wasn't all magic and glory.

My muscles throbbed by the time our fingers found metal. Smooth, two iron sheets were separated by a thin line, but there were no handles. Only two pulsing marks broke the dull gray—Marzanna's Frostmark and Czarnobóg's Darkmark.

I cursed, laying my hand over each mark. Nothing changed despite my attempts to channel over them.

"You try," I told Wacław. "Maybe it needs a Naw, like the portal did."

He looked warily at the Frostmark, flexing his once-marked palm before starting instead with the Darkmark. Nothing changed. Head dropped, his worries pushed through our bond as he switched to rest his hand over the Frostmark.

His worries faded when Marzanna didn't strike him. He stepped back quickly, hand clutched against his chest. "It's not a surprise neither of the corrupted gods wants us to enter."

"Try stabbing it," Kuba said, peeking around us at the doors.

I rolled my eyes. "It's *metal*, Kuba. You wouldn't ram the tip of a sword into a shield and expect results either."

"But Moonblades can cut anything. They might work on this too."

Wacław shifted his coat as he eyed the nearby souls. "It's risky."

Narcyz stepped past me. "I'll do it."

"Wait!" I exclaimed, but it was too late.

Kwiecień's golden light blinded me as Narcyz drove it into Czarnobóg's mark. Moonstone pierced metal with ease, and he shouted in glee until the humming in my chest deepened to an audible tremor. His hands shook on the blade. The whole ground jolted, throwing us from our feet as Kwiecień faded to a dull brown.

Rage burned through my shock as I dug my fingers into the sharp sand. Narcyz had just needed to wait for *one moment* for us to consider the options. Sneering, I tapped Sierpień at my ear and summoned it as a Moonblade. Without my channeling, my light spear was beyond my reach, but a sword was better than nothing.

"Iron-brained idiot!" Ta muttered from beside me.

I sneered. "I doubt he has even that."

My bond to Wacław snapped tight. Where was he? I scrambled to my feet, but the earthquake had sent a thick sand haze over us, stinging my eyes. Most of the group was near. That feeling, though, meant danger.

Hot pain stung my back.

I spun out of instinct, slicing sloppily with Sierpień. It found only air, but laughter answered. Ringing, haunting, it danced about at great speed in the haze.

"I feared we would never meet again," a twisted feminine voice said. "Our last encounter was not so fair to me, but at least I took someone in return for my life."

The familiarity of her voice struck me as she swept closer, decay consuming her near-white skin and ghastly blue eyes. Hair as bright as Dadźbóg's sun tangled with bones and fell to a tattered dress that left little of her rusałka body to the imagination. She'd appear as beautiful as a goddess to any man. To me, she was the rat who'd nearly ruined everything.

"Yuliya," I spat, touching the crescent scar Marzanna's szeptucha had left upon my cheek. She'd killed Kuba and nearly done the same to me. Kuba's javelin had slain her in-turn, but Minna's revival had shown that Marzanna didn't appreciate losing her pets so easily.

Yuliya bared her cracked teeth, sinew and blood staining what bits remained. "Lady Marzanna did not tell me before that you were Dziewanna's little daughter… It doesn't matter. I'll enjoy devouring you all the more now."

An arrow zipped into her shoulder, spurring a snarl. She snapped her gaze to Ara as the huntress shouldered her bow and drew the gray blade of Październik. I flanked to the other side.

"Your friends wield the Betrayer's blades," Yuliya hissed. "They will not save you."

Ara and I struck together. Our swords sliced through the haze, but Yuliya was faster, darting toward the doorway. I made chase as she tore through the door and disappeared inside.

I'm going in, I told Wacław, Ara, and Sabina through our Moon-marked bonds. Wherever Wacław was, he'd have to hold off the other demons lurking in the distance. Their shadows shifted ever nearer, but fighting them wasn't my goal. Only grabbing the Moon-stone mattered. That didn't mean I intended to let Yuliya continue her second life.

The air grew cold and stale as I clambered through the door, my boots striking smooth stone that sloped downward. My moonlight pierced the darkness for only a few dozen strides, but the ring of light grew as Ara, Ta, and Sabina joined me.

"So, that was Yuliya again," Ara muttered. "Think my arrow actually wounded her?"

"Like a flea on a dog," I replied, checking for any other old tongue symbols that could signal a trap. There appeared to be none for now.

Ara grinned. "She went toward the Moonstone, so at least we get the chance to kill her again. Kuba would like that."

Metal clanged and snarls echoed from behind. The battle had begun, and I offered Wacław a silent prayer before starting down the slope with Sierpień extended before me. "Marzanna brought Yuliya back for a reason. Let's make sure she doesn't succeed."

12

Wacław

At least this is familiar.

DEMONS CIRCLED ME. Wilkołaki, rusałki, upióry, and even a płanetnik rushed through the haze at Narcyz's calling. Ignoring the others, they drove me toward the Smorodina, whose flames seared the sky like the wildfires of summer.

The Smorodina also confined my retreat, drawing ever nearer as I parried my enemies' attacks. With Grudzień in one hand and Marzanna's Thunderstone dagger in the other, I was as dangerous as the greatest swordsmen, but the winds abandoned me. I needed their boost to my speed. My movements felt sluggish without them, and my foes were faster than any mortal.

Luckily, the demons were also malformed and inexperienced.

It had taken me years to discover the true power of my płanetnik soul, and even then, I had only learned to wield lightning with the prodding of Jaryło. The płanetnik before me sent windblasts, but they were barely strong enough to stagger me for a moment. He couldn't fly. That left him exposed when I dodged his allies' attacks and surprised them by moving toward their pack.

The płanetnik held no weapon, nor any claws to defend himself in melee. He dodged Grudzień's edge with his superior speed, but he didn't see the dagger coming.

My heart ached killing a fellow płanetnik, knowing he was commanded by Marzanna. But I had no choice. All living souls would fall to her if we didn't succeed. So I fought onward, and when Otylia's message about her pursuit of the Moonstone arrived, I pushed back toward the doors.

Except the demons had no interest in allowing me to move further from the Smorodina. It was mere strides away now, and sweat clung my clothes to me, the heat shifting the haze in waves that tricked my eyes. Where there was a demonic shadow one moment, there was nothing the next. My attacks were sloppy, so I kept an old dual-wielding defensive posture Xobas had shown me years before.

Fatigue made even my parries too slow. Claws and teeth managed to find my flesh in brief strikes. Each wound wore me further. And the flames now nipped at my heels.

Narcyz had always been the better swordsman. *Žityje* could heal me though, so I took cut after cut in hopes I had distracted enough of the demons for him to hold the door with the others. Otylia hated relying on our friends, but I was more grateful for them than ever.

There was no time to worry further about the others with every movement risking the Smorodina's wrath. Heat beyond even the brightest bonfire on Kupala Night burned my exposed skin. It kept the demons at bay, too, and that gave me an idea.

I wore layers for the cold, but they slowed my movements and grew heavy from my sweat. So when a wilkołak swept from the side to catch me off guard, I shed my fur coat, entangling the beast within it before kicking its chest. The half-wolf, half-man towered over me, but the force sent it tumbling into the burning river. The screams that followed told me enough about what awaited me if I failed.

Unfortunately, the kick also sent me onto my back as the other demons smelled their meal. Was that why they'd followed me? I had vast amounts of *žityje* still in my soul after consuming the guardians' hearts. Any demons needed it to live.

Another part of me wondered if they knew I was a Naw instead—a threat to Marzanna's control of the Way of Souls. It didn't matter, as they attacked regardless, and despite my trickery, I only managed to trip a rusałka into the fires before the remaining demons pinned me against the river again.

"How many of you fiends are there?" I asked through labored breaths.

The earthquake's haze should've dissipated by now, but the sand lingered to cloud my vision and scratch my eyes. There were so many shadowed figures shifting in the darkness. Surely, they couldn't all be real?

That thought betrayed me. I focused on the demons who'd struck at me already, but a *zap* from a shadow I'd doubted warned me how wrong I'd been.

Lightning burst into my chest and sent me toppling. A chała emerged at full speed, sparks snapping at the ends of her dress of a stormy gray. Electricity filled her eyes, and as I staggered back to my feet, she prepared another strike.

There was nothing I could do to stop it.

I desperately raised Grudzień to deflect her attack, but she was too quick. Dodging past my blade, she jabbed her palm into my chest and smirked. Lightning surged from her fingers. Like a shockwave, it flung me backward, away from the sands and into the flames.

13

Otylia

What other surprises do you have for us, Marzanna?

WACŁAW'S PAIN GAVE ME PAUSE as we continued down the sloped stone path. He grew weary without his powers, but I had to trust in him and the other boys. They fought so that we could pursue the Moonstone. Turning back would do nothing to help them now.

The chill deepened with us, and our breaths soon fogged the air. But there were no signs of any other demons. Yuliya had come this way. Either she lay in wait, or this underground home for the Moonstone was larger than we'd expected.

Nothing Marzanna had done so far was aligned with our expectations, so why would this be any different? This was the death goddess's territory. We played by her rules now.

I signaled for the others to stop when the light from our Moonblades reflected off a surface ahead. Dark, unmoving, it appeared like the glass mirrors in Vastroth, but a dark patch of dried liquid on the stone wall revealed the floor wasn't solid. I approached and prodded the surface with my blade. As expected, it shifted like the viscous liquid in the first river we'd reached.

"Yuliya must've entered here and disturbed the water, or whatever this stuff is," I said, sweeping my blade over the surface to see if anything lurked in the depths. All seemed clear for now.

Ta prodded it with Wrzesień and curled her lip at the substance sticking to its purple blade. "Yeah, I really don't want to step in there. Can't Sabina just fly ahead?"

I met the nymph's gaze, and she gave me a smile as convincing as a wobbling drunkard claiming sobriety. "I… I can do that," she squeaked.

"You don't have to," I insisted, pointing into the darkness. "Whatever's out there could come after you, and we can't help you from back here."

It was harsh, but she needed to hear it. Sabina was no fighter. Though she could certainly scout, these weren't the clear skies above the souls. Marzanna *knew* we were coming and would account for it.

Surprisingly, Sabina puffed up her little chest and plopped her sword onto her shoulder. It was a heavy blade, though, and the motion sent her careening to the side until Ara caught her. "I can do it," she said. "We can still message each other through your mark, so I'll call if something goes wrong."

"May your bravery light the way for us," I said with a proud smile. Oh, how far she'd come since our initial meeting in Nawia.

She took flight, the patter of her wings echoing through the narrow stone tunnel. Czerwiec in her hand cast a bright white light over the waters, but couldn't pierce the surface, leaving it a shimmering black. Most substances like it would've absorbed the light, not reflected it. That alone hinted at some magical trickery that I'd yet to identify.

The path soon curved to take Sabina out of view. I knew worrying would gain me nothing, but I tapped my foot anyway, never taking my gaze off the now dark point she'd disappeared around. All the while, Wacław's pain only grew.

Then he lost consciousness.

The colored lights of our Moonblades spun around me as I staggered. My stomach turned, my mind joining the clouds. I had to drop to a knee to keep from vomiting, and Ara's worried pleas were distant as I called to Wacław through our bond.

What's happening out there? Wašek, where are you?

I hadn't seen him since the earthquake, but I'd assumed he joined with Narcyz, Andrij, and Kuba. Should I have waited longer to help them organize the defense? My need for vengeance against Yuliya had taken over, and now, both Wacław and Sabina were out of my reach.

Ara's assurances failed to calm my racing heart. "What if Marzanna captured him?" I asked, my voice echoing as if I'd screamed, and when Ara stumbled for an answer, I did. It felt good to pour my anxieties into my voice, no matter how silly. We'd stumbled into another trap.

Once again, it was my fault.

"I shouldn't have split the group," I said, fingers digging into my temples. "There were too many demons out there."

"Narcyz stabbed the bloody door," Ta said. "We coulda prepped if he hadn't."

I shook my head. "We were more disorganized, but we didn't know the earthquake would throw us apart. Yes, Narcyz is a fool. That doesn't change that this would've happened anyway. I should've known from my visions."

End had shown me demonic attacks amid what I'd thought to be smoke, but it wasn't the battle over the Smorodina. To even consider reaching the bridge to Nawia, we had to find this Moonstone. We were in far worse shape than End's successful visions had implied. I'd known the cost of using Sierpień too soon and revealing my presence, and now, Marzanna knew our plan.

"We'll figure it out," Ara said, rubbing my back, but her own brow was wrinkled. "Fate has a strange way of ensuring we do."

I stepped away. "Destiny has failed me before. I'm not relying on her to fix this."

Sabina had been gone for long enough, so I reached out to her through my mark. My heart drummed for each moment afterward until her voiced peeped through.

"Sorry, it is quite the long tunnel."

Find anything? I asked, straightening my posture with a relieved sigh. She would be okay.

"I stopped when I saw a hint of light around a corner. Any further, and I feared them seeing my Moonblade's aura."

Smart. Just get back to us safely.

Sabina returned a few minutes later, smiling like she'd just found the fern flower herself on the journey. She hopped on her landing, and I embraced her, much to her surprise.

"Oh," she said. "Lady Otylia, is all well?"

"I'm just glad you're back."

She cocked her head at Ara, who clarified, "Wacław's missing, we think. Seems our favorite goddess is a bit sentimental about us now."

I shot Ara a glare before prodding the liquid with Sierpień again. "Enough about my feelings. Do you think we can walk through this safely? You said it was far, and I don't want to be consumed by some magical pool."

Sabina cringed. "Well, I couldn't tell from the air. There didn't *seem* to be anything dangerous in it, so maybe?"

Perfect... I pulled back my blade and stepped into the pool so that it went no higher than the top of my boot. *Glomp.* The liquid seemed to suck onto the boot's leather, but not hold so tightly that I couldn't shift again. For now, the ground still sloped downward, meaning it would have to go higher than my boot.

"It's not trying to kill me yet," I said, "but let me go a bit further to see. Sabina, be ready to grab my arms if it tries to drag me down."

She faked a smile. "I'm unsure if I can lift—"

"You'll do great."

I chose to have faith in her, because I doubted my own decision making as my second boot slurped into the liquid. The next step would take me beyond the boot's protection. Waiting would only make it harder, so I threw myself into a few more strides until it reached mid-thigh.

And by the gods, it was freezing.

Any water would've formed ice by now, but this just clung to every piece of skin and hair on my legs. Beyond the cold's sting, though, it didn't hurt, but tickled. It would've been ridiculous in any other circumstance. With Wacław missing, I wasn't in a laughing mood, and the pool slowing me down grinded on my little remaining patience. We needed to get the moonstone quickly.

"Come on," I told the others as it leveled out at waist-deep. "It's frigid, but fine besides that."

"I hate the cold," Ta muttered.

Ara dragged her behind. "It's already cold, so it doesn't matter if it's the air or… well, whatever this stuff is… Better we make progress. Otherwise, we'll never get out of this place."

Ta's grumbling continued as she descended. Since she was shorter, the liquid reached up to her chest, and she bared her teeth in the least threatening display I'd ever seen. At least *our* lives weren't at risk for now. I tried to hold onto that relief, but my thoughts slipped back to Wacław.

Be safe, I told him. *We'll get the Moonstone soon, and then we'll both have our powers.*

We trudged our way around the first corner, the pool somehow getting colder the further we went. Whenever I felt like I'd adjusted, it deepened, and my legs numbed to the point that each step resembled falling out of bed in the morning more than walking. I feared how much more we could endure before the end.

"We can't keep going like this," Ara confirmed not a minute later. She shivered with her arms held across her coat, but our layers did nothing in the pool.

"Can't we find a way to dump the Smorodina in here or something?" Ta replied, copying the motion. "Feels like I'm about to have ice for a stomach at this rate."

"Just keep walking," I replied through gritted teeth, but my stumbled steps were hardly brimming with confidence. They were right. Based on Sabina's explanation, we were nearing the halfway point, and the pool showed no signs of warming. "Or go back. I'll face Yuliya and get the Moonstone."

Ara scoffed. "Alone? Not in Oblivion. Yuliya messed with all of us, and I want to see that stinking rusałka suffer."

Ta just mumbled something under her breath, but followed. What had they done to deserve a friend like me? They had both lived somewhat normal lives before, and now, they were traipsing through magically frigid water at the edge of the underworld. That loyalty had to be earned, and I refused to let them falter for my errors.

So we continued. Our pace slowed with the cold, and my shoulders ached from keeping my arms above the pool. I focused on that pain instead of whatever was happening to my lower half. Frostbite would be a real concern, but *žityje* could heal it later. Until then, all I could do was keep moving forward.

As we turned the second-to-last corner, a force struck the air from my lungs. I stumbled back in a coughing fit while the others caught up.

"What's wrong?" Ara asked.

Our Moonblades' lights revealed the surface ahead didn't shift with our movements. I reached out with my free hand, finding a cold, jagged edge that flaked away at my touch.

"It's ice," I said, "or at least something like it. Seems we finally found a place cold enough to freeze this pool."

Ta leaped onto the ice ledge with some effort, the liquid clinging to her as she tried to claw her way up. Only with Sabina pulling from above and both Ara and me pushing her legs did she manage it, but she smiled triumphantly. "Finally! I am so sick of that disgusting…" She scowled at the amount of it still coating her clothes and hands. "Great Mother, show me how to kill that winter witch."

"Shhh," I hissed. "They'll have heard that."

Ta shrugged. "Yuliya *saw* us. She knows we're coming, so why bother pretending we're sneaky?"

Ara and I hauled ourselves up with some effort. The ice cracked with the three of us so close, so we spread our weight throughout the tunnel, shuffling onward as my legs thawed. I wished they wouldn't. With each bit of vanishing numbness, needles pierced deep into me, and I ground my teeth to keep from screaming.

We made quicker progress without the liquid to drag us down. I'd lost track of how long we'd been in the pool, but my legs had forgotten their normal stride, wanting to twist and push against the current that they no longer faced. What use would we be in a fight if we couldn't even walk correctly?

That worry grew as we rounded the final corner and entered the dim ring of light Sabina had seen. Luminescent blue gemstones ringed the top of the tunnel, their glows colliding mid-air with the light of our Moonblades and mixing into an array that was both beautiful and haunting. I'd never seen gems like these. Experience, though, had taught me that new bits of magic like this weren't to be trusted, so I kept my blade ready as we headed toward the light at the tunnel's end.

A circular stone platform rose from the pool amid a larger chamber. Gemstones continued into it in greater quantities based on the intensifying light, and the humming in my chest intensified with it.

Deep light the color of walnut bark created an aura around the platform's center. It pulsed like a heartbeat, swelling and retreating with the hum, and the power within it had become all too familiar.

The Moonstone.

"Be ready," I told the others, creeping forward.

I hated this feeling. For so long, I'd been the wild witch, watching from the shadows of the woods to have the advantage. It was unnerving to stand in the open and wait for my opponent to make the first move, especially without my powers to call upon. Sabina's elevated eyes were our only chance of seeing Yuliya before she struck.

Sabina's wings and our echoed steps broke the silence as we shuffled toward the platform. The ice provided a surprising amount of grip compared to frozen water, which I assumed was because of how sticky the liquid had been. That helped me keep a defensive posture, but at the platform's edge, I would have to climb up. It was the perfect place for an ambush.

"I'm going up," I said. "Sabina, watch to make sure nothing takes advantage."

Her fluttering overhead was enough of a signal, so I leaped to grab hold of the ledge, letting go of Sierpień in the process.

"There is nothing except a brown orb right now," Sabina said. "Maybe Yuliya didn't—"

She cried out as a gemstone shot through one of her wings. Then another.

Her wings gave out, sending her tumbling. My muscles screamed as I reached out for her, I was only halfway onto the ledge—too far. The *crack* of her bones when she struck the platform sent a jolt through my heart.

I screamed, snatching Sierpień and rushing to her as a gemstone *whooshed* past me. Ara and Ta yelped from below, and I cursed myself for leaving them too. Why would the defenses only be on the platform? There were far more gemstones here, but those in the tunnel were plenty enough to strike my friends.

I threw myself over Sabina to protect her from the gemstones. They pierced my back over and over, but I just held tight, her tears dripping onto my gloved hand as she whispered in the nymph tongue.

"It'll be okay," I told her, but my rapid breaths betrayed my panic.

Blood joined the tears as the gemstones' onslaught continued. We were cattle for the slaughter here, but with nowhere to hide, the only way out was to return to the dark area of the tunnel. We'd have to leave the Moonstone.

Or did we?

Staggering to my feet with a dozen gemstones jabbing into my back and limbs, I shouted with all my fury and lifted Sabina. Thank the gods for her slight form. I could barely carry her, but the platform was short, and I managed to haul her to the ledge, dropping her down to Ta below.

"Where's Ara?" I asked, eyeing the gemstones scattered across the ground. Few remained in the tunnel's ceiling, and it was too dark to see further than the light of our Moonblades.

Ta shook her head as she protected Sabina against the platform's wall. "Gone…" She wiped her teary-eyed face with her sleeve. "She protected me, but there were too many. The ice took her when she collapsed."

I lost control.

Spinning toward the Moonstone, I sliced the air with my blade, more gemstones shooting toward me as I yelled, "Fight me! Yuliya, you coward!"

I'd failed again. Ara had stood beside me when no one else would, and now she was gone, because I hadn't realized the threat. Why hadn't End warned me of this? Were we somehow beyond what it had seen? Had I broken its possibilities, straying down a path even worse than those I'd known?

Laughter answered.

"A fair trade, one would think. Listopad for Październik—a Moonstone for a Moonstone. And Lady Marzanna's pets for your own." She cackled again. "Or more than one of your pets… The Naw will add nicely to her collection too."

I pointed my blade toward where the laughter had come from, but Yuliya's voice faded down another tunnel as the last of the gemstones fell. Another two shot into me. The pain was nothing compared to the spines in her words, and *żityje* healed the physical wounds. My arm trembled, my fingers loose on Sierpień's hilt. What had I done?

"YOU COWARD!"

My voice echoed through the now dark chamber, only Moonstone left to light it. I glared at the pure orb hovering at the platform's center. Its pulses still drummed my chest, and my steps followed its beat as I stormed toward the stone.

Taking it should've been a relief. I'd felt the suffering of the souls trapped in Marzanna's corruption through the stone, but as I took it in my hand, emptiness answered.

No humming with power.

No warmth through my bond to Wacław.

No support from Ara.

Just the cold void that filled the chamber. Gemstones shattered underfoot and the taste of blood filled my mouth as I bit my cheek.

We'd gained another shard of Alatyr, the eleventh moon of Listopad, but lost both Ara's Moonstone of Październik and Wacław's of Grudzień. *I'd* lost them.

My visions had shown me the way, and my desperation had led us down a path that I'd known would lead to destruction. Yet, here I stood. My lover was gone. My loyal friend had fallen without me by her side. And we were no closer to securing Alatyr.

"Mother guide me," I whispered into the darkness. "I have lost my way."

14

Narcyz

FIGHTING A SWARM OF DEMONS WAS HARD no matter who was on your side. But it helped a whole lot to have someone who'd killed hundreds of them. It sucked for us, then, that Wacław was nowhere to be seen.

"Get your nasty breath out of my face!" I roared, stabbing some monstrous beast as its jaws clamped down on my wooden shield and tried to rip it from my grasp. Luckily, Moonstone packed a punch, and the demon dropped to the black sands.

The gap that undead witch, Yuliya, had created in the doorway was wide enough for Kuba and my overlapping shields. We held back the tide of demons as Andrij launched flaming arrows from behind.

"Half-Chief abandoned us," I shouted to Kuba. "That's the only answer."

Kuba pushed himself up with my shoulder, plunging the stunningly green blade of Maj through the eye of a diving wiła—an ugly winged thing that looked like Sabina but with way more shrieking.

"Wacław wouldn't do that," he said when he landed. "Besides, you caused this mess."

Kwiecień flashed gold as I struck down another, leaving it coated in demonic black blood. It was the point of a sword, but I despised seeing such well-crafted weapons ruined by beasts. Any trained warrior spent hours ensuring his blade was well taken care of. It took seconds to ruin all that work.

"Yeah," I said, digging in my heels as the demons rushed into our shields. There was no time to regret my haste now. Kuba would no doubt let me forget it later. "I did. But *where is he?*"

Flames lapped at my ears as Andrij shot another arrow between us. His presence was my only reassurance, calming my panic, but unlike me, he didn't grin when his target screeched in agony. "Focus, both of you! These bastards swarmed Wacław. He's doing us a favor by distracting them."

"Yeah, big favor," I muttered.

We'd killed at least twenty demons of any and every kind. Their numbers had thinned since the initial strike, but every part of me was sore from trudging through deep sand and fighting the day before. These were the times that made me dream of sleeping next to the forge, its breaths hot on my face. It was hard to believe that's where I'd been days before.

Wacław had ignored my messages through his Eclipsemark too, so he was either dead or too focused to reply. Neither option was good. All we could do was keep fighting and hope Otylia showed up to tell us what in Oblivion had happened.

Except she never showed.

Two wolf-men rammed us harder than we could fight back, sending us stumbling back into the tunnel. My shield cracked from the blow, and when Andrij helped me back to my feet, I found a gaping hole in it just above the arm hold. Near useless. But it was better than *completely* useless, so I kept it as far away from me as I could as the demons charged down the stone slope.

I cursed how smooth the ground was. It was easy to dig into the sand, but here, my boots slipped. My only luck was that none of the demons held long spears that could strike through the gap in my shield. Instead, they preferred to flail their arms against it like some drunk idiots.

They'd have killed us by now if they fought with any skill or tactics. Most demons were stupid, but these had no clue how their bodies worked. Half the time, they tripped over each other, and the smooth stone only made that worse.

A terrible idea made me smirk.

"Kuba!" I said, deflecting another strike and stabbing back. "Throw whatever you've got left in your canteen across the ground. Take mine too."

He huffed and sliced off a upiór arm that had been headed right for my head. "Are you crazy? What's that gonna do?"

"Just do it!"

The sudden wetness on my leg told me that he'd either listened, or that I'd soiled myself. There was no horrible smell—beyond the demons' reek—so I assumed it was water. Most of it had gone past us. That would give us a footing advantage.

"Push," I told the others. "Together, now!"

Kuba gave no reply but lowered his shoulder into his shield as Andrij jumped in-between us with his fresh shield. At first, nothing happened. The demons snarled and swiped like normal, but then one of the smaller ones slipped on the wet ground, falling into the legs of the one next to it. That one did the same to the ones nearest to it, and soon, ten of them were in a heap of misshapen limbs.

We took advantage, slicing and shooting like madmen as the demons untangled themselves. Those still standing tried to counter our advance, but struggled to find footing amid the writhing mass. Black blood flowed.

"Now retreat," I told the others, shuffling back to a position below the wettest points. The blood, I hoped, would only add to the demons' slips and allow us a second charge.

We waited for the demons to advance through the blood and water, but they just stood there. Some shook their heads as others looked around like they suddenly woke up with no idea where they were.

Then they started wailing.

I gripped Kwiecień, expecting some kind of trick as the dozen remaining demons dropped to their knees. They screamed and wept with voices as horrific as their bodies. But they didn't attack.

"What in Oblivion?" Kuba asked on his tip-toes to peek over my shoulder. "Narcyz can even make demons cry, huh?"

I elbowed him in the stomach. "It's a trick. Keep your shield up."

Footsteps came from behind us. I spun, expecting an ambush, but Otylia emerged from the darkness with Ta and Sabina at her side. Her eyes were swollen and red, and her glare carried the cut of a freshly sharpened blade.

"The trick is already done," she said, squeezing a brown orb at her side.

I lowered Kwiecień and dared to hope the battle was finished. "That the Moonstone?"

She nodded.

"Where's Ara?" Kuba asked as he scrambled to us. "And Wacław? He headed toward the Smorodina, and we haven't seen him since."

Otylia pushed through us, and I knew well enough to give her space. Few people could do more damage than her when angry. If Ara and Wacław were gone…

I should run before she explodes.

Tears streamed down Sabina's cheeks as she followed, but Ta stopped, an arm held across her body. "We ran into a trap," she said. "It 'bout killed all of us, but Ara protected me. The weird water stuff took her."

I shoved Kwiecień into its scabbard and turned away. Gods, it shouldn't have hurt that much. Ara and I had never been all that close, but to die now, after all we'd been through, was a joke. We'd fought demons. We'd fought gods. But a cave had been too much?

"She's dead dead then?" I asked. "Not like kinda dead?"

Andrij placed a hand softly on my back, his voice careful. "I don't think there's such a thing. If her soul is gone, it's gone."

"We're on the *Way of Souls!* You can't tell me her soul shouldn't be somewhere around here then. We'll just bring her back, like we did to Kuba."

"I had to find the fern flower to become human again," Kuba said, tugging at the flower which peeked out of his bag. "There's only one, I think, and I don't think I can use it on her. The spirits had to help get me out of that jackal body."

I stomped my foot. They gave in too easily. We'd faced the odds of the realms before and won, so why would this be any different?

"Otylia will help," I muttered, freeing myself from Andrij's embrace and heading over to her. It was cold away from him, but I didn't need his care right now. I needed to fight back.

The remaining demons gawked around Otylia as her silver light pierced the haze. She rifled through her bag, retrieving herbs, bones, and a fire-starting kit. When she finished, she held her Eclipsemark necklace—mirroring the Moonmark one Wacław wore—to her lips and whispered with her eyes closed. She opened them at my approach.

At times, I'd wondered what Wacław saw in her, but it was clear then. There was fire in those eyes, passion that would burn through anyone keeping her from him. Her glare sent a shock right through my stomach. To another, though, I could see the allure.

"What do you want?" she snapped.

I crossed my arms and took a wide stance. Our tribe's most experienced warrior, Albin, had taught me to show strength when afraid, and it felt appropriate against a goddess who could sever my soul. "To help. The others think Ara's dead, probably Wacław too, but I don't believe it."

The ends of her mouth curled. "Go on."

"Marzanna knows you're the real threat," I said, "but you're a goddess. That makes you tough to kill and even tougher to keep dead. So, why would she kill your lover and your friend when she can use them against you?"

"We've come to the same conclusion," she replied. "End has also shown me as much, now that the Moonstone isn't amplifying the sands' draining abilities. I'm bonded to Wacław and Ara. I would sense if they were dead. Yuliya called this a 'fair trade,' so Marzanna is playing games with me. I *hate* her taking Wacław and Ara, but this offers us an opportunity."

"How? She's got two people we can't let her kill."

Otylia approached a wiła, now landed, and touched her cheek. "She's used the guardians, these demons, and even a Moonstone to weaken us. She was willing to surrender Listopad and lose control of her power to create demonic armies through the Way of Souls. The gods strike down their foes when they have the strength. We've backed her into a corner, and she knows it. Her attempt to manipulate me means she knows she might lose."

I huffed. "Your visions tell you that too?"

"No." She turned away from the wiła, moonlight pulsing at her fingertips as she weaved it into some type of image. "End's original visions promised failure if I channeled Sierpień to save us from the guardians, and since then, we've strayed beyond even what it had showed me. I haven't managed to create as powerful a ritual in the few minutes I've had my power back, but I saw the Way's end."

She turned the moonlight image, and it soon became clear that it was a map. We stood on a massive plain of sand along the left side of the Smorodina. Ahead was a series of bridges connecting an island in the Smorodina to the other side.

"Is that the way across?" Andrij asked, approaching and pointing to the first bridge. "Don't the legends say a dragon guards it against intruders entering Nawia?"

Otylia's nose wrinkled. "They do mention a żmij, but Weles's Thread leads that way. Marzanna will have him trapped on her island at Nawia's edge. Probably Wacław and Ara too."

Ta, Kuba, and Sabina joined us around the map, each studying the challenges ahead. We were only halfway to the bridge based on it, and we'd lost nearly a third of our group already. What hope did we have of defeating Marzanna in her fortress if we couldn't withstand some demons on the way?

"We can beat a dragon," Kuba said. "Just like Czarnobóg, we chop off its head."

"Czarnobóg survived our battle," Sabina replied, scrunching in her own neck as if she were a turtle retreating into her shell. "Maybe we should try another method?"

I shrugged. "Dragons have scales that are hard for even our Moonblades to cut. The neck is the most exposed part, and it's hard for them to bite you or boil you when you're attacking it."

"We'll deal with the żmij when we get there," Otylia said, pointing to spikes of silver that rose between us and the bridge. "First, we need to finish crossing this stupid sand. There are mountains blocking areas further from the Smorodina, so we'll have to travel closer to the river."

Andrij studied the mountains, then gestured to the narrow gap between the mountains and river. "That's a choke point if I've ever seen one. If Yuliya is looking for an ambush spot, it'll be there."

"Why don't we just fly over the mountains?" Ta asked. "Or over the river? The flames can't go *that* high."

Otylia eyed the Smorodina's fires in the distance. "The Smorodina was made to protect against beings exactly like us from entering Nawia. You might have a point with the mountains, though."

"They appear like a block here," Sabina said. "Are there any lower points?"

"End didn't show me all the details," Otylia said. "Most of its visions had us going through the pass, and yes, facing ambushes of one kind or another."

Kuba raised his brow. "Most? So there's a chance we don't have to deal with an ambush?"

But Otylia shook her head, dismissing the map into twirling silver wisps. "The other visions had us either already dead, or dead before we reach the pass. None showed what happens if we try to go over the mountains, but that's why I want to conduct another ritual. End can show me what gives us a chance, if we have one."

"Is that wise for your health?" Sabina asked as she walked to Otylia's side and laid her head on her shoulder. The nymph's wings were bloodied, but looked as if they would heal in time. "You have toiled beneath the weight of knowing we are already in a tumultuous situation. Seeking the future further could only strain you more."

Otylia tensed, but didn't move away from her. "I've seen enough to give Death himself nightmares. What more could one vision do?"

"You could say the same about one nymph or mortal, yet here we are, fighting when the gods rest in Prawia. One small thing can alter the future."

"I need to know what happens," Otylia replied. "Marzanna will have the advantage otherwise."

I grabbed a fistful of sand and threw it between us. "She's already got the advantage! Don't mess with your head and make it worse."

She scanned us, and from her flinch, I assumed she'd looked for Wacław's reaction. Her pain made sense. It had been our responsibility to fight by Wacław's side, but we'd lost him in the haze. Maybe it could've been different if we'd found him. Maybe not. In the end, thinking about what might've happened was a waste of time.

Otylia shook her head, but threw her ritual elements back into her pack. "I won't do it, then, but we need to go. This sand is draining us, even with the Moonstone not taking our powers anymore."

"Won't the path ahead be sand too?" Andrij asked before nodding to Ta. She was shivering violently. "We just went through Oblivion to retrieve that Moonstone, and a few hours' rest should be enough to stop us from falling over at least."

Otylia's eyes widened at Ta's condition. "The cold…"

She ordered me to throw down my bedroll for Ta as she took a few herbs from her bag again. Ta's eyes darkened, and Andrij had to catch her before Otylia was finished grinding down her witch medicine with mortar and pestle. When we rolled up Ta's pantlegs, her already dark skin had turned black as charcoal in spots. Her eyes rolled back.

I shook her. "Keep awake! Otylia, what is this?"

"It's the reason you don't jump in a half-frozen river," she replied, stamping her herbs quick enough to draw sweat from her brow. "Marzanna's Curse has many forms, and Ta just emerged from a pool of the stuff we saw in the river before. My *žityje* healed me, but she obviously hid how badly it had affected her." She waved toward Kuba. "Pour me some of your water."

He paled. "I… er… I used it to make the demons slip."

"Then grab mine!" she snapped. "And Narcyz, stop her from sleeping. The sickness will kill her if we don't stop it."

Ta's eyes fluttered as I shook her again. I normally had no issues beating someone up a bit, but my stomach ached having to do it as violently as she needed to keep awake. She was just a kid. We'd all seen and done terrible things on our journeys lately, but I'd had the chance to grow up first.

Once Kuba got his act together, Otylia stirred her slushy potion together and knelt beside Ta. "Tilt her head back and hold her mouth open. She won't like this."

I did what she said, but Ta's fighting forced me to hold down her legs to stop her from kicking me in the groin. Otylia was done quickly, though, and I released Ta as she descended into a coughing fit. That was good. At least, I assumed it was better than slipping into unconsciousness.

"Keep her awake still," Otylia said, turning back to her mortar and herbs. "The sickness hasn't set in far, so the potion should hold the worst of it back. Frostbite is a different monster."

"Then why didn't you deal with it first?" I asked with more bite to my voice than needed.

Her eyes of daggers tore into me, and I looked away as she replied, "Frostbite will take a finger or a limb, sure, but Marzanna's Curse will take your life. It doesn't matter how many fingers or toes you have if you're dead."

Andrij patrolled with Kuba as Sabina helped Otylia prepare poultices for the frostbite. I felt useless just keeping Ta awake, but Otylia insisted, and I had little desire to piss off the goddess any more than I already had. Kneeling there gave me too much time to worry. It had been easy to fight when my life was threatened by the demons, but moving forward was harder when our foes didn't have a blade to my throat. Dread's blows were blunt, constant. And worst of all, I couldn't fight back.

Andrij could.

"The souls are heading back to the river," he said, his voice peeling back the weight holding me down—not completely, but enough for me to take a long, relieved breath when he spoke. "They're not wandering anymore, either."

The haze had died down, and beyond our group, the crowd of souls headed directly toward the flames, soon followed by the ones who'd been demons. No more aimless meandering. None gave us even a glance, but I preferred it that way. We'd helped them by getting the Moonstone. That didn't mean I *wanted* a couple thousand undead souls staring at me.

"Maybe they'll grab Wacław for us," Kuba said, waving at each soul despite their ignorance.

"Doubt it," I muttered before moving out of the way for Otylia and Sabina to apply the poultices. Warriors had come back from campaigns with frostbite when wars raged into the winter. Those bits of it—like the frostbite Wacław had taken at the ends of his fingers to help Otylia moons ago—were nothing compared to this. Patches across Ta's legs resembled Czarnobóg's black scales more than skin, and I feared even Otylia's healing wouldn't be enough.

Andrij meandered to us and pressed his hands into my back. A hundred knots within it answered, both loosening and releasing a waved of pain, but I leaned back into his touch. "I wish there were a way for us to ask the souls for help," he said. "We freed them, but unless we stop Marzanna, then they'll walk right back into her control in Nawia."

"They had no consciousness when I touched their wisps before," Otylia replied. "It's likely they aren't fully reborn until they reach Nawia."

"What about the demons?" Kuba asked, groaning as he stared at the sky. "Sure, they're not attacking us anymore, but we could use *something!*"

I shook my head. "You heard them scream. They'd suffer if we tried to use them against Marzanna. Those could've been our tribe's dead. Let them rest in peace." Then I stood and grabbed Kwiecień. "Leaves more of Marzanna for me to stab."

Part 2
The Queen of Death

15

Wacław

Flaming water is officially worse than normal water.

I BOILED ALIVE.

We'd all seen a hunk of meat bobbing in a pot of soup over the fire. The aroma of Mom's soup alone was enough to pull me in from a half-mile away, excitement for a meal making my stomach rumble. I'd never considered in those moments what it felt like for that hunk of meat.

The answer was *torture*. Like a thousand blades pricking me all at once, then driving deeper, the Smorodina's flaming waters sought to destroy my battered body. All I saw was fire. And it turned me to ash.

No salvation came no matter how I flailed. The shore was a distant horizon, the winds some alien force miles away, and it seemed my agony would never end.

Until something grabbed hold of my coat by the collar and dragged me ashore, coughing and spitting up water that burned my throat raw. Black sand dug into every burned nook and cranny to amplify my pain. *Žityje* poured from my soul to heal the wounds as figures moved through my blurred vision, but how much remained? I'd feasted upon the guardian chorty's hearts. So long upon the black sands had drained me, though, and I could barely feel the winds.

I feel them!

That realization tore me from my malaise for a moment. Either I was too far from the dampening Moonstone, or Otylia had succeeded. That gave me some chance to resist whatever had a hold of me, but with my eyes slow to heal, I couldn't comprehend the shifting shapes in front of me.

"Who are you?" I mumbled, my tongue burned too from swallowing the water.

"Keep quiet," a woman's voice commanded. A hand shoved the back of my head and forced me to stare at my feet and stumble on. Something rattled ahead as the Smorodina's heat fell away, but the cold brought its own sting. "I'd cut out your tongue, but Lady Marzanna wishes to speak with you."

I spat in the direction of the woman. "I don't much care for Marzanna's wishes."

She didn't reply, but my returning vision gave me plenty to focus on. A hulking utopiec and wilkołak flanked me on either side, their reek worse than the deepest swamp. Unlike most demons, though, they wore matching sets of armor that resembled Czarnobóg's dark scales. So, too, did the two upióry pulling a full wagon in front of me. The beasts grew the more hearts and blood they consumed, and this pair were three times my height, easily pulling the wagon through knee-deep sand.

From iron blades to ceramics and split wood, items of every kind filled the wagon beyond its walls, as if stretching toward the living realm above. Except the sky was a swirling blackness that expelled the usual gray of the Way of Souls. Only the owl-like wings of a strzyga met the winds above, Grudzień hanging in her grasp.

I recognized her.

Long hair the color of the Smorodina's flames draped over her broad, armored shoulders. She noticed my gaze, and a sneer crossed her gaunt face, her lips smeared with fresh blood beneath her fangs. Life flickered in her eyes. That made her corpse-like form all the more frightening as she turned to face me with a flap of her owl wings.

"You recover quickly," she said, amused. "I shouldn't be surprised after that escape you pulled with Lady Marzanna's sister. We thought you were finished when my brothers and sisters trapped you, but you batted them away as if they were nothing, your wounds closing like a god's. For that, I must thank you. I failed to understand the full strength of a Naw until that day."

Awe and fear alike filled me at the sight of another Naw… or Nawie. Based on my other captors' expressions and the *żityje* in their souls, they were like us too. I had gone so long without knowing others who experienced the same as me. Now there were five, all bound to Marzanna as I'd once been, and one of them held my Moonstone.

"And in return for your power," I said, looking around at the wastes that stretched every direction, "Marzanna dragged you to the underworld. Nawie were meant to protect the Way of Souls for the natural dead, not curse it! We could be more than this."

The strzyga laughed. "That is adorable, considering that ridiculous mark you bear upon your own arm. You scorn us for joining with a goddess while binding yourself to another. Aren't we all just pawns in their games?"

"Otylia doesn't make me her pawn. I am her equal. You don't have to be slaves!"

I couldn't fight the passion pouring through my voice. Every word burned through my recovering throat, but these were my people. They suffered as I had with the demonic taint, so if anyone could save them, it was me.

"Slaves?" The utopiec beside me laughed, then shoved my head down again. Its… *His* fingers dripped with swamp muck, and it trickled cold down my spine. "Lady Marzanna gives us power," he said. "She feeds us the blood we need for strength and gives us armies to command. We are not slaves. We are her generals."

"She sees you as playthings," I replied. "We're just tools for her to use against the other gods, and against the living. Don't you see what she did to Jawia? She'd kill everyone so that she can lead as the goddess of death!"

The strzyga dropped, sending a puff of sand over me as she snatched my throat. Her claws broke the skin, but the trickle of black blood that followed was almost pleasant compared to the Smorodina.

"You had your chance to rule the realms alongside us," she hissed. Those fangs flashed in the remaining light from the flames, and hunger lingered in her eyes. Hunger that I knew too well. "Your betrayal has cost both Lady Marzanna and our kind. We Nawie are few, corrupted by the gods who abandoned us. Don't claim that Perun or Weles had any care for what we endure. Our lady sees us, knows our pain."

She released me with a last jab of her thumb into my throat. "Speak again, and I'll use your Moonblade to remove your fingers. Lady Marzanna may need your tongue, but I doubt she'd complain about missing digits."

I let a demonic growl slip through my lips, but didn't reply. As much as I hated them for abandoning what we should've been, I'd fallen for Marzanna's lies more than once. That hunger, that hatred, held a power that I struggled to resist even now. These Nawie didn't have Otylia to lessen their burden. If anything, their goddess amplified the demon's call.

Pain struck me like a punch to the gut.

"Where are you?" Otylia said through our bond. *"Wašek, I swear to the gods, answer!"*

I coughed, recovering from the sudden reconnecting of our bond, but spurring a glare from the Nawie. *I'm somewhere down the river,* I replied silently. *A group of Marzanna's Nawie captured me, and I think they're taking me to her.*

"Are there mountains near you?"

With the strzyga flying again, I chanced a glance to my left, away from the Smorodina. We were walking parallel to the river now, and the opposite direction was nothing but flat sand. No souls wandered here. Except for us of course.

I can't see far in this darkness, but I don't think there are mountains near. Why?

Her disheartened sigh met my chest. *"End showed me what's ahead. You must be beyond the path we need to take. We can't reach you in time, and Marzanna took Ara too."*

As I'd expected. Though my fall into the Smorodina had seemed a timeless eternity, it was clear enough the flow had carried me far. Had Marzanna expected me to fall into the flames, or was it sheer luck—or lack of it—that her Nawie found me?

Keep going, I told her. *I'll let you know if—*

Another force struck my mind, paralyzing me mid-stride and causing me to fall. I caught myself on my knees, but a searing headache made any comprehension difficult. It burned cold like a spear of pure ice. And Otylia's presence disappeared at its touch.

The utopiec's grimy hand pulled me to my feet again. I scowled at it, only to receive a punch to the cheek that broke my jaw with an audible *snap*. Gods, I'd failed to realize what abilities a Naw in utopiec form would have. While I had my winds, this man had enough muscle to shatter my strengthened soul-form with a single blow.

My jaw hung loose as *żityje* did its work, taking another precious chunk of my supply. Demonic hunger filled the gap. It wouldn't be long before I needed to feed again, and I doubted Marzanna would be eager to help me.

The reason for my sudden pain became apparent when I recovered from the blow. A castle of pure ice loomed behind the flames of the Smorodina ahead, its towers and walls reaching into the swirling darkness above. The arcing keep at its rear seemed to dance between sheer black and the reflected fiery red of the river, as if Czarnobóg himself rested upon its battlements. The home of Marzanna. She was here. Not an avatar or visage like we'd faced alongside Koschei, but the goddess of winter and death herself.

A shiver ran across my skin, my hairs raising at the realization of my foe. For moons, I'd anticipated this moment, but I was unarmed, alone. I was no longer predator, but prey. This was the den of the ice wolves, and like a mother to her pups, she would tear me apart for them to feast.

16

Zakir

What forces allow this, I wonder?

A COLD RAIN FELL AS ICE ADVANCED up the rooted legs of the goddess Dziewanna. The streaks of emerald that once extended from her fingertips had frozen in the days after her ritual, and each day only made it worse.

We had two weeks at most until the frost consumed her.

I triple-checked my mental calculations in Dwie Rzeki's village center, noting the additional five finger-widths of ice compared to the day before. It was the same time as the day before, of course. Failing to account for the moment of the record would lead to a skewed result. Even then, it was an approximation. Each day varied between two and four finger-widths, but the rate seemed to be increasing based on today's measurement.

Unless yesterday's measurement was short.

My foot tapped the muddied ground, but I ignored the splashes. Ara would be concerned about my attire as marzban being ruined. Except she was gone on the expedition. That allowed me the freedom to dress as I wished, which was to say that I didn't much care.

There was too much to comprehend about the realm we called Jawia to bother with how muddied my pants were. Mud itself could be fascinating, with its changing composition based on the soil of the area…

I paused, glancing at the muck beneath my feet. Could the increased density of the wet earth impact the ice's advance? Did it offer a conduit for the goddess Marzanna's winter force?

My bag flopped open at my hand's absent asking. I scanned the pockets Ara's mother had sewn within it to keep my components organized. The furthest right contained rolls of sheep-skin parchment tied with a knot she claimed was used to set traps for rabbits. It seemed to have entrapped the paper well enough.

The parchment was rough to the touch. As I shielded it from the rain, pieces of its back flaked onto my fingers, which I brushed off onto my pantleg with a shudder. There must've been a better way to make it, but that would have to be for another time. Ara insisted that my pursuits needed to help the people now.

Thinking of her made my hands shake. I lacked the Moonmark that allowed her to contact Otylia, but I wished for some way to know she was well. The living realm relied on her and the others far more than my people relied on me. Xobas and I sought solutions for the small problems in our village. Those wouldn't matter if the goddess Marzanna could not be stopped.

I added to my notes regarding the ice's advancement. My stylus pressed wax into the parchment to create the markings. We had no established writing among the clans, but only I needed to understand these.

The notes confirmed my suspicions. The ice had increased its rate of growth over time, but its pattern deviated enough to imply something else impacted it. What of Jawia's many forces could be at play? Most in the village waved their hands and pled "magic." That was unsatisfying to me, as there was always an answer, even when the gods' forces were involved. They channeled already existing powers, which meant interactions between those powers remained relevant.

Water concentration, humidity, wind, soil composition, or an increasing presence of Marzanna's power in this realm?

I kept my notes in detailed, separate columns to ensure different tracts of thought did not intersect. Among my friends, I saw often how such deviations distorted and delayed their intended path. There was a place for each thought. A crucial position that, if altered, could topple the construction of ideation.

"I must test," I muttered to myself as I tucked my stylus and parchment away. Droplets had fallen upon them unfortunately, and it would take hours of drying over the fire to ensure no moisture remained. *So much to do…*

"What kind of test?"

I jolted. My young assistant, Gastein, had silently stood by my side the entire time. In my focus, I'd forgotten about him, and he shivered in his light jacket, his matted black curls all too familiar. The face of my deceased brother, Bidaês, replaced his too often, so I tried not to look at him. My brother had been a monster. Was that supposed to make me feel shame? Anguish? Anger? Ara said all were natural, but I didn't know, so I avoided the topic altogether.

"We will start with moisture levels," I replied, keeping my gaze on the goddess Dziewanna. Bidaês's confident smile lurked in my peripheries anyway. Haunting me. "Collect wood from the villagers. When the rain ends, we'll build fires around the goddess to keep back water and cold. Then, we will see if the goddess Marzanna's ice can advance without water to draw upon."

Gastein touched his second and third fingers to his nose, then extended them toward me in a formal Simukie gesture. "Yes, Marzban." He ran off in the manner of a child about to soil themselves.

Youth are strange.

I was only two years older than him, but my expeditions with Ara and the others had given me more experience than all the years before. Every day brought discoveries now. No longer did I toil in an ill-prepared tent, far too small and unclean to ensure the purity of my experiments. People listened to me too. Often, too much.

My mental notetaking kept me there awhile longer as the rain intensified. This goat-skin coat was hardly enough to keep out the chill, but I didn't flee the cold. The other villagers laughed and ran back to their houses and tents. They had families, homes. Without Ara, I had only my discoveries, and each moment I watched the goddess Dziewanna in that drumming downfall, I pierced the layers of veiled magic to the forces that lay beneath.

I was no god. No Naw. No spirit.

The threads that Otylia claimed weaved through the realms were invisible to me, but mortality didn't make me useless. It allowed me to see that channeling the forces was not all there was. Each droplet of rain or flicker of fire was as mortal as me. I didn't need to live forever to study them or what consumed the goddess Dziewanna now.

I needed only my mind.

17

Otylia

Enough of these games.

THE OTHERS HAD CONVINCED ME NOT TO SEEK End's visions again, but I refused to walk into another of Marzanna's traps. Every path End had shown me before took us through the narrow mountain pass closer to the Smorodina River. Ambush always followed.

So I took us the opposite direction.

"Do we *have* to be this high?" Ta asked, one hand over her mouth and another over her stomach. "The ground's so far…"

Against her wishes, the moon's pull arced us higher than I'd ever flown. The towering mountains ahead marked a formidable obstacle, and Wacław had explained in his experience that a gentle climb was easier to handle than a sharp one with the air thinning. Ta had vomited once already and Narcyz was visibly green. I felt no difference, but that was yet another reminder that Ascension had changed more for me than I dared to accept.

"How do we know there's not something more dangerous waiting in the mountains?" Narcyz blurted through his sickness.

I shot him a glare, deepening his grimace. "All you've done is complain! Try the ambush if you want. Marzanna has Wacław and Ara, so I'm not risking us getting delayed or caught."

"But—"

Summoning my light spear silenced him. I kept it in-hand as we approached the range's lowest peaks, but unlike the mountains of Perun's Crown east of Krowik, there were no foothills separating them from the flat plains. Their obscene heights dropped off at each end too, leaving none of the mountains connected. It was as if swords had been driven from beneath the ground at random in just this area.

Another river flowed between the peaks. Confined by the range on either side, the frozen Kryzhana River filled the gorges formed by the sheer cliffs, carrying chunks of ice toward the Smorodina. We were too far to see what happened at their meeting.

Ta gawked at the legendary Kryzhana with an instinctive touch of her frostbitten leg. "Never mind, let's keep flying," she said. "I've had enough frozen rivers lately."

Guilt panged my chest. My poultices and channeling had ensured she'd healed well in most areas, but I'd held back to ensure I didn't run out of *žityje* mid-flight. Without my powers, my friends were vulnerable. That weighed heavily on me as I considered what Marzanna may have prepared for us.

So far, she'd managed to break my bond with Wacław when he approached her island. I no longer sensed Ara either, and I hoped Marzanna's power was the cause, not the alternative.

Her death would've struck me through my mark, I assured myself. *Marzanna won't kill her while she's useful.*

Still, their absences left a void in my soul for doubt to fill. Memories of failures recent and long past gripped me. I fought them, trying to focus on clearing the greatest heights, but they weighed me down enough to miss the sudden drop of temperature.

Spires of ice burst from the river far below, crossing the divide in a blink. Andrij cried out first as one entrapped his legs and torso, and before I could free him, spires snatched me too.

The spires retreated once they'd caught their prey. I released a Moonblast, shattering mine, but the others tore my friends toward the river in different directions. Marzanna knew I'd try to free them! I only had time for one more Moonblast, but they were too scattered.

Flames erupted around Narcyz as Andrij channeled Mother's power, the winds doing little for Narcyz and Kuba by themselves. Ta channeled her own earthen spires to tear at the ice without success. Sabina… Why couldn't she break free with my power?

Moonblast! I told her through my mark, summoning my *żbyje* as I tried to figure out who to save.

Guilt pulled me to launch my power towards Ta. Silver flashed between us, missing the other spires, but slicing through Ta's captor with ease. Ice shards scattered into the surrounding cliffs as she managed to summon an earthen barrier to catch her just above the Kryzhana's flow.

The others weren't so lucky.

Andrij had split his channeling. His flames damaged Narcyz's spire enough for him to split the last of it with a lightning bolt, allowing me to catch him with my power, but Andrij's melting spire held. He disappeared beneath the surface along with Kuba.

A tug struck my chest, then vanished. *Sabina!* I called through my mark, but she didn't reply.

My power slipped, and I dropped toward the river, my blood running cold. Eight of us had entered the Way of Souls together. Eight friends who were my responsibility. I was the goddess. I was the one who they relied upon to know what lay ahead. But I'd been wrong, and now, only three of us remained.

I caught myself mere feet above the river's ice flows. Part of me wanted to plunge into it and suffer as my friends had, but that would lead me to Marzanna's shackles. That helped none of us.

Narcyz growled nearby. His cheeks burned red as he drew Kwiecień and yelled, cutting an ice chunk clean in half.

"HE'S GONE!"

His voice echoed through the canyons. Andrij had sacrificed himself to save the man he loved, and Narcyz wouldn't forgive him for it. Wacław and I were no strangers to risking our lives for each other, but like Narcyz, I *despised* that Wacław had almost died for me. We werc supposed to be strong. Knowing our lovers suffered because of us tore us to the core.

But it was more than that for me. I'd made a choice, and it had doomed the others to Marzanna's icy grip.

Ta stared back at me with her face twisted. It asked why I'd saved her, but there were no words to describe it. I'd had only a moment to decide. Whether guilt had been the right motivator, I didn't know, but what was done was done. The three of us had to find the others.

"No!" Narcyz objected as I pulled all of us back up with my moonlight. "We can't just leave them!"

He flailed with his sword, but I raised my spear to keep him beyond his blade's reach. "They're gone, Narcyz," I insisted, biting my cheek. "I couldn't save them, okay? Marzanna caught me off guard because *you* insisted I don't listen to End's visions."

"It wasn't just me!" he roared, Kwiecień's golden point jabbed toward my chest. "End didn't save us the first time anyway. You act like you can know everything, but we're all dying!"

"They're not dead!"

He scoffed. "Right, because three of us can beat Marzanna's army in her own castle. End was right about one thing—we're doomed."

"I should've never left Sheresy," Ta said, tucking in her legs to her chest as she floated beside me. It was a silly posture, but I couldn't laugh. It took all my will just to keep us floating when all I wanted was to close my eyes and pretend this was a nightmare.

No one contested her complaint. We'd been away from Dwie Rzeki for mere days, but it was a whole realm away. This wasn't our world. The Way of Souls wasn't meant for the living, yet we'd come anyway. Wacław with his Naw soul was the only one of us whom this strange border realm recognized. The demons had come for him, though, and even his soul's home hadn't saved him.

"Let's get past these mountains before they strike again," I mumbled. My light spear was little threat with it dangling loosely from my fingers, and absentmindedness would ruin any chance of us making it across.

Five of us had fallen to Marzanna's traps, but it was up to me that the rest of us made it. So I pulled together what remained of my will and hauled us over the highest peaks. The air thinned. I didn't care. We needed as much distance between us and the Kryzhana as possible.

Except when we emerged from the other side of the range, the river split from it too, cutting through the black sand on its arc toward the Smorodina and Marzanna's castle. Dark, dead, no souls followed its icy flow. While the Smorodina forged the dead into new life, its frozen twin trapped our friends for winter's mistress.

Ice towers rose from the confluence of the two rivers. Marzanna's bulwarks shimmered on an island beyond, as if sweating against the Smorodina's heat, and beneath End's power, wisps of sky blue, white, and black shifted about the castle's peaks. A warning? A show of dominance? Or a natural eminence of the power Marzanna now wielded?

"Whoa," Ta gasped, spinning one of her glass spiral blades as she followed my gaze. "That's her castle?"

"That's it," I confirmed.

Narcyz growled and pushed forward. "Let's get them back!" He gripped Kwiecień hard enough to turn his knuckles whiter than Marzanna's snow, and it only tightened when I snatched his arm.

"No."

He tried to tear himself free, but I flared my power, taking hold of his Thread of Life. Fear burst through it. Moons before, I would've succumbed to the visions washing over me once. I chose what to see now.

I let myself endure Narcyz's emotions, his ends, both future and past. Burns struck my arms and legs where no one would see. His ironsmith father's face flashed with them with all the fury of his forge, and that fire ignited son like father. It seared all who came close, all who dared to challenge Narcyz. All until he met the one who'd been through the flames enough to feel no pain.

Andrij hadn't extinguished Narcyz's fires, but he'd calmed them, tended them. Then, he'd taken them and given back warmth.

Touches that had once meant assault by Narcyz's father were now gentle, endearing.

I released the Thread before I felt too much. Intimate moments were private for a reason, and I'd have despised anyone prying into mine with Wacław.

Narcyz staggered away sloppily on the winds, pushing away from my moonlight that had kept him aloft before. "What was that?"

"We'll get him back," I replied. "I promise you. But we paid the cost for ignoring End already. Let me refill my *žityje* from sacrifices, then conduct my ritual while you two rest. We'll figure out the best attack once I know more."

"Do it without touching me, alright?"

I huffed, but nodded.

"Otylia's plan is better than rushing in and dying quick," Ta said. "I'm kinda sick of barely surviving."

Narcyz regarded her, then lowered his blade as he met my gaze. Flames scarred his eyes a sharp red. It was a rage I knew far too well. "How long you need?" he asked.

I started toward the ground with them tailing. "Long enough for you to fall asleep, but short enough for you not to get anything out of it."

"Great…"

The black sand seemed to hiss at our arrival, but I was almost grateful to find the empty Thunderstone again. When nothing was certain, at least the ground never left. Wacław loved soaring among the clouds. I no longer served Mother, but I would always prefer the wild thickets.

There were no wilds here. Just sheer cliffs giving way to flat, unending sand. Nawia lay on the other side of the Smorodina, but what would we find if we were to continue on this way? Did Perun and Weles's desolation have an end?

Everything ends, I told myself, but doubts lingered.

Hadn't Rod remained beyond his death? He'd come to me through End's power, unless that had been another trick…

As Narcyz settled on his bedroll, I replenished my *žityje* from a summoned blood altar made of silver light. The blood was a constant reminder of the sacrifices my worshippers made to grant me my power, and I used that motivation as I grabbed my supplies and built a ritual circle to keep my thoughts at bay. One step at a time, we'd figure this out. All I could do was work to fix it. And I *would* fix it.

After a minute, I froze at the sight of a bone amulet where I hadn't placed it. Each component of the ritual followed a pattern, and this one belonged further to the side, not between herbs whose ends I burned for their purifying smoke. The light *crunch* beside me answered the question before I could ask.

"Ta, you're a szeptucha," I said. "You should know better than to interfere with a ritual."

She plopped down in one of the gaps of the pattern, her foot smudging one of my lines. "You're a goddess. It's different."

I scoffed. "So you can ruin a goddess's ritual, but not a szeptucha's?"

"Makes sense." She flicked her wrist and shifted the sand nearby with Mokosz's earth channeling, far enough not to break the circle's edge. *That* would've been dangerous. "Doubt you even need this ritual. End's your force, right? Just tell it to show you. Szeptuchy need to *ask*, but a goddess *commands*."

How could she be so rude yet make such a strong point? I crossed my arms, shifting back and forth as I examined my circle. She was right about my interactions with End. I'd acted like it was in charge, and I was its vessel. What if I told it what to do for once?

Stepping out of the circle, I closed my eyes and concentrated on the force pulsing inside me. My chest rose and fell with its call, the echo of wisps both eternal and temporal. Souls bound us to the Three Realms, and they carried all we'd experienced and what Destiny had ordained. Some ends were fixed. Others could be altered. More still were fragments, forgotten to time. All of them, though, changed our lives, and I reached out as time's pull tickled the ends of my fingers.

"Show me Marzanna's end," I demanded. "Show me mine."

18

Otylia

What is the end?

AIR FLED MY LUNGS, warmth replacing the dull chill of the Way's sands.

I floated in time's current when I opened my eyes, and wisps drifted past, each entangled with dozens of Threads I hadn't seen during the Trials of Will and Destiny. They bound each moment with vibrant colors unlike any in nature or human villages. All was a web. The Threads bound the wisps' fragile memories and futures in a desperate fight to hold to Destiny's path, spoken by her three old Sudiczki fates.

Since my Ascension, I had resisted End's call, listened to its whispers, touched its wisps and Threads, but had never delved into its depths. Here was the heart of it. Time was nothing without ends to one cycle and beginnings to others. *This* was what I'd been missing.

But time's home was darker than before. The Threads added more dynamism, but the numerous wisps no longer bumped into one another like a packed crowd. Dim, near colorless wisps hung still instead, not a bit of *žityje* humming within them. So many had fallen to Marzanna and Czarnobóg's wraths. Each death stole a living soul, a fragment of Destiny's will.

For the first time since my Ascension, my mind was clear. End guided me wordlessly, granting me sight into each connection dancing through time's flow like darting fish in a clear river. Before me was all that was, all that had been, and all that *could* come to pass.

"To seek one's own end is a dangerous feat," a woman said, every word spoken as if it were a different person.

A shiver ran down my spine as I turned to meet Will and Destiny, two forces all the same. She walked toward me upon the nothingness as if it were stone. A haggard crone one moment and a towering warrior clad in iron the next, her form shifted with every blink, and the wisps molded around her fingers. Without looking, she joined and split them into new moments and chances. New ends. New beginnings. New desires and new fates.

I crossed my arms and gave her a wary glare. "I don't ask lightly."

"The goddess of endings," she mused, stopping beside me and admiring the wisps with a sparkle in her eyes. There was no source of light here, but both we and the wisps were as clear as beneath the midday sun. "One so young, yet one burdened with the fates of each realm. It is cruel for you to be in such a position."

"Isn't that your role? You define our destinies."

She chuckled and flicked her wrist, suddenly branching the flow before us into two paths, then six, then hundreds. Wisps twirled and drifted between them. Some split early and traveled down each path, but others only traveled down a few, or only one. A tug on my heart knew they were the possible paths for each soul—many destinies, shaped by many wills.

But each path was not the same. Most dimmed far more than where we stood, few wisps marking those paths' indistinct edges. Only a dozen held many wisps, and a mere handful were as vibrant as the river I'd seen during my Trials.

"Does that appear 'defined' to you?" Destiny quipped, solidifying into the form of a tanned, wrinkled woman who leaned heavily on a wooden staff. Etchings in the old tongue crossed it and lit up at random before fading again. "As I told you before your Ascension, the wills of those both mortal and immortal shape what is to pass. The gods chose the path we now follow through their actions and inactions, but with one split comes a thousand more. Your little ritual showed you flashes of some paths. Such refusal to fully embrace into your power, however, ensures you will never truly see."

I dropped my head. "I was afraid."

"That is natural." She shuffled closer, the stamp of her cane against the unseen ground ringing through time's flow. "Yet fear answers little without admittance of *why* you fear."

"I wanted to be in control, to choose my own path," I said as I met her gaze. "End's visions showed me pain, anger, and death, so I ran from it. Even when I realized I needed it, though, I clung to my szeptuchy ways, channeling it as if it were another's force."

Destiny nodded. "The force you call End is not merely a force to be wielded. It is joined with your very soul, guiding you. That does not steal your will. Nor does it define how you wish to follow that guidance, but to not embrace it into your heart and mind is to deny who you are. Becoming a goddess is not like the job of a farmer or hunter. It is not a profession, but an Ascension into something greater."

I closed my eyes as guilt struck my heart. "What if I'm not something greater? I feel like a drowning child beneath the weight of the Three Realms."

"That is because you are a child compared to the ancient history of all that has been," she replied, laughing once again with all the joy of an elder watching a babe fall as they learned to walk. "Even Rod struggled to understand at first, and he had the greatest weight of all."

"I failed him, just like I failed my friends." I clenched my fists at my sides and fought back tears. "Those paths with more wisps show that we can succeed, right?"

The symbols on Destiny's staff flashed, igniting paths beside our own. Some held similar wisps to ours, but many were empty except for the still wisps of dead souls. "Shall I show you what was to unfold if you had failed to uphold your promise to Death?" she asked.

I stepped back. "No, I've seen enough of the consequences."

"For those you love, yes, but you fail to realize that your decision was one powerful force where Will within me defeated Destiny. Many paths called for the death of the living realm. You chose otherwise."

"Why are you telling me this?" I asked. "I told End to show me Marzanna's end and mine, not everything in the Three Realms."

Destiny smiled and waved a hand, dismissing the diverging paths of the past. "Those are one in the same. Your choices will determine which of these paths the Three Realms follow, and your end is not yet written in its fullest." She snapped her fingers, and a wisp formed between us. "If you choose to seek the parts that End may show you anyway, then so be it."

Her form shifted again as she drifted away, soon turning to a wisp herself, lost among all the others in time's flow.

Only the wisp she'd summoned remained with me. Green swirled with silver within it, and my Thread of Life drifted toward it, as if drawn to a familiar call. I raised my fingers to it before shying away.

Is this what I want? To know how it ends?

I'd changed the future before, but a lump in my stomach told me some parts of time were fixed. Gods did not come and go with the breeze. Our ends shifted everything, like a great willow's branches shading all others who dared come near. I still feared that truth.

But without fear, there wasn't bravery.

I snatched the wisp and plunged my power into it. "Show me."

Ice cracked along my skin as a swirling blizzard banished time's flow. I pulled back my hand, but the wisp was gone, and each movement fought against the ever-thickening icesheet that covered my body. The air fogged more and more with my breaths until I could see nothing beyond the tip of my nose.

A familiar force tugged on my soul. Gentle, like a warm breath upon my cheeks.

Wašek?

I poured out my *žityje*, shredding the ice before stumbling after the force. My Thread no longer split in many directions, Instead, a single strand pulled me onward, and its sparks flickered from it like a thousand fireflies piercing the mists.

The air was unusually heavy. My lungs labored for each breath, and my shoulders curled beneath a weight that sought to drag me into the snow. But I fought onward, grabbing hold of my Thread and pulling myself through the storm. Memories came with it. Familiar and not, they repeated the joys and suffering Wacław and I had endured—or would endure.

That flood would've been too much for my mind before, but End spun the images into a coherent pattern, revealing the paths that lay ahead.

All led here.

The mists scattered as the blizzard gave way to a whirlwind that threatened to tear me from my feet. All above was darkness, all below pure light that stung my eyes. Between them, Wacław channeled the whirlwind from one knee, defying a power that ripped shreds of darkness from the sky and plunged them into his core.

"Wašek!

I pushed onward with the moon protecting me, never allowing me to be swept away in the gales. Wacław's tattered cloak draped around him, but could not cover his wounds which dripped black blood upon the snow. He did not raise his head. And all that burst through our bond was determination, fury.

No matter how many times I called, the winds stole my voice as I drew closer. My own clothes shifted to radiant silver with tassels sweeping at the hems—unmarked, undamaged, untamed. Moonlight burst from me to join the ground's gold in a dance that only the soul could comprehend. It was beautiful. It was *terrifying*.

But I pushed into the eye of the storm and dropped before Wacław with my chest heaving for breath. Some distant memory told me time was of the essence. Here, though, time stood still.

Neither the winds nor the shreds of falling darkness shifted in the slightest. All was silent. Only my whimpered breaths broke the calm, and even Wacław made no noise as he raised his head.

One eye was black. A wound slashed through the other.

Slashes ripped through my vision, sending me spinning back through the nothingness until I fell into time's flow. A cold sweat stung my skin, and I shuddered at the image of Wacław's dark gaze burned into my mind. Destiny had said that not all was yet written. Was this?

"This didn't help!" I screamed.

The entire current shook from the force of my voice. No answer came, though, and I fumed at Destiny's sudden absence. She'd told me so much, just to leave when I needed her guidance most.

Something poked at my mind. Not a physical sensation, but one inside my very thoughts, interrupting each as they formed, as if trying to weasel its way into my consciousness.

"You were supposed to show me my end and Marzanna's," I snapped at End. "You were supposed to show me how to *fix* what I've broken!"

The poke turned to a shove, so I relented to the force, assuming it to be End's response.

A memory followed.

Father's wooden staff rasped the frame of my room in our Dwie Rzeki home. He never asked permission, but warned of entry so that I could ensure I was properly clothed. Once I'd scrambled to change from my shift to a bone gray szeptucha's dress, I called for him to enter.

He pushed aside the curtain separating the main room from mine, his hair still holding its old black, only streaks of gray beginning to creep in. Between the bones and twine lying on my nightstand beside Mother's black hellebore and the pulsing Bowmark on my neck, I was fourteen at least. But why was End showing me such a mundane memory?

"Clear the tears from your eyes," Father commanded. He studied me like a farmer seeking new cattle stock, then paced toward the hellebore. "It is a szeptucha's duty to *serve* their deity, not to lounge and weep in grief."

"The thaw just reminds me of her," I said, reaching for Mother's hellebore with my wild channeling. It perked up, as it always did with a boost of *žityje*. "Why don't you mourn?"

He sighed. "Grief lingers for a time, but allowing it to fester accomplishes nothing. Your mother is gone, child. Fury and brazen determination cannot mend all Jawia's ills."

"But—"

The vision snapped away before I could reply, throwing me back into time's river. End no longer prodded at my mind. When I tried to ask the force for another reply, it shied away further.

"Even when I command you, you're temperamental," I muttered, but Father's words hung with me. Could I not save my friends and right the path I'd followed? Destiny showed there were ways…

I took a long breath, refocusing on what lay ahead. Marzanna and my ends were too convoluted to help, but what if I was more specific?

"Show me the end of our journey to Marzanna's castle," I said. "Show me the end of the Way of Souls."

19

Wacław

This must be how ants feel staring up at a house.

THE WAY OF SOULS ENDED AT A BRIDGE crossing both the Smorodina and its frozen sibling. Rivers were not meant to meet like trails and split again, but these did, bubbling and boiling beneath the bridge as flames crossed frigid waters. The Smorodina passed from right to left while the frozen Kryzhana mirrored it around the other side of Marzanna's castle.

The cart ahead rumbled onto the arched wooden bridge, the supports below somehow not burning against the flames which lapped at them like eager dogs. With items overflowing the cart's low walls, a trunk slipped over the edge. It clattered against the railing, and only a quick catch by one of the upióry saved it from tumbling into the rivers.

"Don't follow the trunk," the lumbering utopiec said, jabbing me toward the rail. "The Kryzhana's ice ain't much better than the Smorodina's fires."

"Lady Marzanna will send *you* over the Kalinov Bridge's side if you lose us her prize catch," the strzyga muttered from overhead. She kept back with us, no longer leading the way.

I shrugged. "Couldn't be worse than my last adventure down the Smorodina."

The utopiec and wilkołak cackled together. "He doesn't know!" the swamp beast exclaimed. "He's got to say hi at least, don't he?"

"Vlad," the strzyga replied, "I swear to all that is holy in Lady Marzanna's name that I will feed you to Chudo-Yudo myself if you don't shut up."

I swallowed. *Do I want to know what a Chudo-Yudo is?* Andrij had mentioned a żmij, a powerful dragon, from the legends, but could one really lurk in the flames?

Vlad the utopiec definitely knew, because he quieted before shoving me after the cart. It surprised me how much these Nawie had kept of their personalities despite their demonic corruption. Was there still some part of them inside that fought back, or did they truly want this?

"Who were you before Marzanna called you, Vlad?" I asked over my shoulder. "I was a farmer, and she promised me everything. What did she promise you?"

"Stop talking," the strzyga insisted.

I glanced up at her. "What about you? What did it take for Marzanna to drag you into the cold northern wastes to guard a half-dead goddess? Did she reward you for Dziewanna's escape, or did she fall back on her promises like always?"

She dove, talons flashing as she drew blood across my cheek. Not deep enough to wound, but enough to force me to expend *żityje* to heal. "You are a fool, Wacław Lubiewicz."

"That was what my father thought, and maybe he was right." I wiped away the blood and stopped. "What are you called? And why didn't you chase us into the woods that day we escaped with the wild goddess?"

"Gag him," she instructed the wilkołak before flapping her wings sharply and taking off over the cart, which rolled ahead without hesitation.

The wilkołak ripped a shred of its shirt free, but I turned to Vlad before he could tie it over my mouth. "Remember who you were. Remember what it was like to live."

I had no time to see his reaction, as the Wilkołak tore me away and pulled the gag so tight I choked on every breath. He offered neither condemnation nor a beating, dragging me on instead with the bubbling below marking whatever this Chudo-Yudo was. These Nawie feared it. Did that give me an opportunity or yet another foe?

The winds tugged at my hair, eager to be called. With the strzyga ahead with the upióry and the cart, Vlad and the wilkołak were the only ones close enough to stop me before I could flee. Healing from the Smorodina had taken nearly all my *żityje*, though. I wouldn't be able to fly.

Maybe I didn't have to…

I punched the wilkołak's hamstring with the winds' backing. His grip loosened, allowing me to spin away and charge back over the bridge. My knuckles throbbed from the blow as I ripped off the gag, but the punch had given me a head start.

Vlad noticed. Demonic utopiecs were nothing but lumbering swamp beasts, so I leaped over the railing to dodge him, clinging to the side and running with one more burst of wind. *Żityje* slipped away and forced me back after a few strides. I'd cleared him, though, and nothing lay between me and the sea of black sand. I ran toward it with my heart beating out my throat.

The bridge softened like mud in a storm. It caught my foot, sending me tumbling as Vlad closed in. Pity filled his eyes.

A Nawie utopiec can channel?

The fall skinned my palms and forearms, but that was the least of my worries. The strzyga had taken Grudzień and my Thunderstone dagger, leaving me unarmed and near *żityje*-less as the wilkołak charged. Moons before, I'd barely defeated Bidaês with both Moonblade and lightning. Now, I had neither.

Throwing up my arms, I scooted away on my back as the wilkołak's teeth flashed. "I surrender!" I stammered. He needed to believe my fear, and it wasn't difficult to show. A Nawie wilkołak's fury was enough to endure once in my life.

His claws slashed across my arms. I cried out and curled upon myself, holding back the last of my *żityje* to mend only the most severe wounds. Blood already stained my clothes, but black now poured over the bridge, trickling over its edge and into the joined rivers below. The wilkołak lapped it up like a dog before grabbing me by the neck.

"You are nothing!" he roared. "If Lady Marzanna did not demand otherwise, I would tear you limb from limb and leave what's left of you to boil in the Smorodina."

I spat in his face. "Am I nothing? I am a king. I make my own decisions, but you cower beneath Marzanna's power. *You* are nothing but a spear for her to point at her enemies. We were meant for more!"

"Your blood tastes bland, płanetnik." He cackled, tightening his grip until his claws dug into my neck. "Better hope the ice queen gives you *żityje* soon, or none of us will have the chance to kill you ourselves."

I fell limp as he dragged me on. Within me, the demon demanded I resist, but what fight I had left was gone, burned away by the river and the draining Thunderstone sand. This place was supposed to be the home of Nawie. We were its protectors, those bound to ensure the dead souls reached Nawia's paradise. But all the Way of Souls held was torment.

Whatever pain I'd endured was far from over. Beyond the castle's walls of crystalline ice lay the goddess of winter and death herself. A goddess I'd betrayed, whose servants I'd slaughtered by the thousands.

I doubted she'd be happy to see me.

My head grew light from blood loss by the time we passed the ramparts. There was no gate, just a shimmering field of some type of magic that chilled me the moment we entered the castle grounds. After all I'd seen of the Way, I expected emptiness, but a city greeted me instead.

Nawie, demons, nymphs, and souls with half-formed bodies gathered between various buildings, the smallest of which could hold four Dwie Rzeki houses. Skeletal horses' hooves clacked against the icy ground, but did not slip as they carried women clothed in pure white robes. Light shone from strange stones hung above each doorway. It reflected off the ice to grant the grounds a glow like that of the height of summer. People eyed me as we passed, but none snarled or hissed like untamed beasts.

In fact, some seemed almost happy…

The wilkołak dragged me straight through the crowds without regard for who stood in the way. Elbows and knees struck me when people—especially the misshapen souls—couldn't move quickly enough. My vision blurred further, and I comprehended little else until we reached the towering stone doors to the keep.

Marzanna's Frostmark burned hot white across each, searing phantom pain across my once-marked palm. Every muscle in my body writhed against the thought of entering her stronghold. There was little else I could do, though. Torn from my bond to Otylia and without *żityje* or weapons, fighting further would only make things worse for me. Not that my situation was looking all that bright.

Two cloud nymphs flew above the doors, giggling, but their expressions soured at the sight of us. "Who comes to the Lady Marzanna's keep?" one called down.

"Iwo," the wilkołak replied, holding me up by the throat. The skin around his claws had turned raw, and breathing burned. "I've got the płanetnik. Elze should've said we were coming." Heavy, sloppy footfalls approached from behind. "Oh, and Vlad is here too."

"So the Nawie finally did it?" The nymphs giggled together again, their wings fluttering so fast in my distorted vision that a headache added to my pains. "Glad you're of use for once."

They waved their hands, and a dusting of snow fell over us. It crept down my shirt and sent my spine tingling, but I focused only on the doors creeping open before me.

Blue-eyed wolves waited beneath black and white-streaked chandeliers. Creatures of pure ice lurked along the walls of the wide foyer, each a different fragmented shape. Iwo dragged me between them, my blood dripping onto a winter-blue runner which crossed from the doors toward a massive staircase. Flanked by marble columns, it exclaimed glory, beauty, and brilliance—words I'd never have used to describe the goddess who'd met me on that riverbank moons before.

Those steps thumped my dangling legs over and over until we reached their peak. So humiliating. I'd fought gods, defeated armies, and crowned myself king of the lands my father claimed I would never inherit. After moons of striving for this final confrontation with Marzanna, I did so like a sack of wheat.

No, that was unfair to the wheat. I was a bloodied carcass, ready to be carved by my captors.

We continued through another hall with windows high above allowing both the light and stench of the Smorodina to creep through. Smoke curled among the chandeliers, reaching out at all it could stain, but the castle's ice remained pure. What magic had it taken to build such a place? And what fragment of Marzanna's *žityje* was devoted to keeping it?

The strzyga, who Iwo had called Elze, swooped down from one of the chandeliers near the end of the hall. An arching, black sheet of ice seemed like a passageway behind her, but there seemed no way through. After all I'd seen, I had no doubt its cause.

"What took you so long, and why is the prisoner so bloodied?" Elze's words cut the cold like a knife. "Lady Marzanna is waiting!"

Vlad hung his head. "He punched Iwo and ran away. I caught him, but Iwo kept attacking."

"Imbecile!"

Elze swung Grudzień, slicing Iwo's throat before he could reply. I dropped from his grasp with a *thud.* Iwo's blood flowed black like mine, and he could only gargle a wolf's cry before collapsing. A Naw would've healed from a normal blade, but the Moonstone absorbed his *žityje* to be used during its bonded moon.

But why?

Elze glared down at her former ally's corpse, then grinned as she raised Grudzień. "I see why the Betrayer was so fond of his Moonblades, even if this was not his."

"I don't understand," I mumbled, staggering to my knees. "Why kill him? He's one of us! A Naw is a powerful friend."

She huffed. "Oh, you aren't familiar with Lady Marzanna's *gifts*? That'll make this so much more fun." She waved a hand toward Vlad. "Bring Iwo in. He'll make quite the addition to the Lady Marzanna's demonstration."

Demonstration?

"Come, płanetnik," Elze demanded, turning away as a dozen of the ice creatures formed from the very walls around us. "I assume you're not foolish enough to fight your way out of this castle, so make it easy for both of us. Listen to what I tell you."

Curiosity drove me to my feet. I hadn't come this far to be struck down in the hall outside Marzanna's throne room, and if Marzanna had Ara like Otylia claimed, then she needed my help.

I shook my head at myself as I stumbled onward. Pain answered each movement, and my neck ached even craning it to see the black ice beginning to melt away. What help would I be to Ara when I couldn't even free myself? If anything, I was a burden, forcing Otylia to save both of us instead of just one.

Walking shouldn't have been worse than being dragged by my throat, but it was an admittance of my weakness. Iwo had forced me here. Elze exposed me instead, giving me all the freedom to escape while knowing I could not. And from her grin, she enjoyed every moment of it.

"You never told me why you let us go," I said, stopping beside her as we waited for the thaw to finish. "Sure, the wilds were Dziewanna's, but you had an army of strzygi to chase us through that forest."

"Not all the Three Realms are as you see them, Wacław," she replied, blade held before her and her posture stiff. "The Way of Souls stands between the realms of the living and the dead. The two of us never truly joined either, but that's what it is to be a Naw—in-between. Just because I bear a Frostmark doesn't mean I can't think for myself."

"What do—"

Elze flapped her owl-like wings and leaped over the remaining fragments of the black ice. I waited, glancing back at Vlad hauling Iwo over his shoulder. An odd sight. Within it, though, I saw the tense divide among the Nawie—and the one between them and Marzanna. Something else was at play here.

Once the ice had melted enough, I stepped over the remaining fragments. Cracking them underfoot gave me a slice of pleasure that soon faded as I entered the queen's hall.

Sharp, angular beams and columns framed the chamber. They were unlike the stone ones before, a variety of shapes filling them, and when I drew close to the first, my chest tightened. Skulls and bones. Packed so tightly that they resembled an inconstant granite, the remains seeped dark vapors which curled over us. More icy creatures lurked in the shadows along with Nawie in demonic and human forms.

None of Marzanna's servants regarded me. All faced the queen of winter and death herself, seated on a throne of ice with skulls rimming its curved back.

She looked as dead as her decorations.

20

Otylia

Where are you, Yuliya?

THE SKIES SWIRLED BLACK OVER MARZANNA'S DISTANT CASTLE as I let Narcyz and Ta rest, scanning the horizon for threats. End's last vision hung over me.

My power's focus on finality had made me miss the obstacles we'd faced in the middle of our journeys. Whether I'd consulted End or not, my force had guided my choices, but Marzanna had been ready every time. Yuliya had ambushed us at the Moonstone. She'd likely influenced the strike in the mountains too, and as I surveyed the landscape, I swore I saw a shadowed rusałka through the icy Kryzhana River.

She shouldn't have been my focus, but whenever I closed my eyes, listening the End's pulse, my thoughts were drawn to her. Devastation awaited us at Marzanna's palace. Only Yuliya could change that.

More and more glimpses of the supposed shadow greeted me the longer I watched. It drew closer, alone from the look of it, and when it reached the nearest section of the river, it stepped free.

Water dripped from Yuliya's tangled blonde locks before freezing into fractals filled with twists of black vapor. Her eyes pulsed through the dim light, the Frostmark on her neck flaring as the ground froze beneath her bare feet. She was a demon, a beast. But beneath, I sensed her *žityje* flaring.

"Come any closer," I shouted, silver spear in hand, "and I'll sever your soul from your body."

My voice had the desired effect, stirring the others as Yuliya stopped a stone's throw away. "You risk all their lives by coming here," she said.

"Don't pretend you care." I stomped the butt of my spear. "Why are you here?"

She sneered. "I don't care, but the Lady Marzanna does. You all have uses for her, and it is better you come bound rather than slain."

I shot a warning moonblast, forcing her to dodge. "Don't threaten me, demon. I hold Listopad, so nothing's stopping us from channeling now."

"And if I said I had no desire to fight you?"

"I wouldn't believe you."

Bursting forward, I leaped with the moon. Yuliya's Thread was decayed, frail, but fragments of bright yellow pulsed on segments that stretched back toward Jawia. I snatched one.

Yuliya's jaw dropped, and she stammered, arms extended. "Wait!"

"I'm done playing Marzanna's games!" I snapped. "Tell me her plan, or I'll make sure she never brings you back."

She fell to her knees. "There is none. Lady Marzanna is dying."

Her Thread slipped from my fingers as a chill tickled the back of my neck. I had no reason to believe her, but my gut told me she was telling the truth. Destiny had instructed me to trust myself and my force, so I surrendered to the feeling.

"How?" I asked.

The question came out as little more than a gasp. Marzanna was the goddess of death. How could she succumb to Death himself?

"Not all is as it seems," Yuliya said. "Lady Marzanna does not rule the lands of the dead."

Narcyz growled from nearby. "Then who took Andrij?"

"That, she did, but there was a purpose. The dark żmij…" Yuliya coughed, then clutched her side. Black blood coated her fingers. "Lady Marzanna believed she had freed Czarnobóg from Oblivion to be under her command, but he resisted. Influence shifted in his favor when he returned from Prawia with Weles. He'd demanded things of her before. Now…" She shuddered. "Czarnobóg drained Weles's very essence and claimed Nawia as his. When Lady Marzanna protested, he did the same to her, but we managed to drive him away before he stole her power completely."

I glanced toward Marzanna's castle and Nawia beyond. "That doesn't explain why she took our friends or why you're here."

"Lady Marzanna was left with a single Moonstone after Czarnobóg's betrayal—the one she used to take your power. She needed to lure you in to gain others… and to convince you to help her kill Czarnobóg."

"Help Marzanna?" I exclaimed. "Never."

Her expression sharpened. "Then your friends will join the dead and rise as Lady Marzanna's pets."

Narcyz shouted and charged the rusałka, but she dodged, circling behind him.

"My lady awaits my return," she hissed. "Should I not do so, your friends suffer."

Narcyz gave me a pleading look, but I signaled for him to stand down. "Think about Andrij," I said.

"You don't *think* when your lover is taken!" he raged. "You *get them back.*"

Then he backhanded his blade and rammed it through Yuliya's stomach.

21

Wacław

How do you kill the goddess who controls death?

"BRING THE PRISONER FORTH!" A WOMAN DECLARED from beside Marzanna's throne. Robed in white with a glittering veil covering her face down to the lips, the *žityje* of a powerful szeptucha pulsed in her soul. A living one.

Elze tucked in her strzyga wings and bowed, then sharply waved for me to follow, but my attention was fixed on Marzanna herself.

Dark, corrupted veins arced down the winter goddess's temples and neck. Her eyes were droplets in a fountain of black, and her skin stretched so tightly that every bone resembled a prisoner reaching for freedom. Where her funeral gown of a dress met her collar, black blood oozed from a festering wound. She'd once displayed herself with menacing confidence. Now, her back curled like a weary elder's, and her hand trembled violently as she brushed aside her tangled mess of black hair and raised her gaze to me.

"Come, Wacław."

Decrepit or not, her words held power, but they carried neither deceitful charm nor hissed spite. They were melancholic, slow. What had happened here?

I advanced out of curiosity alone. Defiance meant little. This was not the goddess who'd offered me the world in return for my service. No, this was a shadow of a lingering force, gasping for life.

"The Three Realms have not been kind to you," I said, stopping beside Elze. She knelt and gestured for me to do the same, but I refused. "And I won't be either if you don't tell me what you've done to my friends."

A wry smile crept across Marzanna's torn and discolored lips. What teeth she revealed were cracked and bloodied, and her tongue slithered across them. "This is not how I had imagined our reunion, dear płanetnik. These moons have changed much between us, the twisting of fate severing what bond we once held, but fresh betrayals sting more than old scars."

"Why do you gods all insist on dancing around the fire?" I asked. "Let us leap it so that we can end this."

She spun one clawed finger through the air. "Time means little to my ilk. For immortals, we must merely wait for inconveniences to pass and our plans to unfold, but there come times were *pests* like you bite and bite like maggots… Maggots so easily crushed."

"Then crush me," I dared her, arms held out at my sides. "I lack the *żityje* to fight back, and Elze has my Moonblade. After all I have done, I imagine you want nothing more than to kill me."

"Even maggots have their uses."

I spat at the ground between us and locked eyes with her. "I'm done being used by you!"

The Nawie and ice creatures tensed, *żityje* snapping around me as they prepared to channel. Elze had Grudzień at my throat a single breath later, but she had to grip it with both hands to hold aloft the heavy sword.

If they are so quick to protect her, then she is as weak as she looks.

"Do you intend to kill me?" I asked, ignoring Elze and staring down her goddess. "If not, bring out my friends. I'll talk once I know they're safe."

Marzanna curled her lip, but waved down Elze before nodding toward a group of upióry, who ran back into the hall. "You are right to believe that I wish you dead. Unfortunately, matters require cordiality, as we now share a common enemy."

"We've already dealt with Jaryło as best we could," I replied.

"I do not mean the Betrayer."

Footsteps approached from behind, interrupting me before I could reply. The upióry dragged Kuba, Ara, Sabina, and Andrij into the room and threw them each to the ground beside me. Their expressions were grim. Beyond a few visible bruises, though, none seemed badly wounded.

I embraced Kuba and examined him closer for any signs of torture. "Are you all right?"

"I'm good, yeah," he mumbled, his eyes distant. "But they stabbed me with something. I've been dizzy ever since."

"That isn't *good*." I shook my head, then glared at Marzanna. "What did you do to them?"

She leaned forward and plucked a skull from the base of her throne. Black smoke drifted from its eye holes as she threw it at me. I caught it, but held it away to avoid the smoke from pouring over me. It wreaked of rot.

"Are you prepared to listen now?" she asked. "Otherwise, we could wait for your friends to succumb to their ailments, then speak again."

Andrij shot to his feet, grabbing my free arm before the upióry could stop him. "Don't worry about us. We knew the risks when we came to the Way of Souls."

Kuba coughed. "Maybe worry a little, okay?"

I nodded in recognition of their statements before turning back to Marzana. "You've infected them with your death magic, haven't you?" Glancing at the skull, I sighed, then lobbed it toward the wall, as far away from us as possible. An ice creature withered at the smoke's touch, and my hand ached as I continued, "You have my attention, then. What do you want from me that you can't do yourself? You're a goddess and have Nawie aplenty."

"A moon ago," Marzanna replied, sitting back once again, "I possessed an army capable of destroying entire kingdoms in Jawia, thousands of demons, dozens of Nawie, and a beast so fearsome that Prawia shuddered at his very name. Koschei's defeat stole much of that power, leaving me with the Way of Souls and a control of Nawia through Weles… until Czarnobóg broke free of my control." She twitched. "That bastard of a żmij was not content with sharing the realms. He turned against me, stealing much of my power until my servants could intervene and stop his treachery."

I rocked back on my heels. Part of me wished to laugh, but dread overcame it. "Where is he now? After the display I saw in Prawia, I doubt your Nawie were enough to defeat him."

"Czarnobóg is little better than Jaryło," Marzanna said. "All he has, he stole, including my Moonstones. He has taken them and Weles to the shifting depths of Nawia, where darkness embraces all. From there, he seeks to expand his domain into the other realms once he is fully healed from his battles."

She stood with every bone creaking and cracking. It looked as if her entire body restructured itself just to support her weight, and she snarled before continuing, "I cannot face Czarnobóg in this state. It pains me to admit such frailty, but he is a greater threat than any force I have ever experienced in the realms."

"A force that you unleashed!" Ara snapped. Marzanna glared at her, but she held her ground. "I have a heart for mistakes, but how can you appeal to us now when you created this problem?"

"I do not require your forgiveness, or even your acceptance." Marzanna extended her hand to me. "All I require is for you to spare the dying and help me defeat the scourge that plagues us all."

Dying?

I studied her, peering into her godly soul and the *żityje* beneath. Gods usually burst with endless power, but her flame flickered. "Are you actually dying, then? What did Czarnobóg do to you?"

"He is a dragon that feasts on the forces of gods and mortals alike. You have seen what Dziewanna endured after he drained her power for us to share, and I suffered the same process, if not to its completion." She closed her extended hand into a fist. "Death is never permanent for we immortals, as our forces and worshippers renew us in time, but Czarnobóg's severing of that connection… complicates matters. To answer your question, I am fading. If I cannot recover for many moons, I will be all but dead in the eyes of mortals until I have recovered my strength."

"Then what?" I asked. "You'll lash out again, threatening to end the world in your bitterness?"

She sneered, summoning the thrown skull back to her grasp before sitting once again. "I may suffer, but I am still a goddess. Dziewanna and your little mortal friends will succumb if you do not cease with these ridiculous challenges. These mortals have proven their strengths, however, and I will ensure they serve me in their undeath as a reminder that I am not to be trifled with. You wish for the thaw? For the natural cycle to return and for my sister to be free? Then do as I say."

The skull poured black smoke as she pointed it toward Vlad and the dead wilkołak, Iwo, at his feet beside us. Vlad scrambled back at Iwo's writhing amid the smoke. His already twisted half-wolf, half-man form shifted further, his fangs growing, the humanity leaving his eyes as he rose with a vicious look. He focused only on Marzanna, but I sensed his demonic hunger eating away at him.

"Let this be an example of what I may do with the dead," Marzanna continued, "and what will become of your friends if you do not heed my call."

I hesitated at that threat. My pride willed me to resist, but even in her weakened state, Marzanna was a formidable force. If she truly wanted Czarnobóg dead, it would be far easier to have her on our side than against us. Doubts lingered, though, and as long as Otylia remained free, there was hope we didn't need the winter witch's deal.

"What about the Moonstones?" I asked. "You say Czarnobóg stole yours, and then you stole the ones we held. If we help you, we must hold all of them in order to fix the veil that you tore between Oblivion and the Three Realms. Otherwise, Czarnobóg will return again."

She smirked. "It is impressive how much godly knowledge you have discovered so quickly. Of course, the veil cannot be mended without Alatyr's Moonstones falling into alignment. They did so when Jaryło agreed to help me release Czarnobóg, and they will do so again when both you and I hold six shards."

"You used those stones to smother entire cities and nearly conquer Jawia," I replied. "I can't let you hold them, let alone gain more than the five you had before."

"It is fair!" she snarled. "Jaryło left me with less than his seven, but I rule half the year. Let Dziewanna or your precious Otylia hold the other six for all I care, but I *will* retain my domain."

I shrugged. "Then we don't have a deal. Do with us what you will, but know Otylia isn't far, and she'll punish you tenfold whatever you do to us."

"You will regret this."

Pulling all the lessons I'd learned from watching Otylia, I faked a grin. Of course, I held no evidence that she could free us, but I needed none. There was little that could stand in Otylia's way when she was angry, and gods knew Marzanna kidnapping Ara, Sabina, and me would have her *furious*.

"There are many things I regret, Marzanna," I said. "Defying you is not one of them."

22

Otylia

No option now.

I RUBBED MY TEMPLES as the sand consumed Yuliya's corpse, black blood staining her stomach where Kwiecień's gold had plunged through moments before. The rusałka had come offering a deal.

But Narcyz's blade ended that.

"Destiny showed me many paths," I told him with my fingernails dug into my palms. "You better hope that you didn't just sever the good ones."

He shook his head and stomped toward the castle in the distance. "C'mon. We've got a goddess to kill."

Ta just shrugged and followed alongside me. She wore the violet Wrzesień Moonblade sheathed at her hip, and with her short stature, its tip nearly dragged through the sand if she didn't hold it tilted. That snagged her cloak, but she didn't seem to mind as she grinned at me.

"You would've done the same thing back in Vastroth," she said. "Since when are you so cautious?"

I hung my head and remembered the dark timelines ahead. "Only a couple of Destiny's paths showed me futures where many people still live. There was a time I wouldn't have cared about all those strangers, but Ascending has showed me how many people rely on me. They aren't strangers anymore."

"What are they, then? They can't *all* be your friends."

"No, they're each a Thread in the fabric of time, creating a future, an ending that all of us must endure. I'm one of the few who can see those Threads and weave them into that end." I took a long breath and opened my eyes to the Threads, but besides ours and Narcyz's, there were only distant strands loosely binding the dead souls to Jawia and Nawia. "I can't know each of them, but in the same way, with a single touch, I can experience their pasts, presents, and futures more than even their closest loved ones. That gives me responsibility."

"Oh, wow…" She rubbed the back of her neck. "That's a lot to deal with."

"It is, but I'm glad I'm not alone. Wacław and I both bear each other's burdens, and we need friends like you to remind us this is all worth it."

"Don't get all soppy on me."

I jabbed her in the arm. "I wouldn't dare. We'll need to be as tough as a rock of Mokosz to defeat Marzanna."

She jabbed me back, but I dodged, circling her as she tried again and again. When I settled beside her again, she flicked my neck—where my Bowmark had once been. "You ever wish you were a szeptucha again? There's a lot to do, but it's a lot less than what you deal with now."

"I do," I confessed, rubbing where she'd flicked as phantom pain from the old mark rose. "I probably look back too fondly on my time as a szeptucha. I was bitter, unhappy. This power is a burden, but it's also a chance to make things better."

"What'll you make better when we kick in Marzanna and Czarnobóg's skulls—all four of 'em?"

I shook my head. "I haven't thought much about what the world will look like once we're finished. Wacław is king. He can rule for all I care. I just want to stop this corruption from rising ever again."

After a while, Narcyz stopped with his hands on his sides. "I'm sick of trudging through this mire. Can we fly instead?"

Marzanna's castle loomed ahead now, shrouded in smoke from the Smorodina's flames and glinting like a melting icicle. Flying would get us there quicker, but Marzanna would expect it.

"It's a risk," I said. "But I'll admit, I'm sick of this too. The others are waiting for us, and even without Czarnobóg, Marzanna could be doing gods know what to them."

A shadow crept over his face. "Do you really think she'll turn them into demons?"

Ta drew her sword. "Let's not find out."

"We chose to fight, so let's fight," I said with a nod.

I called my silver spear with Listopad, the Moonstone Marzanna had used to dull our powers, as its sharp tip. Sierpień formed a crescent blade on the opposing end to offer another option in battle. I'd yet to figure out how Marzanna could wield fragments of a Moonstone's power outside its moon, so for now, using them as weapons would have to do.

Narcyz burst into the air on the winds, but I caught up quickly, lifting Ta with my moonlight. Each grasp of my power made me wonder of its consequences now. Had we shifted toward the path of endured life, or would the Three Realms fall silent because of my failures?

Focus, I told myself. *Wašek needs you. Ara needs you.*

All of Jawia needed me, but focusing on saving my lover and closest friend was an easier task than figuring out how to mend the veil between Oblivion and the Three Realms. We would fix what Marzanna had broken. One step at a time.

The legendary Kalinov Bridge crossed the confluence of the two rivers, its arching wooden frame forming a barrier between the towering Smorodina flames and the bubbling steam of superheated ice. Wisps of countless souls—dead, undead, and alive—swirled over the castle beyond it. Just a single wisp remained here. Slow, it meandered through the steam among the bridge's supports, but I saw no owner.

"Keep an eye out," I told the others. "Legends say a great żmij named Chudo-Yudo guards Nawia, and if any part of that is true, he may be here."

Narcyz held out his sword. "Good. I'm in the mood to cut a beast."

"Chudo-Whato definitely will cut you first," Ta quipped. "Vastroth didn't have a name for him, but the Daughters of the Earth used to say he'd burn cities where they didn't respect the dead."

"Then I'll cut him *respectfully*."

I rolled my eyes. "Mother help us…"

I guided us toward the Kryzhana River. Frozen, flying over it should be safer than the Smorodina, and I held a foolish hope that it would allow us to bypass the bridge entirely. We'd faced enough dragons in recent moons. All of them had been trouble, and despite a rush of new *żityje* from my worshippers in Jawia, I was hardly in the mood to deal with another of Marzanna's pets.

The Kryzhana had other plans.

The moment we neared the bank, black spires shot from the river to form an impenetrable web of ice. Narcyz and Ta hacked at it with their Moonblades as I blasted it with all my power, but not a shard split away. What was this that could deflect a god's blade?

"Let's just fly higher," Narcyz insisted, shooting upward. But the spires followed far faster than he could fly, and soon, the web was dense enough that there wasn't even the tiniest of holes to see the other side.

Ta spun one of her round throwing blades and stared up at the web. "Well, the ice brains know we're here now, but at least we decorated for them. Was awful bland around here before."

"That's one way to look at it," I replied.

We turned back toward the Kalinov Bridge. A group of dark forms patrolled the far bank now, and a strzyga swept overhead, gripping Grudzień's distinctive jagged blade streaked with colors through its black. My blood boiled. They held Wacław somewhere within the castle's walls, and I would free him.

I nodded to Narcyz, readying my spear. "Let's cut some beasts, then."

The cool air couldn't temper my fury as we dove toward the bridge. Marzanna had stolen my mother, my childhood, and my heart.

So I'd kill her dragon.

A raven burst from the Smorodina's flames and circled before us, its *caw* echoing through the entire Way of Souls. Smoke billowed behind it. Covering the bridge and the air above, it forced us to stop out of fear of choking. Even Narcyz's winds couldn't disperse the haze, and the raven's call mocked our failure.

Twelve red eyes pierced the smoke. They darted about the bridge, but did not rise above it as six voices boomed together, "Dare you to challenge the path of the dead? Come one, come many, but none whose heart tremors shall pass."

"Is he calling me a coward?" Narcyz muttered.

"Marzanna is the one who challenged the dead," I called down to the żmij. "We freed them to continue on their natural path to Nawia, and we will end her and Czarnobóg's corruption of the underworld."

Chudo-Yudo huffed, his flames curling through the smoke, but it remained too thick to see him. "All who the queen of death chooses are lifeless in my eyes. I care not for what happens to such souls, only that those who do not belong shall join the dead before they step foot in its realm."

Narcyz pushed away the smoke with the winds to reveal a beast with six dragon heads and the body of a man with green scales instead of skin. Riding atop a massive steed, he wore a heavy iron breastplate with pauldrons as large as a Krowikie shield, and the sharp tip of his slithering tail glinted in the firelight. Each of his eyes were fixed on me.

"Face me, daughter of the wildfire," he demanded. "Leave the mortals ashore. Should you fail, I will allow them the mercy of fleeing once Lady Marzanna's forces pluck those Moonblades from their soft fingers."

"What about Marzanna's servants?" I asked. "It's not a duel if they join the fight."

He reeled back, laughing. "Lady Marzanna's cowards would not dare step foot on this bridge as long as I stand. They fear me more than their goddess herself."

Good.

"C'mon," I told my friends. "They might be afraid to face a żmij, but I know you aren't."

We dove together, weapons flashing and *żityje* zipping about like a swarm of hornets. Narcyz's lightning struck one of Chudo-Yudo's necks as Ta leaped between her summoned boulders. She threw spinning blades, drawing blood, but the dragon didn't flinch. His flames rushed toward me as I landed and slammed my spear into the bridge.

A shield of light burst before me to deflect the flames. Such channeling had nearly drained me against Czarnobóg in the Trial of Life and Death, but I batted away fire with ease now. It created a channel for me to burst through, spear flashing straight through his center neck.

His claws followed. Flames rippled behind them like a firebird's talons as they slashed across my shoulder. One of the claws seared red-hot, and it cauterized its wound. That should've been good, but the remaining scar festered, burning as if the fire had entered my very veins.

I screamed through the pain and countered at his necks. They bled profusely from each of our blows, some falling still in mere seconds.

But Chudo-Yudo just laughed. He pushed his horse onward with his flaming claw stabbing at anyone who drew near, and smoke billowed with his every breath, stinging my lungs.

I threw myself against the railing just to avoid being trampled by the charger. Narcyz had described well his experience of being struck by a horse during one of Koschei's raids, and despite being a goddess, I had no desire to endure such a blow. Every fragment of *żityje* I lost healing was power I couldn't face Marzanna with. I let even my wounded shoulder bleed for now, anticipating a greater strike from our immediate foe.

A series of Ta's thrown blades cut straight through another of Chudo-Yudo's necks, leaving only the furthest right one standing. Narcyz sparred with it before being driven into the air by the rearing horse.

"That thing's got a kick!" he exclaimed. He swiped Kwiecień at Chudo-Yudo's shoulder in another pass, but the dragon dodged the body blow with surprising quickness.

Why does he not care for his heads?

There was no time to ponder, as Chudo-Yudo snapped his tail around Ta. She yelped and swiped with Wrzesień, violet blade sawing through bright green scales with ease, but that only prompted him to release his flames toward her. I blocked them with a moon shield, then charged.

"You're not taking another of my friends!"

He scoffed and batted aside my spear. "I offered you the chance to fight with honor."

Honor was useless against such corruption, though, so I pulled a dirty trick. Spinning around my spear, I swung with Sierpień's curved blade at the other end. He'd not watched the back of the weapon, and his remaining eyes widened as it struck.

The crescent snapped through scale, muscle, and bone with ease. Chudo-Yudo's final head dropped over the bridge's edge, charring as it tumbled into the Smorodina.

Narcyz rested Kwiecień on his shoulder. "That's it?" He turned his gaze to the strzyga who wielded Grudzień above. "You next?"

His surprise reflected mine, and I let myself smile. *This* had been the legendary protector of the Kalinov Bridge? I healed my shoulder, preparing for the battle against the Nawie on the opposing shore. It seemed even they would be a greater challenge than their żmij.

"Uh… Otylia?"

Ta tugged at my sleeve, pointing at the steaming remnants of Chudo-Yudo atop his horse. The creature remained still despite its master's death, but the dragon's sliced necks spasmed. Scales split. Wounds closed.

"Stab him in the chest!" I exclaimed.

But it was too late. By the time we rushed to try and pierce his armor, twice as many heads had sprouted from the remnants of the previous six. They snapped at each of us, and we retreated out of fear of both teeth and flames.

Narcyz groaned as he deflected the tail and took flight again. "Twelve bloody heads! And I thought Czarnobóg's three were too many."

"Don't cut them off," I warned. "The last thing we need is more of them."

It felt like Chudo-Yudo had grown a thousand from the swarm of skulls before me. Fire leaped from one head as three more tried to block my escape. They forced me to moonblast my way through just to avoid severe burns, and that removed another head, badly damaging another.

This is what he wants…

We'd fallen right into Chudo-Yudo's trap, and he laughed from ever-more maws by the second. I ducked and dodged my way toward his chest. Every time I got close, though, I had to devote my attention to defending myself or my friends. I could handle healing from the flames. Ta's curled hair was already singed, and Narcyz bled from scrapes across one of his legs. Too much of that, and I'd be the only one left.

I needed to take a risk. All this time, End's visions had frightened me into the wrong decisions, but my gut screamed to throw up a shield and charge his heart. I trusted that feeling as my force's guidance.

Right or wrong, I followed that call. My shield burst forth with blinding silver light that scattered Chudo-Yudo's heads. His tail and claws both tried to pierce it, but could do nothing as I charged behind, spear ready. The tunnel to the dragon's heart closed by the second. It suffocated me, and I held my breath as I rammed Listopad's deep brown spearhead through Chudo-Yudo's armor.

No triumph followed, as the countless heads unleashed flame and fury over me in their master's final breath. My hair burned. My clothes seared to my skin. And smoke stole my breath.

"Otylia!" Ta called out as Chudo-Yudo fell.

He toppled over me, the weight of twenty-something dragon necks and a horse crushing my already battered body. Sweat and gore stung my nose. No one ever mentioned the noxious gasses of a żmij's belly when it fell, and I swore it doubled my pain. *Žiłyje* worked quickly, but wings beat overhead.

"Come out, daughter of Dziewanna," a voice taunted as swords clashed. "Your lover's blade calls for your blood."

I gritted my teeth and moonblasted through the pain, throwing Chudo-Yudo off me to reveal the strzyga hovering above. Grudzień flashed in her grasp, but I didn't wait for her to strike.

The black blade's teeth struck the bridge a finger length from my face as I rolled to my feet. Narcyz and Ta held back a group of upióry who advanced with an utopiec at their rear. These were no mere demons, and they rose to twice my height with Nawie power pouring from their souls.

"I let you escape once," the strzyga snapped, Grudzień sparking against my silver spear as we sparred through the air. "I will not do so again."

I swept around to strike with Sierpień's crescent, but she anticipated the move. Neither of us managed a significant blow, and when Moonstone nicked our skin, *żiłyje* healed us immediately. She was no goddess. Her command of her blade, though, was far superior to my ability with a spear, so I turned to channeling.

Moonlight deflected her blade mid-slash as I shot overhead. I'd used far more of my strength in these fights than I'd wished to, but my friends couldn't hold out forever. They fell back out of the corner of my eye, so I delivered what I hoped to be the lethal strike.

Ice latched onto my spear and froze it just before it struck the strzyga's back. We tumbled, each of us trying to break free until we struck the bridge among the scrum of upióry. Fangs and claws were everywhere I looked as I retreated to Ta and Narcyz, crimson and black blood pooling underfoot.

The strzyga raised her blade. "Leave the goddess to me," she commanded her Nawie allies. "Take the mortals for Lady Marzanna."

Their charging steps shook the bridge, but a looming figure outpaced them from behind. The towering utopiec had kept back most of the battle. Now, he grabbed hold of the last upiór, swamp water dripping from his body and the stench of rotten eggs emanating around him. The strzyga protested, but the utopiec only raised the upiór by his neck before launching him into the bridge's railing.

The strzyga whirled about with her jaw gaping. "Vlad, what in Oblivion are you doing?"

"I've had enough!" the utopiec roared. "Lady Marzanna knew we'd die out here, but she don't care a bit. Why should I care what she says?"

"She will save us!"

Vlad gripped the dark Naw's forearm. "She won't, Elze," he appealed to her. "You saw what happened to Iwo! We'll just die like the others and get turned into some worse monster."

I stepped toward them and dismissed my spear. The pain in their eyes was obvious—the same pain I'd watched Wacław endure for moons. "You don't need saving. Nawie were born with a second soul to protect the Way of Souls for the natural dead. The demonic part of you needs to be contained, bound so that you can wield it instead of it wielding you, but Marzanna can't do that for you. I can. It just takes you understanding what attracted the demon to you in the first place."

Vlad hung his head. "My sister drowned when we were playing by the river. We shouldn't have been there, and I was too slow to save her." He looked to the strzyga who he'd called Elze. "Your ma tried to marry you off to a man twice your age from another village."

"I know!" she snapped, baring two rows of jagged teeth. "Don't remind me of that beast of a man. He deserved his death."

"Regret and anger feed the demon," I said. "That pain is real, but you can't let it consume you if you want to help others."

"I just want to be out of this terrible body!" Elze replied. "Wacław is a płanetnik. He's lucky to look human, but I need the sun to do so. There's no sun here…"

Vlad huffed and nodded to the squirming upiór he'd thrown into the railing. "At least the smell of you can't kill someone."

"Otylia," Narcyz whispered at my side, his voice like a wicked wind. "What are you doing? We need to kill them and get Andrij. We're just wasting time!"

"Unless they can help us," I said before turning my attention back to the Nawie. "Wacław is always in his demonic soul-form because his mortal soul is dead. I can't change what you look like, but I can bring you back to Jawia. We have demons in our tribe now whose hunger I tamed. Let me help you."

Elze sneered as Vlad approached me. He held a hand over his heart, as if expecting me to stab it, and the motion revealed Marzanna's Frostmark across his bicep. In a utopiec's form, his arms were as thick as logs, and the Frostmark's X was larger than my head. "It's taken a long time to lose my regret, but I'm ready. Do it."

He towered over me, and I had to hold my breath to avoid choking as I opened my power to the Threads of Life. Vlad's Thread was dark and limp beyond a vibrant yellow section close to his chest. I grabbed hold of it. If I wanted, I could've killed him then and severed his soul, but I plunged my light into it instead, focusing on the natural end for a Naw. He was a protector. No matter how disgusting his Naw appearance, he'd been born to help the natural dead who'd suffered like his sister. I found that memory in him and pushed through it.

"You're not responsible," I told him as I watched his sister stumble from the shore. His sorrow and regret coursed through me, but I swept them away, focusing on him now. "You couldn't save her, but you can help all the others who endure the Smorodina's current."

"For Halyna," he stammered, his eyes glazed over. "I'll do it."

I released the light and stepped back. His Thread now burst from him, stretching up the Smorodina toward Jawia and those left among the living. A single strand also crossed the bridge to Nawia, and he followed it with sorrowful eyes. "She's there. I never said goodbye."

"Marzanna trapped you," I said. "Help us free our friends; then go to your sister. You have an immortal soul, so you have time to heal."

He bowed his head, the Frostmark fading from his arm, releasing Marzanna's hold. "Thank you, goddess." Then he turned back to the others. "Do this with me, Elze. It's better. I feel it already… lighter."

Elze's posture stiffened. "I'm not ready like you. Lady Marzanna has given others her blessing. She entrusted me with Grudzień, and her blessings will never end when I bring her the scalp of Dziewanna's daughter."

"Don't make me kill you," I warned her. "Give up the Moonstone and leave."

But her owl wings swept out, throwing her at me. I hadn't expected her to attack so quickly.

Ta had.

As I summoned a hasty shield to deflect Elze's blade, a blade whipped past my ear. Three sharp edges spun like a whirlwind that plunged into Elze's unprotected neck. The shock in her eyes exposed that she'd forgotten I wasn't alone. It was too late, and by the time her *żityje* started to heal the wounds, I summoned my spear and sent it straight through her chest.

"May your end be better than Marzanna's," I prayed as she collapsed.

Vlad choked, falling back into the railing. "Why? It didn't have to happen. We should've been done, free."

"She made her choice," I said. The upiór who Vlad had thrown into the railing shied away when I raised my gaze to him, my eyes burning with all the Smorodina's heat. Gods, I was so *sick* of all this death. Even when I tried mercy, fate forced my hand. "Accept my help or leave. I'm only this merciful because of Wacław, so don't test my patience."

The upiór fled past us, eyes downcast as he disappeared into the black sands of the Way. I watched him go with a firm grip on my spear. Marzanna and her allies had surprised me too often, and I refused to let them do so again. We were too close.

"Now what?" Narcyz asked. He kept his distance from Vlad, his nostrils flared. "We've got another Naw, but how we getting in there?"

Vlad pointed to Grudzień, which lay under Elze's corpse. "You take it and pretend to run away. I go in and let out your friends. The other servants listen to Nawie, so it should be easy."

"No!" Narcyz insisted, his face growing redder by the second. "We got this far. I'm not letting them figure out how to block this bridge again before we can kill Marzanna."

I looked to Ta, but she just crossed her arms and shrugged. "He's got a point."

"You're both bleeding," I replied.

In sync, they both covered the scrapes on their limbs like children hiding muddied clothes from their parents. Blood told its own tale, though, and enough of it dripped to the bridge to have me worried. Even I had used more *žityje* than I cared to admit. Fighting Marzanna in her own castle would be difficult enough in good condition, but we were far from an optimal state.

Vlad glanced back toward the castle, but Chudo-Yudo's lingering smoke obscured it. "Decide. The smoke will be gone soon, and they will ask questions if they see."

Narcyz sliced his sword through the air. "We should fight our way through. The longer we wait, the more time Marzanna has to torture the others."

"Nah," Ta replied. "Let's sneak."

"How?" Narcyz waved toward the distant castle. "It's a *fortress*! You can't just put on a hood and hope no one knows it's us."

I twirled a wisp of moonlight around my fingers. "No, but we could use illusions."

23

Wacław

She'll come. She always does.

BLOOD SPLATTERED ACROSS MY CELL WALL as the Nawie wilkołak, Iwo, slashed his claws across my cheek for what could've been the tenth or hundredth time. Without *żityje* to heal, I bled until black stained my clothes and the floor. My mind drifted like a leaf in the gales, and I barely heard Iwo repeating his demand.

"Accept Lady Marzanna's request!" his now ravenous voice echoed through the room. "You have no *żityje* left, so you will die from blood loss soon. As will your friends."

I drooped, held up only by the chains that shackled my arms to the stone wall. Broken in more place than one, my legs were a distant pain as my mind numbed to the agony. There was nothing I wanted more than relief from the beatings, and based on the screams echoing through the dungeon, my friends suffered the same. They weren't Nawie…

Kuba's voice rang in my mind. Imagined or not, it refused to falter, his pure fear ripping at my heart. He'd died for me once already. Could I really allow him to do so again because of my stubborn resistance?

The cell's cold reality faded to the soft spring warmth of the forest's memories.

Mud coated my face instead of blood, and the pain in my legs came from Kuba wrestling them back, trying to force me to surrender. He laughed at my flailing until I finally gave in.

By the leg, he dragged me onto higher, dryer ground, smirking all the way. I lay unceremoniously beneath the boughs of an old birch with my tunic dragged up to my chest and my trousers pulling on my nether regions. But I laughed anyway. Despite wrestling hardly being my greatest skill, a friendly competition often pulled Kuba out of his joking deflections and made him admit what he was truly thinking. The shadows beneath his eyes revealed more than mere exhaustion.

He plopped himself at the base of the tree, arms behind his head as if there wasn't a care in the world. His uncombed hair draped over his eyes, but he didn't bother to bat it away. "We're brothers to the end, you and me. Not like your stupid half ones. Blood's not everything."

"Brothers," I confirmed, pushing myself up and clasping hands with him. It was still caked with mud, but he took it anyway. "I'd trade you for Miko any day."

Miko…

Time froze. I stepped back, my boot not making a sound in the thick mud as a shadow slipped from behind the birch. It took on Mikołaj's broad-shouldered form, but his face was hollowed, his eyes the pits of Oblivion.

I reached out for him, but when my fingers met the shadow, he dissolved. Wisps of darkness swept around the tree, leaving behind the stern gaze of a man I'd hoped never to see again.

"Father?" I asked, my heart stuttering.

The hulking man who'd once been High Chief Jacek looked me up and down. I was no longer in the younger body from my memory, but my płanetnik soul-form—corrupted veins and all. My wounds had returned too, and I resembled a man beaten in a drunken brawl more than a king.

"You never cared for my lineage," he spat, his cheeks turning as red as poppies. "Demon! Fiend! You choose a witch over your father, your high chief, then allow your own brother to perish. Now, you claim my throne and call yourself king, bearing your mother's name. Natasza was right about you. I should have sent you to the flames!"

I closed my eyes and took a deep breath as the demon stirred within me. No, I would not bow to its rage. Jacek's blood was mine, but he'd never been my father. A father cared. To him, I'd been nothing but a burden from birth.

Peace held me as I opened my eyes. He didn't deserve the gift of my fury. My choice had saved Otylia and sent him to Weles, and she had shown me more love in mere moons than Jacek had in my entire life.

Darkness drifted from my fingertips as I pointed away. "Return to Nawia," I commanded.

The darkness swirled about him. It was familiar, the same instinctive pull to wield it that I'd felt opening the entrance to the Way of Souls at the bottom of the Wyzra, and something fell into alignment within me as Jacek faded into the dark's embrace. Another force moved with the winds. Like a gentle rhythm growing ever louder, it pulled my mind out of my memories, out of Jawia.

And back into the path of the dead.

I clung to that strange peace as torment returned, my body straining as Iwo clutched my throat. "Lady Marzanna is calling for you. Better say your prayers to that little goddess of yours."

A hum emanated from the Way of Souls and reverberated through my core. Deep, like the throat songs of the eastern clans, it carried power through the old tongue. My demonic abilities drained my *żityje*, but this… It was a fire-warmed mug of water during the frost. A trickle of power entered my soul. Though only a little, it was constant, and it gave me hope all the same.

Iwo dragged me through the halls of Marzanna's castle, each blending into the others until we reached the throne room again.

Blood loss threatened to throw me unconscious, but I held back my *żityje*. They couldn't know. Not yet.

To my surprise, it wasn't Marzanna who met me in the throne room, but my captured friends. They formed two rows along the path to the throne with a Naw standing guard behind each.

None showed any signs of torture.

Kuba cried out at the sight of me. As I probably resembled a corpse more than a man, I couldn't blame him. My health wasn't my concern, though, and I took relief knowing they were all right.

That memory returned as I met his gaze and mouthed, *"Trust me, Brother."*

Whatever magic Marzanna had in the castle had cut our ability to communicate through my Eclipsemark, but his subtle nod was enough of a reply. If any of them would do something to force Marzanna's hand to kill all of us, it was Kuba. Having him be patient was a weapon in itself.

Iwo threw me to my knees before the empty throne, its skulls like thousands of deathless eyes boring into me. It was silent here, but a cacophony echoed from beyond the slits in the ice ceiling. To my fatigued mind, it resembled a dragon's roar and the pulsing *thump* of a moonblast. Had Otylia come? Or was I scraping for another bit of hope beyond my meager supply of *żityje?*

"Where are Elze and Vlad?" I asked Iwo, my voice like death.

Hot pain stabbed the base of my spine before slicing up my back. Like a dagger of ice, it shifted to a frigid shiver away from the point of impact, and I bit my cheek so hard I tasted blood as my hairs rose. All my instincts screamed of danger. I didn't need the warning.

Marzanna had arrived.

The goddess laughed as she trailed a single claw across my wounded cheek. It stung, I but didn't pull away, spitting blood over her heeled shoes of sparkling ice.

"Let the others go," I muttered, beginning my deceit. "I'll do it. I'll spare you and hunt down Czarnobóg. Six of the Moonstones will be yours, but you must swear upon them that you will not harm my friends, or my people."

She snatched my chin and forced me to look at her. "I have heard enough of your lies, foolish little Naw. You see your companions arrayed here like cattle for butchering? That is because your words mean nothing to me—not when your lover slays my żmij and is infiltrating my castle this very minute." Her gaze snapped to Iwo. "Vladimir has betrayed us, and Elze is dead because of it."

The wilkołak cursed. "He always doubted you."

"As did you, Wacław." She threw me back. "Your insolence has pushed me too far, so though I need you, your friends are of little use to me alive."

Marzanna approached the throne and waved toward the Nawie. "Bring me the one who serves my sister."

I slowly released my newfound *żityje* to heal my worst injuries as a upiór dragged Andrij to her. Surprisingly, he didn't resist, keeping his chin high despite the terrified look in his eyes. With Marzanna's attention fixed on him, my wounds closed, but her wicked grin had me frozen.

"You smell of Dziewanna's smoke," she said as darkness swept around her feet. "Yet you hold the composure she never possessed. Yes, you will make a fine thrall." Her smile widened. "All of you will."

"No!"

I yanked myself free of Iwo's grip with a burst of wind, draining the rest of my *żityje*. I had offered my surrender to stop this exact thing. Even if it had been a lie, I couldn't let her turn Andrij or the others into her demons. But a snap of cold across my ankles stopped me dead in my tracks.

Ice snatched my legs, wrapping ever higher as Marzanna laid her palm against Andrij's forehead. His body convulsed at her touch. Black veins crossed his skin as his muscles expanded, his tunic tearing and his teeth flashing sharp fangs.

The others echoed his cries as they suffered the same fate. They twisted and writhed, shifting into demons of every kind. Whether covered in feathers, scales, or fur, each bore razor sharp claws and darkened eyes that bore into me. They'd appeared unharmed when

I entered, but this was the horrid truth. While Iwo had tortured me into succumbing to Marzanna's will, the goddess herself had bent those I loved into her corrupted fiends.

And the only way to her was through them.

24

Otylia

This can't be good.

MARZANNA'S DUNGEONS WERE EMPTY except for a few crazed women who kept repeating the same lines, and their words haunted me as Vlad guided us through the hollow stone halls.

"Life becomes death. Death becomes undeath. Undeath becomes eternity."

A chill ran down my spine. We wore moonlight Nawie disguises—Ta and I as strzygi and Narcyz as an upiór—but End's silent press upon my soul said we were far from hidden. This was Marzanna's home. She was bound to her Frostmarked. And I channeled to keep our illusions up. Why would she not know frauds had entered her halls?

I grabbed Vlad's arm, wincing at the swampy utopiec slime upon it. "Where are our friends? Where has she taken them?"

"The throne room," Vlad replied with his head hung. "She's turning them."

Ta gasped. "*Turning* them?"

My stomach churned. Gods, what had we done? "Go! Show us to them, now!"

"They will know," Vlad objected.

I pushed onward, glaring back at him. "I don't care! We came here to save them and kill a goddess. Both are in the throne room, so that's where we're going."

A heavy silence hung over us until Vlad sighed and pointed down another path. "Then you're headed the wrong direction. This way."

We rushed through the maze of cells until a staircase appeared, its dark stone giving way to near white above. Two creatures of pure ice blocked the path, and they turned with curious gazes at our haste. I hoped Vlad had some explanation.

He didn't.

Lowering his shoulder, Vlad plowed straight through the creatures and shattered them in a single blow. The sound echoed through the narrow corridor and spurred shouts from above. I cursed as I dismissed our illusions, calling my spear instead.

"Stealth got us this far, but it won't kill a goddess."

Narcyz stomped his feet and tightened his grip on Kwiecień in one hand and Grudzień in the other. "No, but I will."

We made a racket rushing up the stairs, but based on the gathered ice servants when we reached the top, they'd known we were coming. Shaped like all kinds of savage animals, they clawed and slashed at us. Moonstone weapons cut down the magic beasts with ease. Demons soon followed, though, and we struggled to force our way to the throne room with melee alone.

So I called upon the Threads of Life.

Visions of agonizing deaths and torture at Marzanna's hand met me as I grabbed hold of the demons' blackened Threads. Their pain became mine, but this power was also mine to rule. I allowed the emotions to fuel my strength, my will. Not to destroy the demons, but to free them.

"You will have your vengeance!" I declared, rising above on the moonlight, their Threads entangling me like a fly caught in a spiderweb. "Marzanna corrupted you, ended your lives. So we will end her."

I poured *žityje* into my words. Light emanated with them, shredding through the dark Threads and leaving fragments of color behind.

Eyes of black turned to brown, blue, hazel, and green. Like those in Sheresy, the demons remained in their corrupted forms, but life filled them once again. They stopped mid-attack, gasping up at me. Fear and awe filled their gazes.

"Bringer of light," a miawka cried from her knees. "What do we call you?"

"My birth name is Otylia," I said, casting a glance at Ta, "but many call me Nemiza, Calamity. I'm here to bring that calamity upon Marzanna for the pain she's caused all of us."

The demons bowed deeper, and another replied, "Then we will aid you. The queen of death must fall."

I nodded. "Then hurry with us. My friends are in danger."

From four to many, we charged through the halls of Marzanna's castle, banishing the creatures of ice and slaying the Nawie who refused to join us. All kept their worship of Marzanna.

Vlad winced as each Naw fell. We'd seen only a few of their kind before, but dozens were here. Wacław would cry for me to save them. I couldn't. My power healed demons by confronting who or what had corrupted them. Nawie, though, needed to be willing, and Wacław had shown their corruption was far deeper, never fully gone. I held part of his in my soul, but I couldn't do the same for Vlad and the others. For them, the fight was beyond just a single goddess. They needed to know their own heart and defy the corruption that sought to control it.

Two final Nawie—a wilkołak and a płanetnik—guarded what Vlad claimed was the entrance to the throne room, but dark ice formed a wall that blocked the way.

"She suspected you would come," the płanetnik said, holding a rope tight between fingers with blackened veins. "I'd fight you, but I ain't got a dream of dying."

He waved a hand, and the ice wall melted away, the remnant water disappearing into the floor. The horror beyond stopped me dead in my tracks.

Wacław rose amid a tower of ice, consumed completely by it. He bore no weapon, and though I sensed the *žityje* in his soul, the winds did not answer him. I'd hoped Ara, Sabina, and the others would be with him. But they were nowhere to be seen.

A sickening feeling crept over me as I eyed the ring of demons separating Wacław from a throne of skulls. The queen upon it stole my attention. Her face was a war between youth and venerable age, and frigid crystals of eyes glared back at me from its center. A menacing smirk flicked across the end of her narrow lips, her left hand dancing through wisps of black and icy blue like a skilled weaver. Waves of pure white fabric followed the movements, and her dress seemed to carry the weight of a thousand snowfalls as she rose.

"*Lady* Otylia," Marzanna began mockingly. "Your friends have been far from gracious guests, and your lover even less so. Poor Wacław cannot join our first meeting, but it is only fair. After all, I spent moons in his mind. It is you I am far more curious of."

I readied both spear and *žityje* to strike. "Release him, now!"

"*Tsk tsk tsk.* Do not act this way." She opened her right hand to display Ara's gray Moonstone of Październik. "He is not the one whom you should be concerned for."

My blood chilled. "What did you do to her? Tell me!"

Her smile widened, exposing jagged teeth as she looked down at the demons arrayed before her—five of them. The grotesque strzyga to her right bared fangs and stretched her owl-like wings, but my gut knew the truth. She still had her widow's peak and the smile lines deep into her cheeks. Yes, she'd been transformed, but it was her.

Ara was a demon.

I screamed and charged, slashing Sierpień's bladed end of my spear through the ice that contained Wacław. Marzanna was weakened, but that didn't change that she was a goddess. To free Ara and the others, I needed Wacław by my side.

Narcyz needed no command to follow. He roared at the sight of Andrij twisted and contorted into an upiór, and the winds carried him over the demons. Laughing, Marzanna darted to the side, calling the green Moonstone of Maj to her grasp as a sickle. Ice shards pelted Narcyz as he made chase.

"Fight me!" he demanded. "Or are you afraid of a mortal?"

The demons—our friends—surrounded him, slashing and biting at his exposed flanks. Ta and Vlad joined him, but there was no way to fight them. A slice from our Moonstone would be potentially lethal. Only killing Marzanna could free them from her grip.

Unless…

I shattered the ice servants who advanced as Wacław collapsed into me. They were mere distractions, but Marzanna summoned a blizzard, strengthening by the second. Heavy fog fell over us. Blinded, I called upon End to guide me as icicles speared into me. Only my light shield could deflect those, but End's wisps revealed the demons' moves before they happened.

My friends' souls burned within those demons. Their wisps were still vibrant, but my free hand burned when I grabbed hold of Ara's Threads of Life. Frostbite seared across my palm, reflecting the power I poured into her to banish the corruption.

Ara's fangs snapped ever-closer. Bloodlust filled her dark eyes, not the care of the friend who'd stood by me for years. This closeness could kill me, but I held firm, refusing to let her slip away again.

"I'm sorry!" I pleaded. "I failed you. I should have protected you."

Marzanna's laughter split through the fog, echoing as if she were on every side of me at once. "She is *mine* now. Your insignificant force cannot free her!"

A shot of cold threw me back from Ara's Thread. My hand stung, *žityje* healing the frostbite, but a skin wound wasn't my concern. Ice shards ensured I had plenty of those already, and many plunged deeper, forcing me to expand my shields over Narcyz and Ta too.

"We need to kill Marzanna," Wacław stammered, freeing himself from my hold. He was frigid and sopping wet, but his sky-blue eyes were alight. "I've heard her voice in my mind. This close, her grip on them is too strong to break."

The ice servants struck again before I could warn him. His vision was impaired without End's help, and he had no sword, making his limbs easy targets for the servants. Black blood covered both of us, but a new source of *żityje* grew inside him. I'd never sensed such a constant source. He seemed unbothered by it, though, so I turned my focus to his defense as he threw out his arms.

Wind banished fog and ice shards alike to reveal our still living friends fighting desperately in the far corner. Narcyz noticed Wacław with a grin.

"Catch, Half-Chief!"

He launched Grudzień at Wacław with pure recklessness, the blade slicing an inch from my nose before Wacław's winds guided it into his grasp. Marzanna's castle had dampened our bond, but Wacław's joy at his Moonblade's return was a jolt of energy I badly needed. We fell into battle stances beside each other. Despite our wounds and the horror of our friends' transformations, this… this felt *right*. Wacław and I were united against the goddess who'd caused so many of our ills.

And we'd defeat her together.

"Keep their attention," I shouted to Narcyz, Ta, and Vlad. Their wide eyes were enough of an objection, but I released my own shield, granting it to them as Wacław's winds kept us protected from the countless shards.

We couldn't risk aggressive magic against Marzanna with our demonic friends protecting her, but Vlad shouldered into them. Like wolves to fresh meet, they circled, striking at my light shield. It held for now, so we took our chance.

Wacław and I struck together, splitting Marzanna's servants. The goddess herself met our advance with Maj raised. Her parries were swift, her slashes precise, and her sickle blade drank greedily of my *żityje* when it pierced my forearm and clanged off Weles's band of silver and wood upon it.

My motions slowed, but Wacław came to my aid. Deflecting a blow, he threw Marzanna off balance, giving him time the draw the Thunderstone dagger in his free hand. The two black blades twirled around him with the wind amplifying his speed. Marzanna had only one blade, and when she blocked Grudzień, Wacław dove, slicing his dagger straight across her thigh.

Black blood sprayed from the wound. Not like a god's or mortal's, she had truly fallen to corruption, and she only laughed as darkness billowed from Październik's Moonstone in her off-hand.

Żityje could not quickly heal a wound caused by a Moonblade, so pain gripped my arm as I joined Wacław's advance. Spear and blade sliced Marzanna over and over. Yet she showed no signs of faltering, and her haze circled me like a pack of wolves who smelled blood.

Then, as I raised my spear and prepared a moonblast, her deathly vapors plunged into my wound.

I staggered, vision fading. My body turned distant, and instead of pain, there was only a vast void pulling me in. Gentle warmth overcame me. Wacław's cry pierced the veil, but even he faded until I floated in the familiar flow of time.

Except it was empty.

Time's current pulled on me as it always had, but there were no wisps or Threads. Only an endless expanse and the silver light emanating from my skin. I attempted to move, but found my arms trapped at my side by a pulsing green Thread that began at my chest. It frayed.

End prodded at my thoughts, wordless. I needed no words, though, to understand what this was: the end… my end.

"NO!" I screamed into the void. "Not yet! We were so close!"

"Careful, little goddess," an everchanging voice replied. "Your voice can pierce the realms, and now more than ever, they are fragile things."

Destiny's voice drifted, as if struggling against time's current. I fought to pursue her, but my Thread held me tight.

"I need to go back," I pleaded. "You showed me what happens if I fail!"

The Thread unwound, releasing me, but sending me tumbling through the abyss until I grabbed hold of it. My muscles ached. My mind spun. I held on anyway and tried to focus on the Thread's hum. *Žityje* flowed through it—a connection to the living realm, to Wacław.

"Marzanna is bound to Death," Destiny whispered. "His power seeps through your very veins. To defy such a force is unwise, but he is well pleased with you after your deeds in Prawia."

Heat rushed across my skin. I needed to be free! "Then tell him to release me."

"You are only here because Death has allowed you to linger already. This is the place of endings, your domain. It is up to you to accept your end or deny it."

"Tell me how!" I demanded.

A single wisp slipped through the darkness, hovering before me as its color shifted from red to green to a bright pink. "To deny your own end, you must first embrace that you control *endings*, not how they come about. Focus entirely upon the journey, and you lose sight of why you travel."

I pulled harder on my Thread, pouring my energy into the pulse within. "I know why I'm fighting. Jawia needs me. Mother needs me."

Destiny sighed. "Desires for others are suitable ends, but more powerful still is where *you* intend to travel. Life will carry on for you many years beyond your tribe and friends. Even Wacław may perish by the blade before you. Find purpose in your own soul. Only this may bring you to the truth of your force and return you to your allies."

Purpose in my own soul?

I closed my eyes, picturing life in Dwie Rzeki before this mess had begun. I'd been spiteful then, so I looked further. Before the wolf attack. Before Mother's death. Before my agony and loss.

All I found was a lie—a child's hopes and dreams, split by her father's condemnation and her tribe's accusations. Witch. Wildling. Untamed. No matter where I searched, I found hatred and pain. The only safety I found in my memories were Mother, Wacław, and my friends. They'd stood by me when I failed, relied on me when I was strong. We supported each other. Protected each other.

Protected.

That word found roots within me, embracing my soul. Yes, I cared for my loved ones, but more than that, I fought to protect those who were like me—those caught between society and the corruption seeping into the defenseless, the desperate. I'd defended the wilds, freed demons who'd been corrupted because of others, taken a piece of Wacław's corruption to purify his soul, and granted light during the night that would not end.

Weightlessness washed over me. My body no longer strained to hold my Thread, and time's current no longer yearned to pull me along. I was eternal, ascendant, free.

"I will protect the lost and the dead from corruption," I spoke into the nothingness. "I will offer them a peaceful end, safe from Marzanna's deception, Weles's manipulations, and Czarnobóg's corruption. Where all things end, I will stand with my spear ready to face Oblivion. There will be moonlight in the darkest nights to guide them to paradise."

Destiny laughed joyously, like Mother had whenever I successfully brewed one of her potions. "That will do, little goddess. Now, you have found your will. Go and pursue your destiny."

Reality returned like a dive into the frozen Kryzhana.

Marzanna's chill ripped away time's gentle warmth as my wounds seared with each movement. Wacław fought in a whirlwind before me. Each time Marzanna made to strike at me, he was there first, deflecting her blade or taking a wound—anything to ensure I did not fall.

The dark vapors curled around him. He darted this way and that, but they sought his wounds as they had mine. Though Death had granted me another chance, I doubted he'd be so kind to Wacław.

I had no idea how to best Marzanna, but Destiny's words rang in my mind. For our entire journey on the Way of Souls, I'd obsessed over *how* to avoid the defeats End had shown. That had led my friends to ruin and me to question my every move. I didn't need to know how at every moment. I just needed to focus on why I fought, and who I sought to become.

Light poured from me. It shone so bright that my eyes burned from reflections off the ice walls, but I reveled in that power—my power.

Marzanna sneered as I charged to Wacław's side. The Threads of Life flashed before me, hers charred and dead. It choked her like a noose, and when Wacław attacked with Grudzień's jagged blade forcing her to defend, I took hold of her Thread.

Rage and sorrow flooded over me. She'd once been a graceful goddess of nature before Jaryło's betrayal, but no joy or desire for growth remained in her soul. All was scarred, broken by vengeance. I devoted my *żityje* to purifying her, but for someone so far lost, she needed to want freedom from its grip. Instead, she longed for corruption's comforting lies, its suffocating power. There was no saving her.

I redirected my *żityje* from purifying her soul to severing it. Though she hacked at me with her sickle, Wacław deflected the blows, his hair shining gold in my moonlight, but his dark veins scarring him as deeply as Marzanna. She'd surrendered to corruption. He fought it with each breath.

And her submission would mean her end.

My power severed her Thread, leaving it frayed as she cried out. But unlike those before, the severing didn't kill her by itself. Her godly soul clung to life. Ice shot from the ground and struck us from every angle, an entire blizzard caught within the throne room until Wacław lunged.

Sparks flew as Grudzień met Marzanna's sickle Moonblade. Locked together, the swords left an opening at Marzanna's chest, and Wacław plunged the Thunderstone dagger straight into her heart.

Marzanna shrieked, her servants and defenses shattering. Demons and Nawie alike stopped and watched their goddess fall. Maj's sickle blade slipped from her fingers, and she grasped at Wacław's hand on the hilt of the dagger, as if hoping he'd somehow let her live.

"You dare slay me with the dagger I gave you to exact my revenge?" she spat, blood seeping from her lips. "Jaryło yet lives. Czarnobóg corrupts the recesses of Nawia. But you reject my deal and pierce my heart with my grandfather's dagger, forged for the love I have lost!"

His expression softened. Wisps of black drifted from her like ethereal blood, and light returned to her eyes as she collapsed on her throne. The dagger still stuck from her heart, but she gave it no heed, instead turning her gaze to me as blood seeped from her lips. "Otylia, bringer of the end. Tell your mother I did not wish for her to suffer as she has. Jaryło betrayed me, but she saw his ills too."

She waved a hand, and a sudden warmth rushed over me. Her fingers trembled with the motion, but an almost motherly smile pulled at the ends of her mouth. "I release Dziewanna and Jawia. I release your friends, my sworn Nawie, and those consumed by corruption on the Way of Souls. This… This was not what I wanted for the Three Realms. Believe me, child. All I wanted was for Jaryło to suffer."

Exclamations tore my attention from her, and I choked up at the sight of my friends freed from their demonic forms. I rushed to Ara, embracing her before taking her cheeks in my hands.

"Are you well?" I asked. "Is the demon gone?"

She beamed with tears streaming down her cheeks. "I'm okay… I'm okay. Though, Narcyz did give me a *nasty* cut on the side."

We laughed together, casting a shared glare at Narcyz, who stood there like a dog who'd stolen meat off the table. Sabina knelt between us.

"Sabina?" I said, joining her, but she turned away.

"I've never been so angry." Her voice was barely audible, tremoring as she looked to Ta. "I… I almost killed you. I'm so sorry."

Ta just tossed and caught one of her circular throwing blades. "Just don't try again, and I think we're all good. It's hard when the winter witch has your mind."

Wacław watched us with a stunned expression, unable to smile as Andrij rose to hug Narcyz. His shoulders sagged, and his sorrow struck with our bond re-forming. We'd done it. We'd killed Marzanna.

But this was far from over.

"We made Jaryło suffer," he told Marzanna. "He holds no Moonstones, and he will never rule Jawia again. Neither will you."

The goddess scoffed, her eyes heavy and her voice frail. "I see the corruption that suffocated me now. Such power…" She coughed, but didn't cover her wound, the blood pooling at her feet. "Leave me to suffer in peace. I am immortal, but Thunderstone leaves its mark. You will not be troubled by my winter until the next year to come, and I shall not break my seasons' bounds. The cycle… Dziewanna and I need not kill as I have done to Jaryło, and he to me. Let this end. I will open a way back to Jawia so that you may reunite with Dziewanna. Take the Moonstones, find Czarnobóg, and mend what I have wrought. When you are ready to enter Nawia, return to the place where I found you after the equinox."

Wacław looked from me to Kuba, his fist uncurling at his side. "Get your Moonblades," he told the others, "and then let's leave. We're done here."

Kuba cocked his head. "But she—"

"Is a goddess," Wacław insisted. "She's fading, and stabbing her again won't change that. If she fails to keep her promises, we know how to make her pay."

Marzanna's Thread now pulsed a snowy white, and though her *żityje* faded, life seemed to grow within her. I trusted Wacław's instincts. More than anything, I wanted Marzanna to suffer, but if she'd lost her strength and truly regretted what she'd done, there was nothing more we could accomplish here. Czarnobóg lurked in Nawia's depths. We needed to stop him before he threatened all of the Three Realms.

With only mumbled protests from Narcyz and Kuba, we collected the Moonstones Marzanna had stolen, then pushed through the rubble to a swirling portal by the throne room's entrance. Vlad watched it with fear.

"I can't go back."

Wacław took his arm. "I know how hard it is to be a Naw among normal people, but our people will accept you." He looked past Vlad to the other Nawie who Marzanna had freed from her corruptive influence. "All of you. We have former demons among us. We have people from every tribe. Please, come with us."

But Vlad shook his head and stepped back. "No. We belong here. Nawie defend the dead on the Way of Souls. You showed me that, and it's better than serving Marzanna."

Wacław clasped his arm, then laughed at the utopiec slime that coated his hand. "One day, I'll return to join you. There are so few of us left, so thank you for standing with us. We may not be here if it weren't for you."

When they parted, I took Wacław's hand—the one not covered with slime. "Ready to go home?"

"It hurts to know we'll have to leave so quickly," he replied, that deep sorrow still filling his soul. "I'm so tired of fighting…"

Kuba nudged him. "Hey, at least you didn't spend the last hour as a demon!"

"He was born one, stupid," Narcyz muttered.

"Right…" Kuba rubbed the back of his neck, then smacked Wacław on the back. "I'll get ya an oskoła back at home. Gods know we could all use one."

Wacław rolled his eyes but a smile slipped through as he surveyed the carnage we'd left behind. In its center, Marzanna died slowly, her head falling further by the second.

"You're right," he said. "Let's go home. Then, let's send Czarnobóg back to Oblivion."

25

Wacław

I killed winter.

IT DIDN'T FEEL REAL. One moment, I was encased in ice. The next, I fought by Otylia's side, taking advantage of the greatest burst of power I'd ever seen from her to stab Marzanna in the heart. The eternal winter was over.

Now, all I wanted to do was collapse.

We stumbled into Dwie Rzeki's village center. The air was warm, the ground coating my boots with muck. Home stunk of animals and leather tanning and workers' sweat, but it was *home*. And everyone was staring at us.

Why wouldn't they? A group of armed, bloodied teenagers had stumbled out of a portal in front of their frozen goddess. Oh, and among those teenagers was their king and yet another goddess.

"By the gods!" an older man exclaimed, dropping to his knees. "They've returned!"

Many others in the crowd copied him. Despite covering their legs in mud in the process, they smiled or wept with joy, and I was at a loss for words.

Had they actually missed us that much? Dziewanna's ritual had repelled much of winter's influence, but in our time away, I sensed a loss in the vibrant life that had filled Jawia. People appeared less starved than before, and some held morsels of hunted meat. Dziewanna herself, though, remained trapped in vines, ice now encasing her as she pressed her palm to the earth. The green lines stretching from her were faded but still pulsing with *žityje*—the last fragments of her ritual's power.

"Mother!"

Otylia rushed to the frozen goddess, her raven black hair carrying a single silver streak that glistened in the midday sun. The sun… I hadn't realized how much I missed it until its heat seared my sweat to my cheeks. Discomfort mattered little when all was as it should be, not trapped in the dark abyss of the Way of Souls.

Dziewanna showed no visible signs of life at Otylia's touch, but the *žityje* within her shifted. Drifting out from her core, it created flowers and vines that blossomed across her skin and cracked the ice. More and more grew until all that was visible of Dziewanna herself was her antlers, marking her as queen of the wilds. She stepped from her winter cage as the flowers wove into a dress that carried every color of the spring bloom.

The wild queen of Jawia was free. Unbound. Unbroken.

Dziewanna swept Otylia into her arms as if she were a toddler. "My little wildling!"

They both wept, Dziewanna stroking her daughter's cheek for a long while before her smile dropped. She surveyed us. "You freed me, which means Marzanna is dead, or something has gone terribly wrong. Where are the other Moonstones?"

"Czarnobóg stole them," Otylia replied. "He betrayed Marzanna and almost killed her for us."

As the two talked, I waved for the villagers to stand. Having them stare at us from their knees felt so unnerving, no matter my position. I didn't want people to kneel. They deserved to live their lives without fear of anyone—their king and goddess included.

"She kidnapped us and turned us into demons!" Kuba exclaimed, rushing up to Dziewanna and hopping on the tips of his toes. "I've been a jackal, but this was *so much worse*."

Dziewanna raised her brow, a wry smile tugging at her lips. "Perhaps this is a conversation to have in private, then." She nodded toward the longhouse before kissing Otylia on the head. "Come, let us talk inside. You all have had quite the journey, and I have been frozen solid for long enough this year."

I longed to find Mom and tell her all that had happened, but she was nowhere among the nearest crowd. We'd find her after we finished with Dziewanna, I told myself. There was little time for pleasantries with Czarnobóg now lurking on Nawia's throne with Weles and three moonstones in his grasp.

Narcyz and Ta grinned as we found seats at the wooden table stretching down the center of the longhouse. The rest of us trudged along, wiping blood and sweat from our brows. I wished I could be happy with what we'd done, but it wasn't that simple. Marzanna had marked me, hurt those I loved, and slaughtered more people than I could count. Defeating her didn't feel like a victory. We'd barely survived recent months, and her sudden regret left me wondering if things could've been different.

Otylia squeezed my hand under the table. "It was actually Wacław who killed her. He stabbed her with the same dagger she used to mark him, but I swear, she changed when I tried to sever her Thread of Life."

"That is not a surprise," Dziewanna replied, seated across from us. She'd thawed mere minutes before, but she glowed with godly power. "Your connection to people's Threads and their endings is complex, bound to desires and destiny. Perhaps a part of her deep beneath the corruption did desire purification. I hope so, as it will make future seasons far simpler, but that is irrelevant unless we can ensure Czarnobóg does not threaten Jawia and Prawia."

Otylia dug the fingers of her free hand into the table. "We *must* protect the dead in Nawia too! I swore to Destiny I would, and if Czarnobóg controls the dead, the demons will never stop."

"And no one will ever find peace," I added.

Sabina nodded slowly. Tears still stained her cheeks, and her voice trembled. "Weles was not a good master, but he respected the dead. They don't deserve to feel like we did. So angry…"

Squeezing my hand once more, Otylia let go and joined Sabina, embracing her and cradling her head. "No one deserves that. We'll make it right. I promise."

"Czarnobóg threatens more than the dead," Dziewanna said, her face shadowed. "As long as the veil between Oblivion and the Three Realms remains open, nothing will stop demons from flooding into Jawia. No one here is safe." She looked at each of our friends. "You all have been brave, but what lies ahead is the work of gods. Wacław is a Naw and more resilient. The rest of you must remain here to protect what we have built, ensuring the living survive for whatever comes after Czarnobóg's death."

Narcyz sheathed Maj with a grunt. "No."

Dziewanna's eyes burned bright red. "That was not a suggestion."

He just swallowed and lowered his head as Andrij patted his back. Though Kuba and Ta gave defiant looks for a moment, both nodded when Dziewanna met their gazes. All our friends had faced enough already. They didn't deserve whatever struggle awaited us in Nawia, and having them here to protect our fledgling kingdom gave me some relief.

"You all will serve an important role," I said, rising. "With us gone, our people will be without their goddesses and king. They need your guidance and protection against the foes that only we truly understand."

Kuba tapped his foot. "And what if you don't come back?"

"Then you do what you must to keep these people safe," Dziewanna replied, "for as long as necessary." She stood as well, nodding to me. "We will leave in two days. It is not long to recover, but *żityje* does wonders for healing. I give you time more for your minds and souls than your bodies."

We said our parting words to our friends, who went on their ways to reunite with their loved ones. Once they left, Dziewanna stared toward the door. "I will head into the wilds tonight to gather my strength. Whatever offerings we can collect from our people will make the fights ahead easier, but I shiver at the thought of what power Czarnobóg now holds. He sapped my power before, and I fear he has done the same to Weles."

"Before you go," I said as Otylia took my hand. "I felt something strange on the Way of Souls when I was imprisoned by Marzanna. It was as if the Way itself was feeding my *żityje* when I had none left."

Dziewanna extended her arms, allowing flames to curl across one and vines to creep across the other. "You are not a god, but all beings carry nature's forces in our souls—some more than others. It is when we are in alignment with that beating power within us that we are who we are meant to be, and that is why I seek the wilds this eve. My daughter finds her strength beneath the moon and in the ends which weave through all of time. You are a creature of the in-between. It makes perfect sense, then, that your soul found alignment in the place between life and death, where those who are pure of heart needed you most."

"And in Nawia?" I asked. "The Way of Souls can't help me there."

 She smiled and took my and Otylia's joined hands. "I did not tell you to come because you are invulnerable, but because you two together are as strong as any deity in the Three Realms or beyond. You have overcome many trials. I will need both of you in order to face Czarnobóg and free Weles, even if the old fool deserves imprisonment for what he did with Jaryło."

"And did to you," Otylia retorted.

Dziewanna furrowed her brow. "We will handle such things when the Three Realms are not at stake. Go, rest and wash yourselves. You smell of death."

Otylia and I retreated into the longhouse's private quarters to do exactly that. I cleaned my face and hands in our chamber's wash bucket before taking off my ruined tunic. My skin was red and cracked across my chest and back, the muscles beneath even worse. *Żityje* could heal the most potent wounds, but soreness remained.

Whether it was just in my head or not, I sat on the edge of my bed and stared ahead at the wall, focusing on each point of pain. It distracted from what we still had to do. What we still had to suffer.

Otylia's touch loosened my back, even if it was just to shove me back to my feet.

"We're going to the Krowik," she said as she took my hand and dragged me toward the door, having changed into one of her old szeptucha dresses. "It's been nearly a year since I washed in a river that isn't frigid. I can't sit in the bathhouse when the wilds have awoken, and you are coming with me, whether you want to or not."

"I learned not to deny you a long time ago," I replied, pulling her in for a quick kiss. "You know, I didn't get the chance to thank you for saving me from that ice in the throne room."

She smirked before spinning away. "You can reward me by keeping your reek away from me until you're clean. Gods, you smell worse than an utopiec."

I threw on a spare shirt and followed her through the longhouse halls, unable to jest back. Though her hair was a tangled mess and sweat glistened on her brow, there was nothing I wanted more than to be beside her. It didn't matter whether we were in the river or the depths of Nawia. I wanted to be with her always.

"What?" she asked with a smirk as we darted out of the light of the longhouse and headed west toward the Krowik.

Letting the winds carry me, I sprinted ahead of her, my legs suddenly light and my muscles free. There were plenty of people about despite the sun's setting, but they only gave us passing glances. Most were too busy celebrating winter's end with mugs of oskoła and enough drunken dancing to worry about anyone else, let alone realize who the running couple even was.

"It's just good to be home," I replied when we burst into the woods. "With you, away from danger for once."

She rounded a wide beech tree, its branches drooping over us and the moonlight splitting through its leaves. The winds shook them and sent droplets scattering over us like the autumn rain, and as I stepped toward Otylia, the first fallen leaves crinkled underfoot. I swept them aside with a silly smile.

"Dance with me, Otylka. Like we did when we were young and didn't have the weight of the Three Realms on our shoulders."

Otylia raised her brow. "The last time we danced in these woods, wolves ambushed us."

I took her hand and pulled her close, swaying to the rhythm of the wind among the trees. "My love, you are a goddess, but if you fear a few wolves, I promise I'll keep you safe."

"That little boy with nothing more than a sharpened stick said the same thing," she quipped, but she didn't resist. Most dances in our tribe were ecstatic affairs full of hopping and glee. We were tired, though, and settled for a melancholic shuffling as she leaned her head against my chest. "You don't need to protect me. That is my responsibility. I saw with Destiny what I have to do—protect those at their ends so they can find peace away from Czarnobóg and his corruption."

With a kiss on the top of her head, I smiled. "While you are busy keeping others safe, someone needs to watch your back. There are always those who want to slay the gods."

"Says the god slayer himself. Your blade pierced Marzanna's heart, remember?"

"Her own blade ended her," I replied, fighting the sinking in my chest. "I was just the messenger. Do you think she saw the truth enough in the end? Will she honor her promise to Dziewanna?"

Her grip tightened. "She released the Nawie, but there's rage deep inside her. I can relate. It consumes you, makes you bitter and desperate. We may have banished Oblivion's corruption from her, but I doubt she's finished searching for vengeance against Jaryło. Immortal grudges last centuries."

"Then it's good we'll last beyond them."

When Otylia stepped back, I spun her, calling the winds to pick up the leaves and circle the ends of her twirling dress. She scoffed at first, but then summoned her Ascension dress with its cape of autumn leaves. Light abounded from her. The leaves seemed to sweep through the entire beech tree, carrying silver instead of deadened brown, and all I could do was watch in awe until Otylia met my arms again.

Her touch was both stronger and more tender than before. Confidence flared in her sharp green eyes when she channeled, and our bond revealed her satisfaction. Each beat of her heart joined mine, each burst of her light sending my winds into a frenzy.

"If immortal grudges last centuries, does immortal love?" I asked.

She furrowed her brow. "Not if you betray me like Jaryło did to Marzanna."

"I wouldn't dare."

She kissed me long and slow as we swayed, holding each other in that moment of bliss. There, beneath those branches, we were in our own world apart from warring gods and corrupting darkness. I didn't want to leave.

Eventually, though, we parted, and she gave me a wry smile as she wrinkled her nose. "Remember what I said about you stinking? Next time, let's dance *after* we bathe."

"We should hurry, then," I said, grabbing her hand and pulling her toward the Krowik. "Who knows when the wolves will arrive?".

26

Otylia

Why does home seem imaginary now?

MY SKIN TICKLED FROM HOW MUCH THUNDERSTONE SAND I'd scrubbed from my pores. Washing in the Krowik River had been refreshing for my mind, body, and soul, but I couldn't get over how strange it felt to be safe. Our time on the Way of Souls had left me on edge. Yet here, there were no demons, guardians, or Nawie lurking.

Well, except for the one who refused to leave my side.

I sat at Lubena's table with Wacław's arm around my waist as his mother beamed. Two now empty bowls of soup sat before us, yet another reminder of life's simplicity before all this. It was late, and only the candle between us and the stone stove in the corner gave any light. So I allowed a little *żityje* to pulse from my skin. Lubena clapped at that.

"It is *amazing* what you can do!" she said as she took my hands. Her golden hair was radiant, and her eyes twinkled like Wacław's when he stared at me, thinking I didn't notice. "Our village has changed so much in recent moons, but nothing has changed as much as you two. You must tell me about this Way of Souls. If it is anything like Prawia or Nawia, I'm sure it was full of excitement."

Wacław and I swapped glances. "It…" I wasn't sure where to begin. The Way had been anything but exciting, but I didn't want to ruin her mood.

Thankfully, Wacław noticed my hesitation and jumped in. "It was a strange place to say the least. So much of it was cold and dead, except for the flaming Smorodina River, and Marzanna's influence dampened our powers for a long time." He let go of me, holding his hands in his lap with his chin tucked to his chest. "Marzanna captured me, then Ara, Kuba, Andrij, and Sabina, turning them into demons to try and force us to help her. If it wasn't for Otylia rescuing us, we'd still be there."

Lubena gasped. "Demons? Are your friends all right? Kuba was a jackal, so I can't imagine he took well to being transformed again."

"They're fine," I said. "Sabina is shaken up at how angry she felt as a demon, but Marzanna changed them back when Wacław killed her. Something—either my channeling, the Thunderstone dagger, or both—pushed out her corruption." I clenched my fists, my shoulders sinking. "It wasn't Wacław's fault that she captured them. *I* saw the future through End's visions, and I became obsessed with avoiding them instead of focusing on what we needed to accomplish."

"I see the pain you endured." Tears welled in Lubena's eyes. She released my hands and wiped them away before grabbing the bowls, but her hands shook. "That place is supposed to be where your soul is from, Wašek?"

He rose to help her, placing the bowls aside and gently guiding her back to her seat. Her head hung as he crouched before her and mustered a smile, but our bond revealed his pain. So did his own tears.

"Nawie like me were born to protect the dead souls on their path to Nawia," he said. "The Smorodina forges their souls into new bodies, but there are forces beyond even Marzanna. Weles and Perun's battles scarred the Way. With Oblivion open to the Three Realms, others could seek to harm it too with Marzanna gone."

"What are you saying?" she asked.

Wacław sniffled, but forced himself to push through his sorrow. "I may be king here for now, but for this kingdom to survive, it needs a mortal ruler. Gods keep from ruling over humans for a reason, and I shouldn't either. In the end, my soul felt at home on the Way of Souls. I regained *žityje* by just existing, and I think I could figure out how to enter and leave it at will. Going there wouldn't be goodbye, but it's where I belong."

My heart ached with him. Lubena had given everything for him, and no mother wished to see their child leave. On this, though, Wacław was right. Whatever came next, Jawia needed its mortals to band together and decide for themselves what they wanted. I was a goddess and he a Naw. We could aid them against the corruption that had already escaped Oblivion, but I couldn't be god-queen of the Kingdom of the Wild Moon and fulfill the promise I'd made to Destiny. All people deserved their natural ends to be protected, not just those in our borders.

Tears streamed down Lubena's cheeks, but she laughed through it. "If that is where you're needed, then it's where you must go." She gave me a pleading look. "And you will go with him, right? I know you aren't wedded yet, but—"

"Don't worry," I insisted, shifting uncomfortably. There was nothing I could do to reassure her. Wacław would leave once—*if*—we survived our battle with Czarnobóg, and she would mourn that no matter what I said. "I don't know where I'll be, but it'll never be far from his side. I promise."

"I worry for you both," she replied. "This year has revealed how many threats are out there, and I can't have you facing them alone."

Wacław pulled his two necklaces from beneath his tunic: Moonmark and Mothermark both. "You gifted me these to ensure no matter where I am, those who I love are close to my heart. You and Otylia will never leave me, and I'll never be gone for long. Where else am I going to get the best soups and pierogi when I'm feeling down?"

Lubena's smile returned as she wiped away her tears again and kissed him on the brow. "I love you, Wašek. There will always be a warm hearth and plenty of food whenever you return, but I would appreciate if it were for longer than this visit. You've hardly recovered from slaying one god before going off to fight another."

"I hope it's our last," he said with a glance at me. "I don't know about you, but I am tired of war among the gods."

I grinned. "When we're done, I'm sleeping for at least a year before trying to kill another one."

"A year isn't long enough," he quipped, popping back to his feet, arms extended. "Make it a decade. That's plenty of time to get used to dreaming instead of rising whenever I sleep, and maybe after Czarnobóg is dead, I'll have something other than nightmares."

"Oh, please." I circled the table to him and wrapped him in my arms. "I know you dream of me."

He tugged playfully at my ears and clothes. "Yeah, with little dragon ears and wings like a nymph. And that's not to mention the demonic veins."

His true fear of those nightmares lingered beneath his jokes, but I went along with it, elbowing him in the stomach. "I deal with *your* demonic veins. It's not like I can look like a moonlit goddess all the time."

"You always are to me," he said with a smile as wide as the moon itself.

Lubena held a hand over her heart. "You two are adorable."

"My father won't see it the same way," I replied as a pit formed in my stomach, "but we should see him anyway."

I'd Ascended to godhood, defeated a goddess, and slain the eldest god himself, but facing Dariusz never became less daunting. Despite not sharing his blood, he'd raised me with the flexibility of a board. Pride was not his first emotion when I walked through the door.

"Go and do your familial duties," Lubena said with a sorrowful glance. No mother wanted to see her child leave.

That sorrow faded as Wacław wrapped her in his arms again. "We'll be back before leaving for Nawia. I promise."

"A king's promise! I'll consider it like gold then."

Wacław's chestnut gelding, Tanek, rushed across the pasture at the sound of our footsteps on the path out. Nostalgia washed over me at that threshold. For so many years, I'd waited there for Wacław to emerge in his soul-form so we could explore late at night. Father had despised it, but those nights were freedom before Jacek tore us apart. We hadn't understood Wacław's power then. Part of me missed that innocent mystery, when we hadn't worried about demonic corruption or endless winters.

We each blew into Tanek's nostrils in greeting—a trick Mother had taught me, which made sense now as mares were one of her godly animals. Tanek's wounds from the zmora attack the night of the equinox had healed well with some help from my poultices. Wacław's sudden burst of płanetnik power had saved both him and his horse that night, and nothing had been the same since.

Something shifted in the pasture's shadows.

I summoned my silver spear and hopped the fence. Flaring my moonlight, I prepared for a demonic ambush. Instead, I found a tall, unnaturally pale man clad in a long navy coat spinning a wooden flute between his fingers.

"My my my, if it isn't Calamity herself, come to bring the end of Czarnobóg of the darkness." Kyustendil, the demigod of the northwest wind, removed his pointed hat which resembled an arrow more than anything to protect his face from the elements. He leaped over Tanek, who was too focused on tearing apart the ripe grass to notice, and waved his flute at Wacław. "And you, Naw, killed the most *preposterous* deity in the Three Realms."

Wacław crossed his arms, but a smirk tugged at his lips. "I did."

"SPLENDID!" Kyustendil flung his arms around Wacław and lifted them both into the air, twirling about like leaves caught in a whirlwind. The motion sent Wacław's hair astray, so Kyustendil fixed it up before patting him on the head. "You have done all of us a great service, and I must say, won me quite the bragging rights over my siblings."

I rolled my eyes. "You made a bet on a god's death? Why am I surprised?"

Kyustendil released Wacław, forcing him to catch himself on the winds as the demigod drifted back toward me. "Me, place a bet? Perhaps… But can you blame me? Many of my siblings were slain by that bastard Czarnobóg, and you already have a record of stabbing gods—may Rod rest in paradise. I have played my part to aid you, I might add, so it seemed best to scribe my name among the legends that will be told about you two."

"The goddess of the endings and moon, the płanetnik, and the insolent wind that showed up when it was convenient for him," I muttered. "Yes, I'm sure the legends will be kind to you."

He tapped me on the nose with his flute, then played a tune that swept around us, his wind carrying the salty smell of the northern sea. With silver hair and a face of sharp features and smooth skin, he looked venerable and boyish at the same time. I often wondered his age compared to Mother, who was already younger than her siblings—Jaryło and Marzanna—not to mention the elder gods of Rod, Swaróg, and Łada. Had centuries driven him insane, or had he always been this annoying?

Where is Narcyz when I need him to stab someone?

"As much as we appreciate the visit," Wacław said, stepping between Kyustendil and me, "do you have a reason for being here? You disappeared before the fight against Koschei, so I doubt you want to join us against Czarnobóg."

Kyustendil dropped his flute. "How little fun you two ended up being. I came to offer you insights into the intentions of Otylia's grandfather and uncle in Prawia, but if you have no interest in hearing from me, I will *gladly* return to Buyan to relax and watch the battle unfold."

I pushed Wacław aside and snatched Kyustendil by his coat. "Unfold? What do you know? We have to find Czarnobóg in Nawia, not fight him here."

"Your Aunt Marzanna's death and Weles's capture have created quite the opening," Kyustendil replied. "Perun may have promised to leave Jawia to Dziewanna, but Nawia… Well, let us say that he has sought paradise for centuries, desiring power for his lost son.

Jaryło cannot hold Jawia, but why not Marzanna's throne or Weles's?"

I released him, biting my cheek. Jaryło had betrayed us, nearly killed me. I'd forgiven his breaking of our blood oath to avoid Perun's ire, but if my grandfather wanted Nawia from Weles, my blood father would ensure there would be no peace.

"Jaryło was a broken mess when we left Prawia," I snapped. "And Perun might want Nawia, but he's done nothing to help us besides protect his own realm."

Kyustendil backed away with his arms extended at his sides. "I am but a messenger. The wise Lady Mokosz seemed to believe you and Dziewanna would wish to know, and believe it or not, you are a more grateful recipient than your mother."

"That is all she said?" I asked, my shoulders drooping. Mokosz's support had been crucial in Vastroth and Prawia, so I'd hoped she would send more than just a demigod with gossip.

He tapped his flute against his lips. "Hmm. Perhaps there was something else... What was it?"

Light flared from my hands. "Kyustendil!"

"Oh! Yes... How could I have forgotten?"

Flipping off his hat once again, Kyustendil plucked an acorn from within it and held it in my moonlight. "She believed this may be of use."

Wacław cocked his head. "An acorn? What use could that be against the god of darkness?"

"Her only instructions were to plant it 'where the false tree once stood, and its fruits shall grant your promise.' " Kyustendil plopped the acorn into my hand. "Whatever that means."

I closed my fist over the acorn. "I know exactly what it means. Go. Send my grandmother my regards, and tell her I have no intentions of letting Jaryło take anything."

"Quite as she expected." Kyustendil tugged on his jacket and fixed his hat before placing it back on his head. "Now, if you will excuse me, I have duties to attend to."

A *whoosh* of wind scattered my hair as he took flight, disappearing into the night. Wacław chuckled watching him go with a shake of his head. "What a strange god."

"*Demigod*," I corrected. The acorn weighed more heavily than it should've, so I opened my hand and held it between us. From the outside, it didn't look special at all. "Why would Mokosz send him of all people?"

Wacław took my hand, holding the acorn between us. "Imagine the gods seeing him go by. If you were Perun, would you worry that he was a threat to your plans?"

"I see the point."

"What do you think the acorn will grow? A new oak?"

I pulled him down the trail toward Dwie Rzeki. "Only one way to find out. We'll grab Father along the way, so I don't have to deal with him in his own house. He can't yell at me in front of my worshippers."

"What about Dziewanna?" he asked as we entered the woods. "Won't she want to see what her mother has sent?"

I gripped the acorn tighter. "There's no telling where she is, and if this is Mokosz's answer to Czarnobóg's threat, I'm not waiting to see what it is."

So we ran like we were children who weren't supposed to be in the woods. Our bond revealed Wacław's concern at the surprise, but Mokosz had only helped us. Unlike the other gods, she'd cared, showing how her power connected to every living person. That limited her concentrated strength, but it was foolish to doubt the Great Mother.

The drunken revelers we'd passed on our way to the river were long gone—except for the idiot face-down in the mud outside a house's threshold. I shook my head at him.

Czarnobóg threatens to end the Three Realms as we know it, but some would rather stick their heads in the dirt than face the truth.

Celebrations weren't without merit. We'd killed the goddess of winter and ended starvation, but what worried me now wasn't eternal cold. As long as Oblivion remained open, Czarnobóg could call a demonic army to corrupt all who stood in his way. He controlled the realm of the dead. How many demons could he create from all the souls who couldn't flee his influence?

I shook away that thought as we passed through the east gate. All I could do was keep moving forward, keep fighting. Mother always said that worry caused the failure you were focused on. Like a rider focused on their destination, I needed to focus on defeating Czarnobóg.

But the comforts of home dulled the blade in my heart: Wacław's gentle touch, Lubena's kindness, and the forests that held my childhood dreams. I so badly wanted rest.

Wacław pulled me to a stop just outside Father's house. His brows were raised, his hand held to my cheek. "I know you won't admit it, but there's another reason for your rush, isn't there?"

"You're right," I said, placing my hand on his, then pulling it off my cheek. "I won't admit it."

I felt his longing gaze on the back of my head as I threw open the door. Father leaned against the rectangular table at the room's center and prayed over a Forgemark amulet of Swaróg. His hair was grayer and his forehead wrinkles deeper than ever. They deepened further as he raised his gaze to me, prayers turning to mumbled curses.

"What 'calamity' have you come to bring me tonight, Daughter?"

His tone raised the hairs on my arms, and it took all my strength not to call moonlight to my hand. Not to attack, but to prove a point. I was a goddess. Dariusz had raised me at Mother's request, but that had never been a legitimate excuse for his spite.

Wacław sensed my agitation and stepped to my side, a hand on my back. "Just a Naw without a weapon," he said.

"You are plenty a calamity without a blade." Father huffed, but a smirk tugged at the edges of his mouth. "I hear the two of you have ridded us of winter. Swaróg may scorn me for cursing his granddaughter, but it is better that Marzanna is dead." He rounded the table and bowed to each of us. "Forgive me. I forget my place at times, as you must remember I have seen both of you grow through much."

I crossed my arms. "You should be happy I'm home, goddess or not. I *choose* to come see you."

"I will be long dead before you realize what I did for you, my dear Otylia, but I tire of our old distasteful spats." He gestured to a chair at the table. "Would both of you join me? These days, I am a lonely old priest who is of little use when szeptuchy are everywhere and gods walk among us."

I winced. Had we made him useless? Did no one pray with him to the other gods? It did make sense, considering how few of the gods had bothered to help us outside of protecting their own homes. Still, I pitied him. He'd been a poor Father, but I had no desire to see him in such a state.

Glancing down at Mokosz's acorn, I sighed. "As long as you have a place for Wacław too, we'll stay and talk."

Wacław's eyes widened as he spoke silently through our bond. *"But I thought you wanted to plant the acorn as soon as possible?"*

We have time, I replied. *Father needs this.*

27

Wacław

How can an acorn defeat the dark dragon?

OTYLIA'S TENSION HAD MY OWN MUSCLES WOUND INTO KNOTS so tight only a blade could free them. She curled her toes and clenched her fists as Dariusz ranted about Zurgowie infidels, "horse-obsessed" Simukie, and demons residing among the living. He didn't mention it directly, but it was clear enough that he critiqued our decisions that had brought radical change to Dwie Rzeki and what had once been the Tribe of Krowik.

Though I had my arm around Otylia the whole time, she felt more like a coiled serpent than a stunning, graceful goddess. Good. Otylia found strength in her fury as much as her glory, and there was nothing more beautiful than the deadly look in her eyes, the color of the vibrant wilds.

She tamed those wilds despite her father's arrogance. Sitting tall, she met his gaze and pursed her lips, but did not protest. Dariusz had his thoughts, but she no longer needed his approval. That didn't mean she wanted him to suffer alone.

Dariusz wore out both of our nerves, though, and we were eager to leave. After some amount of time between ten minutes and an eternity, we found our chance when he asked what we intended to do next.

"Mokosz sent us a message," Otylia said, the words tumbling from her mouth. "She said to plant this acorn where Jaryło's Heart of Jawia had been."

He furrowed his brow. "The one Wacław cut down with a Moonstone once wielded by Marzanna?"

I gave a wry smile, but Otylia interrupted me through our bond before I could contest his accusation. *"He's not worth it."*

So I just shrugged and rose. "It's probably best that we don't wait to see what gift the Great Mother has sent. Perun and Jaryło may have lied about the truth of the old oak, but I doubt Mokosz would do the same."

"Some things must be forged in iron," Dariusz said, following my lead and strapping his amulet to Swaróg onto his headband. "Others must be sown in the soil."

Otylia grinned at me before leading us through Dwie Rzeki's trails to the village center. Few were awake now, but those who were followed us. It was an odd thing. Without a clue what we were doing, they saw their goddess, king, and high priest walking with a purpose. Life in the village could be boring at times, so perhaps they hoped we'd offer some entertainment in the late night.

That thought made me chuckle. Sure, our titles were important, but they were about to watch us plant an acorn. Whether there would be any excitement after that… Well, that depended on what Mokosz had in store for us.

It wasn't long before Kuba and Ara joined us too, each of them eyeing us with the same keen interest as the villagers.

"Thought you would keep us from the fun?" Kuba asked with his arms crossed. He must've been either sleeping or about to be, because he wore a long nightshirt, and his hair pointed every which way.

Otylia rolled her eyes as she strode toward the center of the clearing, standing over the place Jaryło's Oak had once been. "Do you even know why we're here?"

Kuba shrugged. "Dunno. Ara woke me up and said it's important."

"Hey!" Ara hissed, jabbing him in the side. "Zakir was asleep, so I had to bring *someone* else. Besides, it's hard to sleep when you were a demon a few hours ago."

"Believe me, I understand," I said.

The crowd grew with each passing second, so I nudged Otylia to hurry up. Dealing with the gods' magic was difficult enough without prying eyes. I hated to admit Dariusz was right, but Czarnobóg had shown himself to be cunning. He no doubt had spies among us.

Otylia missed the point.

"This acorn is a gift from Mokosz!" she declared with light pouring from her and illuminating the entire crowd. The acorn itself glowed an ethereal silver, drawing exclamations from the crowd. "The goddess Dziewanna, King Wacław, and I will descend into Nawia to face Czarnobóg and end his corrupting darkness. But we are not alone. The Great Mother is within each one of us—each of you—and her eternal gifts grant us strength."

She knelt and dug away the dirt before placing the acorn in the hole. Her whispers to Mokosz split the silence, and even the winds stood still as she covered the acorn.

When she stood, she took my hand and squeezed. I didn't need our bonded emotions to know her worries when every bone in my hand screamed for help. Surely, whatever Mokosz had planned would happen quickly to relieve Otylia, but each rapid beat of our hearts marked another moment where nothing happened.

So we waited.

And waited.

And waited.

Murmurs among the crowd turned to grumbles, then the sound of retreating footsteps. Otylia's frustration only grew, her impatience washing away my only concerns.

"Why isn't it working?" she asked through our bond.

Maybe it needs more time?

"Or I'm doing something wrong." She snapped her gaze to Dariusz and spoke aloud. "Father, do you have any ideas?"

It pained her, but I was proud of her willingness to ask for help, even if it was rare. Most deities we'd met were stubborn and arrogant. Sure, she could be stubborn herself, but she'd struggled to get to where she was. She knew what it was to fight alone and with others.

"It sounds simplistic," Dariusz replied, scratching the gray-black hairs upon his chin, "but any tree requires soil, water, and sunlight. We lack light beyond your moonlight, but perhaps water would be enough. Mokosz is the goddess of the wet earth after all."

Otylia tilted back her head with a silent curse on her lips. "Gods, how did I miss that?"

"Fatigue, youthfulness, and haste," Dariusz said. "That is why you trust in others and the thoughts given to us by the gods."

Scanning the crowd, Otylia waved to Ara, who came running to us. "Fetch water," Otylia told her. "I'd do it myself, but standing here for so long has me looking weak already."

Ara smirked and leaned in to whisper, "Can I make Kuba come with me?"

"Tell him it's crucial that he doesn't let a drop spill," I said, holding in a laugh. "I'm not sure he's physically capable of doing it."

She swept aside her cloak as she bowed, then ran off to grab Kuba. He gave me a confused glance, but followed, dragging his feet. After the chaos of recent days, we all needed a reason to laugh, and Kuba was the most likely to laugh at himself once he realized what we'd done.

It wasn't long before Ara returned with a half-full bucket. Her grin said our trick had worked, and sure enough, Kuba appeared a minute later, taking every step with incredible care. Sweat coated his brow, which furrowed in deep focus.

Should I topple it with the winds? I asked Otylia silently.

She glanced at me, a smile creeping through. *"You've had your fun. This is serious."*

Of course, she was right, but I took incredible joy watching Kuba approach. Ara stared at him, then trickled a stream out of her bucket. "Oops."

His jaw dropped. "You rusałka!"

"Thank you for the water," Otylia said before the two could debate, taking Kuba's bucket and dumping it over the buried acorn. She prayed again to Mokosz as she did the same with Ara's bucket.

"What now?" Kuba asked when she was finished.

"Now, we wai—"

The ground rumbled, sending us stumbling back. Dark shapes surged from the earth and hovered overhead. My vision blurred for a moment, but when I shook my head and staggered to my feet, the laugh I'd been holding in slipped out.

"That's one eager acorn!"

In Otylia's moonlight, the giant oak's branches stretched ten strides each direction, and its trunk was thicker than trees over a century old. More brilliant than its size, though, were the golden apples dangling over us. Each shimmered brighter than our tribe's greatest jewels. The last I'd seen one, Perun had thrown it at Czarnobóg's hide, showering him in godly lightning.

I reached for one on my tip-toes. "Perun sent a gift?"

"No," Otylia said with a devious grin, flying up to snatch it from me. "Mokosz stole it."

Ara's bucket slipped from her fingers. "And these can help you beat Czarnobóg?"

"Mokosz believes they will, so I do too," Otylia said as she ran her thumb over its golden surface. Static sparked across her hand, forcing her to drop it. "They definitely pack a punch."

I circled the tree and counted twelve apples. A reference to the twelve Moonstones, or luck? After so many long days, my mind was too tired to wonder, so I took up the winds to collect them from the higher branches. They sparked in my hand like they had with Otylia, but my płanetnik abilities protected me from any damage. Czarnobóg wouldn't be so lucky.

"Mokosz stole from the king of the gods for us," I said as I descended with a basket of apples and presented it to Otylia. "It seems I have three queens to honor now."

Otylia huffed, but took the basket. "I'm not technically your queen yet."

I took her cheek in my hand. "Considering we could die in the coming days, there's not much time for a royal wedding."

"I'll have plenty of time to keep you for myself," she replied. "Until then, we have a basket of apples to kill a żmij more powerful than any we've faced before."

"Quite the romantic adventure." I eyed those who'd remained in the crowd. "You should speak to your worshippers. They've waited long enough after all."

She plucked a single apple from the basket and stuck it into my hand that had been on her cheek. "You're their king. This is an invasion into another realm, and you're much better at giving people hope."

"That isn't true."

Her brows raised as she stepped back, then bowed. "Do it anyway, my liege."

My skin itched with everyone's eyes on me. These people expected me to lead, not just fight. They needed Otylia as their goddess, but they also needed their king to show that mortals didn't have to fear what lay ahead. So I raised the apple.

"The Great Mother gifts us the weapons of Perun!"

My voice echoed across the village, the winds breaking their silence as they swept around us. I imagined Kyustendil's glee among them. Always there, but only helping directly when convenient.

The crowd cheered at the display as I drifted up on the winds. *Let them believe I'm confident we'll win.* Their excitement gave me strength, reminded me why we fought. This was about more than just those I loved. If we failed, all who remained in the Kingdom of the Wild Moon were at risk, and each of them was my responsibility to protect.

And I would do exactly that.

28

Otylia

Will Mokosz's gift be enough?

I GRIPPED ONE OF MOKOSZ'S GOLDEN APPLES, its static sparking over my fingers. Mother's old alder tree—her Heart of Jawia—rose behind me with its bark pressed against my back. It bore blackened scars from Marzanna's curse, but thrived now despite what it had suffered.

This place had been the focus of my work as a szeptucha for years. Purifying the wild swamps and forests around Dziewanna's Heart of demons, diseases, and other threats had taken focus and time. It had allowed me to pour myself into my work. Only brewing Mother's potion recipes for the ill had pulled me from these trees. Had things been better that way, without so many people relying on me?

"My mother rarely acts so boldly," Mother's biting voice said from ahead. She stepped easily through the underbrush to avoid the muck without taking her gaze off me.

In hunter trousers and an earth-brown shirt with green embroidery trimming it like vines creeping up a tree, she looked as one with the forest. Sunlight split through the branches to shimmer across her antlers and ivy eyes.

I'd not seen her since our meeting in the longhouse, and that day had made all the difference. Whatever she'd done during her time alone in the wilds had rejuvenated her after weeks trapped in Marzanna's grip.

"They say the apple doesn't fall far from the tree," I quipped, tossing the apple to her. It sparked as she caught it with some surprise . "You rebelled against Perun, so maybe that came from her?"

Mother smirked and slid down next to me. She tilted her head back to allow her wavy willow hair to drape over the bear pelt across her shoulders. "Your grandmother is anything but a rebel. Her choosing to aid us in Prawia proved how far Perun has strayed. To steal an acorn from his favorite oak, though, is unheard of. Only a single tree in Prawia bears such fruit. He shall be furious that his golden apples now grow in Jawia."

I laughed, running my fingers through the soft earth beside me. Unlike her, I wore one of my old szeptucha dresses that would be thoroughly muddied, but I didn't care. There were few places I could be alone with my thoughts anymore. The only difference now was that Dziewanna was beside me instead of just in my mind.

"He hasn't struck us down yet," I said, "so either he's weak or a coward."

"Or strategic."

I wrinkled my brow. "You think he'll tolerate this if we win?"

Mother sighed and leaned her head into mine. She smelled of spring rain that woke the plants from their slumbers. "Your grandfather wants us to slay the foe *his* father locked away millennia ago. Swaróg failed to eliminate Czarnobóg forever. If we do so, that would make Perun's life easier and expose Weles's weakness." She winced at the mention of her husband and my blood father's name.

"Kyustendil said Perun wants Jaryło to rule Nawia."

"Ah, so even Strzybóg's grandson knows about Perun's plans." She chuckled. "If one person knows a truth in Prawia, it is a secret. If two know, it is blackmail. If three know, it is but a night before all of Prawia learns of it, *especially* once the winds hear."

My chest tightened. "But it doesn't matter who knows. We can't stop him if he claims it for Jaryło. Weles is weak, and…"

I cut myself off before I insulted Weles so directly. Mother had been cagey about the details of their relationship, but it was obvious she felt *some* pain at his capture.

"And you don't want him to rule anyway," she replied with a knowing smile. "Don't act surprised, my dear child. I may not have been there in your teenage years, but I did rear you for your first twelve. Weles is exactly the kind of being you despise, and he has done plenty to strain my own relationship with him as well. He told you how he turned himself into a basil flower to calm my fury, yes?"

I nodded.

"That figures." She let out a long breath through her teeth. "His stories always make it appear that he is a charismatic and caring man. But he is little better than Perun. It was not a lie that he turned himself into a basil flower to keep me from tearing Nawia asunder to break free from him. What his story fails to mention, however, is that he only acted as such when I threatened to leave—which was often enough."

Her fingers intertwined with mine, gripping like she'd fall into the depths if she let go. "My marriage was destined to be loveless from its inception, but we *were* allies. It was my father who punished me by forcing our marriage, so I was determined to elevate Weles to challenge him."

"Elevating you with him," I said, imagining her fighting by Weles's side. Had he always been such a decrepit old man? "Like how Czarnobóg used Marzanna to weaken the gods, then take her place."

Her alder tree shuddered. Leaves scattered over us as she frowned, her grip tightening further. "Do not compare me to that beast! I would not have killed Weles. For all his ills, he did wish the best for me, even if he could not love me. His actions were patronizing, so I often chose my own paths, but my own actions were to aid us both. The more powerful he became, the more powerful I was as his queen. You have seen how I gathered allies among his realm and protected the mortal man I had loved during his life."

I wrinkled my nose. Imagining her being *with* anyone made my skin crawl. "Ivan was a bear most of the time, but he was brave. We wouldn't have escaped the island where I Ascended if it weren't for him."

She burst out laughing, then wrapped her arms around me. I fought back, but she tickled my sides until I laughed too. "It is all right to be uncomfortable talking about your mother's lover. I often wish that Ivan were your father instead of Weles, but I was not ready for a child yet. It sounds ridiculous; I know. Most women are forced to bear children far before they are ready, and I had centuries to prepare." Warmth flowed from my core as she rested her chin on my shoulder, then kissed me on the cheek. "I regret how I left you, how I did not allow you to live your childhood as a goddess."

"Regret means you've lived," I whispered with a hand over my heart. "I have more regrets from the last few moons than the rest of my life combined, but I'd do all of it again if I had the choice to go back to my old life." My nose burned, and tears stung my eyes. "I tell myself I let the mortals and purified demons of our kingdom down. They've been through endless winter, war, and days where Dadźbóg didn't bring the sun, all because I couldn't defeat Marzanna fast enough. Then I see how they look at me. It's like my moonlight glows in their eyes, and I realize I must do this. Not because of destiny. But because I chose this."

She stroked my hair. "You are not that spiteful child anymore. Despite the habits you learned from me, you found a lover, friends who would give everything for you, and a community. Perhaps it was best, then, that you spent so long as a mortal. Gods often lack empathy for those who see decades when we see millennia. Do not lose that care you hold for them."

I leaned into her, closing my eyes until her embrace was the world for a few heartbeats. Comfort was so alien these days. It took focus to let myself accept it.

"What comes after?" I mused, imagining the realms without Marzanna and Czarnobóg's threats. End offered visions, but even they were indistinct, unsure with varying paths.

"Assuming we slay the dark żmij," Mother replied, "then that will be up to you. Jawia is mine to oversee and nurture, but I have rejected the shards of Alatyr. Bring the twelve Moonstones back to Garafena on Buyan and seal away Oblivion for good. What you choose to do with the united Alatyr then is up to you."

I tugged at Sierpień and Listopad, each hanging as Moonmark temple rings from my headband. "I've channeled the power of one Moonstone during its moon, but I can't even imagine all of them combined. Swaróg created most of the gods with Alatyr... What could I fix with it?"

"Do not assume all the realms' power in your hands will allow you to better things." Mother released me and held out her hand to catch a drifting leaf. "When a single being, no matter how well-intentioned, holds infinite power, even the slightest breath can topple mountains."

"But—"

"No, my Otylka. I know the cost of power better than most. End showed you what I became in my worst hours, when I allowed that power to guide me to destruction in the pursuit of bettering Jawia. I will not allow the same to happen to you."

Sighing, I relented and stood, taking in the wilds—caught between natural autumn and sudden spring. Amber and fiery leaves barely had time to fall before bright green ones replaced them. Marzanna had kept her promise for now. We would have a year free of her winter.

"What would you have me do, then?" I asked. "Garafena was manipulated before, so I don't trust leaving all the Moonstones with that serpent."

"Split them, then," she replied, "as Marzanna and Jaryło did before. That way, no matter what you decide, others must agree."

"But you have already refused to hold one. Besides you, the only immortals I trust are Mokosz and Wacław. No..." I shook my head and opened my mind to End's prodding within me. "We'll divide the Moonstones between us and hide them throughout the Three Realms. No one will know where all the shards are, and no one will hold them."

Her brow raised. "And if a shard is discovered? If the gods seek them for centuries and war for them once found?"

"We are all immortals, so we will watch our hiding places from a distance. Either we prevent them from ever being found, or we ensure they never stray far."

"It is dangerous," she said, but a proud grin crossed her face. "Power is always dangerous, though, and your proposal has its merits. As long as I need not hold a Moonstone myself, I will help."

A knot released between my shoulders. Her resistance to the Moonstones had left me alone to deal with them, and I'd spent enough of my life working alone.

"Thank you, Mother." I hugged her, holding on tight to this last moment of comfort before we prepared to face Czarnobóg in Nawia. "I can't do this without you."

She held the back of my head as she huffed. "That's the thing: You can do anything. You are the end, and you are my beginning. Life became about more than just me when you were born, and I mean it when I say you will far surpass me."

"I'll always be that szeptucha tending to your alder tree," I replied into her chest.

Her tears dripped onto my head. "You tended to this alder as my Heart of Jawia, but my true heart has always been you. I am queen of Jawia now. As you tended to this tree, I must now tend to every oak, maple, and willow, every bush and vine and creature. Through it all, you will remain my reminder of why I push onward."

"We'll beat him, right?" I asked. "We can do this?"

She took a long breath as she stepped back and held my hands. Though she forced a smile, her eyes remained wide. "We will face Czarnobóg with all our fury—for ourselves, those we love, and all those who rely on us. That must be enough."

Part 3
Into the Dark

29

Otylia

We go from my home to the place that could've been my home. How has Czarnobóg twisted paradise to his will?

THOUSANDS GATHERED IN THE VILLAGE CENTER to send Mother, Wacław, and me on our way. Many cheered for us as Wacław and I raised our held hands, but others held out children or pled for us to cure their diseases. Did they see this as their last chance before we died?

I pushed away that fear and showered them with moonlight as appeasement. My power couldn't cure disease or bless children as I was aware, but there was power in belief. Hope had gotten us this far, and my silver-embroidered dress was meant to remind them I was no longer just a szeptucha.

We couldn't depart to Nawia without heading to the Wyzra River, where Marzanna had appeared to Wacław in the days after the equinox and commanded him to kill Jaryło. The alternative was flying to the evening gate that Wacław had taken into Nawia during my Ascension. But Czarnobóg would guard the most obvious path into the realm he now controlled. Marzanna's ice castle lay on the border of the Way of Souls and Nawia. In theory, passing into Nawia would be simple.

That meant it wouldn't be.

Parading through Dwie Rzeki should've been a burst of confidence that our people were behind us, but even now, crowds made my shoulders tighten. Mother was the same way, and Wacław grew extra quiet at the cacophony of noise. It wasn't until we were beyond the gate that we could finally relax. All that lay between us and Marzanna's portal was Mother's wilds. *That* was home to me.

No one said a word. The winds and trees spoke for us, bristling with each gust as autumn and spring colors mixed. Marzanna had suffocated the world, and Mother's sudden spring left nature confused. I would've laughed if that fragile life weren't threatened by a three-headed, shapeshifting żmij who'd nearly destroyed the world thousands of years before.

Wacław's hand in mine brought my thoughts back to the Frostmark that had once scarred his palm. I'd been furious when he revealed his surrender to Marzanna's temptations, but I understood a god's power now. It was far more than a boy deep in the woods could resist.

That Frostmark and his demonic soul had almost taken him from me. It was proof of the corruption that came with obsessive revenge, and I shuddered wondering who Mother had used in her own revolution against Perun.

Centuries twisted events into legends. What would they say of our fight when all who experienced it were long dead?

For that, we needed all our weapons to survive first. We carried twelve of Perun's golden apples, Mother's godly hunting bow, and eight Moonstones. Wacław held Grudzień and Kwiecień as Moonblades while I kept the rest as amulets that hung from my headband as my Moonmark, Mother's Bowmark, and Mokosz's Mothermark. Sierpień and Listopad hung over my temples and could form the two ends of my silver spear when the time came. Until then, the amulets rattled around my head. The noise was distracting, but they reminded me that I carried the strength of my mother and grandmother along with my own.

There was some irony in Wacław wielding a Moonblade from both Jaryło's and Marzanna's moons. He held a demonic soul, but he'd shown himself worthy of a god's blade. Kwiecień had answered his call to save Lubena from Bidaês. Whether that was because of the sliver of my soul that I'd accidentally traded for a sliver of his mortal one all those moons ago, I still didn't know.

But becoming a goddess didn't mean having all the answers. It just gave me the chance to pursue the mysteries.

Water lapped over the Wyzra's muddy shore and trickled around the rocks, which formed a path toward the river's center. Birds sang overhead as a fawn bolted from the far shore at the sight of us. Mother laughed and crouched at the riverside, fingers extended.

"Do not fear me."

Her face shone like the sun as the deer stopped and turned back toward her. Head cocked, it considered whether she was friend or foe, then carefully hopped across the rocks. Grace wasn't its strength, but it arrived anyway. Mother offered it her hand.

"You are right to fear a human with a bow," she whispered sweetly. "But I am not a human. Perhaps being the goddess of the hunt is worse for you. Today, though, I just wish to be your friend."

She raised her hand to her lips and blew. When she offered it to the doe again, ripe berries filled her palm, and the doe ate eagerly.

"We fight for more than just your people," Mother said with her voice carrying through the shimmer of the leaves. "All life relies on us."

A tawny owl's *huhuhuhooo* answered.

Wacław tensed, a hand gripping Grudzień's hilt at his back. He eyed the branches, and static snapped around us as his eyes pulsed with electricity.

I summoned my spear and scanned the forest with him. Nothing seemed off. "What's wrong?"

"That same owl call announced Marzanna's arrival last time." His eyes sharpened as his words turned to rolling fog between us. The owl repeated its call and took flight, its flight silent and its wide eyes glaring like daggers from above. "I get chills whenever I hear one now."

"It is not paranoia," Mother replied, shooing away the doe. "Marzanna's power is diminished as she clings to the remnant of life you left for her, but her presence lingers here—the portal she promised."

End nudged at my mind. I resisted, for now. "This feels wrong. How do we know she's sending us back to her palace? Or even if she is, she could have more Nawie waiting for us."

She studied me, her tone sharp. "Your force calls to you?" I nodded. "Then answer! Do not fear what it has to say. What lies ahead is pure darkness, no matter what path we choose. Only you can offer light."

I bit my cheek, but surrendered the point. End's prodding grew by the moment, so I closed my eyes and let its visions take me.

A feverous chill ran up my arms before striking down my spine. Piercing, it stabbed through the skin and deep into my core. All was frost, all was pain so cold it burned.

All was darkness.

Even the deepest night offered dim moonlight or the twinkle of the stars in the sky—each a living soul guiding us on our ways. Neither offered their relief here. I couldn't even see the tip of my nose, and my stomach churned as I stepped forward and slipped on the uneven ground.

The earth shifted with me, gravity pulling me aside instead of forward. I trudged onward, but my feet slid as the ground shifted further still. My hands found ridges of hard stone just as it turned too steep to stand. *Something* crawled over them. No, hundreds of somethings. They chittered like the giant scorpions of Vastroth and scattered over my arms.

I reached out to them with my power. End connected me to creatures of decay, but these were unbidden, advancing despite my commands. Insects had never scared me before, but losing sight had my heart racing.

The Threads of Life burst into an array. I hadn't called them, but End's will flowed through me, illuminating my skin in silver moonlight.

A sea of beetles, wasps, ants, and spiders sprawled over me. None bit or stung me, but the dark voids of their eyes created a terrifying reflection of my moonlight. Those eyes twisted and merged, the Threads for each scurrying creature turning to bands of gray.

A familiar face formed among them, standing horizontally beside me as if gravity didn't affect him. Death. His eyes were empty voids, his maw filled with scorpion tails for teeth and his fingers buzzing with wasp venom dripping from their ends. Beetles joined along his front to form carapace armor, and snakes carrying daggers in their mouths slithered into wavy yet jagged hair.

Death stared at me with those empty eye holes. Head cocked, he resembled an unwashed teenage boy who'd wrestled for too long in the mud more than the embodiment of the most fearsome force.

"What do you want?" I spat, my fingers beginning to bleed as the rock face tore into them.

A ledge mocked me from only a few feet above, but my shoulders strained just hanging from the shallow holds. Despite my moonlight pushing away the darkness, End apparently couldn't grant me flight here.

"You impress me, Nemiza."

Death spoke with a dozen forked tongues, his words echoed by thousands of tiny mouths as his servants covered my body. *Nemiza* hung in the air. Like the venom that brought victims to him, it pulsed through my veins with each rapid *thump* of my heart. I had never been Otylia to him. Just Nemiza… Just Calamity.

"I don't care what you think," I replied, but my words were unconvincing. Sweat clung to my brow along with the spiders' expanding web, pulling tighter and tighter.

He smiled with a hand over his nonexistent heart. "You wound me. For one who has served me so well, it is a surprise you don't wish to hear my guidance."

"I do *not* serve you! We made a trade, nothing more."

"Yes…" His tongues flicked over his scorpion teeth, as if tasting blood. "The Naw's life for a single promise; a promise which you upheld. Rod fed me well, and much blood has spilt among the living, dead, and godly alike because of your actions. We are so very close, yet one stands in our way."

I yelled, pulling myself up with a burst of *żityje*. My boots and hands scrambled across the otherwise smooth cliff face, but the leap was enough for me to grab hold of the ledge. Arms aching, I clambered over it and glared down at Death.

The cold silver shaft of my spear met my palm. Listopad's bronze tip and Sierpień's crescent blade shone from each end. They were gods' weapons, but could they slay Death himself?

"There is no *we*," I insisted. "I did what I did to save Wacław and my friends."

"Loyalty is admirable," Death replied, striding up the cliff face without issue. His creatures relented, and I took a long, shaky breath with them off me. Phantom creeping remained. "I kept my promises, as you have kept yours. Others have not done so."

He thrust out his hand away from the cliff. The creatures scattered over the stone, which turned to flaky, uneven terrain before reaching the end of what seemed like an island in my moonlight. There, they formed another figure dressed in pure white, covered by raven black hair. Exotic, blue-winged bugs formed her eyes.

A shiver down my spine. "Marzanna was the embodiment of your force," I said. "Like End is to me."

"Death has many forms," he replied, stepping closer. "I am the terror that haunts the warriors, the mothers, and the young. I am the comfort that frees the suffering, the weary, and the hopeless. I am the vessel that brings mortality to paradise."

The creatures forming his head dropped away, dissolving into thousands of colorful wisps. They spun together until they formed strands of white, gray, and black which wove into three separate heads of mist—one for each shade. His body turned deep gray with heavy robes covering up to the base of his neck.

The black head stared back at me from his right with eyes like obsidian, its pupils as deep as blood. "I am the end," he said, not an ounce of color upon his lips.

"I am the new beginning," the white one followed from his left. Blood streaked across its marble-etched cheeks, lips of gold speaking his words.

Death advanced further, the center head's eyes covered by a simple gray rag that matched its skin. It had no hair, but curling horns like a goat arced from each of its temples. Thin cracks across its brow filled with an array of colors to split the empty gray. "I am the eternal cycle. All which has been. All that will be."

"There must be darkness," the white face said. "There must be finality."

"There must be light," said the black. "There must be rebirth."

"And the cycle must continue," the gray one finished.

My heart dropped into my stomach. I staggered back, catching my ankle in a hole, and my spear clattered to the ground as I fell. But I didn't reach for it, focusing instead on the entity before me. Not just Death. Not just Marzanna's force.

"End?" I gasped. "No… You're not my force. I don't serve Death!"

He reached out for me, his misty hand taking on the same gray skin sliced with colors. When he replied, the faces spoke together. "Mortals, deities, and spirits alike have called me many names, but my true one is Trygław. I see what has been and what will be. The sins required to reach those ends, however, are not mine to judge."

Heat rushed to my cheeks. All Death had done to me… all he'd made me do. It had been End all along. "What do you want with me? Why didn't you tell me who you were?"

"Would you have listened to my guidance if I had?" Trygław replied.

"No." I glanced at his hand, then stood by myself. My spear lay too far to grab immediately, but close enough if I needed to fight. "You can see the future, so you obviously wanted me to act in a certain way. Why?"

He pointed toward the disgusting figure of Marzanna. "Like you, she was one who bore an element of my power. She abused it, thwarted the cycle in hopes of clinging to eternal reign. The death she wrought was corrupted and out of my grasp. I needed more influence to grasp the Threads of the future that have become so tangled, so I took Rod through you."

"You lied to me!" I surged forward, pushing him away. "You used me to kill the eldest god."

His heads dropped, and his shoulders fell with them. "I gave Wacław mercy when he rested at my threshold. My actions pursue the necessity of the cycle, not my own will. I am not Destiny. I do not weave the future, but seek to shape it for the betterment of the Three Realms. For that, I must feed. This, you understand."

"I do."

"Then know Rod gave himself willingly. As a god cannot gain *żityje* from an unwilling source—unless they are corrupted as Marzanna was—I cannot feed unless it is part of my realm." He straightened his posture again. "Rod's death, and now Marzanna's, have opened the way forward, but I did not foresee Czarnobóg betraying her. He has so thoroughly corrupted the lands of the dead that I suffocate by the moment. I cannot offer the dead new lives if I lack the sustenance I gain from the dying."

I crossed my arms, but grinned. "So Death wants us to win. I didn't see that coming."

The black head chuckled. "As I said, Death is just a portion of my essence."

"Fine, then. *Trygław*, what can you do to help? Why call me here and tell me this?"

His robes fluttered about him as he rose into the darkness. "It is better that I show you. Czarnobóg's power permeates all of Nawia now, but we reside on its edge. Deeper, no light can pierce his veil."

I followed him, the moon suddenly able to pull me again. Could Trygław grant and eliminate my power at will? My nose wrinkled at that thought. Szeptuchy channeled their god's power, never fully having their own will behind their magic. Rod's explanation of my force had been vague at best, but I'd hoped for more independence than *this*. I didn't care that Death was only one fragment of Trygław. Death himself holding me in the palm of his hand was enough to make me feel like a stranger in my own body.

"How do we fight someone we can't see?" I asked as the air thickened. Choking, it smothered my light and filled my throat with humid vapors that gave me the sensation of rain inside my stomach. I hated it.

Trygław stopped at the edge of my waning light. Shadow cast over his white head as it spoke. "You are gifted with sight beyond your eyes. Seek the Threads that bind souls and the Essences that reveal their truths."

"Do you have a soul?"

A wry smile crept across each of his faces. "I have Essence like all beings. Souls are for the living."

I gestured at his body. "So what are you, then? Dead? A spirit?"

"Words do not exist in your tongue to name what I am, and it is better that way. It is the gods who rule the Three Realms." He paused, considering his words carefully and lowering his voice to a whisper through only his gray head. "Those like me should not intervene so directly, except in the most extreme cases."

"Like the end of the Three Realms," I suggested.

His smiles turned to sneers. "Indeed. Come, Otylia. My time here wanes, and I have seen what must come if my haste fails."

I called to the Threads and wisps as he disappeared into the darkness. The three wisps—or Essences, as he'd called them—guided me in silence. More of the strange cliff faces skimmed my shoulders or knees occasionally, but I couldn't tell if we were passing through a narrow area or if Trygław was testing me.

Gravity shifts countered my flight at random, throwing me into the cliffs more than once. I let *żitÿje* heal the bruises and kept my focus on Trygław ahead. He moved in strange arcing patterns. Could he see through the darkness? The cliffs had no wisps, so how else could he ensure we kept going the right direction? How would I when he was gone?

"Your obsession with beings will be your undoing in this place," Trygław said, slowing. Disappointment slipped into his tone. It echoed Father's criticisms in my head. "You have wielded my force to see your enemies' actions before they happen, and you must do the same now. Connect to the elements which compose the floating islands around us. They have no soul, no direct will or Essence, but they have endings nonetheless."

I closed my eyes—not that I could really tell the difference—and took a long breath. A natural warmth came when I reached out for souls' wisps, but here, there was only the thick, unending darkness broken by walls of stone. Where were the dead? Where were the nymphs who'd served Weles?

"You cannot find the cliffs when you think only of the dead," Trygław chided.

Can you read my mind?

He didn't reply, but that didn't prove anything. So, I turned my attention back to the cliffs and their motions. Nawia was the realm of the dead, yes, but it was also the realm of chaos, of change. Weles had allowed some of that shift in Nawia's landscape while ensuring his power held. Now…

Silver mists formed ahead. Like ash drifting through the forest during the Battle of Kynnytsia, but no flames seared my skin now. All was remarkably still, the flakes of silver not finding purchase. Until they did.

They burst to the right as one, forming a wall that approached at a sprinter's pace. Its ledge wasn't far above, so I shot upward just fast enough for my heel to clip it. Stones scattered across the ledge. Odd, as the others before had been smooth and solid, but the silver flakes revealed grooves and winding patterns—like roots.

My eyes widened as the silver streamed up to outline the boughs of a grandmother willow, its arching branches nearly as wide as our longhouse. Except when the silver reached the far half, they dropped suddenly.

I ran my fingers along the familiar grooves of the willow bark before turning to that far side. Solid wood gave way to oozing fungus, connected to me as a form of decay. I sensed it pulsing with hunger as it fed on the willow's dying strength. It yearned to expand, to thrive.

I'd sensed similar among ants and other fungi before. But this was different. Visceral, ravenous, my stomach curled upon itself as an endless pit burrowed within me. I didn't need food. I needed blood and the pure *żityje* within, but some part of me knew it would never fill the hole. That deep ache would remain.

A hand fell on my shoulder.

Teeth bared, I spun about, ready to dig my canines into the attacker's arm. But wisps slipped around me—black, white, gray. They controlled my flight and held me still as the silver flakes outlined a figure with three heads, his brows furrowed.

"Much in this place is not as you will have remembered." Trygław's voice echoed through the islands, his wisps scattering with the sound before returning to their master. "Nawia changes often, but Czarnobóg has sent the realm into a frenzy that feeds upon itself. *Żityje* is never destroyed. For a lack of a better expression in your tongue, it merely burns hotter and hotter until it combusts."

I pulled my free hand back to my heart. Racing as fast as my head, it scrambled my thoughts. That hunger…

"Nawia will destroy itself?" I asked, flexing my hand to get the oozing fungus off it. None remained. Just the phantom starvation that had driven me mad in an instant.

The three heads hummed together. Trygław released my arm, and his silver-outlined form drifted away with the sound. "Our destination is near."

He surged further into the darkness. Thicker and thicker, it coated my skin and made every breath more difficult. The silver flakes kept me from hitting further islands as Trygław flew faster, and the islands were closer together now, forcing me to change directions rapidly.

Trygław had no trouble, and he slipped ahead before stopping atop a massive island—the only one that didn't shift through the darkness. Wind battered me as I reached its edge. I raised my arms to protect me, calling a light shield, but a force squeezed upon it until it shattered.

"What is this?" I shouted as the winds threw me back into another cliff. My *żityje* waned against the pressure crushing my bones.

Trygław's voices carried through the gales. Ethereal, eternal. "This is the core of Czarnobóg's power. Fueled by the souls of the gods, mortals, and spirits he has drained, he is tearing apart Nawia from this very place. The veil between here and Oblivion will dissolve, and the dead realm will be pulled into the depths. Jawia will follow. Then Prawia."

I cried out, my ribs cracking. "How do I stop it?"

"Defeat the dark żmij. Repair the veil between the realms and the roots binding Nawia to the World Tree." Light burst forth from Trygław, blinding me, but I lacked the strength to shut my eyes. "Bring Czarnobóg to this core, this place of pure darkness, and unleash your light. In his moment of weakness, you must sever his soul and banish him to Oblivion."

"He'll escape again!"

"Then return to Buyan and reunite Alatyr." His light faded along with his voice. "Complete the cycle, and do not become distracted by attachments. Not to anyone."

30

Wacław

Why did it have to be here?

THE HAIRS ON MY NECK ROSE just standing at the place Marzanna had met me moons before. Her Frostmark's phantom pain still haunted my hand, and a stinging rang across my cheek at the memory of her claws threatening to cut me down. Oh, how foolish I'd been to fall into her trap.

Here we were, not a year later, and the same goddess who'd created this mess was our way back into Nawia. That irony grew thicker by the moment as Dziewanna waited for Otylia to awaken from her visions.

Perhaps I should've gotten used to her eyes shifting to pure white. Sometimes she collapsed into my arms—which at least gave me something to do—but now, she stood as rigid as a log. I glanced at her expressionless face, that crescent scar on her cheek glowing like the moon itself.

Gods, she was beautiful, but I shuddered seeing her like that. Her confusion rushing through our bond didn't help matters. What was End showing her?

Dziewanna's constant gaze only made me sweat more. She was a huntress, and as her daughter's lover, I couldn't help but feel like prey when we were alone.

"Any guess what End is showing her?" I asked to break the silence.

She trudged through the shallows, thoroughly drenching her deep green dress, but flames flickered at its hems. By the time she neared me, she was bone dry. Those same fires burned in her eyes.

"I unnerve you, Wacław," she mused, forehead wrinkled. "It is difficult to imagine how you must feel in your situation. An outcast who was crowned king. A young man whose childhood love Ascended to godhood. A Naw forced to wait alongside that lover's mother." I chuckled as she finally turned away with a wry smile. "Know that though I am Otylia's mother and have lived centuries, you need not fear me. You have learned that I once loved a mortal, so I do not disapprove of my daughter's choice. Despite losing half your souls, from what I can tell, you have lost none of your heart. I fear I ripped out much of Otylia's many years ago."

I raised a hand to the Moonmark amulet hanging at my collar, tracing its edges that joined with my Eclipsemark. "We've all lost bits of ourselves and replaced them with what we could along the way. Otylia has endured more than most, but ever since we found you, she's seemed a bit like her old self again. Neither of us are children anymore. She has some of her light back, though—and not just her moonlight."

Dziewanna snatched my hand with both of hers and squeezed. Her smile vanished, replaced by an intensity that seared straight through my core.

"You bear a fragment of her soul in yours," she insisted. "Such an act may have been an accident, but it is no small feat, Wacław. As I have seen, you have proven yourself worthy of that fragment. Your lives will be long, however. Each year, each moon, each breath, you must strive to earn it again."

I squeezed back, but hardly matched her strength. "I will. I swear it."

"A promise from a man." She released me, smiling once again. "Yours is one of the few that I have believed—demonic soul or not."

The Thread binding me to Otylia snapped tight. I rushed to her, catching her in my arms as she stumbled back, shaking.

"What happened?" I asked with a hand to her cheek. Her skin burned, and sweat glistened on her forehead. "What did End show you?"

"End isn't End," she huffed.

I raised my brows. "I don't understand."

"I have often wondered about your force," Dziewanna said. "Did you finally find the answers you sought?"

Otylia gritted her teeth and stepped away from me, fists clenched at her sides. "I wish I hadn't. But End isn't important now. I know how to stop Czarnobóg."

My heart strained. Why was she hiding the truth from us? If it were something she didn't want Dziewanna to hear, she'd have told me through our bond, but she refused to even meet my gaze. Instead, she circled toward the river.

"Where's this portal Marzanna promised?"

Searing pain arced across my palm. I winced, but held it out, cursing at the Frostmark pulsing upon it. "I swear, if you marked me again, Marzanna, I'll send you to Oblivion."

Thehe hot white light surged from my hand. Shooting over the rocks crossing the river, it formed a shimmering doorway of ice just a foot above the Wyzra's flow. No mark remained on my palm, but pain lingered. A hundred memories reminded me of the suffering I'd caused through that mark. Otylia and my joined marks on my arm had freed me from Marzanna's corruption; though, it hadn't ridded me of the nightmares.

Otylia nodded sharply. "That answers that." She eyed me before turning back to the doorway just as quickly. "Ready?"

"Can you ever be ready to fight the god of darkness?" I asked.

Dziewanna leaped onto the first rock and drew her bow, never taking her eye off Marzanna's magic. Her flames flared as she neared the threshold. "Yes."

Without further clarification, she bounded through the portal. Otylia and I swapped glances. Dziewanna had reached for her quiver in that final moment, and Marzanna was nearly defenseless against another goddess in her current state. Had Dziewanna sought revenge, or was she merely being careful?

Otylia grimaced. "I hate to say it, but we need to make sure she doesn't finish off Marzanna."

"I will leave that to you," I replied, holding out an arm for her to pass. "She made it clear I shouldn't be afraid of her, but it didn't work."

"Coward."

She summoned her silver spear and ran toward the doorway with me two steps behind. My stomach churned knowing we were about to return to the castle where I'd been tortured, trapped by the goddess who'd manipulated me for moons. Nothing about it felt right, but what choice did we have?

Frigid cold tingled up my arms as we emerged into Marzanna's frozen throne room. Shattered shards of what had once been walls and columns lay strewn about. Ice servants hauled them about in a disorganized fashion as their queen sat upon her throne, chin rested on her fist and the bloodied Thunderstone dagger sitting on her lap. Despite it staining her dress, she appeared unbothered. Even her vengeful sister couldn't raise her drooping eyes.

"I have struck a deal with your daughter already," Marzanna said, her voice cracked and weak. "Leave me be, Sister, or would you like the Way to descend into Czarnobóg's darkness without my last fragments holding it together?"

Fire rippled around Dziewanna's feet and tipped her nocked arrow—aimed directly at the winter goddess's head. "You may have claimed that you shall willingly surrender power at winter's end for every coming year, but I am not inclined to believe you." She *slightly* lowered the bow. "My instincts confirm what Otylia has told me, however. Something has changed in your soul. I have not sensed this much purity in you since before Jaryło's adultery."

Marzanna scowled. "I will yet have my revenge on that insolent coward, but yes, what corruption had a hold on me has vanished. My judgment was clouded. You should understand how such obsession leads to destruction."

"I do." Dziewanna glanced about at the damage. "Except when I fell, Father did not allow me to retain my palace."

Marzanna shot to her feet, the dagger clanging to the ground in her haste. Strain covered her face, and she leaned on the throne's arm to keep from falling. "This is hardly comparable to Prawia! Father and Weles turned half the Way of Souls into a wasteland of Thunderstone. Yes, you were forced to wed Weles, but you resided in *paradise* while I rotted in my annual battle with Jaryło. Every year you traveled by his side to slaughter me yet again. You knew of his betrayal, yet you sided with him nonetheless. What, for Father's favor?"

Dziewanna turned away with eyes bloodshot and tears streaming down her cheeks. "I had little fondness for our foolish brother, but it is my role, my duty, to ensure spring's arrival. It was not my choice for you to murder each other in the endless cycle! You have no idea how I pled with him to show mercy. But you know him. Prideful as ever."

"He was so easy to manipulate," Marzanna said. She stared at the dagger, her legs swaying from the effort. " 'Free the dark dragon,' I told him, 'and then you will be king of all the realms when you strike him down. For even Swaróg could not defeat Czarnobóg forever.' "

"I should have seen it sooner."

Marzanna slumped back onto her throne. "No, you should have never trusted him. And I never should have loved him." She waved toward the side, where the half-demolished wall exposed the bridge over the Smorodina River into Nawia beyond. "Go. Let the realms be finished with the wake of my treachery. You have seen today that my promise is kept, and it shall be so until Dadźbóg no longer arrives in the east and flees in the west—in your realm of the living, that is."

"Break that promise," Otylia said as she stepped to her mother's side, wearing a glare sharp enough to pierce metal, "and there won't be mercy next time."

Dziewanna laid a hand on her shoulder, then nodded toward Nawia. The throne room's chill faded with every step we took away from Marzanna, even as we traversed the maze of her castle. From what I could tell, the rest of the Nawie had left with Vlad, and only ice servants remained to guide us to a pair of hefty stone doors at the rear of the castle's keep.

The nymphs, demons, and other stray souls, too, were nowhere to be seen through the arrow slits over the courtyards. I'd done more than drive a dagger into Marzanna's heart. Her hold over her vast network of servants and slaves had shattered, and I hoped they had found their way to safety instead of into Czarnobóg's grasp.

The ice servants' limbs cracked from the effort as they shoved open the stone doors. In the end, they stopped when there was a crack just wide enough for us to side-shuffle through, and Dziewanna shot them a glare as she slipped past. I kept Grudzień at the ready in case they tried anything, but neither servant moved in the slightest until all of us were outside the castle.

Snow mixed with black sand at our feet. Sweat clung cold to my face as the winds whipped over the frozen Kryzhana River which arced around the castle to our left. The Smorodina's flames mirrored it, but felt an eternity away from the remnant ring of Marzanna's power.

Beyond that ring stretched Nawia's paradise—or what *should* have been paradise. This far from the Heart of Nawia, the rolling landscape was untamed with trees, shrubs, and grasses of a hundred colors stretching every which way. These weren't the hundred-foot forests deeper into the realm. Still, they were expansive and should've been teeming with Nawia's strange life after death.

They drooped instead, vibrancy fading as tendrils of darkness curled through their branches and roots. The few nymphs drifting among them had glazed-over expressions, as if caught in a trance.

"He has poisoned my home," Dziewanna said through clenched teeth. "These wilds were mine to tend while Weles focused on the souls."

Otylia pounded her spear into the sand. "I've seen what's ahead. It gets worse."

A rickety bridge of rope and rotten boards crossed the rivers where they joined ahead. The Smorodina carried dead souls into Nawia from here, bubbling, but no longer ablaze. Once, they would have found a gentle end to the fires which formed their new bodies. Now… I swallowed. If Otylia refused to admit what she'd seen, it couldn't have been good.

Otylia raised a hand as we neared the bridge. She inspected its construction, then looked over the ledge, as if expecting Chudo-Yudo to emerge on the other side of the castle.

The Threads of Life revealed just how few beings remained within Marzanna's domain. Wisps swirled around us, but none came from below. Otylia had killed the dragon who'd guarded the route to Nawia. Surely, he couldn't have recovered so quickly from a Moonstone-tipped spear?

Dziewanna snagged Otylia by the back of her dress and yanked her to her feet. "You worry too much. We have a long way to go. If we spend our time and energy inspecting every potential threat, Czarnobóg will have corrupted the Three Realms by the time we reach Nawia's core."

Otylia grimaced, but nodded. "Focus on the ending."

Taking a sharp breath, she led us across the bridge. I'd hoped it would be sturdier than it looked, but it was far worse. Every weight shift sent it swaying to and fro with enough force to threaten throwing me into the waters far below. I had no intentions of letting that happen. One journey down the excruciating Smorodina had been plenty enough.

I clung to the ropes and used the winds to steady the bridge. Its movements were erratic, as if wanting us to fall, so I closed my eyes and reacted to the shifts the moment I felt them. Oh, how badly I wanted to take flight, but Otylia had told me how the rivers rebuffed her every attempt before. It still didn't explain why spirits and gods could do no better than a bridge any tribe would be ashamed of.

My winds stabilized the bridge more than before, but keeping my eyes shut had bile rising in my throat. I had flown thousands of miles, fought dragons, demons and gods. *This* is what my body decided was enough to make me vomit?

Otylia's relief greeted me minutes later as she stepped to safety. Unfortunately, I needed relief too, and when I stumbled onto solid ground, I emptied the contents of my stomach into the Smorodina.

"Wonderful," Dziewanna quipped, pinching her nose. "Boiled vomit is quite the stench."

Otylia couldn't hold back an ironic smirk as she helped me stand. "You okay?"

I clutched my stomach. The knot in my gut had only tightened, and the worlds spun around me as the cold sweat turned to a blizzard against my skin.

"Gods…" I muttered, curling over. "What in Oblivion did Marzanna do to me?"

"I'll make her suffer!" Otylia stomped back toward the bridge, but Dziewanna interrupted her.

"Wait, my dear." Dziewanna studied me before turning towards the forest. She extended her arms, and the nearest tendrils of darkness twirled around them, seeping into her skin. "Gods have the resilience to pass through these different realms quickly, especially when they are tainted by such corruption. Wacław is but a Naw. I had not considered the jarring effect such a transition would have on his body."

I shook my head and tried to put on a confident face, but it was no use. Otylia felt my pain through our bond anyway. She'd shown no ill from it yet, but as she returned to us, she coughed, holding a hand over her mouth.

"Gods, this has to be the worst you've felt since Vastroth," she said. "Get over this, or you'll make me sick too."

I wiped my mouth with my sleeve. "This isn't helping me keep the demon quiet." That effort was enough to send my head spinning again, and I fell onto my bottom, head in hands. "Just… er… Just give me a minute. I'll be fine."

"Liar." Otylia rolled her eyes before pulling Dziewanna aside to whisper. I couldn't hear what they said, but Otylia's frown deepened. When they returned, Otylia put her hands on her hips. "Mother says you'll acclimate in a few hours."

"*Should*," Dziewanna clarified. "I have little experience with Nawie or realms this tainted with corruption, but you are much stronger than a mortal at least." She glanced around. "We are far too exposed here to rest, but the forest should offer us cover with some coaxing."

I'd never felt more useless in my life as Otylia threw my arm over her shoulder and hauled me into the woods. Those dark tendrils curled overhead like claws digging ever deeper into flesh, and my stomach and head alike acted like those claws had embedded themselves in me. A wave of heat swept through my body. The chills that followed burrowed deep, and I stumbled into a tree, ready to vomit again despite nothing remaining in my stomach.

"It's getting worse!" I spat. My fingers dug into the tree's bark until they bled, and the winds pulsed beyond. They flooded my thoughts with every object for a mile each direction—a thousand pin pricks on my exposed mind.

Beneath it all, a force stirred.

Otylia tried to hold me up, but I cowered away from that *thing* inside me. The demon. The Płanetnik.

"Fight it," she demanded, kneeling beside me with a soft hand on my cheek. "I took part of your corruption, remember? I feel it too. I know Czarnobóg's calling to it, but you're stronger than that!"

I groaned and curled my fingers into fists. The winds went mad, tearing through the trees at a deafening gale. "I'll never… hurt… you."

I choked on my own whirlwind as the demon within fought viciously against its cage. Eyes shut, I devoted my strength to holding it back.

Otylia gripped my head with both hands and shook violently. "Look at me, Wašek! We've come too far for you to surrender now.

Remember everyone who needs us, everyone who fought and died so that we could be here to protect those who are left."

The demon lashed out, and I screamed, resisting her hold. But she just pulled me closer. Light burst from her skin and banished the tendrils which circled us. It grew brighter and brighter until my whole world was silver. Only her spring green eyes broke that sea, and I dared not look away. To lose sight of her was to lose sight of the last fragment of my human soul within her. More than that. She was the reason I fought, the reason I kept struggling against my darkness. All our kingdom needed me, but more than that, *she* needed me.

And I couldn't fail her.

I slammed shut the demon's cage, fortifying my mind with my *żityje*. So quickly, I'd already expended too much, but it wouldn't matter how much strength I had if the Płanetnik was back in control. Memories of the bloodied innocents he'd killed... I'd killed... stained my mind.

Never again.

Otylia tensed as I held the back of her hands with my shaking ones. Nawia's corruption still coursed through my veins, weakening me, and I spoke through haggard breaths. "He's gone, for now." She stopped me from moving my head, but I flicked away my gaze. "I won't let him hurt you again."

"I don't care about me right now," she replied sternly. "What was that?"

"Something more than just sickness from traveling the realms." I released her and leaned my head back against the tree. My fingers stung from digging into its bark, but *żityje* had mended the worst of the damage without me asking. "I think the corruption here strengthened the demon, like it was answering a call."

She let go, swapping glances with her mother. "We need to pick somewhere close. I'm not letting him go further like this."

I tried to push myself up. "I can—"

"No!" She put her hands on my chest and held me back into the tree. It brought us close, and despite the situation's severity, my heart drummed faster at her touch. "The demon almost broke free. I won't let that happen."

Dziewanna studied me from a few paces away, arms crossed. "If I did not believe we needed you, I would send you back. It would be the best for all of us, but unfortunately, Otylia's soul is not united without you there. She will need all her power if we are to defeat the dark dragon."

"That makes me feel a lot better," I grumbled. "I'm only here because I stole part of her soul."

Dziewanna huffed. "That fragment of her soul allowed you to tap into Kwiecień to save your mother, but your skill with the Moonblades and your demonic powers are of use, no matter the state of your soul." She turned sharply and waved a hand toward the deeper forest. "Here is as good a place as any to rest for now."

"The darkness deepens further into Nawia," Otylia added. "I doubt Czarnobóg's corruption will get any easier."

I settled back, clutching a leg to my chest. "I'll be all right once I adjust, I think. I'm already feeling better."

That was a lie, but I was reassuring myself as much as I was her. We'd come so far. Failing now wasn't an option. No matter what happened to me, I would ensure Otylia and Dziewanna had their chance to slay Czarnobóg and bring the Three Realms back to peace.

31

Otylia

I can't lose him again.

MOTHER AND I LEFT WACŁAW TO REST. Nawia constantly altered its form under normal circumstances, but as we scouted the path ahead, it became clear those shifts were far more rapid now.

Cracks formed in the earth at random, separating before crashing back together with enough force to make me stumble. Mother eyed those gaps with distrust, but never changed her pace.

She stepped on the balls of her feet like a huntress. Her leather-clad fingers held her bow's string as its grip pressed into the web between her thumb and index finger. An arrow tipped with sleek Thunderstone rested within, and it scraped eagerly against the bow whenever Mother tensed.

"You don't seem worried about Wacław," I said, clutching my silver spear. A dull light emanated from it, and the dark tendrils curled away like a hissing cat.

Mother lifted the bear pelt from her shoulders to place the bear's head over hers. Her eyes narrowed as she knelt, tracing a dormant crack. "Many things worry me. His struggle with his soul's remnant corruption is but a minor one." She rose and stepped over the crack.

"This realm was my home, and it is now consumed by the very corruption I helped protect your village from. Weles, I may have never loved, but I cannot say the same for Nawia."

"Fine, but don't dismiss my—"

A chittering came from deeper into the woods. Like bones snapping against each other, it drew closer over a nearby ridge before falling silent. No living wisps signaled other souls, but deep gray ones curled among the treetops. Frayed, dying leaves fluttered through them as a brisk breeze carried the Smorodina's warmth.

Mother nodded to me and raised her bow, ready to draw her string. I flared my *žityje* and prepared both Sierpień and Listopad at my spear's ends. A grin tugged at my lips. Demons didn't frighten me anymore, and I itched for the chance to fight alongside Mother. Things were simpler when it was us against the world.

That itch dropped the moment the *thing* crept over the ridge.

A dozen horns protruded from the beast's mask of bone, behind which eyes of obsidian glared down upon us from twice my height. Layered bone pauldrons and plate armor covered its torso, and mangled, bleeding muscles peeked from the cracks between them. Each rapid movement made another *clack* that echoed through the woods. More chittering followed.

"Get out of my woods!" Mother shouted at the beast, launching the first flaming arrow straight into its forehead, but it did not waver.

I raised my hand and mirrored her attack with a blast of light that cracked its plate. "What in Oblivion is that thing?"

"A corrupted leszy, if I had to hazard a guess." She cursed before loosing a series of arrows in a blur. "Czarnobóg has tainted the very spirit of these wilds."

The leszy shot down the slope far faster than any beast of its size should've moved. Arrows peppered its plate, smoke scarring bone, but they did nothing to slow it as more beasts emerged from the ridge.

Zmory, their familiar chittering and decrepit forms bursting forth in a dark sea. Countless of them.

I threw blasts of light and reached for any creatures of decay that I could command. Fungi thrived in the corrupted landscape, and their spores showered down upon the advancing horde. Many of the zmory slowed as mushrooms and mold ate away at what remained of their bodies.

None of my channeling pierced the leszy's armor. The ground shook as it bounded toward us, sweeping out its massive arms and forcing me to throw up my defenses.

"*Pri!*" I shouted in the old tongue, a forcefield of light forming before us and deflecting its attack. But the shield shattered from the single blow.

"Focus on the zmory!" Mother called as she leaped forward. Brown fur grew across her arms and face, claws arcing from her hands. She bared her razor-sharp teeth and tackled the leszy. Her bear pelt no longer hung over her head, as she'd become the great beast she shared with Weles.

A rotting stench choked me as the zmory encircled us. The beasts who caused nightmares lived up to their names, striking furiously, but with little organization.

My silver spear flashed and spun in my hands. More from instinct than skill, I drove Listopad's spear head through one demon's sternum before twirling and slashing another's throat with Sierpień's curved one. It was difficult enough to defend myself, but Mother had her hands full as she wrestled with the towering leszy. If the zmory reached her, she'd struggle to fight all of them at once.

Her flames seared through the leszy's bone as I threw out my arms and moonblasted away the nearest of the zmory. Trees tumbled against Mother's power and the leszy's weight, crashing through the waves of demons. All moved too fast. I used my power to foresee their next actions through End's wisps, but still wasted *żityje* sending blasts at shadows.

Claws raked through my side. I'd missed one of the zmory, and it ran its disgusting tongue over its claws—covered with my blood. I drove my spear straight through its mouth as punishment, but for every kill, another demon followed.

Until the leszy cried out.

Mother had torn through its plate and mask to expose the hollow figure within. With the body of an aged man and a long gray beard filled with wooden amulets, he was the exact figure of a leszy from Mother's tales. Except this spirit didn't protect the woods with tricks and wildlife magic. Czarnobóg had ruined him without a goddess to purify his corruption.

"Mother, wait!" I cried out, knocking aside another zmora and rushing to her as she raised a bloodied claw. I grabbed hold of her bear arm before she could strike. "Let me try and save him, please!"

The zmory advanced as she considered, so I covered us with another *pri* shield, my arms shaking with adrenaline. "Hold off the others," I told her, "and maybe he can use the forest against them. We have to try!"

Mother stared back at me with half-human, half-beast eyes, then nodded. "No longer a szeptucha, but always a protector."

She turned and roared at the zmory, charging into them with the strength of a bear and goddess combined. My ears rang from the zmory's desperate shrieking as I knelt over their master.

"This isn't your fault," I told him with light bursting from my skin. Though a spirit, he had a Thread of Life like any living being, its ends frayed and blackened as I trapped it in one hand and placed the other over his heart. "Search for your purpose, your heart in these wilds."

He stared at me, those blackened eyes glinting in my moonlight. But I swore there was some recognition of my words, so I pushed my *żityje* into his Thread and burned away the corruption within. If Nawia had fallen as far as Trygław had shown me, each fragment of its purity we could retain was crucial. This spirit was bound to this forest like a nymph was to her tree. These lands were nothing without him, and only he could repair this place to what it had been before.

The chaos of battle faded. All that remained was the beating of the leszy's heart and his slow breaths. His Thread pulsed in my grasp, resisting the light that I poured within until his eyes shot open.

"THE DARK DRAGON COMES!" he boomed like thunder.

A shockwave burst across the woods, rustling the trees and sending fallen leaves scattering into the winds. I flew back into a great trunk. My back ached and the bark chewed into my spine, but I shouted in glee as vines and leaves grew across the leszy's body. His horns turned to great antlers that mirrored Mother's. A mask of wood replaced that of bone. And his eyes radiated vibrant green.

Mother echoed my laughter. Roaring and impaling a zmora on a particularly sharp branch of a nearby tree, she charged down the beasts who'd fallen to the leszy's cry.

The wilds charged with her.

Branches, roots, and vines entangled and impaled the zmory who dared threaten Mother's flank. Goddess of the wilds, queen of the hunt. She tore the zmory to shreds with fang and claw until those that remained shrieked, fleeing over the ridge.

They left behind a destroyed clearing. Trees lay strewn about, the earth beneath their roots shattered like ice and black blood staining the fallen leaves. Over a hundred demons rotted amid it all, and the roots drew their corpses into the crevices. Where they took the undead, I didn't care. Death was a mercy for demons too lost to their corruption to ever be redeemed.

My heart raced as I knelt beside one of the zmory the roots had left behind. Wacław would need *żityje*-filled blood to recover, and pulling free the demons' hearts distracted me from the horror surrounding us.

I huffed at that thought. Tearing out a creature's heart *was* horrific, whether undead or not. We'd spent moons dealing with my offerings turning to blood at my godly altar and tempering Wacław's hunger. Such things weren't normal, but neither were we anymore.

Mother returned to her human form as she tended to the leszy, speaking with him in hushed whispers. He cast me a nervous glance, but snapped his attention away when he noticed me staring. His jaw shivered beneath his mask.

"Are there others like you?" I asked him, wrapping the hearts and tucking them away in my bag. Their *żityje* would fade significantly by the time we returned to Wacław. For now, though, there were few other sources of life to give him while Czarnobóg's corruption held.

The leszy stood with Mother's help. Barely reaching my naval, he looked almost silly compared to the towering depictions of leszy in Wacław's story and Father's legends. Spirits often looked harmless to avoid revealing their intentions, but this one's wisp of bright green shifted hesitantly, as if his meekness was genuine.

"I am called Lew," the leszy said to me, ignoring my question. "Yet, all the same, you are remarkably familiar."

His voice rumbled through the roots underfoot, and Nawia's quakes seemed to echo his power. I knelt on one knee before him. "I am Otylia, goddess of endings and moon. Dziewanna is my mother."

Lew narrowed his eyes, considering that. "You hold far too much *żityje* to be a mere demigod." He glanced at Mother. "Is she of Lord Weles's blood?"

"Blood is the only gift he's ever given me," I replied before Mother could. My heels dug into the dirt. Friendly spirit or not, I couldn't trust anyone who freely called Weles "lord."

Sabina called him her master once, I reminded myself.

But she'd been forced to do so. Leszy were greater spirits, practically deities over their forest. Either Lew didn't want to offend Mother, or he still held loyalty to Weles. His reaction wiped away my doubts.

"You hold your mother's spite!" he exclaimed, chuckling. "Worry not about my opinions of Weles. He is lord of this realm, and I call him such, but Nawia is a place of change…" His voice trailed off until he scowled at the ridge he'd surged over. "The others either succumbed like me or were slaughtered by Czarnobóg. I thank you both for freeing me from the darkness, but plead with you to abandon your quest. Nawia is lost. At its furthest edge, I will seek to repair this portion of it, but I fear there is no piercing the corruption at its core."

"I've seen it," I said, "but I don't understand why Trygł—" I caught myself and faked a cough, "—why End didn't show me what was happening to Nawia's spirits."

Mother's gaze shot to me with all the intensity of a wildfire. Sweat beaded on my brow, and I averted my gaze to not surrender anything more. But she'd heard enough of Trygław's name. My heart burrowing into my gut knew she did.

"Stopping Czarnobóg here is our only hope," she said through gritted teeth, still glaring at me. "He will come for the other realms next."

Lew bowed. "Yes, my lady. I will do what is within my power, but I am not as powerful as I would have hoped."

Vines emerged around him, consuming his legs and torso. Seconds later, he was gone, and I so badly wished he wasn't. My slip had exposed the truth about End—a truth I wasn't ready to admit to myself, let alone Mother.

Maybe she didn't notice.

I gave a crooked smile and patted my bag. "We should get back to Wacław before these hearts become useless."

Mother snatched my arm. Her nose wrinkled, mirroring mine. "Why did you not tell me?"

My heart shot from my gut straight into my throat. I stammered, fists clenched at my side. Who was she to question me keeping secrets when she'd hidden the truth of my birth and her false death for so long? She never shared her relationship with her force despite me helping her restore her connection to it. I'd only learned about Trygław hours before, and it had been far too much to wrap my mind around so quickly.

"I would've eventually!" I tried to tear my arm from her grip, but she held firm. "I only found out today."

"Trygław is not simply some force you can ignore."

"I'm not!"

She groaned. "You do not understand. You cannot yet understand!" Loosening her hold, she held me close, and her voice wavered.

"Trygław knows more than any god or spirit. What he showed you is to influence the realms for his ends alone. He is Death and—"

"Mother, I know," I insisted. "He tricked me, *used* me to kill Rod, but right now, he's helping me kill Czarnobóg. That's all that matters right now."

"If only it were so simple." She released me and began the walk back to Wacław. Her hair was a mangled mess, her dress spouting flames at her heels. A bad sign. "Trygław is older than even Rod. His plans span beyond mortal comprehension, and my little wildling, you are far too young to see much further."

My lip curled. "Like how your plan to leave me was beyond my comprehension? Like how you left me to discover who I was when *Jaryło* showed us to the Lake of Reflection?"

The ground shook, sending us both stumbling into nearby trees. Mother shoved herself away from hers. She bit her lip as flames rushed to her cheeks. "This is not the time!"

I met her gaze, but had nothing more to say. We'd both hidden the truth from each other, yes. The difference was that I'd done so for a few hours while she'd lied my entire life, and I took my turn at stomping away.

Away from her, Wacław's agony returned through our bond. I'd hoped that our time scouting would allow him some time to recover, but that pit in his stomach had deepened. The demon's call waned at least. Behind, it left only a dull, aching hunger that was all too familiar. That was a problem I could solve. It was the ones that I couldn't that irritated me to no end.

Wacław startled at my approach. He snatched Grudzień from the ground beside him, drawing the jagged black blade and staggering to his feet, but his eyes softened at the sight of me.

"Oh, you're back." He faked a smile, which dissipated as his gaze dropped to my blood-spattered clothes. "Gods… What happened? Where's Dziewanna?"

I wrinkled my nose at his mention of Mother, then dropped my bag of hearts beside him. "A corrupted leszy attacked us with a swarm of zmory, but I managed to purify him. I brought you some hearts. Take the *žityje*. You'll need it."

He did so. Though I'd gotten used to him consuming hearts, I still looked away, picking at my nails. Having Mother back filled a gap in my heart, but scars remained. How different could my life have been if she'd told me the truth earlier? Couldn't she have hidden me from Weles while still raising me as a young goddess?

"Stop staring at me," I muttered, catching Wacław's gaze out of the corner of my eye.

A true smile cracked through his discomfort as he wiped blood from the edge of his mouth. "I have many reasons to stare at you, but especially when you're hiding something. What happened between you two?"

I plopped down beside him and leaned back into his tree. "Am I that transparent?"

"I knew something had happened when I felt your adrenaline." He nudged me with his shoulder. "It got worse *after* the fight, though, and only two people can anger you that much: Dziewanna or me."

"Can I ask you to trust me?" I tucked in my legs. "I'm not ready to talk about it."

He nodded, but nuzzled his head into mine. "I trust you. Always."

32

Wacław

HOURS AFTER OTYLIA'S RETURN, MY HEAD STILL SPUN and my guts felt as if they wished to be outside me. I packed up anyway and prepared to continue. Czarnobóg grew stronger every moment we waited. If enduring this corruption got Otylia and Dziewanna where they needed to be, then so be it.

Otylia eyed me distrustfully. Our bond exposed how horrible I felt, but she allowed me to straggle behind her as we followed the route they had scouted.

At least, we followed the route they *thought* they'd scouted. Earthquakes split the ground and led to sections of the landscape rotating around us like some kind of children's toy. A section of trees before us one moment could end up on our right not ten minutes later. It was disorienting, but the dark tendrils stretching from Nawia's center kept us focused on our goal.

"What happens to the souls that end up here?" I wondered aloud. The Smorodina River carried them somewhere to our left, eventually depositing them for Weles's spirits to show them to paradise. Except there were no Weles, spirits, or paradise left.

Otylia looked back with pity. "Oblivion is a better end for them than this place. Believe me, I saw the core of Nawia. It's unrecognizable."

"A hundred zmory attacked us in one fell swoop," Dziewanna replied, her fingers white from gripping her bow. Her eyes snapped from left to right, and her posture resembled a cat preparing to leap. "You need dead souls and bodies to make a demon. The rest, you can imagine."

My breaths caught. I stopped dead in my tracks, staring at the shifting earth. "Please tell me you aren't saying what I think you are. Every dead soul has been corrupted? Everyone we lost in the war against the Horde?" I clenched and unclenched my fists. "No matter what happens, we need to help them."

"I swore I would," Otylia replied.

I raised my brows. "Swore to who?"

She just waved me on, heading deeper into the darkness. A dark fog embraced her. It ebbed and flowed like breaths during the long winter, warm against my skin as I trailed behind. Fifty steps later and I lost sight of the goddesses completely. Only my bond to Otylia kept me from straying, but the thicker the fog, the fainter our connection became.

Light pierced the fog just as I opened my mouth to call out to her. Moonlight, pure and silver. It gave her raven black hair an ethereal glow that seemed deeper than the heart of Oblivion. That witch turned goddess made my heart race with just a single glance, and I trusted her more than anyone. I did. But why wouldn't she tell me what she'd seen?

"My light is enough now," she said, forging ahead, "but it won't be soon. The ground will start to fracture further to look like Prawia's islands. Use your winds to guide you if we lose track of one another."

"Keep your vision open to the Threads of Life too," I replied. "That way I can follow the one connecting us."

She gave a solemn smile and nodded.

Not an hour later, her prediction came true. A ridgeline ahead shot up at the edge of her ever-dimming moonlight. It towered overhead until a cliff as tall as the ones surrounding Sheresy in Vastroth blocked our path. The winds whipped about it in search of a way around, but the chunk of earth had split away for half a mile either direction. Up would be easiest.

I normally craved the burst of wind that carried me into the air, but dread formed a knot in my stomach instead. That power, my power, belonged to my demonic soul. Being a Naw meant that I controlled it. With Czarnobóg's corruption seeping deeper into me, though, was using the winds only strengthening the caged demon?

Otylia offered to carry Dziewanna with her moonlight, but great wings sprouted from the wild goddess's back. Stretching wider than I was tall each direction, they buffeted me with my own winds as she took flight with a smirk.

"Oh, how I missed this," she said.

Otylia's tales told of how Dziewanna had transformed into many animals during her revolution against Perun, hoping their power would help them outmaneuver her father. So far, she'd opted mostly for the bear. What other animals' forms could she take advantage of?

I imagined her carrying true venom instead of just the bite behind her words. Such a possibility was enough to put fear into any mortal or demon, but what did Czarnobóg care for a bear's claws, an eagle's wings, or a snake's venom? Perhaps her adaptability was another advantage. It didn't chip away at the ball of dread within me, and I drifted slowly up the cliff behind her and Otylia.

That is, until the ground shifted again.

The winds alerted me to a surge from our right. A wall of stone crashed into the cliff before skidding our direction, sending shards slicing through my exposed skin as I warned the others and burst upward. End must've helped Otylia, since she adjusted quickly, but Dziewanna lagged.

I gritted my teeth and sent an updraft to aid her wings. The new island passed just beneath me, sending me straight into the branches of its trees. Dziewanna hadn't followed, and the winds revealed her spiraling into the cliff. Had my gust thrown her astray instead of helping?

Dziewanna is caught! I called out to Otylia through our bond, trying to detangle myself from the branches in the pure darkness. The lateral movement had worsened my nausea, though, and it took all my focus not to be sick again. A deep chill gripped my whole body. The winds fell away with it.

Otylia's silver light shot from above. The colliding cliffs were closing on where Dziewanna clung to a ledge halfway up, and without the winds, I held my breath as Otylia dived right into their paths.

They're goddesses, I told myself. *They'll be fine.*

But Nawia's corruption had turned it strange and unpredictable. This place was not meant for wings. Even the winds had struggled in the shifting darkness, and Dziewanna lacked their insight and Otylia's senses.

I only exhaled once Otylia's light appeared with Dziewanna's winged form gripping her daughter's hand. Sure, I was still caught in a stupid tree, but at least they had made it out. There were surely hundreds more of these islands crashing about. From now on, though, we would be ready... I hoped.

After reaching the top of the cliff far above, Otylia lowered herself to me. She raised one brow while failing to hold back a wry smile. "You seem a little tangled up."

"That's what I get for trying to save Dziewanna, I guess," I quipped before covering my mouth. Talking made my throat burn.

Her smile faded to form a narrow line. "You're hiding how bad the corruption is."

Yes, I replied silently for both fear of my unruly stomach and Dziewanna overhearing. *The demon isn't trying to break free again, yet, but my whole body feels like it's been dumped into Narcyz's forge.*

"What if I took part of the corruption again?" she asked. *"It worked in Vastroth."*

I shook my head and peeled myself from the worst of the branches. The winds returned, allowing me to step onto them and hover before her on wobbly legs. *You need all your strength to face Czar-nobóg. I won't let my soul's struggle drain your power.*

"Wašek," she breathed, clutching my hand. "I won't—"

You will, I insisted. *Being near you makes it easier, but it doesn't matter what happens to me.*

She pulled me into an embrace. "The darkness won't take you from me." Tensing, she sighed. "End showed me how to see the islands with his force. You see the Threads when I do, so if you look closely, you should see the islands outlined in silver. At least the ones close to us."

"You're shaking…"

Cursing, she backed away with her moonlit pull. Her eyes were puffy and red. "Everything changes too quickly. Not us. We'll be together no matter what we face, right?"

I reached out for her, but she just shot up toward Dziewanna. All felt oddly still despite the cliffs crashing and the winds warning me of every shifting tree. Darkness encompassed all like a living being dampening light and sound alike. If it didn't seep into my soul to enrage the demon within, it would've been almost peaceful. One could forget their worries in the darkness. For even when we closed our eyes, we saw light, but here, there was only the pounding of my heart and the demonic whisper in the back of my mind.

"You will not live to see the sun."

33

Otylia

Why didn't you tell me he'd suffer like this?

I CURSED TRYGŁAW AS WE NAVIGATED the dark islands of Nawia. These, he'd warned me of, but he'd failed to mention the twisted leszy or creeping corruption that would consume my lover.

Wacław didn't deserve this. He'd been the gentlest of the boys growing up, always seeking to help others while avoiding his father's wrath. Demons were supposed to punish those who lived their lives unnaturally or who died with a vengeance left unfulfilled. All I could think of was Wacław's joy when we'd finally admitted our feelings and kissed in that field deep in the Mangled Woods. He deserved that joy.

Instead, I felt corruption eating away at him. Maybe he hid it to stop me from worrying or to ensure we didn't turn back. His dread went deeper than the taint Nawia's corruption inflicted upon him, and it threatened to drop me to the ground, never to rise with the light again.

I knew him too well to deny that he would sacrifice himself for me. That made our constant march forward all the more painful. Even Mother had struggled against the realm's demons and shifting islands, and she was a goddess.

Though Wacław had found his true power on the Way of Souls, discovering that Nawia devoured those same souls was heartbreaking. I held the light Trygław claimed could defeat Czarnobóg here, but Wacław had no secret weapon against the dark. He needed the same hope I clung to.

So why couldn't I tell him everything?

He no longer trailed behind, keeping at my side instead with my silver moonlight washing over his face and bright hair. Beneath, darkness crept through him. Demonic veins had crisscrossed his skin ever since I took his mortal soul during the Trial of Loss, but they worsened now. Like tributaries connecting to a greater river, strands of black stretched across his exposed skin in greater numbers every time I looked at him.

Mother saw it too, but she'd given me a look more than once that said, "He's yours to handle."

She'd been wrong about this just being sickness from jumping between realms. Wacław would've recovered at least slightly if that were the case, but his strength waned instead. The winds no longer whipped around us like a protective barrier, and his eyes grew dim.

My heart screamed for me to turn back, to abandon the quest and save him from Nawia. I couldn't. If we failed, there would be nowhere for him or anyone else to run.

"How far?" his raspy voice asked when we crested yet another cliff.

I closed my eyes—not that there was much light anymore—and remembered the suffocating darkness Trygław had shown me at Nawia's core. We were drawing near, but my light still pierced the haze.

Something else drew me away from Nawia's core. Two Threads stretched from Mother and me down and to the side, both heading toward the same target: Weles. Czarnobóg must have trapped him deep within Nawia, but away from the core Trygław had spoken of. Another god would be useful in the fight ahead. Ally or not, Weles was one of the elder gods and the traditional king of Nawia.

"Otylia?" Wacław asked through our bond. *"What do you see? Those Threads?"*

"Weles…" I said aloud, spurring Mother to stop alongside me. Her wings made quite the noise with every flap, but my light already dispersed any chance of stealth. "He's down there."

Wacław's eyes widened, and Mother winced beside him. "We need to free him, don't we?" he asked. "Having Nawia's king captured must be an advantage for Czarnobóg."

"I hate to agree," Mother said, her posture curling and her hands flexed at her sides. "Weles is no perfect god or man, but he despises Czarnobóg as much as any of us. Perun and Swaróg have failed to aid us. Having an elder god's power with us would be a great help."

I crossed my arms. "I thought you'd want him to suffer."

She turned her head into the shadowy mists. "Believe me when I say that no one deserves the kind of torture that Czarnobóg inflicts. There were countless times when I wished I was not immortal, when I screamed into the void for death." Her eyes darkened as she looked back at me. "Weles allowed me to endure that horror, but we are not the same. We must free him."

Trygław's warning echoed in the back of my mind. No distractions. No attachments. What did he know?

I bit my cheek and shook my head. "He tried to kill us! I am his daughter, but he'd have left me broken beneath that volcano. Only Wacław's blood saved me!"

"And you will have lifetimes for revenge," Mother replied. "Stab him with a spear tipped with Alatyr itself for all I care, but Czarnobóg feeds on the gods he holds. He did so to me. He did so to Marzanna. And now he is doing the same to Weles." She flew closer as I averted my gaze. "Unless Trygław had something to say about it?"

My chest ached, and when I looked up, Wacław's face held a pained expression. "Who is Trygław?" he asked.

"Do you want to tell him," Mother said with a bite in her tone, "or shall I?"

I scowled at her, but submitted. She'd backed me into a corner. Lying now would drive a spear right through the trust Wacław and I had built over the moons since the spring equinox. I couldn't do that to him, especially when he was risking everything to fight onward with me.

"End is just a third of a greater entity that is my true force," I admitted, approaching Wacław. "His true name is Trygław, and another part of him is Death."

He reeled back. "The one that forced you to kill Rod?" he stammered. "The one who almost killed me?"

"He tricked me, but revealed the truth in my vision this morning." I reached out my hand, which he reluctantly took. "The only reason I didn't tell you was because I still can't understand it fully myself. Trygław is ancient, more so than even Rod, and he was cryptic with his explanations of what is to come. Well… except one thing."

"Oh?" Mother asked. "You refused to tell me more."

I rolled my eyes. "I would've if you'd given me time to speak about it on my terms, but here we are." I took a few long breaths before meeting Wacław's gaze again. "Trygław said that Czarnobóg's corruption is forcing Nawia into a cycle of rapid change that is expending and then reusing its *żityje* so quickly that it is metaphorically burning hotter and hotter until it will destroy itself. This darkness is eating away at what had once lived here. Once it's all gone, it'll turn on Nawia's core, and whatever chance we had to restore paradise for the dead will be gone."

Wacław looked from me to Mother. "He isn't powerful enough to destroy an entire realm, is he?" He coughed weakly. "It only confirms that we need to move quickly."

"We cannot allow either you or the realm to crumble," Mother said. "Czarnobóg does not have the ability to destroy a realm on purpose, but by exposing it to the depths of Oblivion, he apparently can do so indirectly. I had not dared to consider such possibilities before."

"But it makes sense?" Wacław asked.

She just gave a solemn nod and looked to me. "Is that all?"

"Trygław gave a final warning," I said, running my hand over Weles's gift from my time in Nawia. His intertwined bands of willow wood and silver ran up my left forearm and had warded attacking magic plenty in recent moons. Was that care, or knowledge I was an asset to him? "He told me not to be distracted by attachments."

"Does that mean Weles or me?" Wacław asked with his expression heavy. "Or both?"

"I didn't get a chance to ask. He ended the vision right after that."

Mother flapped her wings heavily and descended. "We need to land and discuss this. Unlike you both, I do not fly often, and I grow weary."

Weary or furious?

She refused to even look at me until we landed atop a fairly stable island. Trygław's streaks of silver revealed a few scattered trees beyond my light, bones and cracked earth between them. I didn't need to touch their branches to know the corruption ate them by the minute. When Mother kicked a rib bone of some long dead predator, she turned back to me with her brow as wrinkled as Rod's.

Definitely furious.

"Trygław's warning implies there is more to consider than merely time," she started, not waiting for Wacław to catch his rough landing beside me. He leaned into me, and I wrapped my arm around him to hold some of his weight. "No doubt, he knows we want to free Weles in one form or another, so it is likely he has laid a trap of some sort."

"He's connected to this realm, isn't he?" Wacław replied. He nodded to me. "You said the leszy you purified managed to gain some power over his old domain, despite the corruption. If Weles can do the same, there is a chance he can push back some of Czarnobóg's corruption and help me keep going. He is the god of magic after all."

Mother scoffed. "He is also the god of trickery." She turned on her heel, arms crossed as she studied me. "You have defied Trygław before, have you not?"

"I have." I flinched at the thought of my failures on the Way of Souls. "Dodging his warnings didn't work, but I've learned I was focusing too much on how to get to where I wanted to be, instead of worrying about the actual end in itself."

"So," Mother threw out her arms, "what then, do you want at the end of this?"

I took a long breath and ignored my thoughts, clinging instead to the instincts guiding my heart. "I want Nawia's corruption gone so that the dead and dying don't fear the paradise that awaits them. I want a place to settle, to remember what it's like to live without the world ending every waking moment." I leaned into Wacław. "And I want those I love to be safe."

Mother considered that as she ran her boots over the broken earth. Nature was gone here, and all that remained was the raging goddess of wildfires. But we needed that anger to survive this.

"Does saving Weles help you accomplish those?" she asked directly.

"I don't know. Could he really help Wacław?"

Her shoulders sagged. "I confess that I do not know either. What is obvious, however, is that Wacław will not be the same at the end of this if we continue as we have."

"I'm right here!" Wacław snapped, forcing himself away from me, but staggering without aid. "Don't talk about me like I'm dying on my bedroll."

Mother looked him up and down before waving a dismissive hand. "You won't be long for this realm, or any."

"Then let's find Weles and see what he knows," Wacław said. "Czarnobóg can try a trap, sure, but what besides the dragon himself can stop two goddesses and a Naw?"

I wrinkled my nose, but considered his argument. It was rare that he got this aggressive without it being the demon's doing. This was about more than my spite. Until Czarnobóg was dead, pride could wait, so I met his gaze and held a hand over my heart. "I trust you. If this is what you need, then we'll go after Weles—as long as I can stab him a few times."

"We will each take our turns," Mother muttered, pacing to the edge and glancing over. "So, we descend further?"

"No." I stepped to the ledge, then stepped over. My voice carried through the darkness as I tumbled. "We fall."

I just hoped it wasn't for a trap.

34

Otylia

WARMTH ENVELOPED ME AS I DARTED HEAD-FIRST through gaps between islands and dodged stray demons in my descent. These were so corrupted that they didn't resemble rusałki, wiły, or even the mutated and ravenous upióry. They had lost all sense of human form. What remained were little more than shadows twisting at the edge of my moonlight, as if afraid they would disappear if they entered its glow.

Too far gone.

I closed my eyes and allowed Trygław's force to guide me. Each of the demons' wisps flew past too quickly for me to reach out for them, but with enough focus, I sensed random moments from their past lives.

A carpenter, his fingers calloused against his saw's worn handle.

A seamstress, her thread pinched beneath her teeth as she carefully worked her loom.

A mother, struggling to nurse her child during a long winter.

A father, smiling as he watched his child leap the fire and become an adult.

I lost count of the images, but clung to a piece of each. These memories were ours to protect for those still living. And with Czarnóbóg gone, I hoped even the most corrupted demons could pass with peace.

The loose Thread binding me to Weles drew tighter and tighter. I wished he weren't my father, that I had only Dziewanna's blood as my mother to thank for my power. Dariusz had hardly been the father any child dreamed of, but he showed me care in his stringent sort of way. He could've ignored Mother's plea through Swaróg to protect me. Maybe he'd just done it for his god, but if nothing else, I was thankful he didn't turn me over to the manipulative king of Nawia. Weles had shown me well what his priorities were.

I was never one of them.

The demonic shadows grew more common the further we dropped, and soon, a crowd of them followed me at the edge of my light. I didn't call my spear, only opening my eyes to check on the others. Wacław glanced at the demons with blade drawn as Mother gripped her bow. But they weren't a threat. Tryglaw's wisps marking each demon's immediate ends showed they didn't intend to attack. At least, not yet.

Wacław couldn't see things so clearly. "Any plan if they attack?" he called out, his voice echoing between the island cliffs until we suddenly smacked into water.

No, not just water—the Smorodina. Its rush of heat explained the increasing warmth I'd felt, but the flaming river didn't burn. Wacław had suffered its blaze on the Way of Souls. Here, though, it had merged with the frozen Kryzhana and become like the pools hunters from far off lands said formed around hot springs.

"I can't swim for long," Wacław said through our bond.

As if she'd heard his silent plea, Mother swam to his side and pressed her hand against his forehead. His eyes widened, but he didn't resist as *żityje* flowed from her fingers. His skin shifted on either side of his neck to form a series of slits. Deep red, they pulsed as Wacław gasped.

Then he breathed.

"Thank you," he mouthed to Mother, tentatively touching the gills before wincing as a shot of pain rushed through our connection.

Gills are sensitive. Good to know.

A more intricate pair grew across Mother's neck, and frog-like webs formed between her fingers as she swam to me. I cringed at her wings morphing *into* her back and disappearing. She must've noticed, because she cast me a sarcastic grin. I'd hardly realized I was drowning until she pressed her palm to my forehead too, and anxiety filled my chest as I instinctually breathed in to find only water.

Nothing felt as strange as my body creating a new organ. Not only did my skin pinch and tickle with the gills' formation, but my lungs and ribs ached as they adjusted to handle the changing arrival of air from the water. My breaths started shallow. Like an infant learning to walk, I stumbled through the process of controlling gills I'd never used before.

Mother didn't remove her hand from my cheek until I took a long, relieved sigh. My chest was still tight and the demons lurked nearby, but at least I wasn't drowning.

One step at a time.

I swam to Wacław and checked him over. His creeping corruption had fallen away from my senses while I'd focused on the demons, but it returned now, turning the Smorodina's heat into a chill that raised every hair across my body. My stomach turned with his. He was doing all he could to resist the corruption, but beneath his agony, his heart was racing with desperation.

We're almost there, I assured him through our bond. *Weles will help. We'll make him.*

He just gave a half-smile before waving his arm downward. I took that as enough, so I led them deeper into the Smorodina.

The river's flow had been rapid in the Way of Souls, but it was near still here. How did it even exist this far down? We were beyond Nawia's fractured earth, and the Smorodina had been at our level when we left Marzanna's castle to enter Nawia. Was there some part of this strange, fractal darkness that we weren't grasping? Or had

Czarnobóg just allowed Nawia to fall into its natural changing chaos as his darkness sped it toward destruction?

Weles's Thread followed the river's flow, but drifted downward. Though we swam together, I found our inability to speak isolating, and the darkness creeping further into my moonlight made it difficult to see Wacław and Mother out of my peripherals. It didn't matter that Wacław and I could speak through each other's minds and feel each other's sensations. My instincts convinced me I was alone.

And I hated it.

I'd preferred solitude just moons ago. A good day meant no people calling me a witch or begging for an old potion Mother had taught me to brew. The equinox hunt for the golden egg had been annoying, forcing me to cooperate with the boy who'd avoided me for years and two children who wandered about with little direction. There had been countless bad days since then, but that one began a change I wouldn't see for a long time.

There was nothing wrong with solitude for a time. But there was comfort, safety in being around those I loved. I'd feared those things after Mother's death and Wacław's retreat. No longer.

So I checked for their presence every few moments. It was silly, but with the shadow demons circling closer as my light faded, I needed to know that they were with me. Whether against Weles or Czarnobóg, they gave me the confidence I needed.

A ring of stone pillars appeared from the deep, each stretching higher than my light could reveal. I stopped at its edge, and the demons kept further back. They hissed through the water. Disunited and deafening, it jarred me as I laid my hand on the stone and reached out with my power to sense any magic at work here.

The answer was blinding. A vast array—or more, disarray—of dark wisps enclosed the stone circle. I couldn't see any demons or other beings attached to them, but *žityje* poured from them so heavily that my heart skipped a beat when they pulsed.

I turned to Mother to explain, but cursed silently when only bubbles and incoherent noises came out. Instead, I settled for silently informing Wacław of the danger, then mimed what I'd seen to

Mother. It was a horrible process, but by the end, her eyes narrowed as she turned to study the circle. She could sense the *żityje* too. It was the unexplained wisps that had me worried, though.

Mother extended her arm. Vines wrapped around her wrist, stretching through the gap in the nearest pillars. They wound vibrantly without resistance until they reached the end of my light. We swapped glances, and she frowned before sending another push of *żityje* through the vines. More shot out.

They soon stopped somewhere in the darkness, wrinkling Mother's brow further. Decay crept across the vines at the end of my light and crumbled them to dust. Mother released what remained before the decay could strike her fingers, but wisps remained.

I dove in front of Mother to stop her from moving into the remnant decay. Whatever it was had fed on the vines in seconds. What would a ravenous force like this do when it tasted a goddess's bountiful *żityje?*

But it was decay… part of my force.

For once, I thanked Trygław's diversity of powers. Some elements of his were less bound to me than others, but his connection to the decay that ended one cycle and began another had saved me multiple times. Now, as I reached out to understand this hunger, a sea of shouts filled my mind.

"PROTECT… MASTER… REBUILD!"

I fell back, drifting as I clutched my head and screamed into the water. Those voices were all there was. Their agony flooded through me in a desperation greater than anything I'd ever felt, ever experienced. It consumed every fiber of these strange beings and aligned them toward a single purpose.

No, this wasn't decay. Decay allowed for new growth to replace it. These *things* were bent on pure destruction until nothing remained within their circle.

I needed to talk with Mother.

Turning to her and then Wacław, I pointed up and began to swim back to the surface. That circle wasn't something I intended to enter without knowing what I faced. I was no vine, but experience told me that even gods could perish against strange magic. Czarnobóg had proven that clearly in Prawia.

Our dive through the waters had felt like hours, but I emerged mere seconds after starting our rise. Real air came with it, sending me into a coughing fit as I adjusted from breathing through the water. The shadowy demons skittered about at my outburst. Why did they still follow me, but not attack? They had obviously sensed the danger in the circle. What did they sense in me?

Mother appeared a moment later and wiped away the sopping hair that stuck to her face. "What did you sense in the stone ring?" she asked, straight to the point.

"That isn't just decay," I replied with a shudder as I remembered the shouts. "There are beings of some kind in there who are desperate to protect their 'master'. Weles, maybe?"

Her lip curled. "Our servants… I will send that bastard of a żmij back to Oblivion!"

"What do you mean?"

"The spirits who stood by Weles and my side through every trial are trapped in there with him." She glanced down, as if she could see the ring from here. "Czarnobóg must have corrupted them, thwarting their forms but retaining the part of their intentions that held them to protection. I doubt they even realize they are the ones trapping him instead."

I followed her gaze. "I doubt they realize much of anything. Their voices in my head sounded like they were being tortured." A pit suddenly formed in my stomach. "Wait… Where is Wacław?"

He hadn't emerged within my moonlight, and I would've heard a splash if he'd come up further away. I focused on our Thread, its bright glow shooting downstream and under the surface.

I dove, not waiting for Mother to answer as I pled through our bond instead. Wacław was in no state to defend himself in this darkness. A blade couldn't cut easily through water, and there was no wind there for him to control. Neither was there a reply.

"Wacław!" I called into the water, but it came out as little more than gargled groans.

Demons swirled about me quicker and quicker. As if they fed off my own desperation, I sensed their remnant *žityje* pulsing like a heart with its veins spread through each of them. One drew too close, so I summoned my spear and lashed out, slicing through it as if it were nothing. It scattered like smoke until all that remained was a trailing whisper of a woman's voice in my mind. A heartbeat later, even that disappeared. Had I freed her, or sent her to suffer in Oblivion?

I shoved away the thought and swam on. Wacław was out there, and wasting time on some random demon would only make things worse. I couldn't save them all. That fact made me burn inside, but I couldn't.

My remarkably quick rise to the surface was a distant afterthought compared to the endless depths I faced now. The darkness stretched on without stone, mud, or anything else to break the Smorodina's creeping flow. I clutched my spear in preparation for some foe to break through my light, but there was only the nothingness. Not even Trygław's silver appeared. I wished it to show me some end, to reveal what happened to Wacław.

Our shared Thread snapped tight. I grabbed hold of it and pulled with all the strength my straining muscles had.

A figure entered the light. Limp, Wacław lay back with his arms drifting at his sides, his light blond hair spread light a raven's wings and his eyes held shut. His Moonmark necklace from Lubena floated free from his tunic, finishing the Eclipsemark hanging from my own neck. That eclipse had made him the Naw he was, but it did *not* define him.

Wake up, I told him through our bond. He remained still, so I swam to his side and shook him. *I'm not letting you give up! Wake!*

I'd have thought him dead, but *žityje* flourished in his soul and his bright blue wisp hopped around me like Sosna when she was excited. His mind felt at peace. Despite the demon's hunger lingering within him, I no longer sensed it pushing its bounds.

Waking him from that rest felt wrong, but he couldn't stay here. The demons surrounding me may not have attacked yet. There would be others, though, and he would be defenseless like this.

I raised a gentle hand to his cheek and pulsed my *žityje* against it. *It's me,* I told his mind. *We can't stay here.*

His eyes fluttered open. He snatched my hand, but released me when he realized what was happening. "I…" he gargled through the water before coughing and switching to our telepathy. *"The darkness was so heavy. You swam away, and when I reached the edge of your light, I couldn't keep going."*

The pit in my chest deepened. *I'm sorry. I won't leave you again.*

He gave a gentle smile. *"Your light can only go so far. It'll get dark eventually, and I need to be able to survive in it by myself."*

You won't be alone.

"I'm never alone." He placed a hand over his heart. *"A part of your soul is in me."*

I scoffed. *Stop being soppy and come with me. We've got an arrogant old man to save.*

His brows arched as he gave a wry smile. He raised his hand to mine and intertwined our fingers. *"We'll save him together."*

35

Wacław

If the demons are afraid of that ring, shouldn't we be?

AFTER RECONVENING WITH DZIEWANNA ON THE SURFACE, we dove again toward the circle imprisoning Weles. The Smorodina flowed toward it no matter which direction we approached from, yet the river itself must have carried further into Nawia somehow. I'd given up trying to understand the realm. It had been a strange place before, and now, the only thing consistent about it was Czarnobóg's suffocating darkness.

It was strange swimming through such a warm river. The water resisted more than normal, but wasn't the viscous black substance we'd encountered on the Way of Souls. No, this darkness cut through the water, thickening it like the air. It had lulled me into a slumber before, and I feared what would happen when I inevitably left Otylia's silver light again.

Weles's Thread of Life guided us ever downward. With Otylia's mark on my arm, I saw her Threads when she called them, and I poured my hope into that line.

This is Weles's realm, even with the corruption, I told myself. *He'll have answers. He has to.*

That did little to ebb my worries. To succeed, Otylia needed me by her side—at least Dziewanna seemed convinced of that. Faltering against the corruption put her at risk, and the rest of the inhabitants of the Three Realms would follow. My body felt as if its guts were being tied in knots. We needed to free Weles quickly.

Dziewanna had explained above the water that the spirits should recognize her. After all, they served her almost as much as they did Weles, and some had likely held more loyalty to her. *Should* and *would* were two different levels of certainty, though. That had my chest tight as the ring of towering stones emerged in Otylia's moonlight once again.

It struck me as strange that the stone seemed to stretch on forever toward the surface, but that we could only find them this deep. With more time we could've investigated what was above. According to the Threads, though, Weles was in the depths, and dealing with him was enough of a curiosity already.

Dziewanna had no stray worries of the stones or their purpose. Hand outreached, she swam toward the closest gap in them with Otylia lurking behind.

I drew Grudzień as I sensed *żityje* swirling beyond the light. Whatever awaited us there likely couldn't be cut by a blade, but it reassured me to know I was ready in case there was something I could swipe at. If Narcyz had taught me anything, it was that it's better to be prepared for a fight that never came than to be unprepared for one that was inevitable.

My gut told me there was little chance Dziewanna could free Weles simply by corrupted spirits knowing her. Czarnobóg was brash, but not foolhardy. He hadn't escaped Oblivion and ravaged the Three Realms by bullheadedness alone.

Dziewanna's hand and then forearm passed into the ring. She hesitated, but seeing nothing change, continued at a tortoise's pace. My patience waned by the time a dark wisp fluttered by the edge of Otylia's light. Mere finger-lengths from Dziewanna's hand.

The wild goddess glanced over her shoulder at us and raised her other hand as a signal to wait. That would limit how far she could go with the limited light, but she kept advancing.

More wisps shot past. They weren't the misty, swirling forms of a normal soul or spirit's wisp, but series of semi-translucent spiny limbs that grasped out at Dziewanna. It was as if crystals deep in the Vastrothie caves had taken flight with bodies somehow made of the air itself, and I wanted to cry out for Dziewanna to stop. Nothing good came from a creature like that, right?

Those spiny limbs entrapped Dziewanna's extended arm as more and more of the creatures appeared. They suffocated all the light at the far edge of Otylia's circle, leaving Dziewanna as a shadow in their midst. But she did not waver.

Dziewanna chanted, her voice pushing through the water, but the words were indistinguishable and distorted. Each seemed to lull the darkness. It loosened enough for her to creep forward without resistance until she reached the last fragment of light.

Where the limbs grabbed her.

I held back Otylia as she lunged to aid her mother, but nothing could stop her frenzy. She tore free and burst into the ring. The light went with her, leaving me no choice but to follow out of fear of the demon's growing pull.

Her Thread guided us deeper and deeper into a sloping pit that filled the ring of stone. Darkness slipped into Otylia's moonlight like a spear piercing a cracked shield, slowing but announcing its imminent danger. Unfortunately, she gave no care for that danger as tendrils of darkness reached out for her spear-arm. The other was protected by Weles's armband, so I swept to her side with a few strong strokes that strained my weakened muscles, then drove Grudzień's blade straight through the tendrils.

The Moonblade shimmered with each color that split across its jagged black blade. Whatever *žitýje* lingered in the corrupted spirits was now consumed by Grudzień, and it hummed with power. This was not its moon to unleash yet, but I took some confidence in the strike working as I turned to Otylia and nodded sharply to her.

Keep going, I said through our bond. *I'll cover you.*

She only nodded, but I needed no thanks. As she chased Dziewanna, all that mattered was keeping the two of them alive. Weles was irrelevant if I lost them.

The back of my neck tingled as the dark creatures appeared before us. Like vines around a mighty tree, they grabbed at Dziewanna from every direction, but she was undeterred. Another figure was trapped in darkness at the edge of the light, and she pushed toward it with Otylia and me charging to slash down the creatures.

Except Dziewanna waved us away. Otylia tried to ignore her, but her mother's glare sent her reeling into me as she gripped her spear hard enough for the pain to shoot through our bond. That pain deepened when Weles's bearded, haggard face became clear in her moonlight.

Bubbles stirred from Otylia's lips as she cursed into the water. That same fury burned in my chest, but tendrils of darkness beyond Dziewanna's creatures forced my attention away. At first, Grudzień sliced through them with ease. More came with each cut, though, and my sluggish movements coupled with the thick water made reacting to their advances near impossible.

Whatever we're doing, I told Otylia, *we need to do it now!*

Her eyes darted from Dziewanna, narrowing as *żityje* pulsed from her hands. *"I'm getting sick of this stupid darkness."*

Moonlight shot from her with enough force to send me tumbling out of the light. The tendrils dissolved, but it was as if they re-formed instantly around my neck. Choking me. Sending darkness itself down my throat.

I couldn't breathe, couldn't cry out. Panic alone scattered the thoughts I tried to send to Otylia, and water joined the darkness flooding my lungs as I forgot how to use Dziewanna's gills.

The demon slammed against its cage within me. My throat screamed as I lashed out with Grudzień, hoping to fend off my invisible foe and free myself from the darkness's grip. It found nothing. Only the blurred shine of Otylia connected me to anything beyond the dark, and I clung to it with all my will.

Swim, I commanded my legs.

Darkness clouded my vision as I kicked sloppily, flailing just to throw myself into the smallest ray of light. A hiss filled my ears with each attempt, and rage burned deep within my core. I was weak. I couldn't save them myself. The demon could save them. The demon could defeat Cz—

NO!

My legs locked as Otylia turned back toward me with her mouth agape. I wanted to swim, to throw myself back into her light, but holding tight the demon's cage took all my strength. I'd drown before I released it. My lungs demanded air, but until the demon relented, I'd give them nothing.

The hissing darkness faded at the touch of Otylia's silver light. I greedily sucked in all the air I could until I coughed through the water. My grip on Grudzień had loosened, but I snatched it back quickly as a cracking sound spread behind me.

Otylia rushed to my side, but Dziewanna lingered behind. Though she'd transformed into some half-crab, half-human beast and struck at the dark spirits containing Weles, she'd only managed to rip a few away. More circled her and latched on to their former master. That gave her little pause, but there was no time to signal for her aid as a chill swept across the Smorodina. The hairs on my arms stood on end. This channeling was all too familiar.

Marzanna's winter.

"She betrayed us!" Otylia snapped in my head, readying her spear for a strike.

That cold burrowed into my chest and burned my racing heart, but something Marzanna had said stuck with me. *No,* I replied. *Czarnobóg stole her force, just as he's done to Dziewanna and probably Weles...* Dread dropped that frost to my stomach. *He can command all the forces they wield: even the spirits who served them.*

"And entomb us in frost!"

Otylia rushed back toward the stone ring. I followed, sheathing Grudzień out of fear of leaving her light again. But we were too late.

Her light refracted as we charged toward the nearest gap in the stones. Ice as thick as a mature oak blocked our path and formed a dome overhead. When I slammed both Grudzień and Kwiecień into it, the Moonblades only left thin cuts that sealed just heartbeats later. My arms ached from the effort already. Out of the water, I could've hacked away to try and outpace the ice's mending, but exhaustion and the water's drag made it impossible.

It was always going to be a trap, I told Otylia, *but we can escape this. Against three gods, a wall of ice is nothing.*

She shook her head, poking the ice with the Moonstone at the end of her spear. *"He's stolen fragments of their power. He will have a counter, and I doubt we're alone."*

I gave a wry smile. *But he hasn't stolen yours. Let's go back and free Weles before whatever's in here kills us, and then you can hit the ice with a moonblast or two.*

"It won't be that simple."

It never is, but it's worth a try.

With a roll of her eyes, she turned back. *"Fine. You have a point. Mother was struggling to free Weles too, so maybe my force—"*

Another round of cracks cut her off as ice shot from the dome in sharp spires. One speared my side, drawing blood before I could dodge, and another aimed for Otylia's head before she shattered it with a light shield that sent shards drifting through the waters. We exchanged worried looks, then swam back to her parents with only her shields stopping us from being impaled.

My black blood drifted behind. *Żityje* worked slowly with my weakness, and it made each stroke feel as if hot irons were being driven into my skin. I assured myself a little blood didn't matter, but the figures circling in my peripherals said otherwise.

The shadowy demons who'd kept their distance from the ring now returned, sweeping through my blood with an excited chittering that echoed through the dark waters.

Otylia! I called out to her. *The demons!*

She scowled, turning back with the curved end of her spear sweeping away the nearest of them. They hissed, but shied back against the intensity of her light. Some among them appeared larger, though. Were these like the upióry who grew when feeding on their victims?

Another spire shattered against her shields as she snatched my hand. *"Don't fall behind. I'm not losing you to this bitter darkness by blood or demon."*

I didn't fall behind, but my limbs were heavy, my strokes weaker and weaker. If the shadowy demons struck again, I doubted I would be of any use. Releasing Weles and ending the realm's corruptive hold on me was my only hope. When we returned to him, though, we found not the trickster god of the underworld and lowlands, but a frail old man.

The dark spirit servants had released him at Dziewanna's willing. That should've been a good thing, but it appeared they were merely content with how much they had drained him, as they swarmed Dziewanna instead.

Flames ripped through the water around the wild goddess's crablike form despite the water. They seared many of the spirits, but others shot right through and clamped onto her. Like leeches, they sucked away her *żityje*. None flowed into them, though, and I feared Czarnobóg's power if all the life force his servants had drained from us fed him directly. It had taken Rod's power to restore Dziewanna's force in an altered state. What would happen to Nawia if Czarnobóg had severed Weles's connection to his force too?

I chose not to dwell on that worry. We had plenty already, and there was nothing I could do to change what had been done to Nawia's king. There was little I could do to help now either, but Otylia ensured that wasn't necessary.

The Threads of Life burst forth around her godly parents. Frayed, blackened ones connected them to their corrupted servants, and Otylia split the gap between them. Spear raised, she used it like a bridge between the tethers, tying corrupted Threads on one end and Dziewanna's on the other with a swirl of *żityje* surging between the Moonstones capping each end.

I could only cover her flank against the circling shadow demons as she worked. My thrusts were slow, barely a prod, but most of the shadows were held together by mere wisps. Only the ones who'd absorbed my blood showed any strength, and they circled, waiting for their allies to leave me vulnerable. But I wouldn't fall. Otylia needed just a few more moments. With twin Moonblades dragging through the river before me, I swore I'd hold on.

The shadows shifted as if they'd heard my promise. Angling from each side, the bulkier, more formed demons swept toward me with forms resembling zmory, upióry, and ravenous wilkołaks. Each as deadly as the other.

My blades refused to answer their challenge, catching like an ax embedded in a tree. Kwiecień in my left hand just graced the edge of one beast as Grudzień's teeth clipped another's head, but there were far more. As the two I struck dispersed into weaker wisps, the others raked claws across my entire torso.

No blood came.

Pain struck me, but no wounds graced my body with their rapid strikes. *Žityje* slipped from my soul instead, its power swirling into them and suddenly turning their shadowy forms to flesh. Human flesh. The shadows that had swarmed me now floated back as people of all ages and tribes, their eyes wide and bubbles drifting from their lips.

It took a young boy wrapping his hands around his throat to make me realize they were drowning. Shadows turned to people. Dziewanna had granted Otylia and me gills, but these people were deep underwater without air.

The air was far above, and far from Otylia's light. There was no other option but to save them, but how?

Burgeoning light interrupted me, followed by more gurgled screams. The dark wisps had vanished from around Dziewanna and Weles to leave nymphs and other spirits half-resembling humans in the same state as the former shadows. And like the shadows, many were drowning.

"We need to rise," Otylia said in my head, grabbing my hand. *"I know you're drained, but the winds must have some power here! Call them with what you have left."*

I can't feel them, I replied.

She squeezed. *"Search for that power flowing from the Way of Souls. The Smorodina carries its souls here, so why couldn't it carry a piece of Nawie power too?"*

The escalating screams couldn't banish my doubt, but closing my eyes, I reached out for the little *żityje* left within me. The demon didn't hold all my power. Though Rod had created Nawie accidentally, we were protectors, and I focused on that desire, that purpose granted to me at birth. The Way of Souls had renewed my strength. It granted the dead a path into this realm, and as I tapped the little *żityje* I had left, its hum found me now. Faint, like a distant song instead of a shamans' earthshaking drums. But that was enough. It had to be.

Air rushed from above. Like a sixth sense, I felt the winds cutting through the water and deflecting it around the pillars forming the arc of Weles's prison. Czarnobóg's ice dome shattered without the water to feed it, and shards scattered around us as I fell to my knees, my soul fighting to form a floor of air between us and the rest of the water beneath.

My head ached. My body burned like it had been dropped into the worst of the Smorodina's flames on the Way again.

I couldn't keep my eyes open, and neither could I resist as someone took me in their arms and lifted me. We rose through my clearing as my *żityje* strained to hold back the water. Each bit I lost was a hole that corruption's call filled, like it had all those moons ago when Otylia traded a portion of her soul to save my own from falling to the demon. The power I'd sensed in the Way could only grant me the smallest fraction, and I clung to it as my final hope until I could hold back the waters no longer.

Cold stone met my skin as my winds failed. The water crashed down, and my consciousness fell with it.

36

Otylia

Great, now we need to babysit a bunch of dead spirits and people.

MY CHEEK BLED FROM HOW HARD I BIT IT, staring down at the Smorodina River from a shifting island of stone not far above.

I should've been pleased. We'd rescued Weles, purified spirits through Mother's connection with them, and somehow given shadowy demons humanity once again through the *żityje* in Wacław's blood. That would've been a success on any other godsforsaken day.

Not this one. In this corrupted realm, it had been hard enough to keep the darkness from devouring Wacław and the demons from overwhelming Mother. We now had a dozen living mortals—well, *living* in the Nawia sense of the word—and nearly fifty scattered spirits to deal with. Not to mention the trickster god who happened to be my blood father.

As Wacław lay unconscious, the *żityje* I'd transferred to him slowly mending the cracks in his soul, I took stock of how much of that life force I had left. The answer unnerved me.

Ascending to godhood had granted me far more strength than I'd ever wielded as a szeptucha, but it was finite. I needed the offerings of my worshippers to restore what I used. It hadn't been long since I'd replenished my strength through a summoned altar in Dwie

Rzeki, though, and I held my breath as I wove together a few strands of light to create another here.

The sphere of protective light surrounding us dimmed with the new drain upon my power. Darkness lapped at its edges like waves approaching high tide, knowing the land would soon give way, and the furthest redeemed mortals skirted inward to avoid becoming lost in Czarnobóg's influence. Nawia changed constantly now. To fall outside the light was to lose track of where you were, or if where you'd left still existed at all.

A shimmering altar of silver light formed before me, holding a bone bowl etched with my Moonmark across its rim. Deep crimson blood filled it—not enough.

No matter the offering my worshippers gave, it appeared here in the form of *żityje*-imbued blood. It was a gruesome experience, but it was what it took to be a god. Through the practice, I heard the pleas of those who needed me, and they gave what they could to help me fulfill those prayers.

That was the theory at least. After such a short time, my szeptuchy and worshippers hadn't managed to collect enough sacrifices to fill the basin, and I'd already used much of my *żityje*.

I took the bowl and raised it to my lips. This was all I had to face Czarnobóg and protect these people. A growing ball in my stomach told me it wouldn't be enough, but I denied that doubt a further hold. It had to be enough, and that's all that mattered.

No amount of practice could stop me wincing when the blood ran down my throat. The flood of *żityje* that followed made it worth it, but gods, I hated this. Gods could only take willingly given sacrifices, but that hardly made it feel any better than demonic hunger.

The fresh pool of *żityje* in my soul did curb the worst of my fears. My growing abilities had also granted me a greater understanding of my remaining supply, though, and at the rate I was depleting it, I wouldn't last more than another day, maybe two if we didn't run into another fight before finding Czarnobóg. And gods knew how much I'd need against him.

Mother noticed my exasperated sigh, circling to approach like a cat to a mouse. She'd lost her strange crab-like form and removed our gills, but flames now lapped at her heels.

"I would say you look far too discontent for someone who just saved so many spirits," she said in a hushed tone as she took a seat along the island's edge, then patted the ground beside her. "But I know *far too well* that discontent is your natural state of being."

I joined her, and though my legs dangled far above the Smorodina, a tingle ran across my heel. As if dark tendrils dared to drag me away. "I'm tired of it," I breathed. "All of it. I need offerings from people who have nothing, only to use that gifted power as a flicker of light in Czarnobóg's darkness. I can't solve their problems. I can't fix Wacław."

I hesitated, pulling one leg in and glancing over my shoulder at Weles. The elderly god conversed with a pair of spirits a few strides away, as my light went little further. His back bent as if he wished to lean upon his old wooden cane, but he had none. Could he not summon it?

"He's powerless, isn't he?" I asked Mother with every ounce of hope slipping from my voice. He'd been our chance to push back the corruption gripping Wacław, but what use was a god without a force to wield?

She followed my gaze. A smile tugged at the edge of her lips, drawing a wrinkle across my brow.

"Why are you smiling?" I muttered as I grabbed her arm. "We need his power."

"There is something sweet about seeing him as nothing more than a frail old man," she replied. The smile vanished. "He has abused his power often. Why should he not endure a few moments without it?"

Her hand patted the back of mine, and her eyes glimmered with an ancient knowing. "It took Czarnobóg moons to sever my connection to the force of the wilds. Weles may be weakened, but his force remains. Close your eyes and feel the flow of power around us. This realm curls around its master, bowing with every fiber of its being, but he will need to restore his *żityje*. Even then, his full strength will take time to return."

I shook my head, releasing her, but I sensed the shift around Weles. His influence on his realm was not yet gone completely. "We don't have time. The darkness is sapping my *żityje*, and if we don't reach Czarnobóg before it runs out, then—"

"We will defeat Czarnobóg because of your power, not Weles's or mine. You are our bastion against the darkness, and you need rest."

"Rest?" I spat. "I just told you my *żityje* will run out before long, and you want me to waste hours asleep while Czarnobóg's hold deepens?"

She pressed two fingers to her temple, then laid her hand over her heart. "Listen to your instincts and your force. Trygław speaks to you when your mind is silent, and you cannot defeat the dark żmij exhausted."

"He seemed threatened during the last vision, like he couldn't stay here."

Weles hobbled closer, and Mother's lips drew to a narrow line as she patted my shoulder. "Listen to what little he can muster, then. His intentions are his own, but he has guided you this far. I must admit when there is one who knows more than me."

"Rare wisdom from my bold wife," Weles said, stopping before us and reaching for her hand, which she pulled back. "I hope you were speaking of my wisdom to free Nawia."

I spun off the ledge and put distance between us. "*Wise* is not the word I'd use to describe you."

He smirked beneath his bushy beard. "Yet you sought my aid nonetheless. Is it about the demonic boy, the one who burned my home in his rage?" His gaze flicked to Wacław, a golden hue flashing across his eyes. "This dark corruption devours him."

I opened my mouth to rebuke him for stating the obvious, but Mother was quicker. "It was our hope you could help Wacław, yes," she said, moving to his side but stiffening as she did so. "Czarnobóg's darkness is not within your power to banish, but the corruption emanates from Oblivion. If you could devote your strength to bolstering Nawia against it, Wacław and the spirits and souls who inhabit here may find relief long enough for us to strike."

"You believe I am not needed to face the dark dragon himself?" Weles asked with his brow raised. "I admit, that is a surprise."

Again, I went to reply, but Mother spoke first. "I know what it is to endure Czarnobóg's torture. What power you have left is dampened, and he has stolen much of your force's strength. As he did the same to me, it must be Otylia to defeat him. You and I must ensure she reaches him unharmed."

Weles threw out an arm toward Wacław. "What of the boy?"

"His soul holds part of mine," I said, the words tumbling from my lips so that Mother didn't have a chance to speak first. Her grin was a knowing one, but she let me continue. "I need him beside me to have my full strength against Czarnobóg, and based on my visions, my moonlight is the only way to do that right now."

"That is a heavy ask after you disavowed me and caused a rebellion within my realm." The elder god's words were slow, careful, but a hint of amusement lingered in that glow in his eyes. "If it were not for you, perhaps I would have had the strength to resist Czarnobóg. Perhaps the three of us could have created a united front to unify the realms."

I bared my teeth. "Unity? You almost killed me! While I lay broken on that island after my Ascension, it took Wacław feeding me his blood to save me. You never cared about me, just revenge against Perun!"

Mother's glare bore into me like one of Marzanna's ice pillars, forcing me to turn away, fists clenched. Why did she defend him now? After all he'd done to us, why protect him?

"We may settle our grievances *after* this is finished," she said through clenched teeth. "What matters is that right now, Otylia needs Wacław at full strength, or as close to it as he can get. Our ambitions and desires are secondary to that."

Weles looked at her, then me. That glint was gone, and his thick brows arched like a startled cat. "What has become of Jaryło? What happened to my son after you slayed Rod and sent us all to ruin?"

"He's alive and with Perun," I muttered. "Forgiving him for breaking our blood pact was the only way Perun would let me leave Prawia, but I hope he's still suffering."

"You are a spiteful child."

I rolled my eyes. "And you are a selfish old man. Believe me, I didn't want to save you, but we need you right now… I need you right now. Do what you want once Czarnobóg is dead. I don't care. Until then, the Three Realms are doomed if we don't finish this quickly."

Weles sighed and stared upward. "Yet Perun sits on his laurels in the realm of the gods, laughing down at me. He takes my place in Prawia and my son, then forces me to defeat his father's old foe. How righteous of him."

"You won't be defeating anything. I don't care for Perun either, but he's not here right now. He's not the king of this realm." I stepped toward him and shoved a finger into his chest. "You are."

Surprisingly, he stumbled back as if I'd shoved him. His face was gaunter, his frame frailer than before, but surely, he couldn't be *that* weak? Mother's body had been less worn than her soul and its severed connection to her force. Was this different?

"Very well," he stammered, his voice far from the ancient god who'd greeted me in Nawia after Jaryło's betrayal. Where was his cunning, his guile? "You have my aid for now, but I shall not forget how you both have turned against me."

Mother circled him, and Weles's breath fled as she lightly touched his shoulder. "We are all aware that your grudges last eternities. Each realm has suffered for it." She waved for me to follow her. "Come, Otylia. Let us find you rest while Weles lends his strength to banishing the corruption from Nawia and Wacław."

37

Wacław

My body lies.

OTYLIA'S SILVER LIGHT GREETED ME AS I WOKE and held a palm to my forehead. I felt *normal*—well, as normal as I'd felt since the death of my mortal soul—and that made me suspicious.

Figures shifted through my blurred vision, forcing me to wipe my eyes as I took stock of my body. The demon lurked beneath, but no longer pounded at my heart. My limbs responded to my commands with ease. *Žityje* no longer fled my soul to fight the corruption.

That was all good, but what had changed? The last thing I remembered was pushing back the waters to protect the people and spirits we'd saved from their corruption.

The answer stood before me in the form of a wrinkled, bent man with hair the color of damp soil that hung wet over his shoulders. Heat rushed through my chest, and I shot to my feet, grabbing him by his robes.

"Weles, what have you done to me?"

The god of tricksters, merchants, the lowlands, and the afterlife stared back at me with eyes carrying the weight of centuries. He made no move to repel my aggression, but I stepped back with my hairs raised, a chill coursing up my arms. Little *žityje* resided in his soul. A god as powerful as him should've blinded my demonic senses, but he had little more than a szeptucha who'd completed her daily duties.

My lips parted, the words more difficult than they should've been. "You... fixed me?" I patted my body down as if there would be some evidence that he'd left some fragment of his power behind to manipulate me later. There was nothing. "Why? Where's Otylia?"

I spotted her a moment later, lying by Dziewanna with her light protecting dozens of spirits and mortals. Relief came with seeing her safe, relaxed even, and I took a long breath before returning my attention to Weles.

He studied me with his head cocked. A strange disapproval crossed his face, like he was a potter and I his misshapen creation.

"Do not make me regret this," he said. Each word carried an emphasis like the one I used when talking to my little half-sister Nevenka, but here, it was obviously demeaning. "Though my work is not complete, at the pleading of my wife and daughter, I have devoted my power to pushing back Czarnobóg's corruption of Nawia. Some fraction of it may still reach for you in the deeper darkness. Whether you fall to it then is not for me to decide, demon."

Against my pride and instincts, I bowed my head. "Thank you. I can't forgive what you did to Otylia, but I'm grateful you've helped us now." I hesitated, then met his gaze again. "I can sense how much effort you have poured into this."

"I do not seek your gratitude." He turned away, but stopped and waved for one of his serving spirits. A gray-skinned nymph ran over and crouched so that the god could put his hand on his shoulder, keeping him upright. "I am curious, however, what you intend to do once this is over. You cannot believe you will be allowed to remain a goddess's lover."

I tapped Grudzień's pommel at my back. "Did you plan on stopping me? Last I remember, your palace burned when you tried that."

"Your victory spanned moments, boy. The vengeance of gods spans centuries, and I know well how to make you wish you bore a mortal life instead of your extended one." He held out his free hand to summon his cane of willow wood, its top curling over itself to form a spiraled handle. Then, with the aid of both cane and nymph, he shuffled back to the rest of his servants.

His threat lingered.

We'd escaped Nawia through guile and luck, and I doubted we'd have done so if it had been Weles and not Jaryło who'd awaited us outside the Heart of Nawia. Only Ivan's distraction had allowed us to flee Weles on the island where Otylia Ascended. Weles was far from his full strength now, but as he'd said, that wouldn't last forever.

That was a worry for a day far from this one. It relied on the assumption we survived our fight with Czarnobóg, collected the last of the shards of Alatyr, and mended the veil separating Oblivion from the Three Realms. Weles was also far from the first god who despised me. Based on my demonic soul, he'd hardly be the last.

Seeking a friendlier face, I joined Dziewanna near the center of our floating island. Collisions and the splitting of others rolled like thunder through the darkness, but ours remained intact within Otylia's moonlight. That would inevitably change, though.

"How long can we stay here with all these people?" I asked the wild goddess, kneeling by Otylia's side. Her exhaustion sunk deep in my core to join with my own. "Weles says he's pushed back the corruption—at least in part—but can we protect so many?"

"That will be the rest of Weles's task," Dziewanna replied. She stood with her arms crossed and her flaming dress flapping at her feet from the inconstant wind. Often, she looked barely older than her early thirties, but her face was heavy now, resembling a wise elder more than the queen of the vibrant wilds. "Otylia will not approve, but I have told him to take the dead souls and any willing spirits back toward the border of Nawia. The corruption and darkness are weakest there, and any others who are protected by Weles's power may join them in that relative safety."

My shoulders slumped. "He won't help us against Czarnobóg?"

She flexed her hand, staring down at the flames dancing between each finger. "I know well the cost of enduring Czarnobóg's torment.

An elder god like him will recover quickly, but our approach to Nawia's core is imminent. We cannot face Czarnobóg with him in this state." Her final words held some hesitancy, as if she wanted to say more as her eyes flicked to Weles for a passing moment. Instead, she gestured to Otylia. "I do not wish to wake her, but time is of the essence. We are lucky she has had the chance to rest for this long."

"Today is it, then?" I asked. "The day we face him and end this?"

"Otylia says her *žityje* will run out if we don't, so we must act quickly."

I stared down at Otylia, admiring how gentle she could appear when asleep. Somehow, that girl who'd played with me in the woods as a child, kissed me in a meadow in the Mangled Woods, and stolen my heart every moment since was our only hope to kill the god of darkness.

Silver light radiated from her very skin. Her tangled black hair, though, was draped over her face in a way that resembled a wilkołak more than a goddess. A smile tugged at my lips. Being near her brought a warmth that banished Nawia's dark chill, calming the worries that plagued my mind. I didn't know what horrors lay ahead, but at least I knew I'd be facing them with her.

"Then it's time to enter the deepest darkness," I told Dziewanna, "and hope her light is enough."

38

Otylia

I know what I must do.

WACŁAW'S GENTLE TOUCH AGAINST MY CHEEK woke me from my restless sleep. Trygław had not appeared again, but his visions showed flashes of Czarnobóg's ends. Both past and potential future.

Alatyr's fall from Prawia and shattering had sent sparks through Jawia's darkness, forming a being of malice. Czarnobóg destroyed and destroyed until Swaróg dared to face him with his mighty hammer. But demonic corruption had spawned with the dark dragon, creating an army to serve him against the elder god. Even with the help of Prawia's other gods, Czarnobóg stood strong.

Until Swaróg and Perun reunited the twelve shards of Alatyr. Even then, they could only create a sub-realm to entrap Czarnobóg and his corruption within, sealing it away from the Three Realms.

I'd already heard these tales, but Czarnobóg's life in Oblivion was another story. Trapped for millennia, he'd fostered the corruption in his soul, growing with its potent strength and awaiting the day when Oblivion's veil fell. His rage became mine. His desire to thrive away from the gods expanded beyond vengeance into a pure *need* to destroy all his foes had created. As long as their mortals, their spirits, and their realms existed, he could never be free. So he would devour it all in his corruptive darkness.

Time had no end for him there, yet the cycles in his mind had many. Madness took his sanity in solitude. Some days he wept for himself and the demons slain by the gods. Others, he lashed out at the veil and screamed until he bled to the bone against its power, his corruptive *żityje* healing him before he could truly feel the pain. He wanted out. He wanted freedom.

He wanted to destroy.

Then the agony ended, the veil suddenly dropping as Marzanna called him into the Three Realms once again. He thought her a fool. Like any manipulative god, she believed she could control him to her own ends, but he'd spent thousands of years crafting his plot. He waited despite his yearning to be free. And when she was at her weakest after Mother and I defeated the fragment of her in Dwie Rzeki, he took advantage.

What I couldn't understand was why he'd left Marzanna instead of draining her more completely. Did he believe she could stop us, give him more time to further Nawia's corruption and expand into Jawia?

The answer didn't matter, but the visions proved he'd planned far ahead. He foresaw our attacks and defenses, further enrooted himself in the darkness while Marzanna's forces tore us apart. He knew my light. He knew we'd come for Weles and Nawia's core. Weles was useless against him, though, and freeing him had taken precious *żityje* I needed to kill Czarnobóg himself.

It all had a purpose to him. Gods played mortals like toys, and he was no different. Except the dark dragon played *gods* against each other like toys, waiting for them to fall before acting himself.

All schemes had flaws, though. Czarnobóg had planned for thousands of years, but he didn't know what happened in the Three Realms during that time. Nor could he see the future ends. He foresaw our attack, but only Trygław's visions revealed the future strands that could lead to our victory or defeat. I'd been so obsessed before with avoiding what could go wrong. Now, I just had to focus on the victory. My light, my connection to endings was the key.

What came next was up to me.

"You're awake?" I asked Wacław, pressing his warm hand against my cheek for a moment longer. "Does that mean Weles did his job?"

He smiled, and for the first time since we'd entered Nawia, I could tell it wasn't a false one. Nothing else made my heart so full. "He threatened to make the rest of my life pure torture, but for now, yes, he pushed back a lot of the corruption."

I tensed. "So there's some left?"

"Otylka, my remaining soul is demonic. There will always be remnant corruption in it, and Czarnóbg is too powerful here for Weles to get rid of all Nawia's taint." He smiled up at Mother, who I realized was standing guard over me with her dress aflame and her glare fixed on Weles. "Weles is going to take the spirits and souls, so it's up to us from here on."

"So my blood father leaves me to mend his realm." I scoffed and rose with a hand from Wacław. Gods, I badly wanted a moment alone with him before we fought for our lives, but there was nowhere to go away from Mother's watchful gaze. "I knew it would be up to me, but Trygław's visions made it clearer."

He studied me, holding our hands between us. "There's something else, isn't there? I know that look."

"I don't know…"

I'd just woken, and hadn't had time to process all I'd seen. Czarnóbg's emotions were real in those visions. Frighteningly, they made sense. He had corrupted Jawia against the gods, but it was the will of his force. He'd never known Prawia's paradise or what a normal mortal life was. That lack of understanding had led to a god war and his eventual confinement for longer than I could comprehend. I shouldn't have pitied him, but I did.

"Is it wrong to say I understand why Czarnóbg hates the gods and the living?" I said as I averted my gaze. "He's corrupted by his rage, but he didn't choose this."

Wacław winced, but nodded. "I know corruption's pull. If he was born of corruption when Alatyr shattered, he never existed without it, but that doesn't change the evil he's caused."

Mother turned from her glaring match with Weles and laid a hand on both of our shoulders. "Every god has made our mistakes—some greater than others—but Czarnobóg will have to find a way to mend his another time. We won't have time to hesitate when it comes to finishing this."

"Then I won't hesitate," I confirmed.

We prepared to leave as Mother's old serving spirits either bowed to or embraced her. Many were nymphs like Sabina, and my heart ached for my friends. Czarnobóg's corruption was spreading beyond Nawia now, so they would form the front line against the demons who sought to punish our allies. Having Wacław and Mother by my side made this easier. There was an unmatchable strength when we fought with all our friends, though, and I yearned to return home to them soon.

We will, I told myself. *Today is the last day of this war. Things will go back to normal after this.*

But what was normal? Wacław as king and I as his goddess lover? That couldn't last forever, as mortals needed to find their own way without immortals to rule them. Besides, Wacław and I had both sworn to protecting the souls of the natural dead in one form or another. Our fledgling kingdom deserved rulers who could devote all their attention to mortal affairs.

Whatever came after this wouldn't be normal. I hadn't been an Ascended goddess for even a year yet, and most of that time had been spent fighting Marzanna and Czarnobóg. It would take time to figure out what it meant to be a goddess outside a time of peril in the Three Realms.

We'd made allies and enemies alike in recent moons. Both would vie for power in the space left behind by Marzanna, Czarnobóg, and the fallen mortal tribes, destroyed by the Frostmarked Horde. For those of us who remained, the realms would be ours to shape for good or ill.

I pulled Wacław aside while the others said their parting words. We wouldn't have long, but this was as close as we'd get to that time alone.

We sat along the edge of the island, Wacław's legs swinging anxiously as he drummed at Kwiecień's pommel on his hip. Stubble covered his chin and jawline, and though Lubena had cut back his overgrown hair in Dwie Rzeki, a few stray strands curled over his ears. He resembled a warrior in the finest sense of the word. Those demonic veins crossing his skin were his battle scars, and his palm was calloused against mine as we squeezed so hard you'd think a force were dragging us apart.

Our people had crowned him as king, but that was the title Jacek had craved, not his son. Wacław had always dreamed of being an adventuring warrior, fighting monsters and protecting the innocent. Ironically, our discovery of his demonic soul had granted him exactly that. Some called him the monster, and he had been for a time. Beyond those moments of corruption's grip, though, he'd spent every moment protecting even those who despised him.

"Is this how you pictured it ending," I asked him, "when you faced Marzanna for the first time by the Wyzra?"

Sorrow filled his eyes. "Falling for her temptations was the most foolish thing I've ever done. Her Frostmark promised me the power and freedom I'd always wanted, but that's her manipulation. Show the desperate what they want, and they'll do anything to get it."

"You got your wish by defying her, not taking that mark." I traced where the Frostmark had once scarred his hand, gone now that our joined Moonmark and Eclipsemark pulsed on our forearms. "I'd been so afraid what would happen to you when that corruption deepened, but you pushed against her power and saved me from her curse." I grinned. "Wašek, I didn't know what to think about you for a long time, but that moment reminded me why I loved you. It was different when we were kids, but even the worst days have always been better with you by my side."

He raised my hand to his lips and kissed it softly. "I never stopped loving you. After Father's threats, I lied to myself that you were better off if I kept away, but I'm glad we found each other again. I want to remain by your side for as long as my strange Nawie life allows me to exist."

Heat rushed to my cheeks, despite it not being an unusual gesture for him. We'd had so little time to be a real couple, and I looked forward to that more than anything. "Good, because I don't plan on letting you out of my sight until I'm sure this corruption is gone."

"Knowing you're watching me is both threatening and alluring." He shifted closer and laughed, his breaths hot against my neck. "Unfortunately, I have to close my eyes and sleep now that you killed my mortal soul, so I can't promise the same to you—though, I'll do my best."

"As long as, when your eyes are shut, you're lying beside me, I'll forgive it."

He bowed his head with a smirk. "Your generosity is overwhelming, my goddess."

"Shut up!" I joked, punching his shoulder before grabbing his tunic and surprising him with a kiss. We parted only far enough for the tips of our noses to touch. "Please, I need you to be a reminder of who I am without these powers."

His fingers graced my cheek and pushed back my hair. "The stubborn witch who could never be tamed. Some things never change."

He returned the kiss, longer this time, and I let myself dwell in our bonded emotions. Our synced heartbeats. Our joy of being together. Our desire for this all to end. For those few precious moments, we were all that mattered. Not Czarnobóg or the fate of the Three Realms.

A cough interrupted us, and I blushed again at the sight of Mother standing over us, her brow raised in amusement. Weles, the spirits, and the souls were gone. That didn't lessen the embarrassment.

"Are you two finished?" she quipped. "Or shall I wait until the corruption deepens again?"

I rose with a sneer, the weight of our task returning like a tree falling on my shoulders. "You told me to rest, so I listened for once."

"I am proud of you for that, my little wildling. Are you rested?"

"Enough." I was still groggy from what was a nap more than a true sleep, and my *żityje* reserves were lower than I wanted them. There was little choice but to forge onward, though.

"And you?" she asked Wacław, who rose beside me with a roll of his shoulders.

"I'm not the important one here," he said. "But the demon's quieter, and my body doesn't feel ready to crumble. I'll take it."

Nodding, Mother extended an arm toward the darkness as her owl-like wings grew from her back once again. That still made my stomach twist, so I summoned my silver light spear and focused instead on our destination. Trygław's visions guided me toward the core of the darkness, where my light could banish him and his power away from the Three Realms. It all seemed so simple. Among the gods, though, nothing was ever so easy.

Wacław and Mother took my flanks as we launched off the island that had been our refuge and soared toward Czarnobóg's core. It tugged through my force, guiding me toward it like my tether to Wacław. Except this one made my insides crawl. And every moment we went on, the edges of my light crept closer until it barely encompassed us all.

"I never thought there could be something darker than the night during a new moon," Wacław said, reaching out beyond the light. His fingers disappeared completely, as if the darkness had teeth that ripped them away.

"This light will be gone by the time we reach the core," I replied. "I'll have to concentrate it into bursts, so be ready to rely on sound and the Threads of Life. I wish Trygław's silver could appear for you too, but our joined marks are limited."

I shrugged. "He's a giant three-headed dragon. If I swing my blades, I'm bound to hit something."

"It will not be so simple to strike him this time," Mother said. "He was the outsider in Prawia, but he has warped this realm to his cause. There will be spirits and demons aiding him. I will attempt to draw his attention away, but you, Wacław, should remain near Otylia's protection. She needs the fragment of her soul which resides in you."

He met my gaze and gave a nervous smile. "Then that's where I'll be."

Nawia's chill grew with the devouring darkness until my skin stung and the flames at the ends of Mother's dress flickered. The darkness smothered even them when they passed beyond my light, and I held to the reminder that Czarnobóg had stolen fragments of Marzanna, Weles, and Mother's powers. Winter had been Marzanna's entire threat. It was but a portion of Czarnobóg's.

My light had all but vanished a few minutes later. Wacław and Mother's faces were little more than shadows, the rest of their bodies engulfed in the darkness.

I started at something touching my free hand before realizing it was Wacław reaching for me one last time. "This is it," he said. "I'll see you when the light returns."

"Don't sound so ominous," I said, squeezing his hand.

"It is appropriate," Mother replied with her shadowy gaze fixed ahead. Only the bases of her antlers were visible, making it look as if some massive creature were perched upon her head. "The fate of the Three Realms rests in our hands, and Destiny herself holds her breath. Perhaps even Trygław will bother to care."

I took a long breath, fighting the growing ball in my chest. "He'll care. For better or worse, he's been guiding me this whole time. Whatever happens will affect his plans."

"Let's hope those plans don't involve me dying again," Wacław muttered.

A rumble shook the entire realm before I could reply. Nearby islands shattered, and Trygław's silver lines exposed stone shards scattering every direction. Most diverted away from us, but when a roar echoed from the depths ahead, they stopped, hovering.

"You have strayed beyond your domain, Otylia of the end," Czarnobóg's heavy, yet smooth voice called from the deep. "There is no moon here, no light, and when I am finished, there will be no remnant of the gods who bent these realms to their will. The Three Realms shall be built anew in the glory of Oblivion's power!"

The shards shot toward us as one, forcing me to summon a *pri* light shield. It protected us on every side with a thin layer of moonlight, but the darkness closed in and enveloped the passive light from my skin. Only that thin shield pierced the black as thousands of stone daggers cracked against its surface.

Each blow was small, but together, they pulled my *žityje* into maintaining the shield. Czarnobóg roared again and again, each shattering more islands and banishing what heat remained in the realm.

Ice and stone rained until my arms ached against the shield and my ears rang from the hammering of the shards. I lost track of time against the torrent, throwing all my energy into the shield as its light flickered at the edges. I couldn't break. Not now. Not when we were so close to Nawia's core. I couldn't let Czarnobóg drag the Three Realms into Oblivion and take all I loved with them. Against the pain, against the onslaught, I would stand.

"We must advance!" Mother shouted over the torrent. "He will shower us with the remnants of the entire realm if we sit here."

She made it sounds so obvious, but my body strained just holding my ground. Pushing onward…

I screamed into the abyss and threw myself forward, the Threads of Life revealing Wacław and Mother keeping beside me. My shield was only so large, and I needed to be careful not to send them outside its bounds. The constant barrage would spell death, even for a goddess. Czarnobóg wielded Weles's control over Nawia and the lowland earth to bend the islands to his will, while using Marzanna's winter to freeze me to the bone and add spires of ice to the mix.

The core of Nawia wasn't far now. I felt it pulling at my soul, as if desperate to be freed, but corruption flooded from it. The veil separating it from Oblivion was torn, so nothing stood in the way of the tainted power and the beings within that flooded the realm.

I caught sight of the creatures just beyond my shield. Dark, winged beasts with fangs and bodies that cracked with the power of a storm—chały. They were no strangers, but my chill deepened at the memory of the tapestry the Daughters of the Earth had in Vastroth. It had told of a time long past when chały blotted out the sky so thick that they devoured the sun. They were chaos, corruption of the very sky, and Wacław's rage at his familiar foes surged through our bond.

His lightning snapped before I could warn him not to waste his strength. Bright blue split around my shield before disappearing into the darkness, and only the shrieks of the beasts beyond revealed his success. It pushed away his fear.

"Drop the shield!" he cried out.

I ground my teeth. "Are you insane?"

But Trygław's silver wisps revealed him dual-wielding Grudzień and Kwiecień as the winds grew around us. "Maybe! But you trust me, right?"

"I do," I muttered through the pain, still trying to push onward at a far too slow rate.

"Then drop the shield."

39

Wacław

I've had better ideas.

MY HEART POUNDED SO HEAVILY THAT MY HEAD ACHED. It was frightening enough being surrounded by complete and utter darkness so thick that neither Otylia's base moonlight nor Dziewanna's flames could pierce it. Add an entire realm's worth of stone and ice shattering against a light shield, and you had terror worse than my darkest nightmares.

Yet, for some reason, I thought it would be best for Otylia to . It was our only thin ring of light and protection against the death barrage beyond, but I felt her *żityje* rapidly depleting. She needed her strength to banish the darkness.

I didn't.

"Then drop the shield," I heard myself call through the calamity, as if they were a stranger's words.

Grudzień and Kwiecień's hilts were frigid against my gloved fingers, and the chill had deepened beyond the worst of Marzanna's winters. Moonblades, they yearned to feast on more *żityje* to store for later use. There was a sea of it in the decrepit winged chały beyond the shield. A płanetnik's natural foe in the sky. My lightning had pierced some, but there were so many more to kill to buy Otylia the time she needed.

The winds circled us as I sensed her releasing the shield. My timing had to be perfect, or we'd all be skewered by shards of stone and spires of ice before we had the chance to heal. So I unleashed my whirlwind early, pouring my fury into the torrent at the tip of each Moonblade.

Otylia's fragment of light vanished with her shield. I caught my breath, waiting for the shards or chały to rip through my whirlwind and slay me before I ever saw light again.

But the winds caught the shards and brought them into their fold. Each thickened my defenses more by accident than design, and as we advanced, the stones cracked against other shards and spires of ice that attempted to break through. I flinched with each deafening sound. They only grew more constant with the growing layers of stone and ice within the whirlwind, drawing my *żityje* against the winds' weights.

I poured all my strength into the whirlwind. If I could only manage to keep Otylia protected until we reached Czarnobóg, it would be enough. The dark dragon had grown far too powerful for me to defeat by lightning or blade.

It seemed an eternity before the flapping of great wings broke through the cacophony. Czarnobóg's roar carried through the eternal darkness, and heat singed my brows as only the sudden reappearance of Otylia's silver shield diverted a blast of his draconic flames.

"Drop the whirlwind!" she shouted aloud.

It was my turn to panic. "Are you sure?"

"Trust me." I sensed her confidence flaring through our bond as she replied in my mind. *"And launch all the shards at him."*

With her shield in place within the whirlwind, I dropped it, circling with the final gust and throwing out the winds. Lightning snapped across my fingers and blades to join the surge of stone and ice. And when I sensed the corruptive horror of the dark ray unleashed by Czarnobóg's middle head, I sent my combined attack straight into the gaping maw which lurked in the darkness beyond.

Rage answered.

Like the power of the Smorodina magnified tenfold, his other two heads unleash blasts of fire which rolled over Otylia's shield. Its heat still burned despite her protection, and I instinctively raised my arms as Otylia grimaced against the power.

"Well, you made him angry!"

Dziewanna drew back her bowstring and released a series of flaming arrows in the direction of the roaring dragon in the darkness. "Angry means mistakes. Do not copy him." Then she swept from Otylia's protection and into the darkness with a single flap of her owl wings.

Another round of flames followed, but only from the right this time. The other head must've been focused on Dziewanna. A distraction, and we needed to take advantage.

We can't just sit back! I told Otylia. *Dziewanna gave us an opportunity.*

The edges of her light shield crackled as she strained from the effort, both hands extended to hold it. *"We need to find the core of the darkness!"*

Trygław can do that, I replied, *but I can't.* I sheathed Kwiecień and opened my pack, pulling out one of the golden apples Mokosz had gifted us. *I'll keep him off you until you're ready.*

"Wait!" she pled, but I was already gone.

Lightning shot all around me and sent the chały fleeing or falling amid a sea of sparks. Beyond, the darkness swallowed everything, pressing against me as if I were buried deep underground. It strained my breaths and slowed my movements, but I willed the winds to counter its force. Except I had no sight of where to go. Czarnobóg's wings flapped to either side—and I'd heard his roars—but all the darkness looked the same.

The roar of dragon fire and twang of Dziewanna's bow traded strikes from my left as Otylia descended with her light shield, her eyes pure white. Threads of Life flashed between us until something blocked sight of her moonlight for just longer than a blink.

That's it!

I dived to the opposing side until her light was no longer visible, ensuring Czarnobóg was between us. But a rush of flames surged over my arms before I was ready. My hand spasmed from the pain, and I cursed as the golden apple slipped into the darkness.

The *crack* from my right alerted me to one of Czarnobóg's maws launching another fire blast, so I surged up as I grabbed another apple. Far below, the one I'd dropped exploded against something with enough power to shake the air even up here. Perun had done great damage to Czarnobóg in Prawia with the apples, so I hoped it would damage the dark dragon too.

When the next wave of flames rushed below me, I threw the golden apple into the maw that had released them.

Another explosion rocked me. Lightning danced up my arms and my mind spun. Normally, I'd have been able to absorb it, but the apples were originally Perun's. They held condensed power far beyond what I could ever wield, and the lightning further burned my skin as *žityje* rushed to heal it.

Czarnobóg was not so easily wounded. No cry or roar followed the apple's blast, and instead, I felt the faintest tinge of heat on my face. Still stunned by the blast, I could neither divert my tumbling path nor raise any kind of defense as it grew to a stinging blaze.

I mustered what will I could to cross my two Moonblades before me and pray Otylia acted quickly. But Czarnobóg's flames didn't care for my prayers. They struck the Moonblades with a mighty force. It took all my strength just to keep them from falling back into my face as my clothes burned, my hair singing to ash as my skin boiled. The blades kept the fireball from killing me directly, but the pain made me cry for Oblivion's release.

Light flashed between us. It revealed a monstrous snout atop teeth as long as my torso and as sharp as Grudzień's jagged fangs. Smoke rose from Czarnobóg's nostrils, but ice, not fire cracked in the back of his maw.

Set me aflame and then freeze me. What fun.

I couldn't face him this way much longer. My *žityje* was failing, barely able to heal the worst of my wounds caused by the flames.

That ice would be the last straw, so I did what Xobas said any wise warrior should do when they were outmatched.

I fled.

Launching both my Moonblades at his snout, I released the winds and dropped. Darkness consumed me as Otylia's flash vanished. The golden apple had struck the surface below a few seconds after it slipped, and I used that precious fall time to recall my blades once they slashed through the thin scale on the nearest head. Another flesh wound, but also another distraction for Otylia.

The Moonblades hummed as they shot back into my grasp, and Otylia's light returned a moment later. *"I found it!"* her voice echoed through my head. A heart attack came with it.

I struck a massive tree's branches at full speed, enduring a dozen minor cuts before tumbling toward the tangled roots. They surrounded the widest trunk I'd ever seen. But this was not the first time I'd seen it.

A man-sized gap formed at the center of the towering World Tree, so dark that even Otylia's blinding glow could not pierce it. The Heart of Nawia had offered us an escape against Weles all those moons ago. Now, it held the core of Czarnobóg's darkness in the realm.

That deep corruption washed over me as Otylia's emergent light faded again. Each demanded a great burst of *życie* from her, and I wondered what it would take to truly purify this place. Weles had banished much of the corruption, but he was far from here. It returned to me now, the demon pounding against its cage in my soul until Otylia's voice returned.

"Wašek, I need you with me! I can't hold on much longer."

I barely summoned the winds enough to cushion my fall before I struck the ground. Grudzień and Kwiecień sliced into the earth with a gruesome *shling* on either side, embedding themselves and forcing me to stagger. My head spun. My soul warred with the demon's hunger. I didn't have the *życie* to fight Czarnobóg when focused, let alone with my soul split.

"Where are you?" I mumbled absently before repeating it through our bond.

A bright blue Thread burst to life, wrapping around my torso before shooting above. Even the darkness couldn't smother it, and I took heart in that as I grabbed my blades and flew toward her. Czarnobóg had other ideas.

The frost returned. A thousand shards of ice sliced across my skin just as I raised the winds, deflecting many more, but distracting from my flight. I dropped into freefall again until Otylia's familiar force caught me.

My ribs and back ached from the sudden stop, joining the rest of my body's bloodied pain. I held onto the Moonblades through instinct more than any purposeful will. Czarnobóg couldn't take them. He already held three of the Alatyr shards somewhere on his dragon form, and if he took mine, we'd be even further from being able to seal Oblivion again.

I took a sharp breath and darted upward on the winds again. Otylia needed her power for herself, not to save me, so I changed my direction at random this time to avoid any potential attacks.

Czarnobóg's wings beat overhead as Dziewanna shouted in rage somewhere behind, my *žityje* senses revealing her own flames washing over the dark dragon. It wasn't enough. I couldn't see Czarnobóg, but the ferocity of his strikes hadn't faltered in the slightest after our attacks.

I was nearly to Otylia before her voice rang out in my head. *"Wašek, claw!"*

I dodged with a gust of wind, but Czarnobóg moved quicker than any creature his size should've. Another flash of moonlight revealed his claws ripping through my burnt tunic and the flesh beneath. My lungs failed. Blood pooled in my mouth, and I sputtered as one last burst of air sent me to Otylia's side.

All but the last of my *žityje* drained to heal my pierced lung. Blood drowned me in the meantime, and I sheathed Kwiecień with my trembling hand before grabbing Otylia's free one.

She was unharmed. Thank the gods, she was unharmed. All the agony and struggle had given her the time she needed, and now, she just needed the piece of her soul that dwelt in me.

"I must purify the Heart," she said in my mind as her light swelled around us. *"Don't leave my side until it's over, or the channeling will break."*

My breaths were weak, shuddered. I stared up at the towering dragon and the wild goddess sparring with him through arrow and flame. One head followed her, but Czarnóg had three. *Czarnóg won't let you,* I replied.

"Let me handle it!" She bared her teeth and extended the tip of her spear toward the World Tree. Listopad shone on its end, and a beam of moonlight shot to the center of the pure darkness consuming the Heart. *"Focus on pulling strength from the Way of Souls. We're not done yet."*

With her light shield protecting us, I closed my eyes and tried to reach out for the Way. It had been difficult before, and we were deeper still into Nawia now. Its flow of power was a whisper amid a thunderstorm here. But I was a płanetnik. The storm was mine, and I quieted my mind as my soul touched the edge of that distant stream.

40

Otylia

How could something be so corrupted?

THE HEART OF NAWIA SPEWED CORRUPTION straight from Oblivion itself. Trygław's final help had warned me that this darkness was beyond even Czarnobóg's great strength. It was the corruption from Alatyr's shattered fall, trapped in a sub-realm for millennia. It had grown and sought an escape with every passing moment. This was its freedom.

And only my moonlight stood in the way.

Cold, heat, and corruptive blasts washed over my shield as I split my *żityje* between it and the beam of light I directed straight into the Heart of Nawia at the World Tree's base. It shocked me how much of my power could slip away so quickly, but it was working. A pinprick of light pierced the Heart's darkness near its edge. Just a tiny shimmer, but a start.

That start had taken far too much *żityje* to create. It would run thin far before the Heart was pure, but Trygław had offered another key in his final visions. Far above in Jawia, the moon had shifted from Sierpień to Wrzesień in the days since we'd left.

I had an entire Moonstone's worth of *żityje* in reserve.

Czarnobóg didn't know, and I'd kept it from Wacław and Mother out of fear of him finding out. Sierpień's power had kept us alive on the Way of Souls. Now, the purple Moonstone Ta had wielded would hold the power to vanquish Czarnobóg's corruption for just long enough to send him back to Oblivion. I just needed the dark dragon to believe he'd won, to lower his guard so we could take his three Moonstones and rebuild the veil.

His laughter carried through the darkness as his claws gashed through Mother's shoulder. She healed, but his corruption washed over her before she could draw back her bowstring once again.

I yearned to help her, but Trygław's warnings held me firm. Ending the darkness at Nawia's core would take all my strength, even with Wrzesień's help. Destiny had shown me the soulless flow of time if I failed, and I refused to let that happen. Mother was a goddess. She would endure the torment and heal with her worshippers. But that didn't rid me of the pit in my stomach as demonic chały swarmed her.

Wacław had scattered and killed many of the chały with his lightning. He was immobile now, his head tilted back as I sensed *żityje* trickling back into his soul, and the chały noticed his absence. Mother wasn't a master of the skies. They would overwhelm her.

Tears stung my eyes watching the demons' lightning burn her skin as their claws tore deep into her torso. She fought and slashed, shifting into a winged version of her half-bear form, but the chały were mere distractions. The dark żmij himself loomed.

An enormous sword entered the edge of my light, its hilt gripped by his draconic claws. Three strands of wintery hues spiraled through it: ice blue, navy, and teal. Three Moonblades formed into one god-slaying blade, and Mother was its target. With the chały tearing at her arms and holding her in place, she had no defense.

I couldn't save her.

Turning away my gaze, I wept as my light pierced the Heart little-by-little. It felt useless. What did it matter if I couldn't save her? Maybe she would recover some day from a Moonblade's strike, but this would be no mortal blow.

The unmistakable sound of metal piercing flesh cut through the realm. All fell impossibly silent. Even Czarnobóg's wings made no sound as Nawia wept for the loss of its queen. Except the Threads of Life revealed not two strands connecting to my chest, but three.

I forced myself to look back toward Mother, gasping at the figure who lay impaled at the end of Czarnobóg's massive Moonblade. Not Nawia's queen.

Its king.

Weles, lord of Nawia, god of the afterlife, trickery, and magic, stared toward me with his eyes agape and blood pooling in his mouth. The chały were gone, and Mother drifted away, safe, as tears ran down her cheeks. Her half-bear form seemed both an omen and an honor for the god who'd born a bond with the beasts.

My blood father. Her husband. There had been no love in our strange godly family, but my heart cried out at the loss anyway. Weles had been all but drained by Czarnobóg, and now, the Moonblades would send him away until his force could piece him back together. He'd been selfish, greedy during my time in Nawia before. But in the face of the greatest corruption to ever face the Three Realms, he'd sacrificed himself to save his wife, his child, and all the realms. Perun sat upon his glory in Prawia. In this moment, he bore no match for the god whose blood coursed through my veins.

Czarnobóg laughed from three heads at once, grabbing Weles with his free claws and ripping him free from the Moonblade. *Žityje* leaked in vibrant wisps from the fallen god, and the Moonblade lapped them up like a parched dog at the river. I couldn't let him have this victory. Weles had bought us time, and I would take advantage.

"Pitiful!" Czarnobóg exclaimed. "The king of Nawia throws himself at a blade's end to grant his loveless wife mere mo—"

I tapped into Wrzesień's power and ignited it.

Blinding silver light burst over the realm, scattering the darkness for a mile each direction. Czarnobóg cried out from the power, but he wasn't my target. I channeled the immense surge through my spear and toward the Heart. Only its edges had strayed from darkness, but when the ray of light expanded with a Moonstone's force, the Heart's dark core shattered.

Shrieks filled Nawia as the corruption within its Heart fought to protect itself. It poured into Wacław and sought the fragment of his soul that was bound with mine, but I held his mortality, not his demon. His eyes remained shut as he filled with the Way's *żityje*, and our souls connected through our joined hands and the marks upon our arms.

Wake up, Wašek, I called to him through that bond. *I need you!*

His eyes shot open, and I tapped into his strength. It united my godly soul, unleashing the last fragment of my power as Czarnobóg realized what was happening.

"You ignorant child!" he shouted as he threw Weles to the World Tree's roots and dove. Mother meant nothing to him now. I was the threat. I was moments from destroying his dark hold over Nawia. And as his great form descended upon me, I knew I didn't have enough time.

"He'll reach us!" Wacław explained, suddenly tense as much of the *żityje* he'd gained poured into me.

Be ready, I warned him. *I'll have to break the beam and restart away from him. Let go in three, two, one…*

We released each other, and he understood the unspoken command to draw Kwiecień with his now free hand. Blades crossed, he charged the now illuminated dragon, aiming for the weak place along the neck we'd exploited in Prawia. I darted the other direction and struck at the furthest right neck. The Threads revealed Mother doing the same to the third.

My initial burst of moonlight had changed Czarnobóg's scales. Before, a magical shimmer had covered them, absorbing or deflecting most blows, but they were dull now. Czarnobóg couldn't react to all three of us at once, despite a torrent of corruptive and ice blasts, and our weapons struck true on each neck.

All three heads cried out as one, sending him crashing to the World Tree's island below. His merged Moonblade split and scattered into three around him. I had my opening, but we needed those last Alatyr shards before I could send him back to Oblivion.

"I'll grab the blades!" Wacław exclaimed, diving after Czarnobóg. "Deal with the Heart!"

Mother didn't follow him. Her face and dress were bloodied, and flames no longer danced at her fingertips. Her *żityje* was all but gone, the last of it used on the final strike. As I pointed my spear at the Heart once again and channeled my light, I hoped she'd be smart enough to keep away from the rest of the fight.

Czarnobóg's form morphed and shrunk as Wacław arrived and grabbed two of the fallen Moonblades. The dark dragon's second and third heads disappeared, his scales retreating back to a pauldron on his shoulder until he resembled nothing more than a man with impossibly black hair and a bare, muscled torso. He noticed Wacław sheathing the two stolen blades, and he snatched up the final teal one before Wacław could arrive.

The Moonblade of Marzec flashed so quickly in Czarnobóg's grasp that Wacław barely parried the strike, then staggered back from the force behind it. The dark dragon had seemed to be defeated a heartbeat before. But he surged forward now with the vigor of a godly warrior.

Wacław had given me the connection to the last piece of my immortal soul for long enough. I only need him to hold back Czarnobóg for a few seconds longer and somehow pry that final blade from his grasp. If he failed in that, I could only hope destroying the Heart's corruption would force Czarnobóg to drop it before Oblivion drew him back in.

Silver cut through the Heart's blackness for all but the center. That core resisted more, sending wave after wave of corruption blasting into me through dark tendrils. They latched onto my limbs and reached into my soul for every bit of rage that dwelt there, but the greatest of it was against their master.

Pain slashing across my shoulder alerted me to Wacław's struggle below. Lightning cracked at the end of his two blades as he stabbed and parried against Czarnobóg, but black blood coated his tunic. He was badly outmatched, and with each blow, the demon grew within.

Mother noticed too, but I waved my free hand in her direction. "Let him hold!"

She was far too drained to confront Czarnobóg again. I couldn't lose her for the third time, and I only needed a few more seconds. Except a deep dread filled my chest.

Trygław's wisps swept around me with the vibrant *żityje* that poured from my soul. They foresaw Czarnobóg's shadowy form slashing through Wacław over and over until a force washed over them from the direction of the Heart. Their wisps disappeared a moment later, and my heart stopped knowing what that meant.

Oblivion would take them.

"Wašek, get away from him!" I shouted, my whole body vibrating from the battle between my moonlight and the Heart's darkness. "He'll drag you to Oblivion!"

Moonblades flashed and clanged, the two warriors sharing their deadly dance. Czarnobóg shot ice spires and more tendrils of darkness towards me with his free hand, but I refused to relent. His corruptive tendrils covered me, stabbing at my mind, body, and soul. I could only endure.

Wacław was no different. Darkness stained his cheeks and the skin exposed by his burned and torn tunic. All he managed against Czarnobóg now were desperate, sloppy blocks and dodges at the last second. His *żityje* faltered. But when he raised his crossed blades to block Czarnobóg's strike with Marzec, his voice did not tremble.

"Do it!" he demanded. "Do what Destiny demands!"

My throat burned. My eyes seared from tears. Finishing the Heart would mean condemning them both to Oblivion, but the veil wouldn't be mended until I returned the Alatyr shards to Buyan, where I'd left Lipiec with Garafena to earn the serpent's trust. Could Wacław escape before then? Could Czarnobóg?

I blinked back the tears, feeling my *žityje* slipping away as Czarnobóg's blade grew ever-closer to Wacław's face.

"DO IT!" Wacław demanded through clenched teeth. "Please, Otylka!"

I lowered my head and reached into that last bit of power within me. Memories sought to overwhelm me, but I forced myself to meet Wacław's gaze. My love. My oldest friend. My eternal ally.

I love you more than the flowers love the spring sun, I told him silently.

Then I unleashed one final blast of moonlight.

The Heart of Nawia exploded, shooting both corruptive darkness and purifying silver rays over the World Tree's base. Awash in the glow, the warring god and Naw before it screamed as their skin burned. Their feet slipped. Their eyes bulged. Light and dark swapped over them to create a strange scene that turned neither recognizable.

The explosion reversed a heartbeat later, drawing back in all the power Oblivion had blown into the realm. Including the creatures birthed of its corruption.

I echoed Wacław's cry as his pain became mine. The strands of both light and dark tore at his very essence, seeking to tear him away to Oblivion. His soul was demonic. Like Czarnobóg, he belonged in that sub-realm of pure corruption, but as he vanished into nothing more than a thousand wisps the color of the cloudless sky, I shouted that I would save him from Oblivion's depths. My power had sent him away.

I would bring him back.

41

Otylia

What have I done?

I KNELT AT THE BASE OF THE WORLD TREE, its towering branches curling over me like a predator's claws. The moon soared even higher as it passed from Jawia and covered this fallen paradise in silver. My moon.

That light revealed Czarnobóg and Wacław's five Moonblades lying at the World Tree's base. Its roots wound over the blades and across the earthen isle before reaching over its edge for a world that no longer existed. Czarnobóg had thrown the broken pieces of every other nearby island at us, leaving the tree and its Heart alone as the realm's king fed it with godly blood.

Mother landed beside me with owl wings stretching from her back. Her boots squished against the blood-soaked earth, and she looked toward me, then Weles's corpse, caught between us.

"You have done what no other god could."

Her hushed voice hung in the still realm, not even a wind gust to break the ethereal silence. Praise. It tore at my frayed nerves, and I dug my fingers into fists in the dirt.

Then I screamed.

There were neither nature's mountains nor man's buildings to echo my voice, yet it carried for an eternity as I shook. Anger, fear, and regret stirred in my heart. Warriors' legends called victory a glorious event, but they failed to mention the agony and loss that came with it. I'd secured the last of the shards of Alatyr—the purest united power of the gods. I'd banished Czarnobóg to Oblivion for a time. I'd purified Nawia of its corruption, preventing the realm's destruction.

None of it felt like a victory. Wacław was trapped in Oblivion with Czarnobóg and his legions of corruption. He had no weapons and little *żityje*. Such a fate was a death sentence for even the most powerful god. I heard nothing from him through our bond, but deep in my soul, I knew he still lived. That bond had revealed his brushes with death before.

"What will happen to Nawia?" I asked Mother, wiping away my unbidden tears. "Weles is dead."

She held herself and shook her head absently. "No god dies forever, but there is no telling how long it will take for him to recover from such a blow. Jaryło barely grazed you with Kwiecień, and it took a great deal of Weles's power to bring you back to your basic state. He was all but drained already…" Forehead wrinkled, she crouched beside me and leaned her head into mine. "My husband is gone, but your lover is not. We must return to Buyan to reunite the Moonstones with Garafena's final one, then seal Oblivion again. There may yet be a chance for you to bring Wacław back from that dreaded place."

I gritted my teeth, but took her hands and forced myself to stand with her. "How?"

"Oblivion calls those born of the corruption trapped within." Her eyes darkened. "That does not prevent a god from entering to pull free one of those entities before the veil returns."

"Then let's go."

I rushed over to the Moonblades, touching each and transforming them into another amulet to hang from my headband. Entering Oblivion sounded like the most terrifying thing to endure, but I'd forced Wacław into it. Hesitation wouldn't save him. Every moment he spent in Oblivion was another resisting Czarnobóg's torture, and I couldn't let him face it alone.

With my silver light spear dismissed, eleven Moonstones now hung from my headband in the form of my Moonmark, Mother's Bowmark, Mokosz's Mothermark, and now, Grudzień and Kwiecień took the form of Wacław's Eclipsemark in his honor. A strange weight came with that. One more, and I would hold every shard of Alatyr. The gods had warred for such power. Mother feared it enough to not even wield one shard. What power, what responsibility, was I accepting?

I shoved away those doubts. This was the only way to keep Czarnobóg from returning. If Mother was right, I could do that *and* save Wacław, and I refused to accept another alternative.

Mother said her parting words to Weles's corpse, then joined me by the Heart of Nawia. She held a hand to the World Tree's trunk on the side of the arch and closed her eyes. "I never thought I would see this realm so destroyed. Its Heart is pure now at least, and that is because of you. Focus on where you wish to go in Jawia. The Heart will take you there."

"You're coming, right?" I asked, brow raised.

She nodded slowly. "Someone must wield Alatyr while you are in Oblivion."

"But you refused to even hold a Moonstone!"

"I know." Her fingers drifted down the trunk and traced each groove in it. "This is what must be done, though, and I will relinquish Alatyr the moment our work is done. I promised myself I would never seek such power again. My rebellion against Perun caused horror that I refuse to ever partake in again."

I offered her a reassuring smile. "You aren't the girl who rebelled anymore."

"Centuries dull the past," she replied before releasing the tree and stepping to me. "They do not erase it. Now, go, and let us finish this vile work. Focus on Buyan and the final Moonstone you gave Garafena. That island is where Alatyr fell, and it will be where we banish the offspring of that fall."

I ran my hand across my Moonstone amulets as I approached the Heart. Moons ago, we'd fled through it without planning and had tumbled out into the deserts of Vastroth. There was no time for misdirection now.

So, I pictured the lush isle of Buyan, the Indrik who I'd tamed, and the giant serpent Garafena, who protected the final Moonstone for my eventual return. It was an island for the spirits and the winds. Even in the deepest depths of winter, Marzanna's power couldn't scar Buyan, and as I stepped into the Heart of Nawia, I prayed it would be safe from Czarnobóg too.

42

Wacław

This place will be my tomb.

A DEEP CHILL WOKE ME. I lay sprawled amid swirling wisps of white, black, and every shade of gray. There was neither sun nor moon, but the wisps emanated light of their various shades. Even the purest black one glowed in a way unlike anything I'd ever seen in the Three Realms. And I'd seen plenty in recent moons.

Aches in every muscle and joint reminded me of the battle I'd just endured as I tried to push myself up. My hands found not dirt beneath me, but… nothing?

I had expected Oblivion to match the eternal darkness of Czarnobóg's Nawia. Instead, a haze covered the realm beyond the nearby wisps, and the pure white ground felt both beneath me and incredibly distant at the same time—as if I were falling, yet the winds had caught me. It was far more stable than the winds, but I stumbled anyway.

Nausea clutched me as I held my hands on my hips just to keep upright. Corruption. It had become all too familiar since our arrival in Nawia, and I warred with myself to keep its call at bay.

I need to find Czarnobóg…

"He will destroy you," a sinister voice replied within me. The demon lashed against its cage in my soul, and its fury surged through my veins. If it hated Czarnobóg as much as me, could I wield it against him? *"Otylia trapped us here. The gods have abandoned us, so our only hope is to kill Czarnobóg before he kills us."*

"You can't kill him," I muttered aloud, then reached for Grudzień, only for my heart to skip a beat.

It was gone, and so were Kwiecień and the other two Moonblades I'd taken from Czarnobóg. Had they remained in Nawia? Had Czarnobóg managed to steal them back somehow?

"We… *I*… definitely can't kill him without a Moonblade."

Who was I talking to? The demon who dwelt deep in my soul, feeding on my worst emotions? This wasn't a debate, and I wouldn't listen to that voice. Not again.

So I tried to contact Otylia through our bond instead. *I'm alive,* I told her. *This place is strange, and its corruption is already affecting me. I don't know what happened to the Alatyr shards or to Nawia, but do what you must. I knew the risk I was taking.*

My fingers and toes curled at that, repulsed at the death I'd accepted. It didn't matter whether I lived seventeen or seven hundred years. Oblivion would always be my end, but I'd hoped for more time with Otylia. Her last words before the Heart exploded were a promise to save me from this place. As I forced my legs to soldier on through the sea of mist and wisps, I didn't know whether she even could.

What did the gods know of this place? Swaróg had created Oblivion to seal away Czarnobóg and other corrupted beings, but had any deity stepped foot in the prison? Jaryło had believed it to be filled with nothing. A gentle breeze split the mists, though, and these strange wisps offered a light that wasn't *nothing* at least. If only I knew what that something was.

After a few minutes, I gave up any hope of hearing from Otylia. I felt her desperation when I closed my eyes, but the connection was faint. I was on my own.

Black joined the white beneath my feet. A trail of it, and my finger wettened as I raised them to my nose. More blood leaked from where Czarnobóg's claws and blade had sliced during the battle—all wounds my *żityje* had already healed.

I clenched my jaw as I reached into the little supply of *żityje* I had left. The winds shifted, whipping around me at the slightest command, but any *żityje* I sent toward healing slipped away as sky blue wisps.

My sickness deepened. I'd become reliant on my Nawie resilience so quickly, and losing it made me feel naked, exposed. My slashed clothes didn't help, but clothes could be replaced. Without healing the deep gashes Czarnobóg had inflicted, I would struggle to walk for long, let alone fight him again.

It occurred to me then that I had no idea where I was. This had been Czarnobóg's home for millennia, and he knew how to escape through the torn veil. If he found it before I found him…

I was bleeding and weak, but I refused to just wander. The winds encircled me as I took flight, seeming to curl defensively like a wolf mother around her pups. They carried me higher without more than a whisper of *żityje*, and I soon rose above the sea of mists.

Wisps of white, gray, and black filled the sky in a terrifying array of clashing shades. They drifted over and through the mists, most keeping far from each other, but following closely behind me. Were they curious entities? Pure forms of *żityje* like that I'd lost during my attempts to heal?

The eight winds scattered at my command, searching the land-scape for any sign of Czarnobóg or other threats. It took time, but they were a sixth sense as they slipped along what felt like hills and valleys. They searched for miles each direction until one brushed against a slimy form that had to be an utopiec. I pushed them further. I wasn't here for simple demons, but when they crossed over a ridge-line together, a force suddenly tore away my connection to them.

My flight slipped for a moment before the winds returned to me. I caught my breath, but the demon screamed at my failure to hold onto the search. Something lurked ahead.

That was enough.

I held my tunic tight against a deep gash in my chest as I followed the winds' path toward the ridge. Mists covered there too, but the sparse wisps grew denser in various places across the landscape. I sent one wind for each group, slowing my approach. Those wisps clumped around beings, and I needed to know whether any could attack a flying target. Even a chała could be fatal in my current state.

I skirted around all the demons, keeping a larger distance from any flying chały, wiły, or strzygi. They grew more common the further I went, but none moved. It was as if they were frozen in wait.

He is planning to use them against Jawia, I guessed. *Corrupt Nawia completely, then use the dead of the underworld and Oblivion's demons to swarm the living together.*

We'd removed Czarnobóg from Nawia, but if a sleeping demonic army awaited him here, his threat was far from finished. The Frostmarked Horde had burned and pillaged much of Jawia. What remained would struggle against a similar force, especially when an immortal żmij led the demonic legions.

A chill soon washed over me, and in the distance, a large mass of wisps grew by the second. Except this one was different. While ones of all shades coalesced around the other demons and me, only the ones emitting blacklight joined the group beyond the ridge where the winds had failed. That could only mean one thing.

The lord of darkness himself.

I instinctively reached for Grudzień, but my scabbard was still empty. No Moonblade. No weapons at all. Yet I faced the corrupted god who made even the elder gods cower in Prawia.

His *żityje* grew with the wisps, so potent that my demonic hunger sensed him from miles away. It reminded the demon within me how little life force I had left. Each drop that fled my veins stole more of it, and my head spun from blood loss. But I had to do something to delay Czarnobóg's return to the Three Realms.

So I advanced. With neither plan nor blade, I pushed toward the swirling wisps of darkness, waiting for some demon or beast to strike me down far before my arrival.

But Czarnobóg needed no demons against me, as Oblivion was the realm of corruption. It was a constant drumming against my skull that only intensified the closer I got to Oblivion's master. The dark veins expanded across my skin until decaying, dead flesh covered more of me than living. Deeper, the demon broke free from its cage to feed on my desperation, fear, and anger.

Czarnobóg had destroyed Nawia's paradise for countless souls. The people we'd lost against Marzanna's Frostmarked Horde were trapped, corrupted, or suffering because of him. People I'd led into battle.

Now, he threatened those who remained, trying to rebuild from the ashes Marzanna left behind. I was their king, and though many among them scorned me as a demon, I couldn't fail them. Nawie were born to protect, born to wield corruption against corruption itself. We couldn't do that without the demon in one of our twin souls.

I had no mortal soul to balance the demon, not anymore. The soul that remained, though, was more than just demonic.

Otylia's godly soul radiated her moonlight within me. It was a mere sliver, but against corruption's eclipse that had made me what I was, she was the thin strand of light piercing the darkness. I rolled up my sleeve to reveal her Moonmark joining with my Eclipsemark. More than just a symbol, it was a pure truth of our bond. No realm or god could separate us. She would always be with me, and I with her.

Until the end.

I traced her Moonmark as the demon fought for control. Free, it surged through the winds, granting me strength beyond my own. To be a płanetnik was to command the storm, but it was also to wield that storm to protect those vulnerable to it and defeat the beasts seeking to destroy.

The demon was right about one thing: I needed to channel my power through my emotions. I was *not* weak without it, because Otylia ensured I wasn't alone. Still, I lacked the strength to become what I needed to be without the full extent of my power. I wasn't a demon, a mortal, or a god. I was a Naw. I was a protector of the balance, of the natural way.

A blizzard struck as I neared the dark wisps. Impossibly dark clouds clashed with my control over the winds, sending me back into the mists as I controlled my descent. The fight wasn't worth losing my limited *żityje* over, so I skidded across the strange, snow-covered ground beneath the wisps.

No other demons lurked here based on the lack of other wisp groups, but I decided to keep low anyway. Czarnobóg's overwhelming power could've torn away any wisps from other demons. Mine kept with me, though, so I hoped that was a good omen. I badly needed one.

When I reached what appeared to be a hill, it gave way slightly to my foot. The give increased with pressure, and soon, a light gray wisp slipped out of the ground where I'd stepped.

I reached for the wisp to try and grasp some understanding of it. My fingers slipped through, its solidity lost, and a tingling ran up my arm. The slightest bit of *żityje* came with it before the wisp zipped away. Behind, it left a gouge in the hill, but my thoughts lingered on that jolt.

I grinned and ran my thumb across my fingers. Oblivion prevented me from healing, but if I could draw a portion of *żityje* from these wisps, I'd have some tool against Czarnobóg. I scrambled for my bag, breathing out a long sigh as my hand found the remaining golden apples. Two tools, then: my lightning and Perun's. They would have to be enough, so I stomped across the hill and pulled as much *żityje* as possible from the fleeing wisps.

The dark clouds swelled overhead as thousands more wisps joined Czarnobóg no more than a few hundred strides away. His *żityje* poured through my demonic senses now, dark tendrils reaching through the blizzard. Were they searching for me?

A horrible thought struck me. What if this was his way of replenishing too? All those wisps surrounded him, and they didn't appear to flee…

With my stomach turning, I decided I'd replenished enough. Czarnobóg's power grew at an impossible rate to match, and I needed to get to him before it surpassed what he needed to escape. He already held far more than I ever could, but there was no other way forward. A plan began to form in my mind as I sprinted toward the center of the spiraling mass.

Hurry, Otylka. I don't know how much longer I have left.

43

Otylia

Let this be the end of this madness.

WARMTH STRUCK ME AS I STEPPED FROM NAWIA'S RUIN onto Buyan's vibrant isle. Jawia was free from Marzanna's embrace, and standing beneath lush trees on the great slope that crossed Buyan, I could've forgotten Czarnobóg's threat looming over the realm.

The Heart of Nawia had dumped me somewhere above the oak where Koschei the Deathless's soul had been buried. Mother was nowhere to be seen, but a quick glance at the Threads of Life revealed she was already down the slope. I ran after her, desperate to get Wacław out of Oblivion before Czarnobóg did something horrible to him.

A flash out of the corner of my eye forced me to summon my silver spear as I ran, but I released it a moment later when a familiar creature slid to a stop before me.

"Otylia of the end, has the time come for Alatyr to be united already?" the Indrik spoke into my mind.

I smiled at the beautiful creature. Deep gray with the head of a horse, body of a bull, and legs of a deer, the Indrik would be considered by some to be a monstrosity. Those people were stupid. There were few creatures as majestic as the Indrik, and I adored the glistening white horn on its head, contrasted with its manicured black mane and tail. It was a pure impossibility that could bound gracefully one moment and shake the ground the next.

"It has," I replied, approaching and scratching its neck. "We've managed to force Czarnobóg back into Oblivion, but he's taken Wacław. If I don't act quickly, the dark żmij will kill him and return to Jawia with his corruption."

The Indrik had leaned into my care, but at my mention of what was to come, it threw back its head. *"Leap onto my back, and I will show you to Garafena. The great serpent is in a far better mood now that it has a shard of Alatyr to protect, but I fear she will not surrender it easily."*

"I won't give her the choice," I muttered, climbing onto its back.

It took off at a gallop without a command. I could only cling to its neck and mane, hoping Mother would find the right place too, but something told me she'd been here before. There was so much I still didn't know about Buyan's secrets. For now, I would settle for the Indrik's swiftness and a final deal with Garafena.

My hair whipped freely behind me as we leaped faster than a hawk's flight. By the time the tree bearing Perun's golden apples appeared, my cheeks stung from windburn and my thighs ached from holding the Indrik's flanks. It skidded to a stop over a distance of fifty strides before swinging its head again.

"Send up your light, and Garafena will come."

So I threw up a hand and released a burst of moonlight into the bright sky. Silver shimmered through the blue, and a distant roar answered. I took that as enough of a sign before reaching for one of the golden apples on the tree. Wacław had taken ours others with him, and if I could just have a couple more...

The apple shriveled at my touch, plopping to the ground and dissolving into mush. I cursed, but the Indrik reared back with a whinny.

"Only Perun himself may wield the golden apples of this tree," it said. *"He planted it himself during his battles with Weles, and Garafena has found offense at its presence ever since. After all, she served your father once."*

I bit my cheek. My instinct had been to snap that Weles wasn't my father, but his sacrifice in Nawia made that feel like an unnecessary jab. "Weles sacrificed himself so that we could keep fighting," I said, surprised at the sudden burning in my nose. I sniffled, baring my teeth. "He was no father to me, but Nawia will suffer without him."

The Indrik bowed its head, a tear rolling down its equine cheek. *"May the master of paradise rest until his return. All realms must find a master. Who, now, will rule Nawia in his absence?"*

Flapping wings interrupted me before I could reply. Garafena's long serpentine form slithered from Buyan's mountains as her two massive wings shifted enough wind to make me stagger back. Her scales were like sandstone, her fangs dripping venom as she swooped over us.

"The master's daughter has returned," she declared.

"I have," I replied before pointing at the Moonstones hanging from my headband. "As promised, I've collected the other eleven shards of Alatyr and return them to you now. My mother and I have repelled Czarnobóg back to Oblivion, and we need Alatyr's strength to seal the veil once again."

Garafena's pupils narrowed to slits, her tongue hissing through her teeth. "What proof have you that you will return such power once you hold it? All gods seek Alatyr, and I sense you have a greater motivation than simply Czarnobóg."

Mother emerged from the forest at a sprint, and I nodded to her before replying, "I don't want Alatyr's power, even for this, but I need it to end Czarnobóg's threat and save the man I love. Wacław is trapped in Oblivion with Czarnobóg. I seek to free him first."

"And who will wield Alatyr while you are in Oblivion?"

Mother stopped at my side, chin raised. "I will."

The serpent scoffed. "She who burned Jawia to defy her father."

"Centuries change us," Mother insisted with her arms crossed. A fire burned in her eyes, but she didn't reach for her bow yet. "I made mistakes, and I have sworn never to wield Alatyr because I know my fury better than any other. For my daughter, though, I am willing to make this single exception."

Garafena's tongue flicked the air, as if tasting her intentions. "I sense you speak the truth, but know that if you do not, I will ensure you suffer."

Mother held a fist over her heart. "I have suffered much, and seek no more. Alatyr will leave my hand the moment Otylia returns with Wacław."

"Then I relinquish back Lipiec to Otylia, daughter of Weles and Dziewanna." Garafena's gaze fell heavy upon me again. "Do not fail, child."

She opened her maw wide, and a beam of pure, colorless *żityje* shot overhead. Lipiec's crimson Moonstone hung within. Once marking the end of my spear, its power had been crucial during our battle against Czarnobóg in Prawia. Now, it would be the final piece to seal him away. Hopefully for forever.

The beam dissipated, allowing Lipiec to drop into my extended hand. It had a significant weight for a stone that could fit in my palm, and I wondered whether that came from its power or merely the rock itself. Either way, it hummed as I removed the first of the other Moonstones from my headband.

Each Moonstone I added to the pile in my hand strengthened the hum. They pulled on each other as if knowing what I intended to do, forming a third of a sphere, then half. Soon, only the twelfth moon of Grudzień remained.

I hesitated with that final shard in my grasp, its Eclipsemark form sending memories of Wacław flashing through my mind. What if I couldn't free him in time? What if Oblivion trapped him for eternity with the god of darkness? Would Czarnobóg twist him until he resembled the Płanetnik more than the Wašek I loved?

I bit my cheek and shoved Grudzień into the rest of Alatyr.

Hesitation only gave Czarnobóg more time and Wacław less. He needed me to be strong, decisive, so I would be. And as the completed orb in my grasp shimmered with brilliant power, I promised him I wasn't far.

Alatyr rose from my hand, vibrating and spewing *żityje* as if it couldn't contain its own power. Twelve colors swirled among old godly symbols both familiar and strange. Twelve Moonstones had shattered with Alatyr's fall. Marzanna had reunited hers with Jaryło's temporarily to release Czarnobóg, and now, I would do the same to mend their horrible mistake.

"The stone that birthed gods," Mother gasped with its radiant light reflecting in her eyes. "For centuries, I never thought I would see it reunited."

I closed my eyes and focused on the rhythm of Alatyr's humming. Symbols of the old tongue flashed against my eyelids, speaking of endless potential. Of creation. Of change. Of balance. Of destruction.

"Show me Oblivion!" I commanded the stone.

Alatyr called me into the air. We drifted upward as the winds whirled through the trees, bringing storm clouds and gales which screamed in defiance. Blue sky shifted to deep gray. Darkness enveloped us, but Alatyr shone with every color, its power pulsing through my moonlit skin until all was bathed in our glow.

And the pure power of Alatyr merged with the *żityje* in my soul. Vibrant, endless. It yearned to be wielded, and part of me mourned using it only to seal away Czarnobóg. There was so much *potential.*

No! I told myself. *This is what tempted the other gods. They fought wars for this power, and by shattering Alatyr, they created Czarnobóg in the first place.*

I breathed in deeply, embracing the power despite my intention to surrender it once we finished. This was greater than godhood. It reached to the forces that we merely wielded and beyond, into the pure essence at the heart of all that was, all that had been, and all that ever would be.

Alatyr flared when we no longer rose. A tremoring force that shook every tree on Buyan, a beam of light shot from the stone which hovered before me. It split the cloud and formed a circle of swirling wisps of white, gray, and black.

A deep throbbing in my soul revealed what I already knew. This was a portal to Oblivion, and nothing stood in its way as corruption surged from that realm. Somewhere within, Wacław was trapped, but he was alive. Our bond revealed that much. Though I couldn't speak to him through the portal, I clung that distant beat of his heart and feared the pain that consumed him.

I glanced down at Mother and extended my free hand. "Mother, take Alatyr until I return. If Czarnobóg tries to break free first, then close the veil."

She rose toward me on her owl wings. The ends of her lips twitched, and she spoke sharply as she took my hand. "I have left you to fend for yourself too often. That place will destroy you, and I cannot allow that."

"This is my choice," I insisted. "Czarnobóg engulfed Nawia, almost destroyed Prawia. I can't let that happen here. My friends don't deserve that."

Her breaths grew heavy, and tears welled in her eyes as she held a hand to my cheek. "Then you must return." She summoned a wooden blade intertwined with thorny vines. "Take this. You may no longer be my szeptucha, but my strength will always be yours."

I stifled a sniffle and took the sword by its hilt. It was no Moonblade, but it would do. "And I'll always be your little wildling."

She smiled, but it faded a moment later as her attention turned to Alatyr. A shadow fell over her. "I never wanted to hold this." Alatyr followed my hand over to hers, and its rush of power vanished the moment it switched to hovering by her. "Be quick."

The sudden absence made being a goddess feel like nothing, but I shook off the malaise. Wacław needed me.

Moonlight shone from my skin as I flew toward the portal. Corruption's pulse quickened, echoing the rapid beat of my heart. Every part of my soul screamed for me to not enter the realm where no god belonged, but one small fragment reminded me why I kept flying. Wacław's last bit of his mortal soul lay in me, and I would never abandon him.

So I plunged into Oblivion.

44

Wacław

Never fight a żmij in its lair.

THE TENDRILS OF DARKNESS REACHED FOR ME as I stumbled my way through Oblivion's blizzard-filled mists. My use of the wisps had granted me some *żityje*, but I resisted using the winds against these remnants of Czarnobóg's power. Not yet, at least.

One advantage of the thickening storm was it blocking any sight of the black blood dripping to my feet. My wounds grew worse by the step, but I couldn't heal in this horrid realm. Only escape could bring survival.

Czarnobóg desired the same thing, but not for survival. I'd passed countless dormant demons on my way here. They would swarm Jawia and overwhelm the vulnerable kingdoms and tribes of the living. I couldn't let my people suffer such a war so soon after the Horde's rampage, and if that meant remaining in this place to keep Czarnobóg trapped, then so be it.

Laughter met me as I reached the edge of a great crater.

"So the Naw has come to defy his purpose," Czarnobóg's voice boomed from the crater's center. He wore only leg armor of black scales and a matching pauldron on his right shoulder, scales arcing from it down the outside of the same arm. His eyes were obsidian, defying the joy of his wide smile. "I sense the demon in you, Wacław. Release that rage and join me against the gods who scorn you."

Dark wisps descended upon him, dissolving against his outstretched hand, and from the look of the blackened snow around his bare feet, the same process had created this crater. How much *żiyje* did he wield? It was far more than I'd sensed in any god, dragon, or spirit.

"Marzanna tried to tempt me the same way," I replied, a hand over my chest to both stop the bleeding and sense the demon within me. It was already free, but its rage was mine. And it wasn't the gods I hated. "I won't let you leave this place."

Another laugh. The żmij extended his arms to his sides, his muscled torso crossed with black veins like mine. He was no longer in his dragon form, but the twisting black tendrils drifting from him were enough to make the better part of me yearn to flee.

"The veil is torn," he declared. "I am free, and soon, I will have the power to subjugate your mortal world, then that of the gods."

The darkness snatched my limbs and pulled me through the air to Czarnobóg. I didn't resist. My plan was a risky one, but it was all I had. I needed to get close to him without immediately being struck down. Maybe, then, I could figure out how he planned to escape this place.

The dark god's eyes burrowed into me as his power grew. My fear grew with it, my breaths turning short, and his smirk said he noticed. I'd walked right into the hands of the foe not even the elder gods could defeat. What threat was I to him?

I flexed my hands at my side to ensure I still had access to my power. The winds shifted in the slightest to confirm, and I breathed a sigh of relief at that. For this to work, I needed what power I had left.

Some of the wisps stopped their descent around Czarnobóg's scaled arm, swirling around his hand to form a whip so dark that no shadows crossed it. The wisps' strange blacklight exuded from it and stole all color. It gave the god himself an ominous glow that flared when he snapped the whip at his side.

"You dared to ruin my plans for Nawia." He snapped the whip again, and my ears rang as it cracked inches before my nose. My will to live forced me to resist, but the tendrils dragged me ever closer. "I will enjoy this greatly."

As he raised the whip, I called my lightning. It struck as pure white in the blacklight and burned away the tendrils as the demon's fury merged with mine. The winds were eager to be free, and they tore between us, granting me the chance to dive away before the *crack* of Czarnobóg's whip struck where I'd been a moment before.

That's step one, I told myself, trying to act confident.

But a cold sweat slicked my hands and dripped from my brow. Breaking free from his tendrils had been the easy part, and before I could reach into my bag for my only remaining tool, Czarnobóg's whip tore through my back.

I collapsed at the crater's base, the new wound's blood joining old around me. My muscles screamed as I tried to stand and face him, but the pain was too much. I spasmed with each movement and clutched my bag. Ten golden apples remained within. Whether they were enough to even hurt him with the power he now wielded, I didn't know, but they were my only hope to buy Otylia the time she needed.

The whip fell again. And again.

Tears stung my eyes as my body numbed to all else. The agony was too much, each strike of the whip burying itself deep as bone. I couldn't heal, couldn't strike back with a Moonblade, so I waited for his approaching footsteps.

"Pitiful," he declared from above me, rolling me over with his boot. "The Naw who believed he could defy the god of darkness. Now, unleash that demon for me, and you might live."

I opened my mouth, but didn't speak. Instead, I rolled with all the strength I had left and poured out the golden apples at his feet. His whip answered across half my face, blinding me and sending me tumbling away into a pool of my own blood. My ears rang and my eyes failed, but I had to hope I had fallen far enough.

With the last of my *žityje,* I called a single bolt of lightning.

A shockwave flashed across my blackened vision. It threw me far into the air, and I had no *žityje* to catch my fall as I crashed into the crater's edge. Stone and ice dug into my exposed wounds. Burning, stabbing at what remained of my willpower.

I'm sorry, Otylia, I said through our bond, hoping somewhere in the realms she'd be able to hear. *I couldn't stop him.*

Though I teetered on consciousness, the demon's rage kept me awake. It demanded I rise and face the żmij whom Alatyr had birthed. My body was broken, my vision lost, and my bones shattered, but I yet lived. So I opened my eyes.

Only one answered the command. I dared not imagine the damage a direct hit from Czarnobóg's whip had caused the other, but one eye was better than none. It gave me a blurred sight of Czarnobóg splitting the mists with one hand absorbing *žityje* from the wisps and another readying his whip for another strike. He was still too far, so I listened to my demon's will, staggering to my feet just enough to lean back against the crater's wall.

My legs were in far better shape than my torso, but even they wobbled as my energy waned. I had nothing left to give. Ten of Perun's golden apples had barely left a mark on the god, and I had no weapon to inflict anything worse. After all I'd faced, though, I refused to die crumpled in a ball.

I raised my chin and met Czarnobóg's dark eyes. There was pity in them. He knew the corruption in my soul better than anyone, but while I'd fought it, he surrendered.

That pity faded as he raised his whip one final time, but as he did, Otylia's Moonmark pulsed across my forearm. Its silver pierced the sea of blacklight. My bond with her snapped tight, her voice echoing in my head.

"I'm here, Wašek! Hold on!"

My mangled and beaten mouth managed a crooked smile. He brought down the whip, but I threw all my strength into holding out my arms, focusing on that bond between Otylia's soul and mine.

A piece of her godly one rested in me. So did her power.

Light flashed between my extended hands, and cold silver formed in them just before the whip cracked across my face. Instead, it wrapped around Otylia's light spear, somehow in my grasp, its moonlight hissing against the dark whip. Czarnobóg yelled in frustration and tried to pull it away. By the time he succeeded, the light had eaten through the whip to leave only a nub behind.

The god of darkness tossed away the whip and summoned a dark sword from the wisps instead. "What is this?" he exclaimed, almost amused. "A Naw who can wield the power of a goddess?"

I couldn't speak through my wounded jaw, but I kept that horrid smile as I stumbled forward with Otylia's spear ready. It was foolish. My mind was spinning, though, and my heart soared knowing Otylia had come for me. I'd held him off long enough.

Czarnobóg charged. My bloodied arms already shook from blocking the whip, and I hadn't the strength to block him again. But I raised the spear anyway to meet his strike.

I hope you spend eternity in this place. Trapped with all the power of the realms, but no escape.

A *clang* echoed through the crater as Czarnobóg's dark blade knocked Otylia's spear from my grasp. It skidded into the mists, far from my reach. But as Czarnobóg readied a decapitating blow, I saw what he couldn't.

Otylia's Thread of Life shot right at us.

A beam of moonlight sent him staggering into the wall beside me before he could swing. Otylia burst from the mists a heartbeat later, eyes as wild as her mother's flames and a vine-wrapped wooden sword in her grasp. She sliced the blade through Czarnobóg's unprotected chest, then launched him into the mists with a moonblast.

I collapsed back into the wall, breaths ragged until she caught my fall. "Wašek?" she pled. "Wašek, why can't you heal?"

This realm stops it, I replied through our bond. *We need to get out of here, but Oblivion feeds his power. He'll just follow us unless we can delay him.*

Her gaze snapped from me to the mists, then back. "I saw this in one of my first visions. It was different, but the future is always changing…" *Żityje* flowed from her soul into mine, and though I resisted, her grip only tightened. "You may not be able to heal, but you can call the winds, right?"

I forced a nod. Even that made every muscle in my back scream.

"Call a whirlwind," she said hastily, "and I'll infuse it with my light. It should stun him for long enough."

And if it doesn't?

"Then we'll deal with it together, like we always do."

She held me up against the wall, her hand pressed against mine and our eyes locked. Part of me couldn't believe she was here. Was this the imagination of my dying mind, or had she actually saved me?

"Call the winds!" she repeated as Czarnobóg's yell echoed through the mists.

I cried out, forcing the *żityje* Otylia had gifted me into the eight winds. They surged, eager as they encircled us with lightning snapping through the whirlwind. Watching it made me dizzy, so I kept my gaze on her. My delirious mind could only think of how beautiful she was with the moonlight radiating from her skin and the winds making her black hair streaked with silver drift behind her like some ethereal flower crown. Those thoughts kept me conscious, so I clung to them.

Czarnobóg's dark figure emerged from the mists in the corner of my vision. I refused to look at him as Otylia curled her fingers tighter around mine. Our hearts raced together, and when she channeled, light poured from us both.

The winds burst into blinding moonlight streaked with lightning as Czarnobóg charged with his dark blade raised. He ran straight into the whirlwind, which threw him back, the light hissing against him. But my *żityje* faded quickly.

I can't keep this up! I told Otylia.

She nodded slowly. *"On three, we'll throw everything in the whirlwind at him in one blast. Then, I'll get us out of here."*

I don't—

"Three, two, one!"

I had no time to think, so I followed her instructions. Wind and lightning swept at Czarnobóg, only knocking him back a few strides until Otylia's light followed. He screamed against it, but showed little signs of damage as he raised his arms.

Otylia tore me into the air before I could see anything more. My body revolted at the sudden jerk, and every wound's searing torment returned as we flew toward the dark clouds swirling above. I wanted to protest. But I could only close my eyes and endure the pain, trusting Otylia knew what she was doing.

The winds whistled past my ears. On them, I almost swore I could hear Kyustendil of the northwest cheer and Cervenko of the east shout in victory. Whether it was my slipping sanity or the truth, it brought me some joy.

I'd held back the god of darkness. It didn't matter to me in that moment whether I bled out in Otylia's arms or lived to hold her for many more years.

Czarnobóg would be trapped here, far from the people I loved. His shouts echoed behind us, and I sensed his corrupted presence making chase. He was too late. A warmth encompassed me as we passed into what must've been the portal back to Jawia.

And we left Oblivion forever.

45

Otylia

Was it enough?

OBLIVION'S CORRUPTION BURNED AGAINST MY SKIN. A realm with neither sun nor moon, its light came from dark wisps that gave Wacław a ghastly image as I dragged him back toward the portal high above.

"We're almost there," I told him, but my voice was lost to the winds.

Gods, he was a mess. His tunic had torn away from Czarnobóg's strikes, and the layer of black blood covering him was so thick I couldn't tell what flesh was wounded and what wasn't. Whatever weapon had left the marks cut deep, each slicing across our connection to alert me of his agony. The worst wound of all ripped down the left side of his face from brow to chin. How had he survived?

But Wacław had done more than survive. He'd risen against Czarnobóg, even somehow calling my light spear through the Moonmark on his arm, and done enough to give me the time to arrive.

I cursed myself for every second I'd wasted talking with Mother and Garafena. Wacław would've been dead if I'd waited any longer. After all he'd sacrificed for me, why couldn't I have been faster to save him from this horror?

He *had* survived, though, and I held onto that fact as we neared the portal. Czarnobóg's immense power flared below. More *žityje* burned in him than any I'd sensed before, and my heart leaped into my throat at what he'd do if he escaped. We couldn't let him follow us, but I'd used the vast majority the *žityje* I had left in that single blast with Wacław.

A dragon's roar echoed through the pit Czarnobóg had dug into the odd ground. Heat rushed up behind me, and I resorted to old tactics, shouting, *"Pri!"* and throwing out a shimmering moonlight shield to repel the dark żmij's flames.

A beam of corruption followed, but by then, we'd reached the swirling portal. Jawia wasn't visible on the other side because of the clouds of pure darkness. The Threads, though, showed me the way back home to those I loved and those I protected. These days, they were all the same, and as we plunged through the portal, I smiled knowing I'd done all I could.

We tumbled back into Jawia amid tendrils of darkness and corruption. Wacław had obviously let the demon free based on the state of his soul, but from what I could tell, he'd resisted Oblivion's corruption. Our pact in Vastroth had held. If we didn't seal the veil once again, though, that same corruption would turn so many innocents into ravenous demons.

"Seal it!" I shouted over the gales to Mother far below, not waiting until I could see her. "He's coming!"

Light answered. Washing over us like an earthquake, Alatyr's power slammed into the portal, and thread-like bonds wove over it as Czarnobóg's roar rumbled beyond. Mother flew on her owl wings above Buyan with Alatyr hovering over her extended hand. Flames danced in her eyes, her hair and dress sweeping in the storm of pure, unfettered power.

"Czarnobóg shall not be free!" she called over the gales, commanding Alatyr. "Hold him in Oblivion until the end of his days."

A great maw snapped at Alatyr's woven threads above. Ice shot from it, missing wildly, but when Czarnobóg's other two heads appeared, they began tearing through the fledgling veil. He would be free before long.

I caught us with the moon's pull when we reached Mother. Wacław's worst wounds had begun to heal, but even with *żityje*, he'd be stuck with grotesque scars. He needed all his power and focus for that healing, so I sent him softly toward Buyan with my power before turning to Mother.

"Do you need me to hold him back?" I asked, sword at the ready.

She shook her head and reached for me. "Take my hand. Let our combined strength be enough."

Her voice trembled more than I'd ever heard it before, and my fear matched hers as I grabbed her hand. Alatyr's power flowed through us both. That sudden return took my breath away, but I bit my cheek and turned all my focus to directing that energy to sealing Oblivion.

The veil grew again through our joined power. Czarnobóg lashed and launched fire, corruption, and ice, but his progress waned. For every thread he tore, two replaced it. Soon, a few flickers of flame were the only visible evidence of the żmij who'd threatened the world. Then the final threads fell into place.

A shockwave shook the air, Alatyr's work and Czarnobóg both vanishing in a blink that left the sky as clear as a summer's day. I stared up at it with a sense of awe.

"That… That can't be it," I stammered. "It's over?"

Mother's shoulders sagged, the fire slipping from her eyes as she leaned into me. "It is done. Take Alatyr from me, my daughter, and never let it enter my sight again."

I took the orb and helped her descend slowly. "Mother? Are you okay?"

"As Wacław wars with his demon for control, so too do I battle with my lesser instincts." She blinked hard. "The force of the wilds loathes that I surrender such power, but I fear what I would do if I were to wield it a moment longer."

"You did what you had to," I assured her, clutching Alatyr tight. Its pulsing lured me, and I shared her desire to be rid of it. But what could we do with a stone that all gods sought? "Your siblings tore the veil, but you sealed it."

Before, Alatyr had been divided between Marzanna and Jaryło to split the year, but obviously, having two opposing gods holding each half wasn't enough to stop them from almost destroying the Three Realms. Could we divide them further? Hide them?

I found Wacław barely conscious beneath the oak with Perun's golden apples, the Indrik nuzzling him. His wounded eye was sealed shut by scarring—and deep gouges covered much of him—but he no longer bled. So much blood loss would've killed a mortal man. From what I could tell through our bond, it had pushed even him to the edge, but he'd fought on in hopes of me coming for him. He'd been willing to die for his people, his friends, and for me. Thank the gods, he hadn't.

"I thought Czarnobóg held more power than anything else," he mumbled, struggling to sit up. "That stone, though, is incomparable."

I patted the Indrik, then crouched before Wacław and inspected each wound. Our travels had taken away most of my time to make potions and poultices, and we rarely needed them with our abilities to heal. Still, I always had a few for emergencies. I pulled them from my bags, holding Wacław forcefully in place when he fought against them.

"Don't worry about me," he said.

I just rolled my eyes and placed each poultice. "You faced the god of darkness in Oblivion, lost an eye, and barely lived. Shut up and stop fighting me. I'm a goddess, and I'll be worried about my lover if I want to be."

A smile cracked across his face, but he winced. "It hurts to smile or even breathe. That whip of his is almost as brutal as your glare." I narrowed my eyes, and he chuckled, then coughed. "Yeah, that one."

I opened my mouth to scold him, but hesitated, running my thumb lightly over his wounded eye instead. The pain he must've endured… It had all been distant while we were a realm apart. Even that faint connection, though, had revealed enough of what he'd suffered for me, and I couldn't help but weep.

"I'm sorry… I wasn't fast enough."

He took a long breath and tilted his head back to stare up at the clear sky. No tears welled in his remaining eye, and our bond revealed only relief within him. "You came at exactly the right time. Czarnobóg thought I was beaten, and that left him vulnerable for just long enough. That pain…" He exhaled and closed his eye, lowering his head again. "I told myself I was prepared to stay and let him inflict whatever torture he wanted for an eternity, but I don't think I could've done it. All it took was a few cracks of a whip to turn me into this disaster."

"Look at me, Wašek." When he refused, I tilted up his chin, and his eye met my gaze. "No one who dares call you a demon or a monster would've stood and faced him after all the punishment you'd taken. You were brave, and your bravery saved us all."

"It's really over, then?" he asked with half-a-laugh. "I keep expecting him to emerge from nothing."

"Czarnobóg's not dead, but I doubt he can be killed with the power he has now. All that matters is that he can't threaten the Three Realms anymore." I held Alatyr between us. "This stone is immensely powerful, but I guess it can't destroy what it created."

His lip twitched at the sight of it. "All of this trouble to reunite a rock which created the gods. I guess this means I can't wield Grudzień anymore."

"That depends entirely on you," Mother said, circling with a distrustful glance at Alatyr. "You both have reunited Alatyr, so it is up to you to decide what to do with it now."

The flapping of dragon wings alerted me to Garafena hovering overhead and casting a shadow over all of us. She lacked legs or arms, so she couldn't land easily, but part of me thought she preferred to hover ominously anyway.

"Return it to my protection," she hissed. "It is my purpose."

"That's too simple," I replied, standing and raising my chin up at her. "The gods know about Buyan, and you cannot stop them if they decide to war for Alatyr again."

"You promised to surrender it!" the serpent snapped.

I spun back toward Mother. "And I will. Mistakes led to Czarnóg's escape, though, and I intend not to make them again." Stepping closer, I studied Mother's pained expression. "What would you do?"

"Divide Alatyr into Moonstones again," she said. "We discussed hiding them before, but with time to ponder it, I believe it is a flawed idea. Split them among friends and foes alike among the gods, Nawie, and spirits. Bind each to a blood pact never to surrender their shard or take another's."

"Enemies?" I muttered. "You want Marzanna and Jaryło to have Moonstones again?"

Her nose wrinkled. "No, I don't, but Rod is dead. Balance in the Three Realms is fragile, and to maintain it, forces of all kinds must have power in their designated time. The pact stops those bearing the Moonstones from taking them from others, but it doesn't prevent them from keeping rogue gods in their place."

The idea didn't sit well with me, but what other choice did we have? Our friends were mortal and couldn't hold the stones forever. Besides, they would become targets of entities far more powerful than them, and I couldn't subject them to such an existence. But gifting Marzanna and Jaryło each a shard after they unleashed Czarnóg?

I turned back to Wacław. "What do you think?"

He stood, leaning on the tree for stability as he clutched his chest. Though it had healed, the ache cut through our bond. "We could use Alatyr to mend Nawia into paradise first, even fix much of the damage to Jawia."

"The power in this stone is too much," I told him. "If I hold it for too long, it *will* turn me into someone I don't want to be. We can't hold onto it."

"Then dividing it with a blood pact is a necessary evil. Like Dziewanna said, if we tried hiding them, someone would find them eventually and cause all of this to happen again." He grimaced. "We can't allow that."

Garafena's hiss objected from above, so I glared up at her again. "Garafena, as a sworn guardian of Alatyr, will you accept a shard to protect under the blood pact Mother described?"

"A single shard?" she replied, her wings beating faster by the second.

"I could offer you none instead. The risks of anyone holding more are too great." I glanced down at Alatyr. "Protecting the Three Realms from destruction is a great purpose and honor in itself."

I tensed as she swept downward, readying to summon my spear, but instead of striking, she bowed her head. "This honor, then, I accept with great humility."

Alatyr hummed as I focused on it with one hand above and another under the hovering orb. Part of me mourned how quickly its power had come and gone. It was ancient beyond a scale I could even imagine, and we would ensure it never reunited again.

"Divide into the twelve Moonstones," I commanded it. "Let each hold their moon's power, and let them never reunite."

I didn't know whether those final words had any hold over Alatyr, but pressing my intentions into it felt right. When the gods spoke, the realms listened. It would still take time before I adjusted completely to who I was and what my life would be.

In a flash of light, Alatyr split and dropped into my hand with cracks throughout it. Each shifting color froze within a separate section. I plucked the bright red one from the orb's top. It curved smoothly along one side, but the other was filled with jagged cracks. Scars from its fall from Prawia.

"You protected Lipiec well while we were gone," I said, holding Lipiec out for Garafena, "so why shouldn't you do so again?"

I cut my free hand with Lipiec and approached Garafena to complete the blood pact with her. Together, we swore to ensure Lipiec wouldn't ever rejoin with the other Moonstones, nor would she seek them. It wasn't greed that worried me with Garafena, but manipulation. Koschei had tricked her before. Could a god do the same?

When we were finished, the serpent accepted Lipiec with another beam of *žityje* from her maw, then flapped her wings and soared away without another word. One shard down. How would the others react to receiving the rest of Alatyr? I didn't look forward to seeing many of the gods again, but luckily, the next two shards were simple.

"Wacław," I said, turning to him. "You worried about losing Grudzień, so it's yours if you want it."

He leaned against the tree with his hand across his chest, staring at me with a pained expression. It was deeper than just the physical wounds he'd endured. Wacław was too careful to not contemplate the weight of this responsibility, but he was no coward. Besides, he loved that sword.

"I am not a god," he said, but a smile tugged at the ends of his lips. "There is no way to ensure I can protect it forever."

I approached and put a hand on his side, sliding Grudzień into his hand with the other. My heart wept at the scars across his face and torso—scars he'd wear for every moment of his life. They would be a reminder every night in our chambers why I loved him. Selfless, brave. He had almost given himself for the realms and for me, and I promised myself I'd do whatever I could to alleviate his enduring pain.

"Then I'll just have to protect *you* forever," I mused. "Now, do I need to craft a blood pact with you, or will that mark on our arms hold our longing trust?"

He huffed. "We've shared enough blood, so no, I don't think we need a pact. I promise not to let you have Grudzień, even if you ask super nicely. Luckily, I don't think that's possible for you."

I'd have jabbed him for that in any other circumstance, but mercy stayed my hand. Rising onto my toes, I kissed his brow and lightly traced the scar over his eye. "Just don't stab me with it either and we have a deal."

"Which Moonstone will you take?"

Stepping back, I considered that. It didn't really matter in the end, but Październik's silver colorations drew me to it. Ara had wielded the tenth moon before, and it marked the descent into autumn. Between that end of warmth and the cape of autumn leaves I'd worn often since my Ascension, it felt right.

Październik answered my touch and formed into my silver light spear immediately. Yes, this would do nicely.

"For my spring," Mother said, studying me, "my daughter chooses autumn. Should I be afraid?"

"You could have a Moonstone of spring," I replied with a pleading look. "With Alatyr divided, you need not fear its power."

But she shook her head and circled the tree with her father's golden apples. Like me, she reached up to touch one, and it shriveled in her grasp. "Even a moon of Alatyr's strength is too much. I swore my oath, and I will abide by it. If you need aid deciding who should receive the others, I will give it, but do not ask me to take one for myself."

"Then we're done here," I said, forcing a smile back at Wacław and dismissing Październik back to an amulet on my headband. He took my free hand, and I sighed with one final look up at where Oblivion's portal had split the sky. "Let's deliver the shards and go home."

46

Otylia

I hope never to do that again.

LIFE AFTER CZARNOBÓG AND MARZANNA'S INVASIONS would never return to what it had been before. That weighed heavily on me as I crossed from my longhouse in Dwie Rzeki and headed across the village center, wearing a formal white tunic with silver and red embroidery across the collar and sleeves. Mokosz's gifted oak granted glorious shade against the sun's heat, but I smiled at the sweat dripping from my brow.

The long winter was over.

Nature's cycles would continue in the coming moons, but for now, we were free from Marzanna's grip. People from old Krowik and many other tribes and clans gathered throughout the village trading wares, treasures from their hunts, and the results of their toils in the fields. Sealing Oblivion had granted them safety from the constant demonic attacks. Some still lurked further in the wilds, but that was why we needed szeptuchy. Common people had no need to worry any longer.

It would take some time before I didn't have the itch that something was lurking. For so many moons, shadows and mists had marked foes of many kinds, but I had no reason to fight now. That would soon change, though.

Mom smiled at me from among a gathered group of children. They sat around her, their eyes wide as she told her favorite legends with Sabina swooping behind her on nymph wings and reenacting the scenes. Her current tale revolved around the trickster leszy who protected the forests from those who sought to harm them.

"King Wacław proves exactly why you shouldn't trifle with a leszy," she explained, wagging a finger at me and spurring the children to giggle. "When one lured him away, the goddess Marzanna tricked him into taking her mark! Now, he has only one eye and veins filled with black blood."

Their giggles faded to gasps, and I crossed my arms. "*Matka*, is this really a story for children so young?"

Her eyes lit up at the challenge, matching her golden hair in the sunlight. "You used to love the most frightening tales. Children are never too young to learn about the mysteries of Jawia. Maybe some of them will grow up to serve a god and face the most *dangerous* of them!"

I chuckled as the children cheered and pulled at her skirts. Sosna rushed from nearby with the excitement, yapping with her fluffy fox tail swooshing into the children. "Another story!" they chanted.

"Perhaps Wacław would like to tell you one about the goddess of the moon," Mom replied with a hopeful look in my direction.

Though I had promised to meet Otylia by the Wyzra River, who was I to deny children their right to a story? So, I waved for them to gather around me as I crouched. My instincts twitched being surrounded with only one good eye to see where they were, but I was slowly adjusting to my shift in sight. Otylia's *żityje* had healed me well after the battle in Oblivion. Czarnobóg's whip, though, had left an eternal mark.

"Otylia was once a witch, brewing potions in the wilds," I began, crafting an overly rosy story of Otylia's journey. With demons and spirits, they had enough to be afraid of. Otylia had become a beacon of hope for mortals of all ages—and one particular Naw too. Even if she hated it, she deserved the praise.

My story carried on for some time, and though I didn't consider myself the most eloquent storyteller, the children seemed to hold either Sosna or their breath through it. I tried to tell a meaningful plot of growth and overcoming trial. At the end, though, three girls approached, holding hands together and giggling.

"Do you *love* her?" they asked together.

I smiled and placed a hand over my heart. "I'm lucky to say I do."

They swapped glances, then the one in the center pulled a strange little creation from her pouch. It appeared to be three different flower petals held together by twine and some creatively applied sap.

"Can you give this to her?" she asked. "We made it!"

"Of course," I replied, taking the flower and sliding it behind my ear for now. "The celebration of our victory is soon, so maybe she'll even put it in her flower crown."

Without another word, the girls giggled among themselves before skipping away and tripping over themselves in their excitement. I couldn't help laughing. Such joy had been rare lately. They deserved the chance to be real children again without the worries of eternal winter hanging over them.

Another girl came the other way down the trail, holding her hands behind her like she was hiding something. My little half-sister, Nevenka, could be as innocent as a fawn and as devious as a crow. I hugged her when she reached me.

"Ready to head to the river?" I asked, jokingly running a finger up her cheek and flipping up her braided hair. "You're not old enough yet to cross those rocks, but luckily, my winds can help."

She nodded rapidly and snatched my hand. "Come on, Waci!" she exclaimed, using the nickname she'd made up for me.

How could a little girl pull with all the force of a wilkołak? Nevenka practically tore me from my spot, and I waved to Mom, who had found yet another group of children to share her stories with. I wondered which ones she told about me behind my back. Would I become a warning for those too young to understand what they'd lived through? A hero? A mythical beast?

Those worries slipped away against Nevenka's fervent pull. I'd done none of this for legacy or fame, but to protect those I loved and others who had no one else to be their shield against winter and corruption. Nevenka deserved every chance of a normal life. Mom deserved to thrive for many more years. Kuba deserved to start a family with the woman he loved. Ara, Zakir, and Xobas deserved to have a place to reestablish their peoples who'd suffered so much. Narcyz and Andrij deserved their chance to find peace.

And all of us deserved a long rest.

Dwie Rzeki's trails were full nowadays, making the once quiet recesses within its walls a bustling scene. People smiled, bowed, or gave me wary glances as I passed. I couldn't blame the skeptics. Between my scarred eye, blackened veins, and the jagged Moonblade sheathed on my back, I was hardly a normal king, and domestic problems remained in our fledgling kingdom.

Soon, though, we passed through the gates and headed toward the Wyzra River. Years in the forests had the trails imprinted on my mind like the veins on the back of my hand. Each held so many memories, and my heart ached knowing I would soon be leaving them behind.

That pain was better than the hopelessness I'd felt staring at dead trees and still, lifeless underbrush. Marzanna had come so close to crushing Jawia's wilds under her frozen boot. Dziewanna ruled now, and warmth filled me as creatures of all kinds skittered across our path. They fled as Nevenka rushed to try and hold each, managing to scurry away before she caught them.

I ruffled her hair. "Maybe Otylia can help you hold a rabbit when we get to the river, all right?"

"Fine…" she muttered, cheeks so puffed she resembled a squirrel who'd found its bounty.

"Do you remember the storks you found last time we were here?" I asked her as we stopped near a pine. Crouching beside her, I pointed up into a towering willow whose roots wove across the mushier ground nearby. "Looks like they came back!"

Nevenka gasped and tried to rush after them too, but I snatched the back of her dress before she descended into the muck. Her mother, Natasza, was a stern woman who had enough reasons to despise me already. The last thing I needed was Nevenka returning to her with mud up to her dress's waist.

"Sometimes, it's better to watch from a distance," I whispered.

Despite her protests, we continued the rest of the way to the river, where we found the stones she'd wished to hop across moons before. A dozen of them led to a larger boulder in the Wyzra's center which was large enough for both of us to stand on. Each jump wouldn't be all that difficult for an adult, but she was young and clumsy. I flexed my free hand, and the winds circled us, at the ready in case she fell.

"Ready?" I asked her as I stepped to the edge and dipped a toe in the Wyzra's rushing flow. Nevenka nodded, so I hopped to the first stone with my arms extended on either side for balance. It was mostly to demonstrate to her how to do it, but it was also more fun that way.

"Step where I step."

Once I hopped to the next stone, I looked back at her with an encouraging smile. She puffed up her chest and put on a tough face—just making her even more adorable—before taking two big steps and jumping to the first stone.

I held my breath, but her feet struck true. Without even a wobble, she stood up straight and grinned at me. "C'mon, Waci! I can do it myself."

So on we went with me more subtly checking on her. Judging each jump's distance while doing so was difficult with only one eye, but we eventually managed to reach the last jump before the boulder. From the shore, it hadn't appeared all that difficult, but it turned out to be quite the leap. I considered our options as I helped Nevenka onto the last stone.

"If you're brave," I said, "my winds will help you make the jump. Do you trust me?"

She furrowed her brow, as if that were a stupid question. "Of course!" Then she leapt without warning.

I yelped and threw out my arms to command the winds. Her attempt took her barely halfway across the gap, and the tips of her boots struck the water before the winds carried her the rest of the way, softly depositing her on the safety of the boulder. With a smug look, she dusted herself off and stared back at me.

"Told you."

I shook my head and flew across the gap without even jumping, then landed beside her and picked her up. "You made that jump all by yourself?" I quipped before raising her up to sit on my shoulders. The Wyzra rushed past us on either side, crashing over many shorter stones and making it so that I had to shout for her to hear. "Maybe you could fly like Sabina someday!"

"No, that's silly," she replied, arms waving through the air. "I can't grow wings, but I can become a szeptucha for Otylia!"

A force tugged at my chest. As if summoned by Nevenka's words, Otylia appeared on the shoreline, arms crossed, but she raised an amused brow. She wore a sweeping dress of silver and autumnal hues with Październik hanging from her neck as a Moonmark amulet. A circlet of winding silver and willow wood crowned her head, matching Weles's bracer that lay hidden under her embroidered sleeve.

She was a queen.

A cape of autumn leaves shimmered at her back as she approached the waters and studied our route. "It was bold to take a child across this," she called over the river's roar.

"This child says she wants to be your szeptucha someday," I replied, hopping to make Nevenka giggle. "Isn't that right?"

She nodded rapidly, but then puffed out her cheeks again. "Mother won't like it."

Otylia's eyes flashed a bright white. Was she looking into Nevenka's future to see what lay ahead if she took a Moonmark? The Threads shimmered to life around us, one connecting me to each of them, and I couldn't think of a better place for Nevenka to be than sworn to Otylia. Though szeptuchy encountered danger often, Otylia was one of the few gods who bothered to help.

"Your destiny is your own to choose," Otylia said when her eyes returned to their usual green. "But I believe you'd make a fine szeptucha."

She eyed the rocks, but shook her head before flying over to us on her silver moonlight instead. Nevenka smacked at my head to let her down so that she could greet Otylia, and she practically jumped from my shoulders before I could do so. That excitement carried into Otylia as they embraced. Otylia rocked back on her heels, barely preventing herself from falling into the river.

We swapped grins as I settled on the boulder's edge and swung my feet out toward the water. "You look beautiful—as always, of course. They're going to love you during the celebration."

"They won't love that we are leaving," Otylia replied, releasing Nevenka and joining me.

"No, but it's for the best…"

Nevenka stuck her head between us, her face heavy. "Why do you have to leave?"

I pursed my lips and stared down at the river. For so long, I'd wanted nothing more than to return home, but there was no normal life for us here anymore. "Dwie Rzeki is safe, but Nawia and the Way of Souls need us now. Czarnobóg and Marzanna destroyed so much of them, and it's up to us now to make the afterlife the paradise it's supposed to be." I wrapped my arm around them both. "Even a realm away, we won't be far, and we'll come back often. Right, Otylia?"

"Right," she confirmed, but her gaze was distant. Her thumb dragged across her palm as she wrinkled her nose.

"Can I visit you too?" Nevenka asked.

I shook my head. "Hopefully, you won't have to see Nawia for a *long* time. Just imagine paradise in the meantime, and do what you can to make Jawia more like that."

She cocked her head and backed up, dancing around the other side of the rock as she played in her own imagination. Her absence created a gap between Otylia and me, so I scooted over to fill it.

What's in your head? I asked through our bond so that Nevenka couldn't overhear. *Sad to be saying goodbye to Dariusz?*

She scoffed. "*Of course not. I just can't stop thinking about the Sudiczki's predictions for my fate. Each time I think I understand them, everything changes. I was to be your queen here, but instead, I'm to become queen of Nawia in Weles's absence. Your corruption was to be my end, but instead, it was the tool that helped us seal away Czarnobóg.*"

I chuckled and bumped her with my shoulder. *We have centuries still for me to descend into corruptive madness.*

"*Don't joke about that.*"

All right, but I'm not joking when I say you'll be a far better ruler of Nawia than Weles ever was. I took her hand in mine and held it tight. *Together, we'll protect the dead souls seeking relief, just like we promised. In their darkest hour, you'll be their light, and I'll be their blade.*

Nevenka stopped and crept toward us, not at all stealthy. "Why are you just sitting there? Mother says you can talk in your heads… Wait!" She rushed to my side and almost knocked me into the river. "Are you avoiding me?"

I kissed Otylia's cheek and stood, sweeping up Nevenka. "Sometimes, couples need to discuss things in private, and our bond lets us do that more easily. Don't worry. We'd never avoid you." I glanced back at Otylia. Shadows from the trees had begun to creep across her face. "The sun is setting, so we should probably get back before we miss our own celebration."

Her eyes lit up as she shot to her feet. Moonlight shone from her skin, and she leaped into the air. "Let's give them an arrival they won't forget."

47

Otylia

The end of one life. The beginning of another.

A ROAR ROSE FROM THE VILLAGE CENTER as Wacław and I appeared overhead, he on his winds and I on my moonlight. Nevenka waved from his arms, and I spotted the former high chieftess, Natasza, glaring at him holding her little girl. Hers was the only sour face in the village.

Everyone else celebrated with mugs and horns full of oskoła, mead, and other drinks from tribes and clans across Jawia. Meats, soups, vegetables, and breads of all kinds were piled upon tables around Mokosz's gifted oak. The setting sun sent a golden hue over the gathering, mixing with my silver as I landed with Wacław on the longhouse's step.

Wacław set down Nevenka, and she scampered into the crowd, skipping. The girl had been a bit of a nuisance. The joy on Wacław's face made every moment with her worth it.

We took each other's hands and headed toward a group of friendly faces gathered around a table. Kuba stood on a single foot atop a stool, waving a drinking horn in the air before downing its contents. His woman, Maja, watched with an amused shake of her head beside Ara, Zakir, and Ta. Narcyz just added to the chaos by passing him another horn as Andrij did his best to stop it.

"Do it for Wacław!" Narcyz declared. "We all know he loves you looking like an idiot."

Wacław looked to the stars, holding back a laugh. "That is, unfortunately, most of the time."

"There he is!" the wobbly Kuba exclaimed. He took a swig of the next drink, but Wacław's arrival had forced him to turn his leg awkwardly. With a yelp, he toppled from the stool, stopping when his face was merely an inch from the ground.

Wacław raised his hand, commanding the winds to put Kuba back on his feet as he approached and smacked his drunken friend on the back. "Celebration is in order, but I would hope you remember my last day as king instead of waking and forgetting our goodbyes."

"Not forever," Kuba muttered before taking another drink. Somehow, he'd managed to keep his horn from tipping in the fall, and I wondered why he valued the alcohol more than his health.

"No, my friend." Wacław embraced him, holding tight as his sorrow rushed through our bond. "Not forever. But I need you to be all right while I'm gone." He glanced at Maja. "It's not just about you anymore, and the kingdom will need people familiar with the dealings of demons and gods."

Kuba stepped back and thumped his chest. "Aye. I'll do it."

"And *I'll* make sure he keeps himself out of trouble," Ara replied, raising her eyebrows in my direction as she dragged Kuba away from a knife he seemed eager to reach for. "It'll be hard, but we've got your marks. We can talk to you whenever we want…"

I gave her a smile, but my eyes and nose suddenly burned. Rushing toward her, I nearly tackled her as tears streamed down my cheeks. "I'm sorry to leave, but you're not alone anymore either." Zakir shied away behind her, so I gave him a sharp look. "Zakir is going to make you *very* happy, right?"

Zakir rubbed the back of his head, then nodded rapidly. Ara wiped her nose as she stepped back and laughed along with me. It was silly being so emotional when we'd see each other often, but we both recognized how much had changed since our times comparing dresses for the equinox. She took Zakir's hand, and for the first time in years, peace settled across her face. That settled my own heart. I wasn't abandoning her.

"What in Oblivion are you wearing?" Narcyz spat as he toppled Kuba's stool and stomped toward Wacław. He plucked the strange flower with three different petals from Wacław's ear and laughed. "It doesn't distract enough from that nasty eye."

Wacław snatched the flower back, then jabbed Narcyz in the stomach so quickly his winds had to be behind it. "It was a gift from some young girls for Otylia's crown." He glanced at me and slipped it into my circlet. "I'd forgotten to give it to her, so thanks for the reminder."

Narcyz sputtered as he fell back, clutching his chest. "Yup. Any-time."

"You deserved that," Andrij said as he threw his arm over Narcyz's shoulder and planted a kiss on his cheek. "Perhaps this can be some motivation to learn some manners. I do have to say, though, that I'll miss you wielding that golden blade of Kwiecień."

I wrinkled my nose at the memory of returning Kwiecień to Jaryło after Czarnobóg's defeat. Even granting the first moon of Styczeń back to Marzanna hadn't been as painful as that. "Why is that sword destined to be held by a brute?" I quipped. "Whether it's you or Jaryło, I seem inclined to smack whoever wields it."

"Hey!" Wacław complained, nudging me. "I held it for a while."

I ran my fingers across his cheek in the way that always made him blush, whispering, "My point exactly."

Ta whistled from her position on a stool. She leaned so far back on it that it teetered on the precipice, and both her black and fur-lined coat drifted behind her as she held out her arms. How was she not burning up in that heavy coat? From the sands of Vastroth, even this heat apparently held a chill for her.

"You two are runnin' off to your own realm," she said with a sharp laugh as her stool shifted, but remained standing with a quick correction from her. "Don't get all touchy in front of us!" I flicked my wrist and sent the lightest bit of a moonblast her direction. It was enough, and she leaped off the stool, landing with a roll before it toppled behind her. "Touched a nerve, huh?"

"You're lucky you're going back to Vastroth," I replied with a challenging look. "I can't follow you with a Moonmark, but I'll make sure Mokosz keeps an eye on you."

Ta crossed her arms, and Ara patted her on the back as she replied, "Gonna miss this place, but home is home. Vastroth needs szeptuchy too after the frost."

"On the topic of home." Andrij coughed, holding Narcyz's hand and dragging him to us like a child asking his parents for forgiveness. "Narcyz has agreed to come back to Astiw with me—or at least, what's left of it. We'll set up a new forge there and help people rebuild. My family…" His head hung. "The Horde destroyed my tribe, but there are many of us left. Whether a part of this new kingdom or an independent one, we'll grow into the future together."

Wacław extended his hand, and they grabbed each other's forearms. "They will have one of Jawia's best commanders to guide them. Dziewanna's flames dancing at your fingertips can't hurt either, but the forests of the east have burned enough already."

"I'll be careful." Andrij glanced at Narcyz. "One of us has to be."

Narcyz looked to grab Wacław's arm once Andrij was done, but Wacław wrapped him in a hug instead. "My Eclipsemark is there for you to protect people," Wacław told him. "You can fly and call lightning. Just make sure the storm strikes the right people, all right?"

"Can lightning forge a blade?" Narcyz asked with his arms fixed alongside himself, rigid as a board. "Just asking for a friend."

I rolled my eyes and shoved a joking finger into Andrij's chest. "Control him. Gods know what he'll try to make, and Mother will blame me if you two set the east alight."

"Well, *she* is the queen of Jawia," Ara said, arms crossed and hip out. "You could say it would be her fault for not controlling her realm. From now on, you're just worried about all of us when we die. Except Kuba. We all know he'll be some kind of ridiculous demon."

Maja gasped and held a hand over Kuba's chest. "Come now. Kuba is silly, but he is no demon."

"A jackal was enough of a punishment," a new voice said, approaching our group from Mokosz's tree. Xobas stood tall in his leather armor that left his arms exposed, and a curved cavalry blade still hung at his side. "If there is punishment for bravery, that is."

Kuba beamed and pointed at Ara. "See!"

Wacław exchanged another hug with Xobas before tapping the hilt of his mentor's sword. "You brought a blade and armor to our celebrations?" He glanced around. "Expecting a demon attack?"

"I am a creature of habit," Xobas replied with a chuckle. He leaned to the side, brow furrowed at Grudzień's pommel before correcting his posture. "It seems I could say the same for you."

"You never know when your mentor might show up and demand a training duel," Wacław said before dropping to a fighter's stance, feigning jabs with an invisible sword. "I noticed you don't try to down me now that I have the winds."

Xobas scratched his bearded chin. "Stop bouncing so much, or your enemy will throw you off your feet. The basics keep you alive when that power of yours runs out." He clapped Wacław on the shoulder. "But you have managed plenty well without my guidance. I'm hardly your mentor now."

Wacław dropped out of the stance and bowed his head. "You'll always be the one who guided me when I had no one else. Thank you, Xobas." When he rose, he stepped closer to his mentor. "I have a favor to ask of you while I'm gone."

Xobas returned the bow. "I'm in your service."

"Nothing that serious," Wacław replied. "But you have known my mom for a long time. Can you keep an eye on her for me? Otherwise, I fear she'll give herself so much to others that she forgets her own needs."

"That care for others is a gift and a curse which she bestowed upon you as well." Xobas placed a hand on his blade's pommel. "Da, I'll make sure Lubena is watched over."

A group stopped by with drinks to ensure neither Wacław nor I went without partaking in the festivities, and we settled around the table with our friends as our conversations lightened. Focusing on the aftermath of Czarnobóg's defeat was exhausting. I'd have the rest of my immortal life to figure out what to do with Nawia and my new godly duties. For now, I wanted one last night of pretending I was a mortal woman just enjoying a night with her friends.

Gods, what friends they were. Through Prawia, the Way of Souls, and the battles of Jawia they'd followed us. We'd lost some, found others, and brought one back from the dead. We'd slain gods, demons, and żmije who ravaged as dragons. All in less than a year's time.

As the night grew old, I stood with my mug raised. I rarely drank alcohol, but on a night like this, I couldn't help but celebrate. It was an end. A bittersweet one, but I promised I would see each of them again many times. My life would span beyond the years I could possibly comprehend. For the rest of their mortal ones, I would ensure they lived to the fullest.

"For endings," I declared. "And for new beginnings. Let tonight mark not the final night of our journeys together, but the start of many new ones. Like a tapestry, we separate and come back together to create a beautiful display of what we experienced."

Silence answered across the table. I worried that I'd said something wrong before Kuba slammed a hand on the table and shouted, "Aye!" before downing his drink amid a chorus from the others.

Wacław's eye was red as he rose beside me and raised his mug, his other hand around my waist. He sniffled and fought through his sorrow to speak.

"I will miss all of you more than words can express—even you, Narcyz. Each of you blessed us with your loyalty, support, and presence through the darkest hours. I…" He cleared his throat, laughing as he wiped his tears. "I know I'll see all of you again many times, but I need you to understand that I wouldn't be here if it weren't for you. Jawia would not be either. *You* are the heroes, the brave who charged into battle without magic to heal your wounds. Let my name fade as some two-souled boy while yours are written into the legends."

"No," Narcyz muttered, shooting to his feet and pointing at Wacław. "That's stupid. Call us whatever, but you marched into Oblivion and faced a god without even a sword. You're Wacław the Twin-Souled, defier of Oblivion, and walker of the Three Realms." He drank from his mug. "Toast to that."

"Thank you," Wacław mumbled through tears, wiping them away with the back of his hand.

The rest of the group stood, and we said our parting words. A knot tightened in my chest with each. There was so much more I wanted to say, but words failed me. So I just held them for longer than I should've, trying to remember this moment. This simplicity.

Wacław's fingers found mine some time later, after he'd found and calmed his sobbing mother. He guided me toward the forests we'd traveled so many times. Then, our palms had been smooth and our faces unblemished. But our scars told of our journeys and battles as we passed beneath familiar branches now. Lessons, regrets, and victories. They would never leave us. Just like we'd never leave each other.

Flickering firelight ahead marked the end of our time in Jawia. Mother stood alongside Sabina in the grove where wolves had attacked Wacław and me as children, her life-giving power returning it to fullness after Wacław had drained the trees' *żityje* moons ago.

Wisps danced before me, reenacting Wacław's desperate fight against the wolves with nothing more than a sharpened stick. He'd fallen, and though my sudden channeling had saved us both, it had been the end of our connection… for a time.

Still in the shadows, I squeezed his hand. "Are you sure you want to come with me? You could—"

"I will be by your side until time's end," he breathed, catching my cheek with his other hand. "Or until you're sick of me."

I kissed him and allowed our joined hearts to beat together for a long moment. Ahead, Nawia lay as a realm for me to rule, but it meant nothing compared to this. As long as I had Wacław with me, the Three Realms fell into alignment.

"I don't foresee that in Trygław's visions," I quipped before rising to my toes to kiss his forehead. "But we'll see after a couple centuries."

Then I dragged him along to Mother and Sabina, who Mother had insisted on us bringing due to her familiarity with Nawia. Mother's antlers towered higher than ever now that her power had returned to its fullest, and she pulsed with *żityje* far greater than she'd ever held when I was her only szeptucha. Oh, how times had changed. It was Jaryło now who was scorned among the spring gods while she was both the champion of spring and queen of the living realm.

Mother rested her hand on the trunk of a silver birch tree, smiling. "This makes a fine place for your Heart of Jawia. We are both barred from Prawia, but as you are the queen of Nawia now, this will bring you to its Heart to begin the realm anew." Her smile faded, and she dragged her fingers down the trunk. "I mourn what became of the realm I once cared for with Weles. It was never mine to rule, but it was home for a time."

"I will do my best to remake it into the paradise it was for fallen souls," I said, taking her hand. "And you will always have a place there."

But she shook her head. "Do not remake it as Weles wanted. Create what it should be without care for his rivalries with Perun or the power he sought through it. You are sworn to protect the dead through their cycle of death and rebirth, so create a place for them to thrive. And you…"

Wacław stumbled back as she snatched his hand too with a radiant look in her eye. "Nawie are bound to the Way of Souls, so you must ensure it remains safe for those souls. As long as Marzanna resides in her castle, you must be vigilant. She will take many years to recover. Her vengeance is not finished, though."

"I will be ready," he replied. "We freed some of Marzanna's Nawie already, but I will search for others to join in the effort. It's no paradise if the dead can't reach Nawia."

"And I will help you both however I can," Sabina said, her wings fluttering nervously. "Lady Dziewanna is convinced my time in Nawia grants me some expertise."

I hugged her tight, but not too tight. She was a frail thing, and it felt as if too much of a squeeze could break the poor nymph. "You *will* be helpful," I insisted. "You'll also make this feel a bit less lonesome."

When we parted, I stared up at the tree I'd marked as my Heart of Jawia. Every god had one, and it felt right for it to be here. It was where part of my life had ended and another had begun. It was close to home, and I needed to know I could visit often with ease.

"I am proud of you," Mother said. "It was far from my desire to see us as queens of Nawia and Jawia, but you have surpassed all I could have dreamed for you to be. Remember, that even a realm away, I am not far. My experience and my power will always be yours."

I smiled and hugged her, fighting another surge of tears. "If anyone dares trifle with Jawia, call for me. Together, we'll make them regret it."

"There's my little wildling." We shared a laugh, and she held my hands as I pulled back. "Remember where you came from and who you are. Mortals' lives are short, but I have learned more from them in recent moons than I have from immortals in centuries." She nodded toward Wacław. "And enjoy life with this one. Love like yours is a rare thing, so hold onto it for as long as Destiny allows."

I took Wacław's hand again, and he nuzzled my head as I replied, "I plan on it."

Mother stepped aside to clear the way to the birch. With the moon's glow splitting through the leaves and radiating from my skin, the tree appeared as a silver tower with its branches stretching across the realms. It was my Heart, binding me to the World Tree at the core of every realm, and it was my way to Nawia.

With one final glance back at Mother, Wacław and I approached the Heart with Sabina close behind. Its trunk split at my willing to form an archway like that in the Heart of Nawia. Power swirled through it, promising a new world and a new journey.

So we stepped together from the realm of the living. Into Nawia. Into the realm we must protect.

Into a new beginning.

END OF THE FROSTMARKED CHRONICLES

A Word From The Author

Whether you're and author or a reader, ending a series is always bitter sweet. The Frostmarked Chronicles will always hold a special place in my heart as my first fantasy series, and I have loved being able to bring the myths of my Polish heritage into these books. I grew up loving the likes of *Percy Jackson*, so it was a bit of a dream to dive into mythology and craft stories with those tales as elements within it.

Thank you to all of you who have read and enjoyed this series. It's been so amazing hearing people's favorite characters, gods, and demons, and I hope you've learned to love Slavic mythology as I do (even if their names are so hard to pronounce!). Your support allows me to do this, so if you've read this *entire series*, please tell your friends about it. Books are better in community!

If you have enjoyed reading this story, please take the time to post an honest review on whatever retailer you purchased this book from. Every review helps new readers discover the series.

To receive your free copy of *The Rider in the Night*—the prequel novella to The Frostmarked Chronicles—other side-novellas attached to the series, and exclusive first looks at upcoming books, join my newsletter at www.Brendan-Noble.com/Free-Books/.

- Brendan

About the Author

Brendan Noble is an American author writing epic fantasy with inspiration from his Polish ancestry, mythology, video games of all types, and Dungeons & Dragons. He loves to explore the complexities of politics and the gray between good and evil.

Shortly after beginning his writing career in 2019, Brendan married his wife Andrea and moved to Rockford, Illinois from his hometown in Michigan. Since then, he has published three series: The Realm Reachers, The Frostmarked Chronicles, and The Prism Files.

Outside of writing, Brendan is a data analyst and soccer referee. His top interests include German, Polish, and American soccer/football, Formula 1, analyzing political elections across the world, playing extremely nerdy strategy video games, exploring with his wife, and reading.